JUL 7 1982 𝒰

D0209259

FIC   Lieberman, Herbert H., 1933-
        Night call from a distant time zone
     : a novel / by Herbert Lieberman. --
     1st ed. -- New York : Crown
     Publishers, c1982.
        p. cm.

        ISBN 0-517-54571-3 $ 12.95

     I. Title.

NIGHT CALL FROM A DISTANT TIME ZONE

ALSO BY HERBERT LIEBERMAN

BOOKS

The Adventures of Dolphin Green
Crawlspace
The Eighth Square
Brilliant Kids
City of the Dead
The Climate of Hell

PLAYS

Matty and the Moron and Madonna
Tigers in Red Weather

NIGHT CALL FROM A DISTANT TIME ZONE

A Novel by

HERBERT LIEBERMAN

CROWN PUBLISHERS, INC. NEW YORK

Library of Congress Cataloging in Publication Data
Lieberman, Herbert H., 1933–
Night call from a distant time zone.
I. Title.
PS3562.I4N5 1982   813'.54   81-9863
AACR2
ISBN: 0-517-545713
Book design by Camilla Filancia
10 9 8 7 6 5 4 3 2 1
First Edition

For BILLY *and* MOE,
in fondest memory

PART I

1

I make war, I make love, I build.
—HENRY OF NAVARRE, 1553–1610

The phone rang three times before he heard it. The fourth ring entered his clouded consciousness and pierced it like a needle perforating gauze. At first he thought it was the alarm and flung his arm out to disengage it. At the fifth ring he was conscious of being prized from a dream, the fleeting contents of which clung to his drowsy consciousness like shreds of torn cloth to grasping fingers. The sixth ring was more insistent.

At the seventh ring he cracked an eye, seeing first the blood-red integers of a bedside digital clock. The numerals were just flashing from 3:32 to 3:33 A.M. He rolled from his left side to his stomach and lifted the receiver from its cradle. Eyes closed, he lay prone, the receiver dangling in space from his wrist. The low drone of a voice flowed from the speaker into the dark, heavily draped room. He listened to it distantly and droused.

Beside him a sleeping figure stirred. An emanation of soap and silk and hair rose in warm waves from beneath the comforter. The figure moaned softly as if on the verge of waking, then sighed, turned and lapsed back into the slow, measured breathing of profound sleep.

The voice crackled once more from the dangling receiver. He heard his name hissed through the darkened room and fumbled the device to his ear.

"Charles Daughtry?"

"Speaking."

"Long distance, Tokyo, calling."

Twisting sidewards, he half rose. "This is Daughtry."

"Go ahead, please."

"Charley—?"

3

"Kanzi?"

"Yes—sorry."

"Christ—what time—"

"—view of the circumstances, and—"

Then came the numbers like a series of detonations. They hammered into his consciousness: 168.0014. The red integers on the digital clock posted 3:35. . . .

Several days before the price of yen against the dollar in Tokyo was over 200.

"Eight percent on 10 mils—overbought dollars. Position untenable. On your instructions. Please advise soonest. Tokyo time 5:36 P.M."

"Where's Sujimoto?" He heard himself speak. "Get hold of Sujimoto, for God's sake."

The phone clicked. The voice receded and disappeared. Only the high ring of the wire persisted, whirling spectrallike through the great dark void of space.

He slammed the phone back onto the cradle. The ringing sound persisted in his ear. Something had happened, he knew. Gone wrong. Something disastrous. It was all there in the integers and decimals still dancing in his head. Yet he could not fathom it. The numbers fluttered downward, cascading over him. He lay back, letting the beginning of panic roll across him like a killing tide.

When the phone rang, he had been dreaming of war. It was the Battle of Rorke's Drift during the Zulu Wars of the late nineteenth century. So vivid was his dream that even as his slumbering mind was dragged rudely back to consciousness by the loud jangle of the phone, he could still hear the crackle of Martini-Henry rifles, the dry rattling screams of Nabuladanzi's Hottentots, and taste the biting tang of cordite in his lungs. In the final frame of his dream he watched Colonel Erskine pitch forward over the Oskarberg Terrace and plummet downward, skewered on the assegai of a waiting Undi corpsman.

It was not unusual for Daughtry to dream of war. In the past

4

several years he had done so with increasing regularity and, on those occasions, invariably he awoke feeling fully refreshed.

Once again the sleeping figure stirred.

"What's up?" a muffled voice inquired from beneath the comforter.

"Nothing. Go back to sleep."

"What time—?"

"Three-forty. Go back to sleep."

"Where are you going?"

The red integers flashed 3:41. "To the office," he said. "Got to get down to the office."

2 *But the age of chivalry is gone. That of sophisters, economists, and calculators, has succeeded.*
—EDMUND BURKE. *Reflections on the Revolution in France,* 1790

At 10:30 A.M. on a typical London business day, five gentlemen gathered in a small, nondescript building in St. Swithin's Lane, not far from the shadows of the Bank of England.

Silently they filed into a small room, furnished sparsely with five small desks. At each desk was placed a hard, unupholstered wooden chair, and upon each desk was a telephone and a small British flag.

Once the five gentlemen, with very little discussion, had taken their seats, the door of the room was closed. A red light went on outside the door and from that moment on, until the red light would again go off, no one would be permitted to enter the room or to interrupt the solemn, matutinal rite that was about to take place. At that moment, the price of gold was going to be "fixed" on the international market.

The place was N. M. Rothschild & Son and the gentlemen

convened there were representatives of each of the five member firms of the gold market: Mocatta & Goldsmith, Ltd.; Sharps Pixley, Ltd.; Johnson Matthey Bankers, Ltd.; Samuel Montague & Co., subsidiary of the Midland Bank, and N. M. Rothschild & Son.

A tallish, rather saturnine-looking gentleman representing Rothschild & Son was positioned at a small rostrum at the head of the room. His name was Strachey. Mr. Strachey took charge at once by suggesting an opening price representing his firm's orders to buy and sell. The only thing he knew at that moment was the net position of his own dealing rooms. His task was to strike a compromise price that could be agreed upon by all five member firms.

For a ceremony, the results of which have such far-reaching implications, the procedure of "fixing" is surprisingly simple. To the untutored it might even appear naïve. The telephones are kept open to maintain constant communication with each of the five home offices. The flags are used to indicate to Mr. Strachey that orders are not yet finalized. In order to hold off fixing a price, a dealer will set his flag upright and shout the word "Flags."

Mr. Strachey may not terminate the proceedings until the last flag is lying flat. It is a process which generally takes a mere ten minutes, although it will most surely take longer when market conditions are volatile.

That morning the "fixing" session endured an incredibly grueling seventy-five minutes with phones ringing hysterically and the small Union Jacks seemingly never put to rest.

At the conclusion of the session the price of gold had been fixed at an astronomical $624 the troy ounce, having soared in a matter of days to those unheard-of heights from a former figure of $508. The huge leap of $116 was attributed to the fact that the dollar was plummeting on all foreign exchange markets, particularly against the yen, where it had nose-dived in one day from 214.0001 to 168.0532.

Confusion reigned. The Mocatta & Goldsmith man exchanged glances with the Sharps Pixley man, as did the representative of Johnson Matthey with the Montague chap. Mr. Strachey, still commanding the podium position, shifted uneasily on his feet, an expression on his face of slightly baffled amusement. It was not their custom, or for that matter their tactics, to communicate with one another during the delicate course of a fixing. This morning, however, both custom and good tactics went out the window.

In commodities trading of precious metals, it is axiomatic that gold rises and falls inversely against the performance of the dollar. When the dollar dives, traders quickly scramble for refuge in the safe harbor of gold. This morning was no different. Typically, however, gold does not soar at such rates in such a brief time span. Nor does the dollar plummet in quite such a fashion as it was plummeting now.

Clearly, something was afoot. More specifically, something appeared to be dreadfully wrong, yet no one in that room—clearly an outpost of top market intelligence—had the faintest inkling of what exactly it was.

3

For great aims we must dare great things.
—CLAUSEWITZ: *Principles of War*, 1812

It was nearly 4:15 A.M. when Daughtry, his hair still damp from a shower, hit the mist-hung pavements in front of his triplex brownstone. There was still an hour and a half before sunrise. The air outside was mizzling and chill, most appropriate for a New York November.

Striding toward Madison Avenue, he pulled the collar of his Burberry up around his ears and retracted his neck against the drizzle that shone in smoky halations about the streetlamps and traffic lights. A faintly lurid illumination from unopened shops and boutiques shimmered in the slick streets, giving the scene some of the dappled luminosity of a pointillist canvas.

Somewhere near the southeast corner of Madison and Sixty-third, he paused at a news kiosk where he was handed a *Wall Street Journal* and a *New York Times*. From there he passed on to an all-night delicatessen where, wordlessly, the counterman handed him a small paper bag containing hot coffee and a hard, buttered roll. Out on the pavement again, a cab, as if by signal, rolled up to the curb before him. The driver mumbled greetings, as a back door swung open and Daughtry stepped in. It was a miracle of timing and precision, figured down to seconds, number of steps walked, and number of words spoken.

Settling back into the dark rank shadows of the cab, Daughtry closed his aching eyes and drowsed. For the past several days he had been feeling a dull persistent ache above his eyelids. Now the ache had grown somewhat more outspoken; a muscle had begun to flutter involuntarily in the corner of his right eyelid.

Moving crosstown at Sixty-fourth Street, the cab rattled through the untrafficked byway and rocketed down toward the river. Shortly they were on the FDR Drive tooling south. In the dim illumination of a rear seat light, Daughtry tried to concentrate his attention on the *Wall Street Journal*. With the strain of reading in that half-light, the muscle flutter in his eyelid increased.

"Overbought. Position untenable . . . please advise." The figures, if they were correct, were catastrophic. So, undoubtedly, they were wrong. There had to be some mistake.

His mind flashed backward. It was February '78 and he was in Tokyo. Sujimoto's mocking features hovered before him, fading and wavering as if underwater, the rheumy, glaucous eyes like those of a dead carp. The cab swept below the Manhattan Bridge and glided along beside the gray sluggish morning tide.

"Long dollars." Voices whispered and fretted about him. "Millions lost. Millions. Dangerously overbought. 168.0014."

The numbers hammered at Daughtry. They pummeled and mauled him like fusilades of heavy cannonade. Numbers were the nature of his work. He heard numbers all day. When he went home at night after work, numbers whispered in his ear and he would hear numbers through his uneasy tossing sleep: 182.0033. 2.0212. 612.1413 up .5 from .1418. In the morning when he woke, the numbers would still be bouncing about in his head, repeating themselves through the course of his day's work. Numbers were the air and water of his life. By profession, he was a currency trader.

Charles Daughtry was a tall wiry fellow with a shock of dark shiny hair and a sallow skin, innocent of sunlight. The small, restive eyes set into deep, bony sockets, a long thin blade of a nose and a spade-shaped beard, well trimmed at the chin, gave him a slightly saturnine mien.

He was shy, at least outwardly so. If he had a family, or if he came from somewhere, you would never have known it. He was the least biographical of men. Not that he was secretive; he simply never volunteered information. If you confronted him directly with a question regarding his past, he would answer you straight on without evasion or duplicity. In this respect he was utterly guileless. Truthful to a fault, he was, however, miserly with information. He needed bringing out.

All that could be said of him with any certainty was that he came from a small town in the Middle West, attended a business college out there of doubtful accreditation, and came east to make his way in the world. With this rather drab, lackluster provenance behind him, the world, needless to say, was scarcely beating a path to his door. The lunacy of Vietnam had been waging itself fearfully for several years. Fortune in New York hadn't beckoned him, and since nothing better presented itself, he volunteered, and was commissioned a second lieutenant in the Army.

In another five months, Charles Daughtry, along with a lot of other young Americans, found himself in Southeast Asia—a newly commissioned tank commander with the 11th Armored Cavalry rattling through Tay Ninh under flares and incendiary fire in a 48-ton M60 tank.

At the conclusion of his service, Daughtry mustered out with a drawerful of medals and citations and a leg lame and permanently shorter from having been shattered by mortar fire. As to his military experience, particularly his encounter with actual battle, he considered it to be the most rewarding and satisfying period of his life.

Returning to New York, his entry into the world of business was as a "two-dollar man" in a slightly shady uptown brokerage house—two-dollar man meaning that he took two dollars going or coming on every $100 placed with him. At that time he was living in a seedy rooming house on Eleventh Street in the West Village, subsisting largely on Ritz crackers and cheap wine. He needed a job badly.

He came to Philliston & Sons, Ltd., with his business college diploma, an honorable discharge from the Army, and no practical business training whatever. The floor manager at Philliston was harried and in a rush and Daughtry could see that the interview was going badly. Outwardly, Daughtry was an unextraordinary man, but he had in his kit one extraordinary gift— the gift of numbers. He could calculate in his head columns of numbers with an almost preternatural rapidity. At a point when all seemed lost, he challenged the manager to devise any six columns of five digit numbers that he, Daughtry, could not multiply in his head. If he missed one by so much as a single digit, then he would go quietly off; but if he got all the figures right, then they must hire him.

At first the manager was skeptical, then amused, then curious enough to take this odd fellow up on the bet. Daughtry executed a half-dozen such mental transactions faultlessly while Philliston's man attempted to debunk the feat as chicanery. By that time five or six other people from the floor had gathered round, checking Daughtry's figures against a huge Amdahl-V7 computer, all looking for, as they said, the gimmick. If there was one, they never found it. Needless to say, Daughtry got the job.

His immediate superior at Philliston was a gray, austere personage with a condescending air by the name of Ludgate. When first introduced to his new assistant, Mr. Ludgate averted his gaze and pursed his thinnish lips, as if he had just sucked a lemon. In the weeks that followed, Mr. Ludgate barely spoke to Daughtry, and his manner was less than civil. Daughtry, for his part, was a model employee. He came early and left late. He took no lunch break. He worked hard and learned fast. Too fast for Mr. Ludgate, it seems, for one month after Philliston had taken young Daughtry on, Mr. Ludgate began to look worried and already a trifle disenthroned.

Several weeks later Ludgate knew he was in heavy water when the tape broke down during a power failure on a day of very heavy trading. The computers went out and the billers and customers men were swamped by a Niagara of transactions that kept pouring in over the phone lines. Chaos and a huge loss of potential profit threatened to ensue.

Ludgate recommended closing down operations until power was restored or at least until secondary generators could be brought into play. It would cost Philliston hundreds of thousands of dollars in unfilled transactions, but it was the only way to handle the situation, Ludgate said.

Daughtry offered an alternate solution. Continue the intake, he said, and bill manually. He himself would be at the center of operations charged with the responsibility for the accurate tabulation of sums and commissions.

Aside from the fact that Daughtry's suggestion was vainglorious, it was also patently impossible. Ludgate disallowed it out of hand. But he was overruled by his superiors who, while as skeptical as Ludgate, were desperate enough to try anything before conceding forfeiture of several hundred thousand dollars in potential billings.

If it is true that the occasion makes the man, Daughtry took over with the air of a man born to the occasion. In less than half an hour the tank commander of Operation Powder in the

Mekong had organized a battery of switchboard operators, customers men and accountants armed with manually operated adding machines, with himself at the center of operations, the linchpin of a makeshift and necessarily rudimentary computer center.

While the bookkeepers fired numbers at him, while phones rang and paper flew and people shouted and careened about the office, coolly and calmly Daughtry's prodigious numerical skills were brought into play. Not only did he keep pace with the staggering flow of figures swamping the phone lines, he also devised and applied spontaneously several formulas based on probability theories for quickly projecting in dollars the total intake of billings. Later these projections proved uncannily accurate.

After that, poor Ludgate never stood a chance. Daughtry's reputation as a guru of numbers traveled like swampfire. Philliston & Sons would have done anything to keep him, and indeed they tried, by lavishing upon him princely sums in the form of salary, commissions and guaranteed bonuses. What they failed to realize was that, unlike other customers men, Daughtry was not primarily a merchant. The romance of sales held very little appeal for him. Untutored, largely unconscious of his own unique thought processes, more than a salesman, he was a theoretical mathematician of uncommon gifts. But, of course, he didn't know that. He didn't give a tinker's damn for the getting and spending of money, the Philliston people were sadly to learn. He was only there because of the peculiar stimulation he got each day from simple numbers and their manipulation. Once he grasped the mystery of the numbers involved in any problem he undertook, he tended to lose interest. Then, shortly, he would have to go out in search of some new and more challenging mystery.

Currency exchange offered him that sort of mystery. In spades. It had not only the numerical complexity he craved but also the volatility, the tactical and strategic dimension of warfare he so enjoyed, plus rapid movement, and the sense of dicing with chance.

Projecting the rise and fall of sterling against dollar, of franc against yen; feeding into these projections the multitude of variables both hidden and perceived; pondering the multiplicity of permutations and combinations ultimately affecting their outcome, exerted upon him the same giddy exhilaration as would, say, producing the perfect Alexandrine or the perfect Spencerian stanza have upon a poet. A sculptor who has wrought in stone some sublimely perfect line or curve, or an astronomer who perceives in a new galaxy some heretofore undiscovered astral principle could not have experienced a more heady sensation than did Charles Daughtry when reducing the unruly capriciousness of currency fluctuation to strict invest-ment principles. He was, in short, some kind of genius.

It was raw genius to be sure, and like all such individuals, he was little understood. His colleagues at the bank where he next went to work viewed him with a mixture of repugnance and awe. He was not one of them and so they did not cultivate him. For them he was not "clubbable" but they were not so foolish as to fail to recognize that his talents were immensely bankable— something that bankers, perhaps more than all others, can appreciate. These talents were soon widely known. If one week Daughtry was buying sterling or selling kroner, it was not unusual to see other currency traders falling quickly into lockstep behind him.

But Daughtry had no social amenities, no interests outside of his numbers. He read little. He listened to no music. He never went to the cinema. He was innocent of any curiosity whatever in the larger political or social scheme of things.

His idea of relaxation, if it could be characterized as such, was to come home after a day's work at the bank and devise small mathematical games and conundrums that would have confounded the likes of a Euclid or a Napier.

"Suppose that 5 percent of the output of a machine is

defective," he would posit for himself while eating tunafish from a can. "From a batch of several thousand products of that machine, 10 samples are chosen at random. What is the probability that (a) at least 1 of the 10 is defective? (b) at least 2 of the 10 are defective? (c) exactly 1 of the 10 is defective?"

OR

"An obstetrician in a large hospital bet $1 even money on every birth in the hospital that the child would be male. He started with a capital of $10 and planned to continue betting until he either lost the $10 or raised his capital to $100. What is the probability that he loses the $10? What is the expected number of bets that he will make? Assume that male and female births are equally likely."

OR

"In a year that is not a leap year, choose a month at random. Let the random variable X = the number of days in the month. Construct a table showing $f(x) = P(X - x)$ for all possible values of X. Find the expectation of the random variable, and so on."

Such was his pleasure. On those rare occasions when he picked up a book it was either a work on military history or strategy, or a piece of low detective fiction, of which the moment he was able to divine the solution to the puzzle (this was generally quite early on), he'd toss the book off into a corner and never look at it again. He knew the ending, and possibly long before the author himself.

But, by far, Daughtry's favorite form of light recreation was to restage on vast dioramas in the basement of his brownstone famous battles of the past—Actium, Quatre Bras, Marengo, Austerlitz, Khartoum, Chancellorsville, Château-Thierry, and so on—these with battalions and regiments of lead soldiers for which he had spent princely sums to acquire. These war games, played with tin soldiers, some might perceive as child's play. But for Daughtry, the strategies implicit in these little *Kriegspiele* had their own kind of poetry, even if it was a poetry of death. On the cardboard dioramas and with his tin soldiers, the game of probability—or "what if?"—could be played out to his heart's content.

One final point. Daughtry had no close friends. Acquaintances, yes. Business colleagues, yes. Of women, there were many. They found him attractive and not a few pursued him. For his part, and with utter consistency, he mostly sought women who posed to him challenges in the form of mystery or puzzle. As with all other conundrums, unfortunately, he was on to them quite fast, with the result that interest quickly lagged.

Peculiarly, too, in romance, he was unable to resist imposing the same rules of strategy and tactics as he applied to *Kriegspiele*. Cold logic; cause and effect, with a gentle nod to divinations—that was his love formula. Understandably, even the most simpatico and durable of his lady friends declined to stand the gaff too long. In sum, he was a single-minded, solitary man who rarely, if ever, felt lonely. His head and heart were totally fixed on work.

It was no surprise, therefore, that Charles Daughtry, at the relatively youthful age of thirty-three, was elevated to high managerial position at the Confederated Trust Bank of New York, where he had come to work as a trader three years before. Venerated and cordially disliked, he was given a wide berth by his colleagues, and left to himself by his superiors, thus giving him a completely free hand to do what he did so well. At that point, having created a Frankenstein monster, they must have feared their creation just a bit. He was making a great deal of money for the bank. The stockholders were delighted with the quarterly statements, and certainly no one was inclined to challenge him. But they never quite knew what to expect from Daughtry. And that was just the way he liked things.

Daughtry's cab hurtled into the tunnel beneath the United Nations, and suddenly for a moment everything went dark. Purple rings with rosy auras whirled before his eyes. Daughtry rolled up the window to block out the chill, faintly putrescent odor of tunnel air. For a moment he saw, or thought he saw, in the lurid glow of a naked light bulb, the figure of a vagrant huddling in one of the shallow recesses along the wet tunnel walls. As the cab shot past, he glimpsed a haggard face framed within a halo of disheveled white hair. It struck him when he saw the face that he had seen it full on with an intensity that was blinding—the eyes cavernous, the temples hollow, a stubble of white whiskers beneath the lower lip multiplied and sharply defined like the venation of an insect wing under powerful magnification. The attitude of the head—thrust back against a dirty, graffiti-scrawled wall, chin held high, the eyes rolling heavenward like a transfigured saint—all of it came to him at once, leaping off the dank wall as if it were an icon painted centuries ago by some anonymous master—dazzling, ephemeral and terrifying. In the next moment it was gone, passed, lost forever.

He whirled in the seat, looking back, but nothing remained in the spot where the face had been, nothing but an ambiguous, elusive mound of shadow and rubbish, soon completely erased by the blur of encroaching cars whooshing past.

By the time the cab drew up before the impressive Stanford White turn-of-the-century structure that was the Confederated building on lower Broadway, a crack of dawn was already glimmering in the gash between the two immense glass shafts of the World Trade Center. Upstairs in the trading rooms of the Confederated Trust Bank, while the rest of the city turned and drowsed in fitful predawn sleep, the Telex, the Teletype and the transatlantic phone were all in use, pounding away relentlessly, "making the market" in sterling, dollars, Deutsche marks and yen.

4

I consider it a great advantage to obtain command young.
—DAVID G. FARRAGUT: *Journal* entry, 1819

"What do you make spot sterling?"

"Forty was just hit for a buck."

"Take a mil at 34. What's the swap rate?"

"Six months. Disco 50–40."

"What are you quoting spot marks?"

"$10/_{20}$."

"What's the book showing?"

"Long marks. Düsseldorf has 13 million DMs worth."

"Tell Bemelmanns I decline to do the whole amount. I take 7."

Daughtry moved through the trading pit, forgetting some of his early morning apprehension in the blur of activity. Motion quieted his nausea. For a while he monitored on a video screen the trading of Canadian dollars, then yen. Next he listened to squawk boxes, checked rate sheets where the latest quotations were posted. People shouted numbers back and forth at the top of their lungs and barked into 24-hour open phone lines. To the uninformed, there was an air of uncontained rage about it—the bellowing of a slaughterhouse. To the seasoned trader it was merely business as usual.

Most of Daughtry's traders had been at their desks since about 4 A.M., synchronizing their arrival at work with the 9:30 A.M. opening of the market in London. Most of them would still be there at 8 P.M. for the next day's opening of Tokyo-Singapore. Similarly, their colleagues on the West Coast in San Francisco would be keeping late hours so they might trade with New York-London on one side and Tokyo-Singapore on the other. The money never sleeps, nor can those who follow it for a livelihood.

17

Quite naturally, therefore, most of these traders were young—under thirty—tough and resilient enough to endure the stress and long hours; most, too, were unmarried and all made a great deal of money.

Daughtry checked his watch. It was now 5 A.M. in New York. On the far wall a bank of clocks posted time in a dozen key financial capitals of the world. Already 10 A.M. in London, it was 11 A.M. in Frankfurt-Paris; 5 A.M. in Toronto; 7 A.M. in Rio, and 1 P.M. in Bahrein. On the other side of the international date line, in Sydney, it was 8 P.M.; in Singapore-Manila, 6 P.M. In Tokyo, however, it was fourteen hours later—7 P.M. and the Money Exchange there had been closed four hours.

Daughtry chatted with several traders, then strolled into the back office where a dozen people mired in ledger paper and cold coffee exchanged payment instructions, value dates and credit information with a myriad of worldwide trading institutions.

Florita Gaynes, Daughtry's secretary, had put up a pot of fresh coffee in his office. On his desk in the large, sunny suite of rooms overlooking the East River, stacks of mail, publications and reports were awaiting him. There were *Interbank Bulletins, Federal Reserve Bulletins, Forbes,* the *London Daily Market Report,* correspondence from the Bundesbank, the Bank of France, the Allgemeine, Suisse National, Mobilare Banco Hispana. There too were the "hot" postings—and daily rate sheets— as of that morning. On his desk calendar were memoranda for luncheon at 1 P.M. and a lecture he was to give at the Metropolitan Club at 4 P.M. There was an invitation to speak at a forum on international finance in London and also a note to say that his reservations at the Palmer House were confirmed for the IMF conference in December.

Daughtry looked up from the papers, and scrawled "Suji" on his calendar. He checked his watch. It was nearly 5:30 A.M. Tokyo had been closed for four and a half hours. He was safe— perhaps for another twelve hours—but not a moment more.

It was a Monday morning, the beginning of the work week.

He had a headache and a net overbought position in spot pounds, value Wednesday. This had to be resolved before anything else. It meant that on Wednesday he had to take delivery of $6 million pound sterling and pay for them with dollars. He also wanted to maintain the net overbought position for one more day until value Thursday because he was certain that the spot pound was going to appreciate against the dollar, and he wanted to be there first with spot pounds when that time came.

He started to scribble on a pad a game plan to obtain an inflow of dollars that day. He also had to work out what he would do with pounds received that day. The problem was how to produce an outflow in pounds and an inflow in dollars for Wednesday, then how to reverse those flows for Thursday.

He had two options: He could sell pounds against dollars, value Wednesday, in order to purchase pounds against dollars, value Thursday. He could go to the money market or invest pounds from Wednesday until Thursday, thus enabling him to borrow dollars from Wednesday until Thursday.

He took a small desk computer out of his drawer and proceeded to work out the net yield of the position rollover computed for each alternative. At the conclusion of his computations it was clear to him that he was better off dealing at exchange rates than at the market's. At exchange rates the spread was in his favor.

In the next moment he reached for his phone, dialed Ricardi, his floor executioner, and instructed him to deal for dollars and pound sterling in the exchange market.

Seated behind his desk, Daughtry now reached for a dictaphone belt from the lower drawer, switched on the microphone, rotated a dial and proceeded to dictate: "Forward purchases of French francs can be made now at attractive levels, particularly in the three- and six-month periods. We would advise that advantage be taken of forward discounts presently available on Swedish kroner in all forward periods.

"Despite our forecasts for intra-snake pressure prior to the EMS formation, we would advise coverage of guilder liabilities throughout . . ."

Mrs. Gaynes entered, placed several reports on his desk, pointed to the top one. It was a long-awaited report from the International Currency Management Group (ICMG) based in London. Without breaking off his dictation, he nodded to her and she smiled and tiptoed out. ". . . our projection period. We recommend a similar strategy for the Deutsche mark.

"Due to the flatness of forward Belgian franc rates and the potential downside risk for the U.S. dollar, we would advise coverage of all BFC liabilities. It is likely that Canadian interest rates will be hiked and forward premiums switched into discounts. This being the case, we would advise caution before selling Canadian dollars at the 84.00 level as this, we feel, will be the bottom for the time frame of . . ."

At the sound of a buzzer, he looked up to see the small red light flashing on his intercom phone. He picked it up to hear Ricardi speaking quickly above a great deal of shouting in the background. The chief trader was calling from the pit to say that there was a sudden rate move in sterling. London was selling sterling for $1.80 and New York for only $1.75. It was one of those rare but irresistible opportunities to turn a neat profit, but they would have to move fast before New York and London had a chance to equalize the discrepancy.

"What are you quoting Deutsche mark?" Daughtry asked.

"2.20 as of a minute ago in Frankfurt."

"What about the sterling-mark cross-rate in London?"

"3.96."

Daughtry scribbled some figures on a pad. After a moment he said, "Take 5 mil pound sterling," and then hung up.

Ricardi was thus authorized to spend $8.75 million to acquire £5 million, in New York. Having negotiated that transaction, the executioner would then turn round instantly and sell the £5 million in London, where the sterling-mark cross-rate was 3.96. For this he would receive 19 million DM in

London, then turn round again and sell his Deutsche marks in Frankfurt at the going rate there of 2.20 DM per dollar. The resulting profit to Confederated would be a quarter of a million dollars. With open phone lines to London-Frankfurt, the entire transaction would take slightly above two minutes. The cost to Confederated—the price of the phone calls and, of course, Karl Ricardi's time. All in all, not a bad piece of work.

Mrs. Gaynes reappeared with fresh coffee. Daughtry lit a cigarette and proceeded to scan the *London Daily Market Report*.

". . . dollar reached all-time lows against DMK, BFC, DKR. . . . DMK remains pinned to its joint float ceiling against all snake currencies with the exception of . . ."

Daughtry put aside the *Report* and took up the *Money Manager*. At a glance he took in German unemployment figures and incoming orders for all manufacturing industries. He checked money supply shrinkage in Holland and its expansion in Japan. From there he moved to the Consumer Price Index in Mexico and the narrowing of the September trade deficit.

After that he was on to spot exchange and Euro Deposit rates in eight different currencies. Then Libor rates in London. The entire financial overview that morning had taken him perhaps eighteen minutes.

He paused, lit a cigarette and sipped coffee. Thinking suddenly of Tokyo, he glanced at his watch. A windchime tinkled in his head and suddenly it was almost three years ago and he was in the cricket-haunted garden in Okitsu.

"We shall have to have more dollars." Sujimoto smiled. They sat in the small jewellike pavilion garden behind the Japanese financier's home off the great Tokaido Road just below the shadow of Satta Mountain. Sujimoto wore a white ceremonial robe and sandals. He handed his American visitor a cup of green tea and a small rice cake which crumbled in his lap as he ate it. Garrulous, cultivated, esoteric and self-absorbed, the old man talked incessantly.

21

"Do not worry about the irregularity, Daughtry. You get the dollars. Leave the irregularities to me."

Daughtry sat quietly as the old man in the white robes rocked slowly in his chair. In the darkness of the garden, with the fireflies flashing like rampant meteors, the robes gave him a somewhat glowing spectral look.

He was a small man, Sujimoto, highly nervous, with hands always busy shaping multicolored squares of high-quality bond into paper boats that he stacked meticulously on his desk and presented to visitors. His carriage, even sitting, was fiercely erect, as if he were conscious of shortness and struggling everlastingly against the irreversible fact of it.

Wherever Sujimoto went, he invariably dominated the landscape, if not by money, power and the force of personality, then by the sheer animal cunning with which he was so richly endowed. When not actually working, he amused himself by playing with his subordinates a number of games of chance. They were for small stakes but he would cheat, if necessary, to win. He could not bear for one moment to be anything less than tops.

Belying the will of iron were soft blue leaky eyes, beneath which puffy sacs of fluid depended. For a man beyond seventy, the umber skin was remarkably smooth and unlined. As to vitality, he had it in quantities characteristic of a man half his age. Only the thick thatch of white hair with the black part running down the center was there to indicate the full spate of years that sat upon his venerable shoulders.

The overall impression Daughtry had that first April night in Okitsu was that of a much revered figure who had lived long and accomplished much. A leading financier-industrialist of a leading industrial nation, Sujimoto was decidedly a world figure.

His forte for many years had been acquiring troubled companies, reorganizing them, then selling them off at a quick profit. An incredibly quick decision-maker, as they were wont to describe him in the trade. "Maybe too quick."

"I bought Mitsu (diversified chemicals) at 80 and sold at 224;

bought Fujitsu (wood products) at 450 and sold for $10 million profit; sold Shiseido (real estate) at $5 million, then acquired Toshiba for a song. Million, million, million, for many years. Now this week I announce the merger of two of my German banks. That's assets of $1.6 billion, my friend," Mr. Sujimoto reported gleefully.

"Who are your ancestors, Mr. Daughtry?" the old man asked suddenly.

"Ancestors?"

"Forebears, Mr. Daughtry. Predecessors."

Daughtry had never thought of himself as having anything quite so lofty as "predecessors."

"No one really."

Sujimoto's eyes narrowed and a small, sardonic smile flickered at the corners of his mouth. "My ancestors were samurai. My grandfather was shogun in the province of Honshu. I find it remarkable that you can characterize your forebears as 'no one.' Were they fishermen? Laborers? Peasants?"

"They were no one special."

"The most trivial life is special, the Buddha teaches. I find you evasive, Mr. Daughtry."

"I don't try to be."

"It's inconceivable to me that a man who can execute binomial and exponential equations in his head hasn't the curiosity to inquire after his own history."

"History? What history? I have no history."

"Then you are sprung full-born, without benefit of progenitors, ay? Parthenogenesized, so to speak, like a lower plant or an invertebrate? As of now, I find you flat, Mr. Daughtry. No perceptible dimension. Do not think you can hide from me long. I'm looking for the subtext in you. I shall be exceedingly disappointed if I do not find one."

Mr. Sujimoto stared hard at the young exchange specialist he had summoned to Tokyo from the Confederated Trust Bank in New York, a bank he had recently acquired. Bringing him into his home and keeping him there, he reasoned, each would learn from the other. The old man's voice had been censorious, but now his eyes twinkled mischievously as if he'd been toying with the younger man but was now willing to grant absolution for all former sins. They stared at each other silently across the dusk-gray garden, both with a wary regard, like two potential adversaries circling each other, each one taking the measure of the other.

5

It is well to learn, even from one's enemy
(Fas est et ab hoste doceri).
—OVID: *Metamorphosis*, IV

For the building of a new Japan
Let's put our strength and minds together,
Doing our best to promote production,
Sending our goods to the people of the world,
Endlessly and continuously,
Like water gushing from a fountain,
Grow, industry, grow, grow, grow.

The refrain echoed in Daughtry's head even as Sujimoto's sad smile undulated before his eye. It was his first week in Japan during the "indoctrination" period at the Sujimoto Automotive Works outside Tokyo.

"You smile, Mr. Daughtry," Sujimoto said as the chanting workers tramped past. "You think it quaint and naïve," the old man went on as they continued to tour the rattling monster serpent of an assembly line. "Yet they sing it every morning as they commence work, and at day's end when they go home. They have translated it into English today especially for you. And what is more, they believe it."

"They must be doing something right." Daughtry smiled. "A

$12.7 billion trade credit is hardly my idea of quaint."

"Ten billion of which is with the United States alone." The old man beamed. "And now your dollar is worth only 63 percent of its yen value two years ago. Don't smile, Mr. Daughtry. Pay heed or we'll red-ink you to death."

"I'm not smiling," Daughtry protested, and for a moment he was tempted to say something unpleasant about Japanese tariff, strict import quotas and an exasperatingly corrupt and anti-quated distribution system, not to mention a maze of pitfalls in customs and product standards on imports. But since Mr. Sujimoto had just acquired 22 percent of the voting stock in the Confederated Trust Bank, what amounted to virtually control-ling interest, thus becoming his new boss, Daughtry thought it prudent to say nothing at all. "I'm not smiling," he said once more and looked quickly at the young woman accompanying them. Her name was Mariko and she was Sujimoto's daughter.

"We already have 40 percent of the U.S. video-recorder market," Sujimoto went on, brandishing figures. "Eighty per-cent of the new plain-paper photo-copiers, and sales of 1.9 million automobiles in the twelve months ending March 31, compared with the piddling 15,000 U.S. auto units exported to Japan. What do you say to that, Mr. Daughtry?" In the week that Daughtry had been there, the old man had sought to challenge him at every turn.

About to respond, Daughtry suddenly caught the girl's eye on him, cool, direct, unselfconscious, unashamedly assessing. "We've much to learn from the Japanese," he said and noted the faint hint of Mariko's amusement in her fleeting smile.

"Indeed you do." Sujimoto bustled ahead, pointing here and there. "Our ethic is work, discipline, self-sacrifice. The typical Japanese worker takes only 40 percent of his allotted vacation. What do you say to that, ay, Mr. Daughtry?"

"Admirable, Mr. Sujimoto. Very admirable."

"America's grown soft, Mr. Daughtry. Fat and soft. The Japanese have an ancient proverb about imitating a neighbor's wise ways. 'The stones of another's hill,' it goes, 'may be excellent for polishing your jade.' Look to your neighbors, Daughtry."

"We're learning to use your stones," Daughtry replied with grave amusement. "Many of our assembly lines have adopted Japanese methods and equipment."

"Not fast enough. Faster, Mr. Daughtry." The old man bustled ahead, pointing here and there. Daughtry slowed his step and Mariko came abreast of him. Her shoulder brushed his. "Our mean overall I.Q. in Japan is 106," the old man went on, spouting figures, unaware. "The highest of any country surveyed. Yours in the U.S. is only 100."

Daughtry ventured a smile at her, but she merely gazed back at him, unflinching, unfazed.

Later they sat outside in a little tentlike pavilion garden with a plashing fountain that gurgled over rocks in a man-made stream. While the temperature was inordinately high for that time of year, it was cool in the garden and, though the spot was no more than seventy-five feet from the huge factory, one would never have guessed that it was there.

A light luncheon of raw fish and rice was served in bright lacquer bowls. Mariko watched Daughtry struggle with chopsticks, offered him a napkin. When he took it, their fingers brushed. He had the distinct impression she had caused them to brush.

"Sell yen against pound sterling at 3 percent discount," Sujimoto droned on tirelessly like a dictaphone. "For value March 1. The outright rate is 2.3940." Sujimoto's eyes narrowed as he caught the American's eye on his daughter. He smiled stiffly. "Mr. Daughtry. If we are to get along, you must pay attention and do exactly as I tell you. There will be time enough for pleasure later."

One night in town at Sujimoto's club, the old man had kept him up till dawn. He'd drunk a whole bottle of rice wine at dinner and was deep into a quart of fine old Rémy. After a while he leaned back in his chair, working his tongue to dislodge a morsel of food from between his teeth. "The best-managed economy is the German. The worst is the U.S. Everyone knows that and counts on the condition continuing indefinitely."

Sujimoto sat back in his chair, lit up a Monte Cristo, and proceeded to regale Daughtry with one of those boozy, rambling anti-American tirades he appeared to relish so. "Of course, we all grow prosperous from American mismanagement, but it is a disgrace. Surplus, abundance and waste has made your people sloppy and undisciplined. Not only in monetary matters, but in every aspect of human affairs, you are known to be wasters and spoilers."

Sujimoto belched drunkenly and splashed some Rémy into Daughtry's glass. "For instance, in May of '42 during the Battle of the Coral Sea, I had the honor to serve under Rear Admiral Aritomo Goto on board the heavy cruiser *Aoba*. We had occasion then to observe firsthand the ineptitude of your forces and armament."

Sujimoto caught Daughtry's eye straying to a distant table. "Do I bore you, Mr. Daughtry?"

Daughtry smiled and gnashed his teeth. "Not at all. I'm all ears, sir."

"Good." Sujimoto's eyes crinkled into an unpleasant grin. "As I was saying, your forces and armament—not terribly impressive for a major power. Not at all."

But we whipped your ass, didn't we? Daughtry thought to himself, while feigning great interest in the old man's thesis. Sujimoto warmed noticeably to his subject.

"We had not only the estimable Mitsubishi A6M2 Zeros, but also the Aichi 99 D3A2 dive bombers—a formidable instrument of war. By contrast, your Douglas Devastator was slow and vulnerable with a cruising speed of only 205 mph as compared to our Zeros with 350 and our Nakajima 97s at 235. Your Grumman F4F3 Wildcat was a pitiful attempt to produce an

27

aircraft which would outrival its Japanese counterpart, the Zero—what your people called the Zeke. The Devastator was never quite up to our Zeke."

We only invented flight, Daughtry reflected inwardly, nodding his agreement at Mr. Sujimoto. We were flying while you people were back in the Age of the Wheel, he wanted to say, but instead he listened politely as the old fellow rambled on.

"Now your Douglas Dauntless was a reasonably accurate weapon. Nothing astounding, mind you, but effective. Still, in general, we thought little of your armament."

But you lost the war, Daughtry's voice roared inside himself. In the end, you lost. We won.

Sujimoto's brow arched; his head cocked toward the younger man as if he'd caught the heretical thought that had just passed there. Impudently, his eyes challenged Daughtry to verbal battle. When nothing of the sort ensued, he drank more Rémy and waxed more eloquent. The vision in his drunken eye of proud armadas, of noble fleets in battle formation, of phantom warships he knew to be reposing now many fathoms deep on the floor of the Pacific—ghostly fans of coral undulating all about them—*Shokaku* and the *Zuikaku* under Admiral Hara, the Fifth Cruiser Division components, Admiral Takagi's *Myoko* and the fierce old *Haguro,* followed by the destroyer flotilla: *Ariake, Yuguri, Shiratsuyo, Shigure, Ushio, Akebono;* followed by the Tulagi group under Shima and the Port Moresby group under his old friend, Rear Admiral Sadamichi Kajioka—all sailed proudly by in formation before his drunken, glassy eyes, pennants and battle flags waving, armament unsheathed, glistening in the fierce Pacific sun.

"Your Admiral Grayville wouldn't fight." Sujimoto suddenly rose and strutted up and down, brandishing his short piston arms with wild rhetorical flourishes. "He had twice, three times our firepower, two carriers, three heavy cruisers, minesweepers and planes, planes, planes—but he wouldn't fight." The old man swilled more cognac. Some of it spilled inadvertently down his collar. "The talent for winning consistently, Mr. Daughtry, is the gift of illusion. Make them think you have more than you do. Like poker, which my friend Pembroke, the American ambassador, taught me. Bluff is 95 percent of the game."

"But after the bluff," Daughtry interposed, "you have to finally put up or shut up."

Momentarily confused, Sujimoto paused. His jaw hung slack and his pale leaky eyes grew cloudy and unfocused. For a moment Daughtry thought he had offended him but, if he had, his anger passed quickly. Arrogance and his own bright vision of glories past swept him ineluctably forward. War was clearly Sujimoto's metaphor, and he lunged now into ever more grandiose and inflated depictions of his naval history—Suji at Leyte, Suji at Kwajalein, Suji in the Solomons, each version more unabashedly self-aggrandizing than the former.

"Grayville wouldn't fight me," Sujimoto ranted. "He hadn't the stomach for it. I came after him. I chased him up and down the Coral Sea. I came after him but he ran." Once more he brandished his arms overhead. "No Balls Grayville, we used to call him. Good sailor—okay? But too conservative." Sujimoto cackled raucously, enjoying the deflation of Americans to his young American assistant. "The Americans have no balls," he muttered sullenly. "They grow softer each year. Drink. Drink, Daughtry."

"I'd rather go to bed."

"Bed? Why bed, so early?"

"Tomorrow is work."

"Work? We go from here to office. No need for bed." As he grew drunker his English grew more slurred. He muttered something fierce and guttural in Japanese. "No, no." He waved his arms and started to sit, missed the chair, then sprawled on the floor. Daughtry caught the expression of injured surprise on his face just as he was going down, then finally passed out. One of the geishas hurried over, followed by the headwaiter. The girl, refined, elegant, was as much perplexed as she was embarrassed. Together they tried to haul him up into a chair, but he was leaden. Shortly they gave up. Instead, they rolled him over, at which point he started to snore, his nose bent against the floor and he burped sourly.

"We've got to get him home," Daughtry said.

The headwaiter shrugged. "He okay. Often like this with him. He stay here. He be fine."

The geisha gave Daughtry a sympathetic look. "He okay," she said, reconfirming her employer's opinion. "I take care. No worry. You go now." She spoke to him assuagingly as if he were an idiot who needed to be consoled.

The place was now nearly empty and Daughtry could see they were anxious for him to go. Only a few woozy strangers lingered there with the weary, long-suffering geishas. Japanese businessmen smashed on Scotch whisky and French cognac.

"But Mr. Sujimoto—" Daughtry protested as they guided him gently through a beaded curtain to the outside door.

"We take care." The headwaiter flashed a strained, toothy smile at the American and signaled the doorman to call a cab.

"But I'm responsible for him."

"We take care Mr. Sujimoto. We put to bed. Not to worry."

Daughtry could see it was fruitless. Obviously, they'd had a great deal of experience with the old man, and they would see to it that he was well cared for. No doubt there was a bed upstairs, with a fresh suit and linens kept in the closet. They were going to have it their way, and Daughtry was too tired to argue the point.

At last the American relented and permitted himself to be whisked outside into a small Toyota cab. The headwaiter ducked his head through the open rear window. "Where you go?"

"Minatoku," Daughtry replied. "Near the French embassy."

The man rattled instructions to the driver and in the next moment they lurched off into the gaudy neon tinsel of the Tokyo night.

The cab whirled him through the lower district near Tokyo harbor. At nearly 3 A.M., the quays and dockside bars were wide open and teeming with life. Street vendors peddled fish and rice out of steamy vats. From open doorways, American disco music throbbed out of jukeboxes at deafening modulations. Life lurked at every corner.

The Japanese clustered together in small, raucous bands of merriment, refusing to relinquish the night. Groups of businessmen, out for an evening, mingled with gangs of sailors off the merchant ships tied up at the docks. Great blond Swedes and burly lascars, bandy-legged Dutchmen, Kanakas, Welshmen and Icelanders, ruddy seamen of the Hebrides, jet-black Ivory Coasters, and small fierce Syrians with furtive eyes, all mingled and coalesced. They lurched along the narrow streets, chanting loud, drunken songs through the teeming night.

On an impulse Daughtry asked the driver to stop at a light. He paid him and got out suddenly eager to lose himself in the whirling pageant. Though he was tired, the seamy spectacle of harbor life was invigorating. In no time the chill air had cleared his head, and he was striding briskly through the kaleidoscopic night, down narrow teeming alleyways where life, cramped and prolific, pullulated like insect colonies.

The sound of a myriad wooden clogs thundered overhead on the Kachidokibashi Bridge. Streetcars racketed toward the Imperial Palace. Shoeshine girls hailed him. On the scummy nearby canal, ponderous unwieldy Japanese barges sat low in the water. Advertising neon lights flashed on and off.

No one in the city apparently ever went to sleep. Enterprise was everywhere. Hawkers stood in front of storefront nightclubs and Western-type bars, proclaiming the rare delights to be found inside. Crowds jammed into coffeehouses and pachinko parlors. Vendors occupying little stands sold tin wind-up toys, knick-knacks, cheap glass and bric-a-brac. Origami crickets, straw turtles, feathery white doves battering their wings against tiny cages, pinkish goldfish suspended in bowls, huge blooms of peonies and chrysanthemums spilling out of flower stalls, prostitutes foraging at every corner—all was commerce.

And along the harbor, on the crowded docks, on huge garish billboards, in the icy blue of calcium lights, along the route to his hotel, the name SUJIMOTO plastered and emblazoned everywhere. Automobiles being off-loaded on the docks were crated in boxes stamped SUJIMOTO. Color television sets, refrigerators, and high-fidelity equipment, electronic instruments, raw steel beams and agricultural machinery, harvesters, reapers and plows—all bearing the name and heraldic insignia of SUJIMOTO —were stacked at every pierside waiting to be craned and pulleyed upward into the great yawning maws of shipholds— ships all owned by SUJIMOTO, LTD, owned by the small disheveled fellow Daughtry had left back there sprawled drunk and disorderly on the sawdust floor of the House of Pink Fish.

6

Discipline is summed up in one word—obedience.
—LORD ST. VINCENT, 1735–1823

One afternoon after Daughtry had been in Tokyo several months, Sujimoto invited him to his beach home at Okitsu. They soaked for an hour together in a great bubbling cedar tubful of soapy water redolent of pine. Steam rose all around them, not unlike a sulfurous pool; only their heads bobbed on the surface as though disembodied.

Sujimoto sat immersed up to his chin with an ice pack on his brow to cool him down. Sweat trickled into his eyes and he talked endlessly of money. Periodically an attendant came by with fresh ice packs. At first Daughtry declined, but as the heat grew more enervating, he found himself lunging for the cool packs when they came around.

Sujimoto rattled on compulsively, nonstop, reciting a list of chores for Daughtry to carry out. "You will secure for me yen, sterling, Swiss francs and DM in forward transactions at the earliest possible time and at the following rates." He then reeled off a long string of figures he had committed to memory and expected Daughtry to do the same. "You will execute these purchases at the Weiler Bank, Zurich," he continued.

Daughtry's head snapped up. "The Weiler?"

"I believe that is what I said."

"But Weiler's your own bank."

Mr. Sujimoto appeared puzzled. "I'm perfectly aware of that. It is controlled by Protocorp, Ltd."

A set of warning bells started to go off in Daughtry's head. "I see," he murmured, his features sallowed in vapory steam. Strong jets of subsurface water pummeled his back.

Sujimoto continued to reel off figures and instructions. "These different currencies you will then sell back to the Weiler at the following rates." The resale rates he then quoted to Daughtry were significantly higher than the price the Confederated had paid for them.

"Why would Weiler buy back currencies at a higher price than they sold them?" Daughtry asked.

"Simply because I will instruct them to do so." The old man beamed happily. "And in this way the Confederated shall be able to post a neat Forex profit for their last quarter earnings report, rather than a loss. A little something for the stockholders, ay, Daughtry?" Sujimoto flashed a gold tooth and chuckled. "And serenity for us."

"But the profit will be fictitious," Daughtry said.

"Fictitious?"

"Yes—not true."

The old rascal put on his most aggrieved expression. "Not true profit, Mr. Daughtry? How so?"

"Because the profits will not express true market exchange rates; only artificially manipulated ones."

"Manipulated? Ah so." Mr. Sujimoto pondered that a moment.

"That's called self-dealing, Mr. Sujimoto."

"Self-dealing?" Sujimoto's splendid control of English suddenly eluded him.

"Yes—manipulating exchange prices with your own banks and holding companies for gain." Daughtry found himself resorting to single words and phrases. "Against the law. Highly irregular. Forbidden."

For all his feigned puzzlement, Sujimoto knew exactly what the young American was saying. "But we have been doing just that for years, Mr. Daughtry. When we wish to cover a loss for a short period of time. Show a profit to our stockholders. Surely no harm . . ."

"No harm? It's illegal."

The two of them sat there in the boiling water, naked and speechless, steam rising all about them, great gouts of piny suds streaming off their backs and shoulders.

"Not illegal for me." Sujimoto suddenly waved his blue-veined hand above the water. "I have always done this. No one ever said no to me. Who dares say so now?"

"I don't speak for your country." Daughtry's tone grew abrupt. "But if you are caught self-dealing in my country, they put you in jail."

"Jail?" First Sujimoto gaped, then he laughed aloud. The laughter was harsh and angry. "No banker goes to jail in United States."

Daughtry was not prepared to argue the point. "All I can say is that such a transaction is highly irregular and I can't be a party to it."

"Can't or won't, Mr. Daughtry?"

Daughtry inhaled deeply, then let the air out of his lungs very slowly. "Won't."

The old Japanese sat quietly for a moment, staring down into the green soapy water as if he were studying something on the bottom. For a moment he appeared very old and fragile. Then he spoke: "You will do this, Mr. Daughtry."

"But that's impossible."

"Kindly do what you are paid to do and leave the impossibilities to me."

"I'm afraid I must first clear this with my superiors."

"I am your superiors."

Daughtry bristled. "I meant my immediate superiors in New York."

"There will be no need for that." Sujimoto's enunciation was clipped. "I have already done that, and I think you will find that your superiors are in complete accord with my wishes."

That evening there was a large dinner party and again he met Sujimoto's daughter. She was seated across from him at table, and once he had fixed his eyes on her he was unable to remove them. Not that she was beautiful. Striking, yes. Arresting. Features of sharp, singular intelligence with strata of depth, and a posture, like her father's, uncompromisingly erect.

Daughtry estimated her age to be somewhere in the upper reaches of the twenties—twenty-seven, or possibly twenty-eight, although with Oriental women, particularly the Japanese, age, for a Westerner at least, is very hard to gauge. For a Japanese woman, too, he noted that her features bore a decidedly Western caste. That is, while he could see clearly the stamp of her father's features upon her, Sujimoto looked unequivocally Japanese; she, on the other hand, did not.

Also, that evening he met Kajumi, the sullen, taciturn son— the one whom you were never to ask questions about. He sat there through the cocktail hour with his hands folded in his lap and his eyes riveted stolidly to the floor. Finally, there was Sujimoto's longtime "companion" since the death of his wife—a rather flamboyantly attractive, slightly untidy Frenchwoman, some twenty years his junior, whom everyone present that evening referred to as Madame de Plevissier.

Daughtry and Mariko barely spoke that evening, but the next morning he followed her down to the beach. She turned on him sharply. "Why do you follow me?"

So sudden and direct was the question, it took his breath away. He was standing about forty feet behind her.

"I saw you. Don't think I didn't. Behind the boulders and the rubble up there. Crouching." She spoke, he noted, in an accent part British, and part that of an American-speaking Japanese. He found it charming.

He made a stab at being amused, but he was ruffled. "I think you must be mistaken," he said. But actually she wasn't. He had been following her. Stalking her as though she were prey. "I came down for a swim." He noted that she'd just emerged from the water and now he watched her as she toweled off her lean, muscular limbs. "May I call you Mariko?"

"I am not mistaken. You were following me. And of course you may call me Mariko."

She rattled off her responses just so, in sharp rapid-fire. It made him think he had done something to offend her. Possibly he was guilty of an unpardonable social gaffe, or perhaps he had neglected to observe some simple Oriental nicety in her presence. He sought now to redress the wrong.

"I'm pleased to see you out here," he went on, still slightly unnerved by what he perceived as her great displeasure. "I've gotten to know everyone in the house except you."

"That's your problem, Mr. Daughtry," she replied. "I certainly do not hold myself aloof. People have only to address me and I respond."

Utterly confounded, he had imagined that Japanese women were all a bit like Madame Butterfly, hiding winsomely behind lacquer fans—timid, docile, infinitely yielding. At a loss for words, he gaped at her helplessly. Having momentarily retreated, he took the initiative again and invited her out to dinner. She accepted directly. It was almost as if she had been awaiting that.

After she'd departed, he stood puzzled and brooding on the beach.

They went out frequently after that. To dinner. To nightclubs. One night she took him to the performance of a Noh play in a Tokyo theater. It started at nearly 11 P.M. and appeared to go on interminably. Bewigged manikins in silken robes with powdered faces and luridly painted mouths moved shrieking and grunting through some grim domestic tragedy. Interpreted through the most stylized and mannered gestures, the story, as seen through Daughtry's eye, recounted the moral descent of a young country girl who is spurned by her lover and, in turn, cast out by her family. Daughtry took it all to be some sort of paradigm. In any event, it was unbearable. He twitched in his seat for nearly four hours.

Later, at a restaurant off the Ginza, she asked him how he enjoyed it.

"Fascinating," he replied in his affably facile way, and saw an expression like curdling milk spread across her features.

"Fascinating?" It was one of those mindless, cocktail party adjectives she loathed.

"Well—" he went on doggedly, "unusual. I've never seen anything quite—"

"Why can't you ever say what you really feel? You were bored to distraction. At one point I looked at you during the performance. You appeared to be in pain. Can't you say that? I won't be disturbed. Insincerity troubles me much more than disinterest."

A long, denunciatory tirade ensued. She accused him of being disingenuous not only with her, but with her father as well. At the conclusion of it all, she called him a shallow, amoral opportunist and stalked out into the night.

Daughtry was still not certain what he had done. By the time he got his bill, paid it, and ran out after her, she had disappeared into the gaudy, rainwashed Tokyo night.

Later that evening he lay stretched on the straw tatami mats in the high vacant shadows of his bedroom in Sujimoto's hilltop villa above the sea. Outside, tall pines whispered like phantoms across the star-blown night. Agitated and sleepless, he watched the shadow figures dance on the shoji screen walls, waiting for he knew not what. Until at last she came, and then it occurred to him he always knew she would.

"Move," the girl said, staring down at him in the shifting shadows. The sea pounded on the beach below.

He rolled aside and she hiked her terry robe and knelt with

37

her bare knees on the straw tatami mats. Gravely, they contemplated each other, then with a small deliberate motion she slipped in beside him. Easy, unselfconscious, she did it all as if it were an action predetermined in a plan worked out on paper. In the next moment she leaned above him and pressed her mouth roughly down on his.

Her lips were cold and at first he was unresponsive. "Your father—" he said.

"Asleep." She kissed him again; still he failed to ignite. She grew irritated. "What's wrong?"

"Nothing. I—"

"I tell you he's sleeping. He's had too much brandy. He won't wake." She sat up and hastily unbelted the white robe, letting it fall open between her breasts. She had just bathed and the smell of talcum rose like floral scents from beneath the robe. Then, in a swift decisive motion, she tossed a leg over his hip and sat astride him, her small, erect breasts thrusting out from beneath the robe. She stared down at him fixedly, her lips parted slightly so that he could see small white teeth glinting between them.

"Why did we go through all that nonsense at the restaurant?" he asked.

She stared hard at him for a moment through narrowed eyes. "It's because I'm fond of you."

She leaned down and kissed him again, forcing his mouth open with the action of her tongue. This time his arms came up around her. He hiked the robe above her hips and felt himself suddenly surge. She bit his lower lip and raked her nails across his back. He caught his breath while they rolled back and forth as if they were fighting.

The action served to arouse him. Rising halfway from the hips, he made an attempt to mount her. She resisted, trying to force him back down. For a moment they clung together like primordial crabs locked in fatal combat at the dawn of time. The muscles of her back trembled against the weight of his body. Then with a shudder, she muttered something in Japanese and

38

slipped beneath him, her legs yawning open as she did so.

Slowly they moved back and forth, the slow, gathering frictive motion itchingly exquisite. Beyond the window the tall pines sighed, the surf roared, and shadowy, formless liquid shapes flowed like fantoccini across the rice-paper screens. Then for a moment, even within the deep swooning intoxication of that embrace, Daughtry heard, or thought he heard, a sandal whisper over the cool bare floor outside the room.

They spent the following morning closeted in Sujimoto's office in the Kabutocho, Daughtry scribbling on a pad while the old man rattled off a series of transactions he wanted Daughtry to consummate before the end of the week.

". . . go for the rollover at 8¼ percent. Secure additional dollars now on forward swaps. All you can. I have it on good information that the Fed will be propping the dollar with bullion sales. Watch particularly interest and Libor rates in London. The progress of sterling over the long haul is for downturn . . ."

"How can you be sure?" Daughtry asked.

"Never mind about my surety." There was an edge of displeasure in Sujimoto's voice. "Just do as I tell you."

Daughtry looked up into a grim, smoldering countenance. "A man who defiles his host's roof is beyond contempt."

Daughtry's heart jolted in his chest.

"Do not pretend innocence, Mr. Daughtry."

"Innocence?" He flushed hopelessly.

"You know very well what I refer to." Sujimoto's shrill voice rose. "What is the nature of your relationship with my daughter?"

"That's easy. I don't have one."

"You are not merely evasive, you are a liar. Never mind. So be it." The old man waved his hands erratically. "Suffice it to say I will not soon forget how you repay my hospitality. I will look for appropriate ways to repay you, too. In the meantime, kindly desist from any further social contact with my daughter. It is a distraction. It confuses your mission here and brings into serious doubt your ability to carry out your transactional responsibilities as an employee of my bank."

Crestfallen, hands clasped limply in his lap, twiddling his thumbs rapidly, old Sujimoto appeared to be on the verge of tears. But in the next moment he cocked a leaky eye in Daughtry's direction. "Oh, by the way, Daughtry. Have you yet consummated our little transaction with Weiler?"

Even as Sujimoto's anxious doleful gaze still flickered in his head, Mrs. Gaynes reappeared with a stack of new reports and a dozen contracts for his signature.

"Your reservations at the Connaught are fine for the end of the month," she said. Something flared in her eye momentarily, then expired like a dying ember. "Mr. Sujimoto's contracts are on top."

He muttered something unintelligible and turned to the documents.

Mrs. Gaynes started out, then turned. He looked up, surprised to see she was still waiting there.

"Yes?"

"Mr. Michaeltree asked if you would stop by his office this afternoon." She seemed flustered.

A fist closed over his heart. He took out the Sujimoto contracts and began to pore over them.

7

If the iron dice roll, may God help us.
—THEOBALD VON BETHMANN-HOLLWEG *to the German Reichstag, as Foreign Minister, August 1, 1914*

"Are you sure?"
"Reasonably."
"How'd they catch it?"

"Routine in-house audit. Just cleaning up details. Pulling contracts at random."

"And?"

"They pulled two or three that were never squared. Been wide open for six weeks."

A police siren wailed mournfully from somewhere below. Daughtry's eyes narrowed and he appeared to inhale deeply. "How much?"

"Eight million Swiss francs, 8 million DM, 9 million yen." Max Michaeltree recited the figures quietly, then added portentously, "So far."

Michaeltree was a senior vice-president of the bank. A money manager with nearly three decades of experience as a trader, and now charged with the responsibility of shaping exchange policy for the Confederated. A jolly, porcine man with a round pasty face, his eyes appeared always to be measuring and mocking, to imply possession of damaging information impinging directly on one's personal fate. "Might be only the tip of the iceberg, they think."

"They?"

"Selig—some kid, down in accounting. Just out of school. Started here three months ago." Michaeltree poured a glass of water from a pewter carafe. As he drank, his twinkling eyes watched Daughtry over the rim of the glass. "Vickers says he's on to something. Doesn't know exactly what it is, but that it's *big*."

Daughtry felt his bowels contract. Outwardly, however, his calm was glacial. "Have you spoken to Leon yet?"

"I'm waiting for the final report from the auditors."

"When's that due?"

"End of the week." Michaeltree rotated the moistened tip of a cigar on his wet bluish lips and ignited it with a desk lighter. "Must have it for the last quarter report."

Two full walls of the office were of floor-to-ceiling plate glass through which the western sky now poured sad autumnal sunshine.

From where Daughtry sat he could see both the Hudson and the East River, the lower tip of the island where they met, and the busy hive of quays on both sides where freighters, tankers, great merchant fleets of mighty trading nations were tied up, taking on and disgorging. Above them, pennants and bright ensigns flapped in the tall masts, denoting the proud commerce of the world.

Daughtry stirred in his seat and cleared his throat. "Where does this sharp young accountant think the losses are coming from?"

Michaeltree contemplated the glowing tip of his cigar. "He's convinced it's in Forex."

"Oh?"

"Can't pinpoint it yet, but he claims we're hemorrhaging reserves from foreign exchange. Hard to believe, isn't it, Charley, since we're posting a 2MM profit in currency operations over the last quarter?"

"Pretty farfetched," Daughtry remarked; his mouth was dry.

"That's what I said. Told him as much. I said I thought it was ridiculous." Michaeltree smiled oddly. "How are the aggregate outstanding contracts running?"

"Normally." Daughtry gazed at the ceiling. "Actually a little below normal."

"Just what I thought." Michaeltree shrugged. "Probably a mistake. Selig's young. Anxious to make an impression."

They were both silent, watching each other warily.

"I'll check it out, anyway," Daughtry said.

"No need to."

"I want to, though."

"Well, I s'pose it can't hurt." Michaeltree puffed thoughtfully. "What about your incoming confirmations?"

"All checked against outgoing."

"And then sent to—?"

"Auditing."

"Always?"

"That's our procedure. Of course I can't be certain—"

"Of course." Michaeltree nodded sympathetically. "There must be hundreds each week. What sort of details do they corroborate on the confirmations?"

"Usual sort of thing." Daughtry stared hard into the manager's flinty eyes. "Name of party. Rates. Amounts borrowed or sold. Currencies involved. Value date. The bank where the amounts are to be received or paid. You know the sort of thing."

"And all discrepancies between incoming and outgoing are appraised?"

"Immediately." A strange, disquieting calm had settled over the room.

A fly, unaware it was November, buzzed petulantly. Michaeltree pondered a moment, then sighed in his chair. "And I suppose all the handwritten contracts are time-stamped by Ricardi?"

"Sometimes Ricardi, sometimes Villiers, sometimes I do it myself. You know that as well as I do, Max. The chief trader time-stamps everything just before preparing the ticket and passing it on for entry into the position book."

"So you're able to do a retroactive comparison between prices quoted on the rate sheets and those on the contracts."

"Precisely—almost on a minute-by-minute basis."

"And of course you're using serially numbered manifold forms for any kind of confirmation?"

"Of course." Daughtry seemed irritated. "What would you think we'd do?"

"And any forms not used are accounted for?"

"Promptly."

Michaeltree leaned back in his chair and puffed contentedly at his cigar. "You understand, Charley, I'm only refreshing myself on standard safeguard procedures. I've been out of the game for so long."

"Of course."

"You trust all your people?"

"Implicitly."

"And Ricardi?"

43

"Tops. The best in the business."

Leaning backward in his chair, Michaeltree's pudgy fingers intertwined comfortably across his ample paunch. "You know, when I started out in this business, forty years ago, we had a trader at the old Hanover Bank by the name of"—his eyes squinted as his mind drifted back over the years—"what was it now? Ellison. That was it. Wally Ellison." Michaeltree chuckled. "You know what this bugger was up to?"

Daughtry leaned slightly forward in his seat.

"He would commit a contract," Michaeltree continued, "mail out the original of a confirmation, then destroy all copies. You know why, of course?"

"So that he could build up a position without the knowledge of management."

"Precisely. Then he would have the incoming confirmation diverted from auditing to himself."

"Which he would then immediately destroy," Daughtry added coolly.

"Correct." Michaeltree smiled. "And then nobody would ever know about the position."

Daughtry took the offensive now. "How would he then *square?*"

"Easy." Michaeltree's eyes twinkled wickedly. "When selling that position again he would make up a ticket for the originally destroyed contract and pass that on, together with the sales contract so that the position was *square* again."

"We'd catch that in a minute," Daughtry reflected. "All of our incoming confirmations are sent directly to an independent audit department."

"But if you don't insist upon an immediate accounting of any missing serially numbered forms—"

"Well, I do." Daughtry rose abruptly. "But you're welcome to check any time you want, Max. You don't just bury $18 million."

Michaeltree chuckled amiably. "I know that, Charley. I'm just recalling old Wally Ellison though. He was something special. A most inoffensive little chap. Used to come to work on a bus. Brought a bag of egg sandwiches with him to the office every day. Took the old Hanover for a million-five before anyone caught on to what the hell he was up to. Million-five meant something in those days."

Michaeltree tilted his head back and roared heartily, then broke off suddenly. A scowl transformed his amiable features. "What have you heard from our friend, Sujimoto?"

Leaving Michaeltree's office, Daughtry walked directly through the trading rooms where the din of bells and numbers sounded like the clash of war.

Ensigns and pennants streaming in the wind. Trumpet fanfares. Hoarse cries. The clank of cavalry. The creak of leather. Overhead the dull, concussive pop of Gatling guns showering blooms of vivid pink sparks down upon the heaving landscape. Lord Chelmsford's 23rd Welsh Borderers swinging into position on the Oskarberg Terrace; the 72nd Duke of Albany's Light Horse moving inexorably forward.

Across the broad Buffalo where the punts drifted aimlessly in the muddy tide, an impi of 4,000 Zulu pikesmen comprised of the Undi Corps and the uDloko under Dabulamanzi started their move. It came with a shuddering motion like that of some large torpid worm just cracking its chrysalis. Behind them lay the scorched slopes of Isandhlwana, stunted and ominous beneath a dirty green haze. All about them, the Valley of the Bashee encroached, serene and uncaring in the heat and choking dust.

Shreds and fragments of his morning's dream rocketed through his head. As he passed Mrs. Gaynes in the anteroom, she handed him several messages, calls that had come in when he was out. "Mr. Wheatley called and his—"

"Cancel my lecture at the Metropolitan Club and accept no further calls today." He swept past her, barged into his office and slammed the door behind him.

Once inside, he slumped heavily back against the wall, and

felt a pulse throb at the base of his neck. His desk was stacked with reports, memoranda and messages that had poured in while he was out. Calls from Washington, London, Manila, Abu Dhabi. Cables from the Bundesbank, and the Mobilare. Old chums, Bradwell, senior VP at Chemical, and Danny Borderguerreaux of the Morgan Guaranty.

Within the tiny stockade at Rorke's Drift the Scottish Highlanders swarmed, erecting barricades of meal bags and ammunition cartons. The air had begun to crackle with musket fire from the Natal Kaffirs up on the parapets firing through a smoky blaze of enfilading fire. Blood ran in deep runnels over the sere shell-pocked earth. But still the Zulu came, unshod, rattling assegais, white shields, huge green monkey-skin earflaps, white ostrich plumes tied behind ringed heads, screaming, shouting, chanting, caterwauling, swinging truncheons and axes, the awful sickening din of battle and dying.

Outside Daughtry's window, lights, toylike and festive, began to twinkle up on the granite face of the Twin Towers soaring remorselessly upward, crashing against the star-blown vault of a cold, evening sky.

. . . *The Mahdi of mass and mutual massacre.*
—SIR B. H. LIDDELL HART: *The Ghost of Napoleon,*
1895

When Daughtry came home that evening she was not there. All of her clothing had been removed from the closets and bureaus. Her perfumes had been taken from the dressing table, her cosmetics, even her lavender soap cakes from the shower. The place had the look of having been subjected to a violent ransacking. She had taken nothing that was not actually hers but she had gone to pains to desecrate anything which she thought was of some special significance to him—ceramics, prints, a Lalique crystal cigarette box. A Chinese vase of chrysanthemums had been upended in a waste basket, and several Javanese shadow puppets ripped off the wall and mutilated. A great number of other things lay shattered in odd corners—nothing of any special value, but little things he liked. He felt no sense of vengeance, only gratitude that she was gone.

He'd known the girl for two months; for Daughtry that was going some. Actually, after the first week he was eager for her departure—the untidiness, the disorder, the clumps of hair in the shower drain and the soiled sanitary napkins, barely wrapped, tossed haphazardly in the waste basket. What an assault it had all been on his overly fastidious ways. A pretty girl he'd met at a party where he'd had too much to drink. They shared a cab home and he'd been imprudent enough to ask her in for a drink. Reckless and unthinking, she accepted, came up, liked the lay of things and never left. But how she had talked and talked, distracted him from work, generated mess and played loud trashy records until he was beside himself. Still, he had not quite the ruthlessness to invite her to leave.

Well, she had done that for herself now and even standing there amid the breakage he felt profoundly grateful. His home was his again, returning to him like an old friend with its worn, familiar look, its lovely silences and solitude.

Even as he'd entered the house that evening, his weary steps turning on the stair, he knew she was gone. The house, unlit except for the dim glow of light in an upstairs bedroom, bore a look of vacancy and desolation. A disquieting stillness hovered unnaturally about the place.

"Annabelle," he called up the stairs, peering at the soft diffusion of orange light spilling out of the bedroom into the hall. His voice sounded ghostly and distant in the upper reaches of the house.

"Annabelle?"

Upstairs he found the empty drawers and closets, the

missing cosmetics and toiletries. In the bathroom, the faint odor of bath oil and scent clung to the porcelain and tile. The shower curtain and thick pile towels strewn about the floor were damp from recent use, and the taps were still dripping. About everything hung the smell of hair and skin and sour laundry. The crowning insult was a message scrawled in lipstick on the bathroom mirror reading "Fuck you, Daughtry."

By morning it would all be gone, praise be, along with all memory of her. With his toe he nudged aside a shard of shattered crockery, stepped over the threshold and, like a returning army long embattled, reoccupied his bedroom.

It was now nearly midnight. He had canceled his luncheon appointment. All he'd had to eat that day was coffee and the few desultory nibbles of roll in the morning cab. Tomorrow the news would be full of Sujimoto's collapse. They would all be after Daughtry then—hammer and tongs—the SEC and the Fed, the FBI and the Currency Comptroller—all yammering loud, bearing down hard. The collapse would shake governments. Reputations would be ruined. Undoubtedly the bank would plead ignorance, and leave him to heaven. He knew precisely the quality of men with whom he dealt each day and just what could be expected from each of them in the pinch. It was not much to look forward to.

The skull-like beatific apparition in the tunnel drive that morning flashed before his eye and it occurred to him that he should eat. He went downstairs into the basement Pullman kitchen with its windows recessed in a well below the level of the street. One could see feet parade by on the pavement above. Occasionally people would stoop down and peer in. Daughtry began to prepare eggs and Worcestershire sauce, then put them aside and took a large dram of Scotch instead.

9

Read and reread the campaigns of Alexander,
Hannibal, Caesar, Gustavus Adolphus, Turenne,
Eugene and Frederick. Make them your models. This
is the only way to become a great captain, and to
master the secrets of the art of war.
—NAPOLEON I: *Maxims of War,* 1831

"Sujimoto?"

Daughtry stirred, hearing his own gruff voice murmuring balefully in the dark. "Sujimoto?" He muttered the name again, half expecting the old man in his white robes to rise wraithlike out of the shadows.

It was past midnight now on Sixty-third Street. It would be past 2 P.M. in Tokyo. He thought of calling Sujimoto to demand clarification—or at least an explanation for this betrayal. He had the private number in Okitsu, as well as the apartment number in Tokyo. But he was certain the old man would not be there to answer calls—particularly his.

The Kabutocho, Tokyo's stock market, had been open for five hours now. Undoubtedly the news of the Sujimoto collapse had already struck there. World markets would be reeling with the seismic impact for weeks; for subsidiaries of the widely diversified international giant, such as the Confederated, it would be a mortal blow. At the bank tomorrow morning there would be chaos. Sujimoto had carefully kept the precarious finances of his empire a well-guarded secret. Now, he had very cynically chosen the value date—the day he was scheduled to perform nearly $45 million in outstanding futures contracts with the Confederated, to declare his own insolvency. By the time the Confederated would learn of it, Sujimoto's doors would be finally, irrevocably shut, and it would be too late then for the bank to react.

The Confederated would be left holding the bag. The bank didn't know that yet, but Selig, the smart young CPA, was going to see to it very shortly that they would. After that, he would

49

show them how their own Charles Daughtry, through conscious complicity with Sujimoto, whether willing or not, had made it all possible.

Stiffly, Daughtry started from his chair, thinking he might go up to bed. Instead, he fixed himself another Scotch in the kitchen and proceeded to amble despondently through the house with his glass. He prowled about like a stranger moving from one room to the next. The house, the place that had come to be home for him for the last four years, the home he had so coveted, was suddenly odious to him. The furnishings (for which he had haunted antique shops and auction galleries and which he'd had shipped from the Orient) rugs, porcelain, celadon ginger jars, jade, lacquer, coromandel screens, priceless old Japanese prints—all this which had been so carefully assembled, piece by piece, now suddenly filled him with a sense of estrangement. If he could have moved it all out of the house, that night, dumped it onto the street, that very moment, he would have done so gladly.

Standing unkempt in his socks, Daughtry found himself in the basement of his brownstone before the vast battlefield dioramas he had erected there several nights before. It was going on 3 A.M. His head ached. His mind was agitated as he observed warily the lead Zulu replicas ringing the infirmary of Rorke's Drift in a fatal knot. Rage and impatience consumed him. Suddenly, he could see Chelmsford's error, his failure to commit the Borderers and the Light Horse at the crucial moment. And then to have left Erskine up there on the parapets, twiddling his thumbs. A smog in his mind suddenly lifted and he could see through to the heart of the mystery.

The British had been dilatory. Too slow to go on the counteroffensive. Daughtry knew that now, having replayed on his battle dioramas the entire bloody carnage of Ulundi, Eshowe, Isandhlwana, and the farce that was Rorke's Drift. His drugged brain grew feverish with strategies. He chafed to regain momentum—move the Borderers up and commit them to a slashing counterattack.

50

Eyes still fixed on the raging battle, he reached back, groping for the half-consumed tumbler of Scotch, and gulped greedily, part of it streaming down his shirt front. He never tasted any of it, such was his absorption in the action before him. Tomorrow would commence a fight for his very life, but right now, as of the moment, no one dare approach him while he was with his battles and warriors—the sacred hour of *Kriegspiele*.

He watched queasily now as the Highlanders fell back before the stampede of charging Zulus. They were streaming over the sandbag barricades and into the infirmary square. The Undi had begun to torch the thatch roofs sloping above the inner verandas. Invalided Borderers came streaming out of the wards, screaming, some of them with nightshirts on fire. The place stank of singed flesh. The Hottentot grooms ran about wildly, like decapitated chickens, spitting themselves suicidally on the uDloko spears, offering their breastbones up for sacrifice.

Metal clanged, rifle fire crackled, assegais soared through the scorched air like swarms of enraged bees. Shields, swords, spears, broken guns, stabbed corpses littered the yard outside the storehouses.

In the next moment the ringing of a phone—sounding far off—pierced Daughtry's woozy consciousness. He shot a last wistful glance at the Highlanders and Erskine up on the parapets, cut off and doomed. The sporadic crackle of the Martini-Henry rifles racketed in his head. DMK—1.9120; SWFR—1.7260; Yen—168.0014; Pound sterling—2.3685 . . . crackling numbers dying in rags of smoke.

The ringing of the phone persisted. It came from upstairs and had possibly been ringing for some time. He rose and lurched stiffly through the half-darkened rooms. "Sujimoto, Sujimoto." He murmured the name, over and over again, almost laughing as he went, thinking the old fox was calling now to tell him the situation was under control—"Not to worry, Daughtry. Not to worry. Overreaction to trivial events surely fatal." At a certain point he banged into a pier table, dislodging a Ming jar.

He did not even look back when it shattered on the floor behind him.

"Yes," he cried, lunging for the phone on a small hall table. There was a pause as he heard someone's startled gasp at the other end.

"Mr. Daughtry?"

"Speaking."

It was a man's voice, faltering and embarrassed. "Bill Craighead of the *Times.*"

"Christ—it's three o'clock in the morning."

"Yes, sir, I realize that. I'm awfully sorry, but I simply had to verify a story that just came in over the Reuters wire from Singapore."

Daughtry's breath caught in his throat. "Singapore."

"Yes, sir—Sujimoto, Ltd., has gone into receivership in Tokyo."

Daughtry stalled for time. His mind was already going a mile a minute. "Receivership?"

"Surely you were aware—had some inkling—"

"No, actually not. No inkling whatsoever." Daughtry heard his own voice many miles distant—lying badly.

"How well do you know Mr. Sujimoto?"

"Sujimoto? Not very well at all."

"Not very well at all?"

Daughtry could hear the skepticism in the reporter's voice.

"What impact do you think this will have on Confederated here?"

"None at all," Daughtry blustered. "Why should it have any impact?"

"But Mr. Daughtry—?"

"Listen, why the hell did you call me anyway?"

"Well, obviously because—"

"You should have called Wainwright or Michaeltree. Someone way up there. Why the hell bother me?"

"Because you're the Forex man," the reporter shouted back, as much infuriated as he was desperate. "Because you determine the bank's exchange policy. The losses are all rumored to be in the area of currency exchange. And of course, Sujimoto's—"

"No comment," Daughtry bellowed into the line.

"Okay. I see. All right." The reporter was momentarily cowed. "Would you care to make a statement about any of this?"

"Absolutely not. I have no further statements to make at this time."

10

As for those cowardly captains of yours, hang them up, for, by God, they deserve it.
—COMMODORE M. DU CASSE: *Letter to Admiral John Benbow, RN, mortally wounded after three days' action against du Casse off Santa Marta, Colombia, August 22, 1702*

"'. . . faked letters of credit and other documents to illegally secure bank loans, the proceeds of which went into speculative real estate investments. Mr. Sujimoto and his group ran into trouble last year when he began to have serious liquidity problems which he attempted to ease through a series of highly volatile Forex transactions.'"

Leon Edelbach, president and board chairman of the Confederated Trust, cleared his throat and looked up from the *Wall Street Journal* page one story to gaze round at the sixteen faces staring raptly in his direction.

Edelbach was a short energetic German immigrant with wiry gray hair and high color. People characterized him as looking in appearance like a block of ice. Still in his early fifties, Edelbach's wing collars and black Oxford shoes were a source of unexpressed amusement to his younger colleagues. He was not the sort of employer with whom one might openly jest.

Having arrived in New York soon after the war with little in the way of formal education, and virtually no one to recommend him, Edelbach's rise had been meteoric. The short stocky frame and the merry, slightly mocking eyes embedded deeply above rose-tinted cheeks gave him a gnomish, fairy-tale appearance, as if he'd sprung whole cloth from the imagination of the Brothers Grimm. But gnomes and fairy tales notwithstanding, Leon Edelbach had a well-known and thoroughly documented reputation for ruthlessness and rough play in hard times.

They were seated in the boardroom of the Confederated around an immense travertine rectangle supported on steel trestles—all sixteen board members, plus Charles Daughtry, who was not a board member. The vast expanse of marble was littered with papers, carafes of water, glass tumblers and heaping ashtrays. Above the table hovered a smog of blue smoke drifting in uneasy currents on the roiled air. Beyond the table, and then farther, beyond the wall of plate glass at the end of the room, the Twin Towers of the World Trade Center soared pitilessly upward into the bright autumnal sky.

Peering round the table from one face to the next, methodically assessing each man seated before him, Edelbach had the look of a stern pedagogue before a group of chastized and badly frightened students. When at last his eyes came to rest on Daughtry, they appeared to fix there heavily, and linger long. If Daughtry was aware of this he didn't show it; instead, his eyes gazed down at a pad on to which he doodled numbers and letters in formulaic pattern.

Mr. Edelbach raised the *Wall Street Journal* once again and resumed his reading. "'Specifically, Mr. Sujimoto is charged with the following malpractices:

"'1. He used his own overseas subsidiaries to issue credit import bills and then used them to apply for loans in Tokyo, Hong Kong, Singapore and Seoul. Once the goods were shipped out, they were again used to draw loans from overseas banking institutions.

"'2. Mr. Sujimoto faked bills of lading and these were issued by his own shipping company to draw loans. Many letters of credit were faked and deposited with the banks here as collateral.

"'3. Mr. Sujimoto diverted millions of dollars into foreign

exchange speculation. When he lost heavily on these speculations, he used his own holding company and banks to engage in a series of self-dealing transactions in order to report heavy losses as gains in bank earnings reports.

"'It is not clear how many banks here have been victimized in the Sujimoto affair. Local business sources believe that the Bank of America, the Morgan Guaranty Trust, and the Confederated Trust Bank have claims in the neighborhood of $300 million, with Mr. Sujimoto's own bank, the Confederated, bearing the brunt of the losses. Officials reached at the bank would neither refute nor verify the claim.

"'It is understood that U.S. government authorities will seek extradition papers against Mr. Sujimoto. Mr. Sujimoto is expected to resist any such attempts. The elderly financier maintains that he is totally innocent of any malfeasance, claiming that he was misled, betrayed and poorly counseled by his own advisers.'"

Edelbach watched Daughtry, still scribbling figures onto a pad, seemingly unmindful of the proceedings around him. Actually, he had already read the *Journal's* report and knew intimately every detail of it.

". . . imperative we assess the full extent of losses," Walter Wainright, senior vice-president, was on his feet talking.

". . . early reports from last quarter audits place it conservatively at $6 million . . ."

"We have to know. We must be exact. We can't possibly go public with losses of this magnitude in the final quarter earnings report." Desmond Bagwell, a rumpled, jowly individual was speaking.

". . . great risk of a run on demand deposits," Max Michaeltree cautioned, ". . . must ascertain at once the extent of FDIC coverage."

". . . drastic liquidity crisis in the event of a run."

". . . our department will recommend that the SEC immediately suspend all trading in Confederated common and preferred issues . . ."

55

Words and phrases burst like shrapnel about the room. Voices droned. People rose and spoke. Others waited to report.

"I personally had no knowledge of . . ."

"I was appalled to learn . . ."

"If only my group had been informed earlier . . ."

The time of alibis had commenced. Everyone had begun to exonerate himself; to proclaim innocence, and wash his hands of any guilt.

Periodically, Daughtry gazed round the table at his colleagues—suave Michaeltree, blustering Villiers, craven sycophantic Bagwell, Wainright, the nonentity and fop—and, of course, Edelbach, potentially the biggest loser of all. None had been close to Daughtry in the past, but at least they had all been professionally civil. Now he sensed them beginning, by almost tacit unanimous agreement, to dissociate themselves from him. To pull away as it were and strand him there alone on the burning decks of a dying ship. The stench of terror was all about.

Daughtry sat doodling cryptic figures onto his pad, seemingly absorbed in some brooding rumination.

Suddenly everyone was speaking at once, papers moved rapidly on the table, voices rose. Innuendo and recrimination flashed through the air.

Daughtry maintained his reserve. He was there, but not really there. Present yet decidedly apart.

At a certain point Edelbach's hand rose signaling silence. Only gradually did the din subside into two final squabbling voices.

"Quiet," Edelbach roared, red in the face. An embarrassed silence fell like a pall over the room.

"If we can't pull together now," Edelbach went on, "God help us when we go up before the Fed." He waited for the effect of his words to register upon them. "That's right—we've been invited to appear in Washington tomorrow before the Treasury Secretary. Invited is a euphemism. We've been summoned there to explain ourselves."

A low murmur of nervous response rippled through the room.

Edelbach continued: "I've been asked to come down with a deputation of five key officers. For our purposes I have selected Walter, Ed, Desmond, Max and Charley."

The selection of the first four—Wainright, Villiers, Bagwell and Michaeltree—was not at all unusual. They were board members with key responsibilities. Daughtry, the final selection, on the other hand, was not. His area of chief responsibility, foreign exchange, while highly profitable to the bank, was not a principal area of board activity. Therefore, Edelbach's choice of Daughtry as one of those to attend the inquiry in Washington, seemed particularly pointed.

"Charley"—Edelbach's white caterpillar brows rose—"I trust you'll be able to join us?"

Daughtry continued to scribble numbers on his pad. They streamed in an unruly fashion across the page spilling onto the edges, denoting in the eyes of their creator some ineluctable truth.

Edelbach spoke again, his voice soft and smoothly consoling. "Charles?"

"I wouldn't dream of missing it," Daughtry spoke at last, a hint of impertinence in the delay.

"There's no question of having to testify, you understand. Our counsel will do all the talking."

"I've no objection to testifying," Daughtry said. For the first time he looked up from his pad directly at Edelbach. "There's nothing to hide. I did nothing other than carry out the instructions of my superiors."

Once more the murmurs came. Papers shifted nervously in the raddled air.

Edelbach's red face purpled. "Your superiors?"

Daughtry nodded. "Yes. Of course. You all knew what Sujimoto was up to."

"I must caution you, Charles," Wainright intruded.

"You all knew about the forged letters of credit. I cabled you,

Walter, on July 3, 1978, to advise of that." Daughtry produced a cable from a sheaf of correspondence and held it up. "You never bothered to reply."

Hot, red blotches erupted on Wainright's hawkish countenance. Daughtry continued to gather a breathtaking momentum as he went on. "On September 22, '78, I cabled Ed Villiers, requesting permission to notify the authorities in Tokyo regarding a number of unauthorized transactions to which I had been instructed to become a party—"

"Are you saying I instructed you to—" Villiers roared. The Adam's apple in his knotty throat bobbled furiously.

"Whether verbally or tacitly instructed, by virtue of never having lifted a finger to interfere in these transactions, it all comes down to the same thing," Daughtry replied crisply. "Among these transactions were a number of arbitragements ordered by Mr. Sujimoto with the Weiler Bank-Switzerland and Protocorp, Ltd., Holding Trust-Liechtenstein. I cabled you that they were of a self-dealing nature. You chose to disregard that and instead authorized the transactions."

"I never in my life authorized—"

"It's all here, Ed." Daughtry patted his sheaf of cable traffic.

"Show me that," Villiers thundered. "You'd better damned well have it right there in black and white." Villiers rose and started round the table.

"Sit down, Ed," Edelbach said.

"By God, he'd better be able to prove that."

"Sit down, Ed." Edelbach's voice took a decidedly ominous turn. "Go on, Charley."

Daughtry sat erect and silent for a moment, gazing impassively at his sheaf of explosive correspondence. Everyone else around the table was now staring at it too, with a sickish fascination.

"Throughout 1979," Daughtry resumed, "and well into 1980, I repeatedly notified Desmond Bagwell, then treasurer, of a persistent pattern of currency speculation in Mr. Sujimoto's directives."

"Now just one minute—" Bagwell rose.

"Shut up, Desmond," Edelbach snapped. "Go on, Charles."

Daughtry, still gazing down, resumed.

"Speculations carried out with funds drawn from demand deposits on hand at Confederated. A total of 9 swap-forward, forward-swap contracts were negotiated on the instructions of Mr. Sujimoto, and never performed at his bank, the Haribachi-Hammamura Bank, Chiyodaku. All the designated value dates were permitted to pass with Desmond's full knowledge."

Across the table, Desmond Bagwell, white with fright, sweated heavily into his shirt.

Daughtry went on mercilessly: "I reported that we were building up a dangerous net exchange position."

"For God's sake," Michaeltree pleaded. "It's Sujimoto's own bank. It's his ball and bat. What did you expect? These were transactions that would never have been countenanced had we been dealing with any other client."

Daughtry hammered forward, going now under the force of his own vindication. "Despite Mr. Sujimoto's position here, I warned each of you that he should have been called to account. Instead, you all opted for a policy of do-nothing. So we adopted a policy of drift. Well, we have now drifted up on the rocks."

"What do you have on your mind, Charles?" Leon Edelbach smiled cheerlessly. "What exactly are you trying to say?"

"Only this." Daughtry smiled back. It was a rather chilling smile. "If you are all so naïve as to think just because my name appears as countersigner to all of these bogus currency transactions, that I'm going to take the rap all by myself, then you're sadly mistaken."

Colonel Erskine, shot in the head by one of his own crazed Borderers, pitched forward over the Oskarberg ramparts and plummeted airily downwards onto the stony barricades below.

"But I—" Wainright made a vain effort to interpose. But this time Daughtry could not be stopped.

"I am not anyone's patsy. Don't forget that. Tomorrow in Washington, if we pull together, we may yet come out. Then again we may not. We may all very well hang together. However I can assure you all—each and every one of you seated here"— he thumped his sheaf of incriminating cable traffic—"I do not intend to hang alone."

11

Soldiers ought to fear their general
more than their enemies.
—MILITARY MAXIM

"*. . . major European markets . . . late dollar rates yesterday . . . Frankfurt 1.9270 marks down from 1.9360 . . . Zurich 1.7337 Swiss francs down from 1.7445 . . . Paris 4.4720 French francs down from 4.4827 . . . Milan 913.25 Italian lire, down from 916.45 . . .*"

In a silk paisley robe and red rubber thongs, Mr. Sujimoto, perched atop a three-legged stool deep within the catacombs beneath his baronial home, in the mountains outside Vaduz, counted money. He had arrived there quite unexpectedly on a private jet from Tokyo the night before.

At an emergency predawn meeting in Tokyo, he had been strongly advised by his counsel that it might be prudent for him to be out of Japan by the time the U.S. extradition papers were served. Liechtenstein was thought to be ideal. Mr. Sujimoto had a home in Liechtenstein; also, happily, the small principality had no extradition treaty with the U.S.

"*. . . the pound was stronger against the dollar in London, ending the day at $2.3665 up from $2.3550 late Friday apparently buoyed by . . .*"

Riyals, dinars, guilders, pesos, kroner, pesetas, lire . . .

He sat at a long oak counting table sifting through mounds of paper currency. Swiss and Belgian francs, Singapore and Israeli pounds, Indonesian rupiah, Deutsche marks and yen. There was a dreamy look of abstraction upon his face. Chilean pesos, Venezuelan bolivars, Brazilian cruzieros, South African rand.

". . . the Canadian dollar traded at 1.1883 U.S. dollars down from 1.1973. Late rates for the dollar in New York . . ."

A high-powered Blaupunkt droned late currency quotations from London. An electric flambeau mounted on the stone wall flickered into the sepulchral gloom of labyrinthine cellars. A studious, bespectacled young Japanese at Mr. Sujimoto's right hand operated alternately a high-speed computer and an ancient abacus as he tabulated currencies by the most recent quotations.

Drachmas, schillings, markkas. Bills of currency, paper tender. Rose. Green. Jade. Yellow. Ultramarine. Soiled and worn through years of commerce. Watermarked. Franked. Paper rolled and wadded, but no less coveted in denominations from paltry to princely. The currency of the world, stuffed and crammed into large wood, steel-belted crates, bins and huge tin coffers, squirreled away over the years beneath dusty joists and moldy rafters, the treasure trove of a miser hoarded away in the damp, dungeon gloom of the Schloss Mendenhall, Mr. Sujimoto's seventeenth-century Alpine château.

Sifting through heaps and mounds of coin, stubby fingers kneading coinage as if they were caressing a beautiful woman's private parts, Mr. Sujimoto counted.

Gold. Silver. Anodized copper. Green patinated lead. Coins of all nations piled in staggering profusion, a chinking happy merry Christmas ring, coins glinting in the half-light of the flambeaux.

Kings. Queens. Presidents. Prime ministers and generals, portraiture, etched, embossed, engraved in rotogravure. Palaces. Monuments. Government buildings. Scales of justice. Zodiacal signs, Masonic emblems, cabalistic markings. Falcons. Gyrfalcons. Quetzal, condor, hawk and eagle. Zoological representations. Mythological figures. Hieroglyphics. Hagiography. Runic. Greek. Coptic. Cyrillic. Aramaic calligraphy. Talmudic talismanic signs. Countless coins, dull, worn, bright, burnished and glinting beneath coffer lids unraised for decades. Even ancient coins. Priceless numismatic treasures. Rarities for the archives. Old sovereigns and doubloons. Golden moidores.

"... *Bullion closed in Zurich at $635.50 a troy ounce, up from $628.625 on reports from New York that the dollar was falling on a broad front against most major currencies....*"

Sujimoto's hand paused in mid-air. Coins spilled in a shimmering cascade through his fingers as he cocked an ear and listened to reports of the plummeting U.S. currency, particularly in Tokyo where it had reached record lows.

"... *168.00 yen compared with Friday's close at 167.65.... At the Tokyo closing today the dollar fetched 168.93 yen—its highest point of the day....*"

Sujimoto listened, then nodded contentedly. All had gone well—for him at least. Much of his dollar holdings had been converted to Deutsche marks and Swiss francs which were now happily rising. But that was, of course, as it should be. As he had intended it to be from the start.

A huge, powerful Japanese called Aito, a giant from the island of Sakhalin, attired in white tunic, loose pantaloons and a leather apron, wrestled crates of gold bars over the stone floors, causing the ancient stones to shriek as if flesh were being torn from them. Setting them round about Sujimoto, Aito prized the lids open with a crowbar, loosing yet another cruel, ripping sound as he did so. Enclosed in each crate, right up to the gunnels, were gold bars each weighing 18 kilos. With a quick grunting sound, the giant stacked the bars in six-foot columns against the moldy walls.

At the same time, the computer on the counting table hummed and purred, tabulating millions at the behest of the lightly flying fingers of Mr. Sujimoto's young assistant.

In that eerie, cavelike gloom, they struck an odd pose, these three—a kind of *tableau vivant*—Mr. Sujimoto and his clerk, the older gentleman in white flowing ceremonial robes, the clerk in loose, flowing blouse and baggy nankeen pantaloons, both perched before the piles of bullion and paper bills. And the tunicked giant from Sakhalin hovering protectively above them both. They looked like an illustration on some ancient Japanese parchment.

Outside in the dazzling sunlight of late morning a sleek gray $30,000 Aston-Martin racing machine, mud-spattered and over-heated from hard driving, stood drawn up beneath the porte cochere, ticking strangely. It had been left there by Sujimoto's thirty-eight-year-old son, Kajumi, just returned from a night of gambling and carousing across the Swiss border, at a casino on Lake Constance, some twenty-five kilometers away.

Kajumi had left the car there and gone straight to bed. Shortly, a German attendant would come and drive the car round the rear to the garages, where he would wash and polish the machine, gas and oil it, and provide whatever maintenance was necessary to have the car in apple-pie order for Mr. Kajumi when he would reappear to reclaim it again at seven o'clock that evening.

Silvery and sleek, the perfect plaything for shiftless, morose Mr. Kajumi, it was a beautiful machine, the Aston-Martin, and in its glove compartment, amid the road maps and sanitized packets of moisturized paper towels, was a 9mm Walther P38 pistol, its magazine loaded and its safety catch off.

In the great kitchen of Mendenhall, a staff of seven—chefs, garmandiere, wine steward, pastry and dessert chefs—were all busily at work preparing lunch. Soufflés, madrilene, fresh pike in a basil aspic, cold tournedos, fresh loaves of crusty bread, chèvre, raspberries, strawberry tart, several well-chilled bottles of a superb Montrachet, and a glorious La Tâche for the tournedos, were all being carefully packed in wicker hampers in preparation for an outing in the mountains—under the supervision of Madame de Plevissier.

Madame de Plevissier, Celestine, as she was called, was a robust, hearty woman in her early fifties, a Gascon aristocrat, the granddaughter of a duke. There was about her a gruff amiability and always a shade too much makeup. Even dressed and coutured for an evening at the casinos, she had a decidedly undone appearance, a hectic, bustling, distracted air, as if she had rushed not yet buttoned from her dressing room, her ash-blond hair barely combed, wisps of it squiggling like serpents in the wind behind her. Well-placed people unfailingly depicted her as "vulgar." She was too familiar with servants.

An ample, earthy, outspoken woman who enjoyed the pleasures of the flesh, Madame de Plevissier had turned her back on home and family to live with the eminent Japanese financier. She had grown a trifle stout over the years with a few creases and folds beginning to appear about her throat. But even so, what remained, still unblemished by time, was quite a bit more than a mere hint of what once had been a strikingly beautiful woman.

Shortly after the war Sujimoto had gone to Paris as part of an industrial fact-finding commission. There, he met the beautiful widow of the celebrated French aviator and war hero, Plevissier, at a dinner party in Rambouillet. At that time she was working as the correspondent of *Le Monde* in the Far East. On coming to Japan for the first time and undergoing an instant affinity for that part of the world, she was able truly to say she had finally come home. She was twenty-some-odd years Sujimoto's junior, a circumstance creating round their courtship a source of scandalous delight within the French diplomatic service.

When Sujimoto's tour of duty in Europe was over, he took Celestine back with him to Tokyo and installed her at the Imperial Hotel. In less than a year's time, it was reported that Madame Sujimoto, his legal wife, was with child and sent home to her parents' farm in the northern region of Hokkaido for the lying-in period. Several months later reports had it she had died in childbirth, but that she had borne a healthy, thriving infant girl.

During the period of Madame Sujimoto's pregnancy, Celestine had *by coincidence* also disappeared from Tokyo. It was said she had gone to Mongolia on assignment for her paper. But shortly after the announcement of Madame Sujimoto's death, she was back again in Tokyo, this time living openly with

Sujimoto in his home, a kind of surrogate mother to his son and new infant daughter.

There was no question that Madame Sujimoto had died under circumstances that were, to say the least, peculiar. The hospital authorities in Sapporo, however, reported her death as accidental, and the police, for reasons never explained, chose not to pursue the matter.

One further footnote to this strange, curiously inconclusive episode. At the time that Madame de Plevissier was rumored to be in Mongolia, a highly placed official of the French diplomatic corps reported having had tea with her in a café in Bangkok. She was a guest at that time of the royal family there and looking, as this official had said, winking all the while, "robust, blushing, and terribly *enceinte*."

Kajumi, the son, only seven or eight at the time, was therefore raised by Madame de Plevissier, but never accepted her as his mother. The boy thought of her as an intruder and played over and over again in his mind an obsessional childish fantasy in which, secreted in a closet, he watched as Madame de Plevissier went through the furtive motions of slowly poisoning his mother.

For her part, Celestine loved Kajumi as if he were her own. One of the great enduring sorrows of her life was that in return for her affection all she ever got from the boy was scorn and rejection. Over the years she had come at last to accept this.

While never marrying, Celestine and Sujimoto enjoyed a happy relationship. They adored each other. Even in their most intimate moments she never ventured to address him in any way other than by the surname "Sujimoto," just as one refers to a divinity or, at the very least, to a very great artist—for her the ultimate accolade. He, for his part, always called her "Madame de Plevissier." It was quaint and playful, but it told a great deal about the nature of their relationship, which, while beautifully intimate, maintained a strict air of formality and mutual respect.

Around Madame de Plevissier Sujimoto was devoted and a good deal more uxorious than is characteristic of Japanese husbands. To her he invariably spoke French. She in turn had learned to speak a tolerable Japanese for him, as well as for his new daughter Mariko, whom she insisted upon raising in the Japanese style.

The central mystery of this seemingly ideal relationship was that Sujimoto never indicated any wish to consummate their relationship in formal marriage. Nor had Madame de Plevissier ever pressed him to do so. While they had never fully discussed the matter, it was tacitly understood by both that at the root of the problem stood Kajumi. As for the daughter, Mariko, the child longed to be acknowledged as the natural offspring of a woman who, while showering love and attention upon her in private, nevertheless in public was only able to claim her as a stepdaughter.

".0716 Austrian schilling: 2.3683 British pounds: .8415 Canadian dollars: .0284 Chilean pesos: .4861 Dutch guilders: .001081 Italian lire: .004508 Japanese yen: .0385 . . ."

The radio sputtered and crackled. Mr. Sujimoto leaned across the counting table and flicked it off. "What are my sterling holdings?" His voice, high and stridulous, reverberated through the cavernous gloom. The assistant ran a slightly deformed index finger down the long tally sheets.

"2,437,582 paper, plus an additional million in coin, sir."

"Deutsche mark?"

"3,400,000 as of this morning's Frankfurt quote, sir."

"Swiss franc?"

"6,892,000, sir."

"Yen?"

"An additional 12 million, sir. Down from the 83 million you'd been holding."

"That figure is apart from my yen position in Zurich and New York?"

"Yes, sir."

"Total?"

Like a serpent's tongue, the crooked finger of the assistant darted over the computer keys causing the machine to rattle and chatter portentously. "$112,231,433, sir."

Mr. Sujimoto closed his eyes and reflected. While he had a high regard for computers, for him the ultimate computer was himself. At last he uttered a grunt of contentment and withdrew a scrap of paper from the pocket of his robe. Grinning with an air of immodest triumph, he handed to his clerk the scrap of paper on which was scrawled a figure—the figure he had computed, after his own fashion, as the grand total of his cellar holdings in Liechtenstein.

The clerk studied the figure and smiled. There was a glow of genuine admiration in his eyes as he handed the scrap of paper back to his employer. The figure written there was exactly what he himself had arrived at after several hours of complex computer operations.

"Very good, sir," he said. "Most admirable, indeed."

Mr. Sujimoto accepted graciously the compliments of his young clerk and at once resumed the more urgent business of tabulations. "Now for the gold," he croaked like a bullfrog into the damp, moldy shadows.

It had been going on like that for several hours, this meticulous, painstaking inventory of the Sujimoto assets—a look at his liquidity as it were, in the tiny principality on the upper Rhine between Austria and Switzerland. The $112 million that Mr. Sujimoto had managed to squirrel away in his cellars in Liechtenstein represented only a small moiety of the financier's total wealth. Hundreds of additional millions in a variety of foreign currencies resided elsewhere round the world—in secret accounts, fiduciary accounts, laundered, stockpiled and far from the greedy, prying hands of creditors, tax collectors and bankruptcy lawyers.

Since the Japanese government expressly forbade, on threat of swift retribution, the removal from the country of significant amounts of foreign currencies, the question inescapably arose, just how did Mr. Sujimoto manage to stockpile his great hoard?

Undoubtedly, he had violated the law. When one has at his disposal one's own fleet of merchant ships, constantly loading and unloading vast cargos in all the world's major ports, it is no difficult matter to falsify a ship's manifest; to store for passage in a ship's hold crates of currency and bullion, described innocuously on bills of lading as toasters, cassettes and transistor radios.

Mr. Sujimoto had been going on like this for years, unrestricted, unchallenged, undetected. Only now, however, with the untimely collapse of his vast empire, the authorities in Tokyo were suddenly scrutinizing every nook and cranny of his financial dealings. And not only the Japanese authorities. Sujimoto, Ltd., was an international operation with vast multinational branches and franchises. That meant that the authorities of a half-dozen other nations were also poking through the chaos and shambles left in the wake of Sujimoto's collapse.

But the sly old financier was now in Liechtenstein, tucked safely away along with his millions in a magical little principality that offered him not only magnificent Alpine scenery, but complete immunity from extradition as well.

Liechtenstein, because of the stable political situation, the absolute bank secrecy, and the low fiscal charges, is a perfect repository for funds one would like to make it difficult to trace. For this reason, more than 25,000 foreign companies and holding corporations (several of them belonging to Mr. Sujimoto himself) maintain nominal offices in the country. Such firms pay no tax on either profit or income. The normal tax rate is one-thousandth on paid-in capital and reserves with an annual minimum of 1,000 Swiss francs. Hardly what one would call burdensome.

Like the superb businessman he was, Sujimoto had the gift of foresight. Nearly twenty years ago, looking ahead to his own retirement, he had purchased the Schloss Mendenhall from an impecunious German baron with a fatal passion for craps. Sujimoto was able to buy the château for a song. Just outside Vaduz, set in parklike grounds and encompassing 500 acres of spectacular Apline woodlands, replete with pheasant, partridge, boar and stag, Sujimoto envisioned the place as the perfect retreat for his retirement years. Cleverly, he had it purchased in his own name with corporate funds as headquarters for Protocorp, his own personal holding company in Western Europe.

With sixty rooms crammed with authentic Louis Quinze, hung with a number of very good late Renaissance and Romantic masters, furnished with every amenity the twentieth century had yet devised, Mendenhall afforded Mr. Sujimoto the ultimate retreat. Here on his private reserve, surrounded by family and buttressed by untold millions, he was certain his fortress was impregnable and he, himself, untouchable.

The only rub was that amidst all the luxury and security he was presently enjoying, Mr. Sujimoto, for all intents and purposes, was a prisoner in Liechtenstein. The moment he set foot beyond the borders of that tiny, 62-square-mile country, the police of six or seven nations would be waiting there to pounce.

12

When princes think more of luxury than of arms,
they lose their state.
—NICCOLÒ MACHIAVELLI, *The Prince*, 1532

"... *dollar continues to plummet on the world foreign exchange market this morning, sliding steadily in wild trading on news of* . . ."

A chauffeur dozed in a silver Bentley parked on the steep slope of a mountain road that climbed over the Dreischwestern massif into Switzerland. The road had a stunning prospect of the snowy Alpine peaks glittering in the distant midday sunlight some twenty miles away.

Several hundred feet off the road, sequestered in the seclusion of a piny, dappled glade, Madame de Plevissier and Sujimoto basked on a large gaily striped picnic blanket in the unseasonably warm mountain sunlight.

Attired in white duck trousers, a faded Basque shirt of blue madras, and a floppy, wide-brimmed straw hat on his head, Mr. Sujimoto lolled on a corner of the blanket sipping cold Taittinger from a crystal flute, while Celestine, on her knees, skirts hiked to her thighs, fed him morsels of pâté and Brie with the chirpy proprietarial delight one associates with the feeding of a pet Pekingese.

In that soft green diffusion of light, filtering through the canopy of trees, sharing food and intimacies, only the Blaupunkt, omnipresent and blaring, was there to recall the restless, jarring turmoil of the world of commerce outside.

"... *1.9232 West German marks, up from 1.8970; 4.4405 French francs, up from 4.3825 ... Gold bullion eased in Zurich to $621.50 a troy ounce from ...*"

The numbers droned ceaselessly into the piny glade clashing with the chirp of birds and the plashing brook. Celestine poured Sujimoto another flute of Taittinger while he closed his eyes and lay back balancing the bubbling glass on his chest. He appeared profoundly pleased with the circumstances of life in his newly adopted country.

"Where is Kajumi?" he asked.

"He might join us later."

"What time did he come in?"

"Around eleven o'clock this morning. He went directly to bed."

They were both silent, knowing what each thought of a rapidly deteriorating situation.

Sujimoto sighed and sipped his champagne. "And Mariko?"

"Off somewhere in the woods with her camera."

"Immortalizing birds and beasts for posterity?"

"Scoff, if you will. She's starting to make money at it—"

Sujimoto laughed and waved his hand in the air. "Twenty-five dollars here and there from dreary little journals. Barely enough to cover expenses. Pathetic."

Madame de Plevissier frowned. "Mariko thinks otherwise. If she wants a career as a photographer, you ought to encourage her, rather than ridicule it."

"When has she ever been able to accept my encouragement

in anything? Like that wonderful *Match* job I arranged for her which, of course, she declined."

An ambiguous smile suffused Celestine's ruddy features. "She's your child. Surely she has the same right to be as stubborn and proud."

Sujimoto closed his eyes and sipped champagne. The second glass had made him drowsy.

"*. . . collapse may have dire implications for the world steel market as well as such related industries as automobiles, shipbuilding . . .*"

Madame de Plevissier reached over to flick off the Blaupunkt. Sujimoto, eyes closed and still supine, stayed her hand.

"Why do you listen to that?" she chided.

"It flatters me to hear my name bruited about over the air waves." He turned the volume up. "Even if they defame me."

"*. . . as a result of flagrant improprieties . . . it appears certain the government will now move to more closely regulate private industry in Japan. . . .*"

Sujimoto fumed. The BBC announcer had one of those smugly self-satisfied voices that infuriated him.

"*. . . huge Middle Eastern oil consortium deeply invested in Sujimoto, Ltd., is moving now to take over and dismember what is left of the vast industrial complex. U.S. and British banks with enormous credit lines to Sujimoto stand to lose hundreds of millions of . . .*"

Madame de Plevissier's frown turned to apprehension as she watched him lying in the grass, listening impassively. "It's all so unfair."

"The truth is seldom fair, madame. Kindly to hush. I want to hear this." Sujimoto rolled over on his side and thrust his ear to the speaker.

"*. . . Officials of the Confederated Trust Bank,*" the BBC chap droned on, "*conceded last night that losses were significant but declined to specify the exact amount. Senior officials disclosed that the bank had been given no warning of the impending failure.*

"*. . . the bank insisted that only one employee, the unidenti-*

fied trader, was involved. But investigators were skeptical. 'It's pretty obvious the foreign exchange loss has to involve hanky-panky by more than one person,' reported one source declining to be identified. 'Or else there has to be almost unbelievable incompetence on the part of the Forex accounting procedures at Confederated to permit such a huge position to be built up unbeknownst to senior management. To incur Forex losses as extensive as the Confederated's, this so-called single trader would have had personally to risk sums in the area of $250 million in currency trades, and at most banks no one could position such sums without having his activities come quickly under the scrutiny of his superiors.

"The conclusions appear inescapable. The unidentified trader worked in tacit collusion with his direct superiors, who, in turn, countenanced the highly speculative trading because they were ordered to do so by the bank's owner and major stockholder—Mr. Hiroji Sujimoto. In Tokyo"—Sujimoto knelt beside the radio, his eyes transfixed in fiery little points— *"authorities issued a warrant for the arrest of Mr. Sujimoto. The warrant alleges irregularities in the 1978–79 balance sheet of the Weiler Bank in Zurich, one of the controversial financier's own banks. Along with the rest of the worldwide Sujimoto financial empire, that bank was closed yesterday. The warrant, completely independent of the Confederated affair, charges Sujimoto with falsifying balance sheets and fraudulent distribution of profits.*

"The millionaire Japanese industrialist-financier disappeared from his Tokyo residence last night. He is rumored to have fled to either Switzerland or Liechtenstein, absconding with sizable amounts of Sujimoto assets and . . ."

Sujimoto's hand slammed down hard on the off button of the Blaupunkt, throttling it with a rude squawk. Inside he was seething. They had lied. They distorted. It wasn't that way at all. Why hadn't they at least had the decency to ask his version of the story? And how dare they spew such a vile, ugly defamation of his character into this primevally lovely glade with its laurel and brooks, its piny, resinous air? Why should his glow of warmth and pleasure be sullied now by the nagging sense that at this very moment the world was reading about a Sujimoto failure rather than a Sujimoto triumph?

Like all Japanese, particularly those of Sujimoto's caste, in whose veins ran the blood of shoguns and samurai, failure, visible public failure, that is, was intolerable; a disgrace that had somehow to be vindicated. One has their *chu,* the venerable Japanese will tell you, meaning of course their duty to their Emperor. One has their *ko,* too—duty to one's ancestors and parents. And, of course, their *giri,* duty to the world. And, for the truly prideful Japanese, dwelling always in the shadow of his ancestors, there is the all-important *ehre,* one's duty to admit failure; one's duty, moreover, to clear one's good name of any insult or imputation of failure.

Old Sujimoto was thoroughly imbued with the full *bushido* of the fighting samurai. The part of him that eagerly aped and coveted Western ways also took delight in scornful mockery of the ancient codes. But still something deep and atavistic made it impossible for him to slough off the old laws completely. Made him both fear and obey them.

Sujimoto was a man who loved victory and scorned defeat. Counting the millions spilling out of his coffers that morning, depositing them in unnumbered accounts in the Landesbank in Essen and the Verwaltungs and Privatbank in Vaduz—that, too, suggested to him a smashing victory. Now this priggish, smarmy BBC chap was gloating, so it seemed, over his misfortunes, accusing him of low, dishonorable practices, blurting the story out to the world, turning his victory to ashes. They made him out a criminal.

"So—now you're angry," Celestine pouted. "They've succeeded in ruining our picnic."

"You heard what he said about me?" Sujimoto fumed. "Lies. Foul lies."

"Ce qu'ils disent à ton sujet n'est pas vrai." They had been speaking Japanese up until that point. Now suddenly Madame de Plevissier's voice dropped a register and she slipped into her husky French.

"Et si c'était vrai?"

73

"*Je ne la croirais pas. Ce sont des mensonges, rien que des mensonges.*"

"*Ma cherie . . . et pourtant, si c'était vrai en partie?*"

"*Ne dis pas ça, Sujimoto. Tu me fais peur.*"

"*Je ne faisais qu'une supposition . . . Mais si c'était . . .*"

"*. . . en ce cas je penserais que ce n'était pas ta faute. Que tu n'avais pas le choix. Que c'était une simple erreur de ta part, mon cheri.*"

"*A, Celeste, je t'adore. Tu es ce que j'ai de plus précieux.*"

Once she had assured him of her belief in his innocence, she then leaned down very close to his ear and whispered something. He laughed. Giggled actually in a high, fatuous way, and pulled her down to him. For a few joyful moments they forgot completely about the BBC man and the Confederated Trust Bank while they stroked and caressed each other, laughing and mauling one another like a pair of affectionate cubs.

Suddenly Madame de Plevissier sat up. Brushing twigs and pine spills from her skirt and blouse, she ran a comb hectically through her luxuriant disheveled hair.

In the next moment a lithely graceful Japanese girl materialized from the forest with the noiseless phantom grace of a spring doe. How long she had been standing there, they could not say. Nor could they judge how much of their conversation she had overheard. Celestine was already on her feet, still brushing her skirt. Sujimoto lumbered stiffly to a sitting position, knocking over as he did so the flute of champagne at his side. Its nearly depleted bubbling contents leaked out over the blanket.

From beneath the great brim of his straw hat, Sujimoto squinted at the figure hovering wraithlike at the perimeter of the glade, where the open grass met the forest. There in shade, halved at the torso by the shadow of a tall fir, stood Mariko Sujimoto. Hands on hips, cameras and film bags slung diagonally across her shoulders, there was something markedly defiant about the way she slouched there and observed them.

They did not speak, but a shudder of palpable tension

vibrated across the narrow band of space between them. Madame de Plevissier needed no one to tell her that Sujimoto's high-spirited, and greatly dissatisfied daughter was spoiling for a fight.

13

To see the right and not to do it is cowardice.
—CONFUCIUS: *Analects*, ii, 24

". . . sold pound sterling and Swiss francs to Haribachi-Hammamura."

"Mr. Sujimoto's bank?"

"Correct . . . and purchased U.S. dollars against . . ."

". . . operating losses in September were $3.1 million, and $1.1 million in October. In addition, Forex trading losses for the two-month period totaled $19.1 million."

Several places down from Daughtry, someone gasped. Voices droned on through the dying afternoon, while Daughtry doodled formulas onto a penny pad. People moved about him. Papers shuffled across tabletops. Water carafes were tipped to fill empty glasses. Lights glared. Yet for Daughtry there was a strange sense of dissociation, an eerie sensation of standing outside and looking in.

They had been there seven hours, sitting round the long oval table in the tower suite of the Federal Reserve Building. It was Sunday afternoon. They had arrived in Washington Friday night, summoned there by top Treasury officials. Daughtry had come with a contingent of eight men. Five were colleagues of his at the bank—Wainwright, Michaeltree, Villiers, Bagwell and president and board chairman Leon Edelbach. The other three men were legal counsel for the Confederated. Latham, the bank's senior counsel, was one of these.

The entire contingent had left New York late Friday afternoon on the Metroliner. As late as 4 P.M. that afternoon no one had any idea they were going to be asked to appear the following day. In the ensuing hour or so, calls had to be made home, appointments broken, apologies made. It was chaos.

Once on the train, in the bar car, they were quite amiable, and seemingly relaxed. They spoke to Daughtry, but he noticed they couldn't look him in the eye. They were civil enough; still there was coolness and a distance there. If they looked upon him then as a sacrificial victim, they were also terrified of him, knowing that what he might say under oath could be ruinous. Daughtry wasn't at all sure if he despised them more than he despised himself.

By the time they'd reached Philadelphia they'd each had several bourbons. There was a good deal of laughter, a forced hilarity with an undercurrent of sick, giddy fright. Rumpled and tired, they wanted desperately to be home around family and hearth in slippers with a drink, or pruning late roses in a greenhouse at dusk before supper.

No one wanted to be there. No one wanted to be next to him. Already he bore ash on his forehead. The mark of the pariah and the leper was upon him. He was to be avoided.

Daughtry had not entered into the desperate gaiety of the trip. Instead, he held back, sipping a drink they'd handed him in New York. He still hadn't finished it when they'd reached Union Station in Washington.

Two long black limousines waited outside to ferry them over to the Jefferson. After they'd checked in, they all planned to go to dinner. Daughtry declined the invitation, preferring to take a light supper in his room, then a shower, and early bed.

Before retiring, he read assorted reports in the *Wall Street Journal,* the *Washington Post,* and the *Star,* detailing the possibility of the Confederated's defaulting on fourth-quarter dividends.

On the TV news, Edelbach's name figured prominently along with Villiers's and Michaeltree's. Sujimoto was given the most play. Daughtry's name was never mentioned, only alluded to as an unidentified currency trader dealing in transactions beyond his authority. He fumed.

Later that evening there was a knock on his door. Daughtry had been lying awake in the dark, his mind several thousand miles from where he was. He flicked on the light, threw on a robe, and went to the door. It was Leon Edelbach. "Rotten dinner," he belched sourly and slouched in.

They sat together on the edge of the bed in the badly overheated hotel room, Daughtry in pajamas and robe, Edelbach in the same rumpled flannel suit he had worn that morning, with collar open and tie loosened round his neck.

The bank president laughed ruefully. "I was supposed to be at the opera tonight." He checked his wristwatch. "Pavarotti in *Turandot*. Instead, here I am in a hot hotel room in Washington." He spoke with a slight, but not unpleasant German accent.

"Looks like you took the wrong train," Daughtry replied.

"I'll say I did." Edelbach laughed ruefully. "A long time ago." Daughtry wasn't at all certain what he'd meant by that. Clearly the bank president had been reflecting on the past, some road not taken, some critical decision not made.

They chatted together in the still gloom, about a myriad of trivial things. Everything but the matter at hand, which Edelbach studiously avoided. Daughtry sensed that this was all intended to be disarming—the prelude to a deal, the scenario of which would go something like this: "You take the rap. Don't make waves. Don't implicate anyone. And we'll take care of you."

Basically, that's exactly what it finally came down to. Not that bald, of course, but essentially that was the gist of it. It started civilly enough. Daughtry knew he was in trouble the moment Edelbach started to call him Charley and compliment him on his talent and extraordinary usefulness to the bank. Then came a number of grand sententious phrases proclaiming the splendors of the American banking system. "All that matters is the integrity of the system, Charley," Edelbach confided and placed a clammy, tremulous hand on his shoulder. "The people

77

trust us and we mustn't betray them." Even Edelbach looked a trifle queasy as that came out.

Daughtry sat silent, unresponding, on the edge of the bed. At the conclusion he merely said: "All I intend to do is tell the truth."

A dark shadow moved across Edelbach's profile. When he spoke at last, the voice was disquietingly soft, and came out of darkness, as if disembodied.

"Do whatever the hell you want. All I can say is that I will not be the one to preside over the first major American bank failure since the Depression. That is not how I've charted my course. That is not what I struggled thirty years for, to be dragged kicking and screaming into retirement by Treasury agents. That is not how I care to have my children remember their father. With this blot on his name. Hear me, Daughtry? I am not going to be the one held up to public ridicule because of lapses in the professional judgment of underlings. This was beyond my control. It is not fair. It is simply not fair."

His voice had taken on a whiny, grating quality. "You hear me, Daughtry? Good Christ. This can't be happening to me. Now don't do anything stupid in there tomorrow, and for God's sake let the lawyers do all the talking."

"Haribachi-Hammamura closed its doors before it had a chance to perform its leg of the transaction."

"Which was?"

$$No = [N_1 N_2 \ldots N_k \ldots]$$

"To pay U.S. dollars on Wednesday morning twelve hours earlier New York time. It was a trick of the time zone. We were zapped by the time zone differential."

The equality $No = [N_1, N_2 \ldots N_k]$ implying that N and No are equivalent sets . . .

"Then it was Mr. Daughtry's responsibility . . ."

"I didn't say that."

"But a moment ago, you did say . . ."

"I beg your pardon. I said no such thing."

"Nevertheless, it was Daughtry who . . ."

$$G(W_1) = G(W_2)$$

Someone nudged him. Whispered in his ear. Affidavits were thrust beneath his gaze. Print swam dizzily before his eyes.

". . . at precisely what time was Mr. Michaeltree informed?"

"I'm sorry. I thought you said . . ."

". . . of contracts unperformed." "Payments outstanding." "Operating outside of his authority." "Shocking negligence." "Criminal action."

"Will Mr. Edelbach please rise?"

Daughtry closed his eyes and heard the rush of water, the ceaseless moil of gravel and sand on the beach at Miho. The dark, rolling waves of the Sea of Japan rushing inward, unfolding like a scroll. The sensation of sand and tumescence in his wet bathing suit. The girl lying wet and quiet beside him.

Then, in the next instant, Daughtry and Sujimoto strolled and conversed on a high cliff above the sea. It was early morning. Mist rose and curled out of the damp grass. The old man wore a pair of white silk pajamas and carried a parasol above his head.

With butterflies fluttering before them, they walked toward a precipice. Above and behind them, the tile-tiered roof of Sujimoto's pagoda-style beach house soared heavenward, swallows darting all about its spires. Several hundred feet below, a sea churned white bashed against the rocks. Waves boomed up the beach like cannon shot.

". . . at Tulagi we taught you Americans a lesson." Sujimoto's smile was one of deep satisfaction. "I was waiting for your people at Gavutu Harbor with two large transports, a small cargo ship, four minesweepers, two destroyers and a single heavy cruiser of the Jentsu class, the *Aoba*. We also had a number of small torpedo craft and five seaplanes moored off Mokambo Island. Nothing great, mind you."

"Will the Currency Comptroller please step forward?"

"Charles, listen to me now. Pay attention. You must pay attention to what's being said. And, above all, keep your mouth shut."

It was Latham, his face looming florid and desperate before

79

him. "You have to pay attention, Charles. You hear me?"

"The American task force was steaming to a rendezvous at lat. 15 degrees S, 160 E, a hundred miles south of the Solomons . . ."

"Charles. For God's sake."

"Your Admiral Grayville had five ships with him, on his own flagship, the carrier *Yorktown* under Captain Buckmaster, the heavy cruisers *Astoria* under Scanlan, the *Chester* under Tom Shock, and the *Portland* under Captain Pearlman. In addition, Grayville had the destroyers *Hammann, Anderson, Russell, Walke, Morris* and *Sims,* with the support of two big oilers, the *Neosho* and the *Tippecanoe.* Task force 11 was to join them at the rendezvous with the carrier *Lexington* under Sherman, the heavy cruisers *Minneapolis* and *New Orleans,* the destroyers *Phelps, Dewey, Farragut, Aylwin* and *Monaghan,* all under the estimable Admiral Fitch. We were under my good friend, Admiral Inoue. Here, let me draw it for you."

Mr. Sujimoto folded his parasol and with its steel finial tip proceeded to carve a schematic of the battle in the dry, porous sand.

"What your intelligence people failed to realize, Daughtry," the old man recounted with relish, "was that the Imperial fleet was split between us at Tulagi, and the others, preparing to advance on Port Moresby on the Australian side of New Guinea . . ."

"Pay attention, Charles," Latham urged. "You must pay attention."

Daughtry nodded and concentrated on a blindingly incandescent point in Sujimoto's reconstruction of the battle.

"And the 22,000 stockholders in Confederated?" A red-faced young Congressman with visions of the Senate pounded the tabletop. "People who have invested their life savings. What about them, Mr. Edelbach? These people stand to lose everything. Isn't that so?"

"Yes," Edelbach murmured. "That's so."

"How much of these losses can be covered by FDIC insurance?" asked another Congressman.

"All, or most of it," Edelbach replied, confidently.

An official of the FDIC rose quickly. "If there's a suggestion of improprieties, we certainly won't say here that we will assume responsibility for the total losses or, for that matter, any part thereof."

Edelbach's desperate eyes sought Latham. They hadn't anticipated that thunderbolt.

The red-faced young Congressman started wagging his finger at the bank president again. "If your earnings have plunged 83 percent in the third quarter from those of a year earlier to a measly 2 cents per share, how can you possibly hope to pay a dividend for the fourth quarter? Now, for God's sake, don't tell me, Mr. Edelbach, that you intend to pass the dividend?"

Edelbach reddened. The interrogation had been moving on toward its eighth hour. At its conclusion the bank president was drained, waxen—his characteristic high flush gone the color of parchment. When at last the committee dismissed him, he was ashen.

"Mr. Daughtry?"

Heads turned in Daughtry's direction. Someone nudged him.

"Mr. Daughtry, please. Is he here?" It was the voice of the Under Secretary seated at the head of the table.

Latham, seated beside Daughtry, rose: "Mr. Daughtry is not prepared to speak to the committee today, Mr. Secretary."

"Is he present? Will Mr. Daughtry raise his hand, please?"

Daughtry's hand rose with a jerky, tentative motion.

"Ah, there you are," the Under Secretary drawled amiably. "Are you all right today, Mr. Daughtry?"

"Mr. Daughtry is suffering nervous exhaustion," Latham quickly interceded.

"Then why the devil is he here?" another Treasury official retorted sharply.

"Merely as an observer, to monitor the proceedings," Latham replied.

The Under Secretary smiled drolly. "Doesn't it occur to you, Mr. Latham, that nervous exhaustion might tend to get in the way of any effective monitoring?"

The Under Secretary turned back to Daughtry. "How do you feel, Mr. Daughtry?"

"As I've said, Mr. Secretary, Mr. Daughtry is in no condition to . . ."

"Mr. Latham. Would you please permit me to be the judge of Mr. Daughtry's ability to address the committee?" The Under Secretary spoke with his eyes fixed on Daughtry. "There is nothing to fear, Mr. Daughtry. None of this is for the record. We're all friends here. We all have a mutual stake in this. Now, tell me, how do you feel?"

Daughtry shot a glance at Edelbach, whose features had petrified into an appalling gray vacancy.

"Well enough, you think, to talk to the committee?"

Daughtry's eyes were fixed on Edelbach who stared unflinchingly straight ahead at empty space. "Well enough," he murmured.

"What did he say?" the Under Secretary inquired of the man at his right. "Will you speak louder, please, Mr. Daughtry?"

Daughtry's voice rose louder and more controlled. "I said, I'm well enough, Mr. Secretary."

"Well now, that's fine."

Latham intruded. "I'm afraid I must strongly protest . . ."

The kindly avuncularity of the Under Secretary's manner underwent a sudden shift. The eyes narrowed and the line of the jaw grew taut. It was a change that was imperceptible to most, but to the senior counsel of the Confederated Trust Bank it conveyed a message that did not go unheeded.

"I think Mr. Daughtry is well enough to speak for himself," the Under Secretary announced with curt finality, and that was that.

In the next moment the table, ringed with SEC and Treasury officials, the Currency Comptroller who had flown in that morning from New York, the Assistant Attorney General from New York, several FBI officials, and the full contingent from the Confederated, suddenly all grew quiet. The air was very still.

"Now, Mr. Daughtry," the Under Secretary resumed in his

mild, relentless, prying way, "would you be so good as to tell us something of your relationship with Mr. Sujimoto?"

14

Woe to the vanquished (Vae victis).
—LIVY: *History,* V, 48

"On the afternoon of November 26, 3 P.M. Tokyo time, 1 A.M. New York time, Mr. Sujimoto chose to declare bankruptcy. No one had any idea it was coming. Not the slightest inkling. Everyone thought it was all hunky-dory in Tokyo because Mr. Sujimoto had never taken the trouble to inform anyone otherwise. He had systematically . . ." Daughtry heard his own voice coming at him over great distances. He spoke in quiet, measured tones, his mind strangely calm.

"We had a series of five key transactions which Mr. Sujimoto had ordered," he went on. "Forward swaps in the cumulative sum of $23 million, or so we thought then. That was only the tip of the iceberg. At the end, when we finally tallied up the serially numbered manifolds, and the net exchange position, which at Mr. Sujimoto's express instruction I had carried forward and never squared, the tab was more like $40 million.

"But we were not the only ones. Mr. Sujimoto had similar contracts with at least three other major banks. Anyone having exchange contracts with Sujimoto, Ltd., maturing Wednesday morning, November 26, New York time, lost 100 percent of the amount involved in these transactions. It was a washout. By virtue of a simple time zone differential, everyone took a bath."

"Except Mr. Sujimoto," the Under Secretary hastened to add.

"Correct." Daughtry nodded. "He was very careful to declare bankruptcy twelve hours, or one banking day, before he was scheduled to perform his leg of the contracts. The loss to all banks involved I would estimate to be in excess of $150 million."

A hushed, almost reverential silence fell like a pall over the room as the figure tumbled out. Several of the Confederated people lowered their gazes and from there on kept them stolidly riveted to papers on the tabletop. Leon Edelbach's much-vaunted military carriage appeared to wilt. He sat now in a most uncharacteristic slouch.

"Remember Pearl Harbor," a mordantly funny Currency Comptroller muttered over the silence and the table roared. It provided the only moment of levity in the day. It lasted but a moment. Instantly, the Under Secretary waved them to silence and proceeded to speak again: "Will you please tell us, Mr. Daughtry, the typical manner in which you operated with Mr. Sujimoto? Did he make suggestions that you purchase or sell certain currencies?"

"No, sir," Daughtry replied emphatically. "Mr. Sujimoto did not suggest. He ordered."

A wave of uneasy murmurs rippled round the table. Outside, a police siren wailed mournfully up Constitution Avenue.

"Were these orders issued in written form, Mr. Daughtry?" asked a tweedy SEC functionary.

"They were issued verbally, over the phone."

"Was that always the case? Did a confirming memo never follow?"

"No, sir. That was always the case. Mr. Sujimoto was careful never to put such orders in writing."

"With a huge exchange position such as you had, Mr. Daughtry, with dangerously overextended contracts"—the Currency Comptroller peered into the bowl of his pipe as he lit it— "why in God's name did you permit yourself to get into a position with all of these contracts maturing on the same date? Good God, man, you're supposed to be a highly experienced trader."

"The answer to that," said Daughtry with quiet self-possession, "is simply that I shouldn't have." He glanced across at Michaeltree, who sat now with his head in his hands. "And I so notified my superiors. I was told that we were to accept a total of 10 million U.S. outstanding in exchange contracts with

Haribachi-Hammamura, and to bear the 10 percent risk on this total. But you're absolutely right. Normal banking practice would have stipulated that no more than U.S. 2 million would be permitted to mature in any single day. However, I think you'll concede that the fact that we were dealing in this case with the chief officer of the bank made normal banking procedures impossible."

"I concede no such thing." The Under Secretary stiffened and peered at him from out of stern, iron-gray brows. "Would you tell us, for the benefit of those of us here who may not know, Mr. Daughtry, exactly what is meant by a fiduciary account?"

Daughtry glanced uneasily at Edelbach. When his eyes came front again, the Under Secretary was gazing at him intently.

"In Switzerland," Daughtry began somewhat haltingly, "it's always been possible to bank in secrecy. With a fiduciary account it's possible to invest in secrecy."

"How does this kind of an account work?"

"Basically it's quite simple. You open a fiduciary account with a Swiss bank. They take your money and invest it, or lend it out—*in their name, not yours.* You take the risk and the profit, if there is one. The bank takes a fee. Your name remains completely unknown outside of the bank."

"And how did Mr. Sujimoto employ this system?"

"With a small, but crucial innovation, he carried the principle of fiduciary accounts one step further. In effect, he stole the money. It worked something like this. At Mr. Sujimoto's instruction, Confederated would open a fiduciary account with a Swiss bank—usually one owned by Mr. Sujimoto. Since the account was in the Confederated's name it remained as an asset on our own books. But, in reality, secret instructions from Mr. Sujimoto himself would direct the Swiss bank to pass on the money to any one of several companies set up by Mr. Sujimoto in one of the world's several tax havens, such as the Bahamas. But most action was with his Protocorp group in Liechtenstein. From that point the money could go anywhere."

As Daughtry's quiet monotone reeled on, Leon Edelbach's

85

face darkened and slowly became a desolation too ghastly to contemplate.

"Frequently," Daughtry went on, "that money was recycled into Japan, used there to finance Mr. Sujimoto's operations on the Tokyo Exchange, and to a much larger extent, his huge speculations in the field of foreign currency. It was a merry-go-round. Without their knowledge, Confederated's depositors were financing Mr. Sujimoto's widespread speculations."

"And this system," the Under Secretary inquired, "was utilized by several of Mr. Sujimoto's banks?"

"Yes, sir."

"Would you say principally the Confederated?"

"Yes, sir, I would."

A low murmur of voices fluttered through the room. The Under Secretary waited for silence, and then continued: "And would you also say, Mr. Daughtry, that the responsibility for such a misuse of funds falls squarely on the managers and directors of the bank?"

Daughtry was silent a moment, as if he were weighing the question. When at last he replied, it was brief and unflinching. "I can't speak for the others here, sir, but I certainly would."

15

In battle, those who are most afraid are always in most danger.
—CATILINE: To his troops in the field, Pistoria, 63 B.C.

In Liechtenstein it was past 11 P.M. In the Schloss Mendenhall a single light burned high up in a corner room beneath the eaves. It was the large bedroom suite shared by Mr. Sujimoto and Madame de Plevissier.

Sujimoto had just stepped from the bath, tying the tasseled sash of an Italian silk robe round his slightly paunchy middle. Madame de Plevissier sat at a vanity applying cold cream to her face. Wearing a blue silk peignoir, her face, covered with a white cream mask, hovered in the oval glass as if disembodied.

Sujimoto in fleece slippers toddled slightly as he moved. The slippers and the richly tapestried robe gave him an ancient, doll-like appearance, rather like an expensive toy. Seldom had he ever looked quite so old, so frail, and oddly vulnerable. Leaning back against a wall, he watched through narrowed eyes Celestine apply her mask of salves and ointments, totally unconscious of his presence there. It struck Sujimoto that she was beautiful, had always been, but that he had never known quite how to properly tell her. His French would have been inadequate for him to convey to her all he felt. And besides, deep down, he knew that such effusions were all rubbish. He relied on the certainty that she knew precisely how he'd felt, no doubt long before it had occurred to him that he indeed even felt that way.

But just then, gazing at her, a surge of uncharacteristic tenderness overtook him, mingled with a sense of depletion and loss. The afternoon which had started so well had ended in an appalling row with Mariko; one in which she had barged out of the glade with a hail of obscenities, leaving Madame de Plevissier dashed and himself mortified.

"Thief. Liar. Betrayer." The words rang in his head, shrill, accusatory and just as raw then as the moment she'd shrieked them. But his desolation was as much a product of that as it was of something that had occurred only moments before in the privacy of his bathroom.

Coming home from the outing that afternoon, Sujimoto had been feeling a great deal of soreness and pain in his stomach. He told himself he'd overdrunk and had too much to eat. However, he'd been feeling that same pain periodically for several months now, and within the area of pain, low in the crease between thigh and pelvis, he could feel a pronounced swelling. But now he had found a large amount of blood in his stool. For months he had been ignoring the pain, the way one does, denying its existence over and over again so as to make it go away. This time, however, the blood was very hard to ignore.

87

He wouldn't of his own volition go to a doctor, certain that if you went to one and weren't sick, the doctor would surely then contrive to make you so. It was their business to make you sick, so they could then heal you at exorbitant cost. Instead, he settled for chewing innumerable antacid tablets and laxatives in the hope these simple nostrums would provide relief.

Still, he had not been frightened. But seeing the blood tonight turning the stool a blackish, tarlike color had shaken him badly. And that is what he was feeling as he watched Celestine's cold-creamed mask, floating eerily in the mirror—fear and the struggle within him against the need to tell her.

It was she who spoke first, glancing up suddenly. She uttered a startled little cry, then laughed, talking to his image reflected in the mirror. "How long have you been standing there?"

She turned and smiled, then saw him lean against the wall, wobbly and tentative on his feet, as if his legs were rubber. She saw pain and fear in his face.

"What is it?"

His mouth worked but he was unable to make words. Instead he smiled queasily. She noted that his lips had an unnaturally bluish cast.

"It's that awful business with Mariko today." She took his hand firmly and led him to the bed. "It's made you sick, hasn't it?"

He trod after her with a pathetic, almost childlike docility.

"It was a nasty row." Celestine bustled forward. "She had no right to say those things. It was unforgivable."

While she chattered and fussed with the tassel of his robe, she guided him skillfully into bed, lifting his spindly legs and guiding them under the comforter. She was an acute woman, Celestine—with a strong vein of Gallic peasant shrewdness. Much did not escape her. "She's been quite upset by the last few days," she rattled on.

"I'm sorry to have inconvenienced her with my sudden turn of bad fortune," he replied snidely. "I'm upset too."

88

"Of course you are, my darling."

"If she thinks I enjoy failure any more than she—"

"Please let us stop all this ridiculous talk about failure."

"I've disgraced her, haven't I?"

"That's absurd and you know it."

"I'm certain all of my sudden notorious celebrity is an embarrassment to her."

"Bad luck for her, then," Celestine fumed. "That child hasn't known an uncomfortable day in her life."

"Madame, I have failed her."

"Oh, come." Celestine rose irritably. "I can't abide self-pity. Hundreds of good men, decent men, confront bankruptcy every day. They don't think of themselves as disgraced."

Slowly Sujimoto's head turned, bringing his woeful features round before her. "But they are not me." He said it with gritted teeth, in Japanese. His native tongue made it sound far more brutal and self-condemnatory than his French could ever hope to.

"What was it she called me?" Sujimoto smiled grievously. "Liar. Thief. Betrayer." He laughed ruefully.

"It was stupid. She's naïve. Hopelessly idealistic."

"By which I take it you mean that I'm cynical—crassly materialistic."

"Now let us stop this," Celestine scolded. "I won't stay here another moment if you're going to go on like this. You're getting yourself all worked up before bed. Let me get you something to help you sleep." She made to press him back on the pillows, but he pushed her hand aside and struggled up. "Don't think I don't know how she's felt about me all these years."

"Sujimoto—"

"The anger. The resentment she's harbored."

"That's not true."

"Against me. For never having married you. Of course it's true."

Celestine's head slumped heavily downward. The cold cream smeared in streaks across her brow gave her a somewhat ludicrous look like that of a tired clown. "Well, what of it," she sighed. "Isn't it enough that I've never felt that way?"

"And now there's this Daughtry fellow. Apparently she was sweet on him."

"Was?" Celestine laughed lightly. "Still is. Very much so. Never says anything about him, but you can see it. Don't you know your own child by this time?"

"I know what she thinks, and I won't have it." Sujimoto's voice grew shrill. "The man's a thief. A swindler. And I was a fool to permit him to mislead me."

"But *he's* the one who faces prosecution. Not you."

The smile on Celestine's face infuriated Sujimoto. He was about to erupt—but then he felt the tender knotty bulge in his abdomen like a sharp sticking sensation and he winced. She caught it at once.

"What is wrong?" she cried. "What is it, my darling?"

"Nothing's wrong. I'm fine. Perfectly fine." He composed himself on the pillows and reached for a well-thumbed Simenon beside his bed.

"You look awful. Tell me, what is it?"

He turned a pair of petrified, childlike eyes upon her, but couldn't speak.

"I'm going to call the doctor," she said, bolting up. "Something hurts you, I can see."

"No." His fingers gripped her upper arm. "No."

"Then tell me what's wrong."

His mouth struggled for words. "Oh, *merde*," he nearly whimpered. "It's that same business of a few years ago."

"What business?"

"That pain. You know. It's back again."

"In your side?"

"Yes."

"Are you sure?"

"Of course, I'm sure. I told you it's my side, didn't I?"

"Of course, my darling. I only—" Her fingers searched beneath his blanket, under his robe, finding the spot and tenderly probing it.

90

"Probably indigestion. I should never have drunk all that wine today," Sujimoto said. "Nothing to worry about, is there, madame?" He laughed uneasily.

"Of course not." Celestine dismissed it. "The doctor told you that three years ago, so stop worrying."

He couldn't bring himself to tell her about the blood.

"All the same," she rattled on distractedly, "we ought to drop by his office tomorrow. You haven't had a checkup recently."

"I don't care to see the doctor." Sujimoto folded his arms and sulked.

"Just a checkup. Nothing more. You're being childish." She fussed over his sheet and blankets, tucking them up about him like a mother fretting over a sickly child. "Tomorrow, first thing we'll—" She sat with him on the edge of the bed, holding his hand as he grew sleepy. So trusting and pathetic he seemed just then, so docile and yielding—Sujimoto, industrialist, financier, world shaker.

Just as she thought he was about to doze off, he muttered, "You're right. She does blame me."

Madame de Plevissier leaned closer. "Nonsense. You make too much of it."

"She blames me for that Daughtry business." Sujimoto flared up momentarily like a dying ash, then rolled his head on the pillow and made a small guttural sound. She sensed he was in great pain.

"We're going to the doctor first thing in the morning."

"She blames me for his present difficulty," he went on obsessively. "She thinks I put him in this fix. That I set him up to betray him."

"And did you?" Celestine's gaze was suddenly heartless and cold.

Sujimoto was caught off balance by the directness of her question. He rolled his head sidewards and gazed for a time at the wall.

"Did you, Sujimoto?"

"Of course not. What do you take me for? He did it to himself entirely. The fool."

She felt he had overreacted, that he had been evasive and self-protective. That made her uneasy.

Later when she'd turned off the light and left him snoring gently, she tiptoed into the bathroom and, seated on the edge of the tub, she wept quietly to herself.

She had seen the terror in his eyes and sensed what he'd been going through. He had been having one of his periodic fits of hypochondria. These generally occurred during periods of stress. Several years ago, suffering from severe pains in his side, he had gone to the doctor convinced that a malignancy was running rampant inside him.

The doctor put him through a battery of tests and concluded that his side pains were no more than gas and stomach acidity related to overeating and overdrinking. He recommended a diet of bland food and nonalcoholic drink, along with liquid antacids. Sujimoto never went on the diet and was more convinced than ever that the doctor had concealed the fatal truth from him; that the malignancy was spreading and that his days were numbered.

By now Celestine was used to these stress-related bouts, but she could never quite get used to the hell of being around him when they struck. Full of dread, she saw one rushing on now like a squall line in the rapidly closing distance.

16

We got a hell of a beating. We got run out of Burma and it is humiliating as hell.
—GEN. JOSEPH W. (VINEGAR JOE) STILWELL:
Statement, May 25, 1942

When they'd left the Federal Reserve Building several hours earlier, the air had snapped cold, and snow darkened the pewter-gray sky.

The conclusions drawn at the emergency session in Washington that afternoon were grim, the implications crystal clear, and the course recommended to avert disaster implacable. The Confederated New York, Corporation for the Confederated Trust Bank had been ordered to approve several major management changes, as well as give their consent to a new $50 million stock issue for the purposes of capital financing. In addition, Mr. E. Daniel Halliday, a former Secretary of the Treasury, had been temporarily appointed, over Leon Edelbach's nearly apoplectic opposition, the new board chairman of Confederated. This came, along with voting rights for all the bank's shares controlled by Confederated New York.

A bitter pill it was for all the Confederated people assembled there that day. Chastisement it was, reproof and humiliation— open testimony to the committee's judgment that the bank's senior management had neither the will nor the capacity to rectify the situation for themselves.

In return for all of the bank's concessions, the Federal Reserve chairman, Mr. Clark Bowie, pledged loans of $1.7 billion to help it overcome its liquidity crisis. Officials from the New York Clearing House present that afternoon were certain that disclosure of the Confederated's huge losses would result in a run on the bank's demand deposits. How extensive a run would depend on how adroitly the situation was handled. The media must not be permitted to hype the situation out of all proportion.

The Under Secretary concluded the hearings with a guarantee that he would prevail upon a number of major banks to pony up an additional $250 million in loans on a secured basis with the backing of the Fed to tide the bank over through a difficult period. "The integrity of the American banking system must be preserved at all costs," he said. Someone far down the table snickered.

Going home late that Sunday evening on the Metroliner, Daughtry sat apart from his colleagues. Gone was any pretense of camaraderie, or even the forced and thoroughly bogus hilarity of the trip out. Instead, it was now simply They and Him. All were badly shaken. Firings were in the air. Resignations were imminent. Anxiety ran rampant like a brushfire. Head-rollings and symbolic executions would have to be carried out, they knew, in order to placate the wrath of the directors and stockholders. Public outrage would have to be assuaged.

Somewhere between Trenton and New York Wainwright resigned, followed shortly by Villiers, who wept openly. Edelbach accepted the resignations. He had no choice, that being the price Edelbach conceded to the Fed for putting together the billion-dollar salvage package to bail out Confederated.

Edelbach sat surrounded by his lieutenants, justifying expedience, affecting humility, like an old sick lion amid its dispirited pride. Napoleon must have looked a bit like that on the retreat from Russia, broken, disconsolate, huddled with his staff, and still uncertain what exactly had gone wrong.

"They would pull through," Daughtry overheard him boast under the spell of several bourbons. "We'll tough it out, but sacrifices will have to be made." He grieved openly and shamelessly. No one, as of yet, had suggested to him that he himself might conceivably become one of the sacrifices.

Several times Daughtry, sitting apart from the others, his mind detached from the events of the day, his conscience strangely at ease, looked up to find Edelbach's gaze upon him— a mixture of rage and hurt hinting at the propinquity of some dark vengeance.

He could not make Daughtry one of the sacrifices. He knew that. At least, not yet. Daughtry, by becoming a pivotal witness against the bank, had ironically secured immunity from retaliatory action against himself. For the time being, that is, Daughtry had survived.

PART II

17

*Going into action today reminds me of a struggle
between two blind men, between two adversaries
who perpetually seek each other but cannot see.*
—FERDINAND FOCH: *Precepts*, 1919

1. Since who I am is of no consequence, therefore,
whatever I do is of no consequence. *Cogito; ergo non
sum.* Action is all.
2. Since the record of my life brings dishonor upon my
ancestors, my life as presently constituted is unacceptable to my living relations.

The first-class stewardess came by and refilled his champagne glass. He did not look up but continued to scribble notes
on a long yellow pad.

. . . and since I give no satisfaction to those I regard most
highly . . . my father being in disgrace, I too am in
disgrace. It follows therefore that the author of this
disgrace must therefore also suffer disgrace.

"Are you ready to order lunch yet?" The stewardess smiled.
A look of puzzled, vacant abstraction pervaded the soft,
rather poetic cast of his eyes. Looking up at her for the first time,
he had the look of a man suddenly recovering from amnesia.
His eyes, large and dark, appeared to expand and brighten.
"Oh?"
"You haven't ordered yet." Seeing the hearing aid in his right
ear, she spoke louder.
"Oh? Is that so? I'm sorry." He was truly contrite.
The stewardess, a pretty young Swiss girl with wheat-white
hair and ash-colored eyes, seemed troubled. The traveler's
comfort was her exclusive charge, which in this case she felt
she had been failing. Not for lack of effort. Actually, she had

gone out of her way to make the gentleman comfortable. It was simply that he appeared so stiff and uneasy, so alien to the large cabin and its many comforts.

The man, however, clearly a Japanese, did not seem unhappy. His passport and tickets identified him as a Mr. I. Matsumura, age 38. Residence, Tokyo-Okitsu.

He drank his champagne silently—five glasses now—and requested little else, although the first-class fare entitled him to a great deal more.

Gazing up at the young stewardess hovering above him, his smile was neither flirtatious nor provocative. It was not designed to overcome her. She was certain of that. In four years of international runs, she had seen more than her share of that sort of thing. This was decidedly different. She knew at once, 30,000 feet above the Atlantic, that he was not about to press his hotel address upon her, invite her for cocktails and possibly dinner. This smile, cultivated and so infinitely weary, was certainly not that. It was simply a smile. No more, no less. It carried no special freight. A smile with a quality of forbearance, it did not ask to be adored.

"There is a veal *blanquette* in Madeira today. *Coquille* of lobster and a *gigot* of lamb that looks quite good." If the recitation seemed a trifle mechanical, the sincerity was at least genuine. "Everyone's eaten already, and we won't be serving again except for a snack."

Again that sad, infinitely forbearing smile. "I'm not very hungry."

She lingered a moment, vaguely troubled and uncertain exactly why she had bothered to try so hard. "Well, if you'd like a sandwich or a snack later . . ." at last she capitulated—"your buzzer is directly overhead."

He nodded and smiled as she went off on her rounds. The smile lingered on his lips a moment longer. He thought about the note he'd left on his bedroom bureau at Mendenhall, saying he was going down to Monte for a week or two of sunshine. Not to worry. But, of course, he wasn't going to Monte at all.

Staring into the darkened cabin, the quiet drone of engines humming in his abdomen, the stuffy, airless sense of drowsy, overfed people all about him, slouched in their seats watching Technicolor figures flickering on a drop screen, Kajumi Sujimoto had the look of a benign creature caught up in some distant pleasant reverie. In the next moment he returned to his pad.

3. Since with each year I am more and more obsessed with the inescapable sense of the undirected, worthlessness of my life . . .

This most recent paragraph to his thesis brought him up sharply. It caused him to reflect on the past and roads not taken. First, there had been failure at the university, followed shortly thereafter by rejection of his application for officers' school in the Imperial Navy on medical grounds—a punctured eardrum with marked hearing loss in the right ear—an abysmally pathetic basis for rejection. Almost despicable in its utter innocuousness. He almost wished it could have been on the grounds of some incurable valvular disease of the heart, or an irreversible kidney dysfunction that would ultimately snuff him out by drowning him in his own fluids. But this punctured eardrum was too absurd. The world must surely perceive him, if it perceived him at all, as ludicrous. And how badly his father had taken it. The old fearless captain of the legendary cruiser, *Aoba*. Heavily decorated, richly honored, old Odysseus back from the wars. But what a pathetic Telemachus his puny, feeble-witted Kajumi made with his wretched, perforated eardrum.

And then of course the final indignity—to have been taken into one's father's business, given a lofty position with a high salary right at the start; given every opportunity to succeed, encouraged, stroked, praised fulsomely for executing simpleminded tasks, and then in spite of all that, to have gone right ahead anyway and failed. It was almost perverse, as if he'd laid his own plans for defeat.

Suddenly he looked up. People all about him were laughing, watching a film with Robert Morley in which the characters spent most of their time eating in four-star Michelin restaurants, while a number of master chefs were mysteriously killed off.

"But this all started long before my failure at university or the Navy or the rest of it," he scribbled hastily, anxious to get it all down as it came to him. "The bottom falls out. The center will not hold." Where have I read that? How I wish I could find the center again. My internal gyroscope. My guidance system through the dark night of my days. When mother lived, I had that. When she died, it slipped away. And then . . ." His pencil paused above the pad as if his hand were in mortal struggle with some invisible force, staying his hand so he couldn't lower it to the paper. "And then . . . and then . . . and then . . . that woman. That Parisian whore, with her whore daughter who dares to call herself my sister."

Suddenly his eyes filled with the dark vision of his mother writhing on the dirt floor of an apple cellar in a farmhouse outside of Sapporo in the distant northern province of Hokkaido. She writhed and twisted, her swollen torso heaving up and banging down on the damp earth with quick sickening thuds. A yellow foam leaked from the corner of her mouth; her eyeballs rolled upward and backward into her head; and a horrible, almost feral growl issued from somewhere deep within her clenched jaws.

Deep within the shadows of that apple cellar, in a large coal scupper, he could see, framed against the dim light of a grimy window, the huge dark silhouette of what was clearly another woman. The face was eclipsed in shadow, but he knew, as he knew his very own self, the identity of that other woman.

"It started with the advent of Celestine in my father's life," he wrote, his fingers suddenly hot and tremulous. "My father's gradual alienation from my mother commenced with her. I was too young to understand what was happening. I tended to blame his increasing aloofness on his disappointment with me. The steady attrition of affection between us, the growing lack of closeness between my mother and him, the long, stiff pauses in conversation, and ultimately my exclusion from his life, I blame on that woman. Clever, she was, and treacherous with her pose of generosity and affection. When she sank her fangs into my father—'Mr. Sujimoto, sir. Would you care to eat? May I puff up that pillow behind you? May I freshen your drink? May I go to your bed and await you there?'—it was she, who cut the floor out from under me. She who insinuated her bastard daughter into his life, and thereby disenfranchised me. She who gelded me. Transformed me into a feckless, inept rich man's son. A pub crawler. A saloon habitué. A casino spectacle. A buffoon. And it was not only me who was transformed, but my father as well— the paramour of the murderess. Possibly her accomplice. Why not? Not so improbable at all. Although I'm sure she did it all by herself. That period when she disappeared and Mariko was born. My sister, who is not my sister. My sister with strangely Caucasian features. Japanese in name only. The daughter of my father's whore. A walking disgrace to the memory of my mother.

"Oh dear and blessed mother. Mother of mine. Heal me. Make me whole again. Give me purpose. Show me what I must do to retrieve myself. Help me to pluck out the scourge from my father's life. Help me to cleanse the sin from my ancestral name. Help me for all the noble line of Sujimotos, then and now and to come . . ."

A thin British lady across the aisle from him cackled. A mirthless, empty vulgar shriek issued from a painted, crooked beak of a mouth. It set his teeth on edge. The pencil clutched in the vise of his talon fingers snapped in half, but he continued to scribble anyway with the broken stump of it, as if the sheer momentum of his rage made it impossible for him to stop. Like a speeding car gone wildly out of control, shrieking brakes, the squeal of burning rubber tires, the broken stump of pencil careened right on, carving gashes into the paper pad, shredding it. "Since I am what I am. And what I am is . . ."

In a matter of a few hours they would be landing at Kennedy Airport. He knew then what he would do. It was a course that struck him as logical, honorable and inevitable. It was all settled then. Good. He leaned back in his seat and signaled the stewardess. Robert Morley was having a second helping of *bombe* at Faugeron. He laughed heartily with all the others. He was ready now for lunch.

18

Let's fly and save our bacon.
—RABELAIS: *Pantagruel*, 1533

That night when Daughtry returned home he started to pack. It was nearly midnight. Although he was exhausted, he didn't go to bed. He didn't even bother changing his clothes. Instead, he pulled a number of cardboard cartons out of the basement, lugged them upstairs and started to fill them with his possessions.

His packing was neither hasty nor disordered, but rather a tidy, deliberate affair. He moved with the sort of certitude and ease that suggests a mind that has reconciled its conflicts, although at that moment Daughtry had not the slightest notion why he was packing or where he might go—only that he would now live out of boxes like one prepared to pull up stakes and decamp at a moment's notice.

All the while throughout that night as he packed and ordered his affairs, he thought of Okitsu and Sujimoto, and strangely and persistently of the girl whose memory now stirred him uneasily.

"Why do you laugh at my father?"

"I? Laugh at your father?"

"Of course you do. At every possible opportunity. I see you smirking. How dare you?"

"You're mistaken."

"I am not mistaken. It's obvious," she fumed. "You find him

quaint and amusing with all of his statistics and pious slogans on the sacred nature of commerce."

"Now, you're laughing yourself."

She grew livid. "I have a right to. He's my father. And besides, I don't do it cruelly."

"Neither do I." He laughed.

"There, you see? You're laughing right now."

"I think you're crazy."

"I am not crazy." She stamped a foot petulantly. "How dare you?"

"How dare I what?"

"What? What? What? What?" She jeered the word back at him. "You can barely express yourself. You're inarticulate. You have no real vocabulary. Your expression is flat, yet you dare to laugh at a man who can express himself in a half-dozen languages—a man who has read the Koran and the Bible and Shakespeare. What have you ever read?"

Daughtry gaped at her. She appeared beside herself, a small, indignant wasp poised to sting. Still he couldn't believe that the source of her rage had anything to do with his opinion of her father. Of course, she happened to be entirely correct. He did find the man preposterous with his mottoes and statistics, all of his pious sententiousness on the glories of Japan's technological miracle. He was like an industrial film—a public relations puff.

Still, his opinion of the quality of her father's genius was not at the heart of her anger. Something else, concealed, as of yet unspoken, lay at the center of this rage: "He is a flawed man. I grant you that. He is pompous, egotistical, self-aggrandizing. But he at least is human. He loves commerce and warfare. Drinks to excess. But he has feelings. He's human. You are not human."

"What the hell am I then?"

The question brought her up sharply. Her jaw dropped and she paused, wanting her response to be apposite.

"You—" She fumed and puffed. "You—you are stillborn. I've never seen anything like you. God knows what the hell you are.

103

A robot or a Martian, possibly. Maybe a freak. It beats me. Take me to dinner, for Christ's sake."

Then, later on the beach, waves bashing the jettylike cannonade—the two of them writhed in a damp, moldy canvas found by an old cabin near the water. Having scissored him between short, piston-legs, her thrusting torso arched up at him. Her eyes rolled heavenward, she spat obscenities and tried to claw his eyes.

The following morning he sat in Sujimoto's office while the old man pressed electric buttons on a console beside his desk, bawled into a dictaphone and barked orders to a badly raddled secretary.

"Why do you persist in defying me, Mr. Daughtry?" the old man whined.

"Defiance is not my intention. It's simply my duty to clear all transactions with my superiors in New York."

"Your superiors in New York, I must remind you, are my subordinates. So you are wasting a good deal of time clearing these transactions with them first. And by the way, Mr. Daughtry, why do these transactions have to be cleared at all?"

"Because they are of a questionable nature."

"Questionable nature?" Sujimoto's voice hit a cracking tremulo. "How so?"

"As I've tried to explain on other occasions, trading currencies with your own banks, instructing them at what prices they will bid and offer is a self-dealing, self-serving operation. The law frowns on this. It is not tolerated."

"The law has been gracious enough to tolerate it in the past."

"All well and good," Daughtry fumed. "I wish you luck. However, if the law suddenly decides to withhold its grace, I don't care to be known as the instrument of these transactions."

Exasperation leaked at every corner of Sujimoto's round, livid face. "We shall see about that," he hissed between clenched teeth. "We shall see. In the meantime, I see that, despite my wishes to the contrary, you continue to spend a great deal of time with my daughter. I must warn you—"

Daughtry's hand rose, a monitory gesture like a traffic cop. "She *is* your daughter, Mr. Sujimoto. I couldn't agree more. Therefore, *you* warn her. She's far beyond the age of consent."

Sujimoto's eyes bulged. He appeared to swell.

"And while we are on the subject," Daughtry continued now in high gear, "I should like to take this opportunity to tender my resignation."

A strangled *yawp* issued from the back of the old man's throat. "You what?"

"I resign."

"Denied!" He pounded his little fists on the desk. "Your resignation is most emphatically denied."

"Very well. In that case, I quit outright."

"You're mad."

"On the contrary, I've never felt quite so sane. I think a long vacation from this job and your daughter will have a salutary effect on my spirits." Daughtry spun sharply on his heel and stalked out.

For a long while after, Sujimoto sat smoldering amid all the highly sophisticated electronic gadgetry surrounding him and the litter of toy paper boats on his desk. His posture, shortly before, distended and purple with indignation, had begun to slowly deflate like a punctured tube. Smaller and smaller he grew, his shoulders gradually slumping until actually he gave the appearance of a furious midget cowering behind the desk.

That evening in Okitsu, as Daughtry tossed clothing into a bag, she came to him.

"Why are you leaving?" she demanded.

"Because I have no wish to go to jail."

"He needs you. He can't get on without you. There's no one here with comparable experience."

"He doesn't heed my judgment. I may as well be in New York." He yanked one of his suits out of a closet and started to cram it into his luggage.

105

"You'll crush everything." She took the suit out and proceeded to carefully fold it. "Please don't go," she said after a moment.

"I can't continue here like this."

"If what he is doing is improper, you can change it. He has great regard for you."

He stayed her hand from nervous folding. "Do you?"

She turned and stared up at him. "I'm asking you to stay, aren't I?" she murmured.

She had never before asked him for anything, much less entreated him in quite so appealing a manner. Ruefully he kissed the sweet cool mouth and felt the lean body melt in upon him a rush of merging liquescence.

"Did he put you up to this?" he said.

"If he knew I were here, there'd be hell to pay. Will you stay now?" Her lips brushed his and they clung together.

"Against my better judgment," he sighed, "but I know I'll rue the day."

Sujimoto's speculations continued, of course, even more flagrantly, but after that night, he never again tried to interfere in his daughter's relationship with the young currency expert.

That was all in September of 1978. Daughtry left Japan two months later in November. He had not set eyes on Mariko in roughly two years.

Laughter echoed through the litter of his bedroom. The drawers were all out, stacks of shirts and socks were piled atop his unmade bed.

Outside on Sixty-third Street, cabs rumbled past the parlor windows. Two drunks had a noisy altercation in front of his door. It was now 4 A.M. and there was a crack of gray in the sky. Several scruffy pigeons commenced their cooing in the dovecote on the adjacent rooftop. Daughtry showered and prepared to face the day. After Washington, a sense of cataclysm was in the air.

19

*Too much success is not wholly desirable: an
occasional beating is good for men—and nations.*
—ALFRED T. MAHAN: *Life of Nelson, IX, 1897*

"Mark 30–38."

"Can you get me a lira, someone? Christ, it's taking a real
run."

"Take. Take. I take."

"64–69."

"Sell—sell."

"Who's talking to Tokyo? The yen's gone nuts."

"Anything new?" Daughtry leaned over and asked Ricardi,
the chief trader on the floor. The moment he'd entered he
noticed a sudden lull in the action, a dropping of voices as he
drew near.

"Fedco wants to buy a bill in marks," Ricardi replied.

"Buy it, then," Daughtry snapped and noted the uncharacteristically stiff self-consciousness in the man's smile. Undoubtedly, he'd been reading the newspapers.

He stalked forward in the direction of his office, Ricardi
trailing at his heel like an attentive watchdog. All throughout
the typing pools, the tellers' cages, it was business as usual, but
there was something in the air—the roiled, uneasy sense of
"something up." Eyes lowered when Daughtry appeared outside
his office. People bent over papers and pretended to work, but he
knew that only moments before tongues had been wagging;
rumors flying. Mrs. Gaynes handed him a sheaf of cables and
the latest rate postings, but that morning her "Good morning,
Mr. Daughtry" struck him as faintly hollow and forced.

"Someone out there is sucking up all the marks this
morning," Ricardi remarked once the door of the office had
closed and they were settled in.

"Doesn't mean a thing," Daughtry said. "Only that some big American company probably needs a shipment of DM to pay off a German supplier. Or maybe some bank has decided to reverse a losing position." Daughtry eyed his chief executioner critically. "Anything special going?"

Ricardi's eyes blinked and he rocked gently in his seat. "There's been a bit of wind about a new 5 percent increase in oil prices plus a big Libyan surcharge." The Argentinian sat opposite Daughtry, crossed his long willowy legs and lit a small panatella. He was still red in the face from shouting into squawk boxes. "They say the OPECs are going to take a bushel of currencies. Anything instead of dollars."

"That's been around for weeks. Forget it." Daughtry scribbled his signature on some documents. He could sense Ricardi watching him warily. Each man was determined to talk about anything but the thing that mattered most. For a moment he had a vision of Leon Edelbach, and wondered how that poor, hapless individual was spending his morning.

The interoffice phone buzzed. It was Mrs. Gaynes to say that a trader in Bonn was trying to reach him. Ricardi watched as Daughtry had the call put through. Given the nature of the weekend he had just endured, and the lack of any real sleep for the past forty-eight hours, Daughtry's mind was remarkably clear. The sense of numbers ricocheting about, the ambience of steady trading, the quiet tick and clatter of big computers, all had a tonic effect upon him.

Daughtry listened as the Bonn trader sought to make a position in Deutsche marks. The man, a trader of course, wouldn't disclose his identity. But Daughtry, recognizing the voice as one he'd dealt with before, had a fairly good idea of who it was. It became increasingly apparent they were both out working for the same client.

The Bonn trader was simply looking for a quote, so he said, with the most elaborate casualness. Naturally, he wouldn't say if he wanted to buy or sell, or whether it was one million or fifty million he had in mind. All that would only be divulged after the rate was quoted and agreed upon. Evaluating what Ricardi had told him about Deutsche marks moments before, he knew in his bones that the man was out shopping, and once he'd quoted the narrow spread of pips, if the Bonn trader took him up on it, he was honor-bound to deliver.

"30–38, for payment 10 days in dollars," he said, without batting an eye. Ricardi recoiled in his chair, rocking slightly as if he'd been pushed.

Daughtry hung up. The deal was struck. The chief executioner shook his head, dumbfounded. "Where the hell do you think you'll find the stuff?"

"Somewhere." Daughtry was flushed with exhilaration. "It's out there somewhere."

Then a sly, knowing smirk broadened on Ricardi's face. "Does it really matter any more?"

Daughtry appeared momentarily angry and bewildered. "It always matters to me. Whatever happens here."

Ricardi looked away, flustered. Shortly, he spoke again. His voice was flat, unemotional. "What happened in Washington?"

"What do you think happened?" The old combativeness returned. "We got what we deserved. They kicked our ass."

Ricardi watched him sign papers for a moment and felt a vague tinge of envy. He held back for a moment, uncertain whether to press further. "They say Wainwright's—"

"Out," Daughtry snapped without looking up.

"And Villiers?"

"Out too. Christ, is that all people do around here? Yak?" He glanced up at Ricardi and divined at once the question in his eye. He fumed. "No, goddamn it. I'm still here. Can't you see that? Don't worry about it any more. We're all still here, if that's what you want to know. The Fed says it's going to bail us out with a billion seven. But if you ask me, it's too little and too late. It's a quarter to midnight. The tiger's at the gates."

"Sujimoto?"

"Somewhere in Liechtenstein counting sterling and yen. Home free while we're sitting here half a block from the Tombs. It'll take an act of God to get him out."

Grievingly, Ricardi shook his head. "But we're still employed?"

"If that's so goddamned important," Daughtry huffed impatiently. "Yes—we're still employed. Business as usual."

"They say the Manny Hanny is talking merger. Takeover."

"They say it's raining in Detroit too. So what?"

"They say Halliday is coming out of retirement to revamp Forex operations."

"He's welcome to it—with my compliments."

"But—"

"Forget it," Daughtry snorted. "Nothing to do with us. Business as usual, I told you. Now get the hell out there and find us some DM. Start with Hein in Düsseldorf. Don't tell him what you want or why, or suddenly you'll find marks getting very scarce."

After Ricardi had left, he suddenly felt exhausted. Alone at his desk, in shirt sleeves, he sat, elbows on table, head cradled in his palms. He felt courage leaking out of every pore. Cataclysm traveled fast in this world. People unaffected directly by it thrived gleefully on other people's bad luck. Once the word got out that the Confederated had been overreaching in speculation, he knew the grapevine would move it fast. The first thing the bank could expect now that the story was all over the newswires would be that other banks would start cutting back on deals with it. In the end they would shun business with the bank entirely.

The next step in this degenerative process would be heavy runs on demand deposits, resulting in a hemorrhage if left unchecked—a hemorrhage that would eventually kill off the Confederated.

The intercom rang again. Florita Gaynes was on. "A Mr. James Hardigan to see you, Mr. Daughtry."

"Hardigan?" Daughtry thumbed his appointments calendar

for that day. "I see no appointment here with any Mr. Hardigan."

"I know," Mrs. Gaynes sounded apologetic. Her voice lowered to a whisper. "He says he's from the FBI."

20

With broken heart and with head bowed in sadness but not in shame, I report . . . that today I must arrange terms for the surrender of the fortified islands of Manila Bay, Corregidor, Fort Hughes, Fort Drum, and . . . [end of message]
—LT. GEN. JONATHAN M. WAINWRIGHT, USA: *Last message from Corregidor, May 6, 1942*

In the immediate period following disclosure of the Confederated Trust Bank's huge losses in currency trading, the following events transpired:

1. The New York Clearing House Association reported that Confederated's deposits had dropped $325 million.
2. The SEC announced immediate suspension of all trading in Confederated stock.
3. The Fitch Investor Service suspended its AA rating on all Confederated New York Corp. stock.
4. When it was disclosed that the Federal Reserve had loaned the Confederated $1.7 billion in an effort to overcome its liquidity pressures, a prominent eastern Congressman, and member of the House Banking Committee, charged that the loan was made at the rate of 8–8½ percent, rather than the normal discount rate of 11–12 percent, suggesting that the loan was the equivalent of a subsidy to the bank at taxpayers' expenses of $600,000–$800,000 per week. This, he maintained, amounted to a scandal.
5. The SEC and the FBI both instituted independent investigations into the causes of Confederated's huge

foreign exchange losses. At the same time, a U.S. Federal judge had taken out extradition papers in the name of Hiroji Sujimoto, while newspapers and TV newscasts were making mysterious and enticing innuendos as to the real identity of the as yet unnamed currency dealer who worked as a conduit for Mr. Sujimoto's unauthorized trading with the Confederated's funds.

It was a time of dismay and uneasiness within the American banking system. The Fed had moved quickly to ease the money supply in an effort to reassure the money market. Far away from New York, at a meeting of the International Monetary conference for American and foreign bankers in Williamsburg, Virginia, the Secretary of the Treasury used the occasion of his address to term "greatly exaggerated" worries over the general soundness of the international banking system. Despite the bank's huge losses in demand deposits, the Secretary urged bankers to resume normal activities with the Confederated in the Federal Fund market. But three weeks to the day of the first disclosure of the bank's deep troubles, the New York Clearing House reported that the outflow of Confederated deposits during the second week of December not only went unabated but had accelerated. This brought the bank's total losses in deposits to $2.31 billion, a decline of $108 million from the preceding week, a staggering decline of 24 percent of the bank's total equity.

The Treasury Secretary's advice went largely unheeded and growing lines formed round the blocks of Confederated's seventy-three New York branches—people chafing to make withdrawals and close out their accounts.

"Hey, Charley." A large-boned amiable-looking gentleman clapped Daughtry on the back and flashed a toothy grin from beneath a bristling red brush mustache.

Seated by himself at a table in a small tavern off Coenties Slip, Daughtry had been taking a solitary lunch. A day before the annual Christmas recess, the atmosphere in the place was festive and boisterous. A fire roared and crackled on the hearth. Mistletoe hung above the bar along with a moth-eaten stag's head gazing benignly down upon the patrons, a large Yule wreath garlanding its six-point antlers.

In a far corner, Daughtry sat before a pint of beer and fresh pink corned beef still barely touched. Beside him, a small Christmas fir tree stood with gingerbread figures embedded in a warm glow of shimmering light.

"How you been?" The man slipped uninvited into the seat opposite Daughtry. At once he recalled the fellow from his Philliston days. At that time Daughtry had no reputation other than that of a kind of clever numbers "freak." Accordingly, this fellow, whom Daughtry recalled as nauseatingly ambitious, had never been too friendly. Now, suddenly seeing Charles Daughtry, who over the years had acquired a certain celebrity within banking circles, the fellow was suddenly the soul of cordiality.

Daughtry had come there for a bit of respite from the thick gloom of the office. He resented the unwanted intrusion into his lunch hour. Nevertheless, he chatted with the fellow whose name was Shields. In his typically laconic way, he answered questions and responded to conversation, rather than initiating it.

They chatted briefly about what each had been up to over the past years, about mutual friends, and about what was good and bad just then in the market. Finally (and Daughtry had been expecting it all along), something sly and a trifle nasty flashed from beneath the red mustache. "Say, what the hell's going on up at Confederated anyway? I hear all kinds of things."

Daughtry, picking indifferently at his corned beef, glanced up. "Like what, for instance?"

"Newspapers are full of it," Shields went on eagerly. "Merger talks with Manny Hanny and the Morg. And," he winked naughtily, "I hear you've got the FBI crawling up your ass."

"Really? Where'd you hear that?"

"Come on, Charley. It's all over the street. It's on the goddamned TV, for Chrissake."

"Is it?" Daughtry sliced a piece of beef and tucked it smartly into his cheek. "I didn't know that."

"It's not exactly a secret, you know." Shields's grin grew impertinent. Foam from his beer clung like frost to the red bristles of his mustache. He leaned closer to Daughtry and whispered, "Who's Mr. X?"

Daughtry frowned. "Mr. X?"

"The mystery chap. The unnamed dealer who's been up to his ears in unauthorized trading."

The careful deliberate carving motion of Daughtry's knife slowed to a halt. He stared impassively back at his interrogator. "I'm afraid I don't know what you're talking about, Clyde."

"So, that's how it is." Shields's eyes danced gleefully behind tinted aviator goggles. "I just wondered if the fellow might be somewhere in this room. Seated near us, right now. You know?"

Daughtry chewed thoughtfully, then he shrugged. "Could be." In the next moment he rose and tipped the remains of his beef and cabbage into Shields's lap. Never once glancing back at the man daubing frantically with a napkin at the mess in his lap, Daughtry strode up to the cashier, paid his check, and departed the tavern.

So swift was his departure that he had not seen, amid a crowd of revelers dallying late at the bar, another solitary patron, this one an Oriental gentleman in his mid-thirties. Oriental gentlemen in the New York financial district are not at all uncommon. The large majority of them are highly successful businessmen and bankers from Singapore, Seoul, Hong Kong and Tokyo.

This particular gentleman had been sitting, small and unobtrusive, before a flute of champagne. While crapulous middle-aged men brayed carols and mildly lewd ballads all around him, he smiled quietly to himself, as if contemplating some private pleasure.

From a position where he could not easily be seen, he had observed the small altercation between Daughtry and Shields—an altercation that had gone largely unnoticed by others in the tavern. The conclusion of it had caused him to smile. He wondered what had transpired between the two men to provoke Daughtry's action. It was clear that Daughtry disliked the man with whom he had been sitting. Kajumi wished that he too were capable of an action so deft and personally satisfying—an action inflicted upon all those whom he disliked, but for far too long had politely suffered.

Back at Daughtry's office a Christmas party was in full swing. Red crepe streamers festooned the place; they drooped over Xerox machines and looped around water coolers. The typing pools were littered with paper cups of liquor and crumbs of cake; salted nuts and cigarette ash were strewn all about. People laughed and sang and danced, but above it all hung the queasy anticipatory air of catastrophe.

On his desk Daughtry found a note scribbled in Leon Edelbach's small, crimped hand. "Please see me before you leave today." The "please" struck him as uncharacteristic and curiously portentous.

Up on the eighteenth floor in the tower suite of the Confederated Trust, Leon Edelbach, the temporarily deposed chairman, sat at his desk, his leather swivel chair swung about so that he faced the window behind him, the better to gaze down at the pre-Christmas bustle of Pearl Street below. There was something solitary and doleful, almost childishly vulnerable about the man as he sat there. Not his typically fastidious self that afternoon, about him was an air of tired dishevelment. Amid the turmoil of paper on his desk stood a half-consumed bottle of bourbon and a solitary paper cup. Brooding down at some spectacle below, Edelbach appeared deep in thought.

Daughtry, standing in the open doorway of the office, cleared his throat. Edelbach glanced up over his shoulder. Seeing Daughtry hovering just beyond the threshold, he frowned.

"There was no one out there—" Daughtry paused—"so I just barged in."

"They're all down at some fool party. Come on in." Edelbach

turned back to the window. "Look there." He pointed down into the street where a long line of Confederated depositors had queued up into a line snaking almost fully round the block, waiting to get into the bank and up to the teller's window. "Been lined up like that since 9 A.M.," Edelbach murmured with an air of quiet awe. A warm blast of bourbon wafted airily from his mouth. "We've taken good care of their money and investments for over one hundred years. Now with the first whiff of trouble they scurry like rats. Sit down." He indicated the chair opposite him and extended the bourbon bottle. "Spot of Christmas cheer?"

Daughtry smiled and waved the bottle away. "A bit too early for me."

Edelbach's red-rimmed eyes regarded him warily. "You're a remarkably disciplined fellow, aren't you, Charley?"

"Not *remarkably*."

"More so than most." Edelbach's gaze lowered. He fidgeted uneasily with papers on his desk. "You could have had an extraordinary career here, you know. I s'pose you still might, if things go well. You're young enough. You have great talent. A brilliant technician. Possibly one of the sharpest traders in the business." He splashed bourbon into his cup, missed partially, and dabbed up drippings with a crumpled handkerchief. "But there's some fatal void in you," he went on. "Don't ask me what the hell it is. I'm not philosophical enough. I have enormous respect for your ability, and I know I'm not alone in that opinion. But I see bottomless chasms in you in which there is absolutely nothing but ice and rock. My feelings have nothing to do with you personally, but I don't think you'll ever sit on Confederated's board." Edelbach smiled ironically, suddenly recalling the people queued up in the street below. "Maybe that's all academic now. I'm not at all sure you'd care to, anyway."

Daughtry sat impassively, observing the burly, bearish figure hunched above his desk, his eyes giving the impression of one who had peered too long into a blast furnace. He continued: "I've never cared very much for you, Charles." His eyes lowered

again. "Am I talking too frankly? Forgive me. I'm a bit tight—
nor do I think I hold a treasured spot in your esteem. I just
wanted to say we're going to have to suffer each other's
company just a little bit longer. At least until the resolution of
this thing one way or the other." He drank, covered his mouth
and belched slightly. "Or at least until the grand jury investigations are concluded. After that I'm pretty certain I'm out and
that son of a bitch Halliday is in. That's if there's still a
Confederated around after all this. Well, Halliday's welcome to
it. The stupid son of a bitch. He'll bury this bank in six months.
Have you noticed that every time the Fed wants to bury some
sick institution they trot out Halliday? He buried Comptons, and
the Buffalo Municipal, you'll recall. And the old Creedy Bank. I
tell you, there's the stink of the mortician about that man.
Well—a pox on all their houses. The Fed. The SEC. The
comptroller. The whole fucking board. I'm sick of the lot of
them. Whining, puling, grousing—egotistical pack of vultures.
May they all roast in hell. They're treating me now like a
criminal. It's as if I'm already convicted." Edelbach rubbed his
red-scorched eyes with the palms of his hands. "A pox on them
all, I say. And a pox on you." He laughed ruefully. "I don't know
what plans they have for you. Depending on the outcome of the
investigations, I s'pose. You may come out all right, but I
wouldn't depend on it. For all that fancy portfolio of yours with
cable traffic from Sujimoto, Wainwright, and all the rest. What
the hell does it prove anyway? You're no Boy Scout either,
Charley. You don't fool me a bit."

Edelbach's red eyes glowed out of his bushy brows like coal
ingots. "'Course, even if they clear you, you've still got to report
to Halliday, and just between you and me, I'd rather report to
Hitler. Heard anything from Sujimoto?"

Abrupt and unexpected, the question caught Daughtry off
guard. "Why would I hear from him? He's scurried down some
hole, hasn't he?"

"He's in Liechtenstein. That's pretty well known now. I'm
told at one time you were close to his daughter." He watched

Daughtry stiffen. "Forgive me. I'm not myself these days. I just wanted to say, they're going to try to extradite him to stand trial here, and you'll of course be called to testify."

"I don't mind that at all."

Edelbach drummed his thickish powerful fingers on the table, watching Daughtry fixedly. "Doesn't bother you? Just a bit?"

"Why should it bother me? I welcome it. It's a chance to tell my side. Clear my name."

"What are you worried about? Your name hasn't even come up yet."

"It's a big secret, isn't it?" Daughtry smiled bitterly. "Wherever I go, people grin at me."

"People are always going to draw their own conclusions. You can't prevent that."

"I don't mind people drawing conclusions." Daughtry's irritation mounted. "I just want to make sure they draw the correct ones."

Edelbach sighed and interlocked his fingers above his paunch. "Sujimoto's a very influential man, you know."

"What of it?" Daughtry snapped impatiently. He failed to see where the remark was leading.

"All sorts of powerful connections."

"Connections?"

"Oh, come now, Charley. You're not a child. Of all people to be called to testify regarding Sujimoto's use of Confederated funds, your testimony is apt to be the most damaging."

"So."

Edelbach smiled wryly. "So, I'm told by people who have cause to know that Sujimoto, when cornered, is apt to play rough. I don't know about you, but frankly, to testify against this man in an open hearing would scare the hell out of me."

In all of Daughtry's hypothesizing probabilities of the outcome of the Sujimoto-Confederated-Daughtry scenario, he had never once factored in the possibility of violence directed against himself as a means of preventing his testifying against Mr.

118

Sujimoto. Now suddenly it occurred to him that all of his careful analysis and computations had been dangerously incomplete.

"Would it, Leon?" Daughtry's question conveyed the full sense of his unguarded surprise.

"It sure would."

21

You medical people will have more lives to answer for in the other world than even we generals.
—NAPOLEON I: *Letter to Barry O'Meara, St. Helena, September 29, 1817*

"Basically, I see nothing remarkable," the doctor observed to Sujimoto. He was a rather phlegmatic, point-blank Swiss who prided himself on his no-nonsense approach to medicine. "There is a small shadow in the area of the colon. But I suspect this is merely a polyp." He might have been describing the implications of a slightly troublesome sinus condition. "We want to watch it, however, for any sign of change. Let's have a look at you again in six months," the Swiss physician went on with almost glacial detachment. "Watch your diet and particularly your drink. No alcohol whatsoever. You might want to try a health spa to get on a new regimen. It can't hurt. I'll give you the name of a good one in Zurich."

Sujimoto nodded as if he were paying attention. But he could not tell the man that he was not free to go to Zurich, or any place else for that matter. That it would be worth his life to leave Liechtenstein, and that the moment he did so, he'd be clapped in irons. Sujimoto, instead, took it all quietly and very well. He was sitting up straight and a trifle stiffly opposite the doctor in the man's consultation room adjoining the examination suite. He never batted an eye, nor did he once interrupt the dry, lengthy recitation of facts issuing from the doctor, as impersonally elocuted as a voice on a dictaphone.

When the consultation was over, Sujimoto shook the doctor's

hand and walked out into the waiting room where Celestine and Mariko waited anxiously.

Vainly, Celestine searched the impassive mask of Mr. Sujimoto's face for some hint of the diagnosis. In the next moment, the doctor called her into the office and had a few words with her. When she emerged again, she appeared tense and rather tired.

An air of gloom hovered over the big Bentley saloon as it negotiated the narrow windy mountain roads snaking its way back to Mendenhall. Sujimoto talked all the way out to the château. He spoke about the market, the soaring price of gold and the continuing plunge of the dollar. He spoke about the unrest in the Middle East and the unrest on the Sino-Soviet border. He hypothesized the geopolitical significance of war between these two giants on world economic order. He spoke about his boyhood in Hokkaido and told an indelicate story at which he laughed harder than anyone else. Then he asked the driver to turn on the radio for the soccer scores from Bonn. He spoke rapidly above the din of the radio and with a dazzling clarity and incisiveness.

Celestine sat grim behind the mesh veil of her hat. Mariko stared phlegmatically at the countryside sliding past the window of the Bentley: the wooded hills, the cow pastures, with the drowsy herd grazing on the hillside, the small Alpine farms that looked toylike and unreal.

Sujimoto continued to expound on a variety of subjects. Every subject, that is, except the subject of his health. This he assiduously avoided. Either because he had determined that the diagnosis was, as the doctor had said, unremarkable or, more probably, as would be the case with minds such as Sujimoto's, that the diagnosis was dire, too dire to tell him directly, and that's why he had called Celestine in afterward.

Once they got home their instinct was to put him directly to bed. But he was having none of that. Though he looked tired, he was going to try some salmon fishing, he said, up in one of the big, fast-moving streams behind Mendenhall. Celestine protested, and that, of course, made him more suspicious. While Celestine and Mariko wrung their hands in a sitting room below, he called for his tackle and gear and went up to his room to change.

Shortly, the eminent Japanese banker-financier reappeared in a jaunty plaid peaked cap, with rubber waders and a straw creel slung over his back. He was all ready to toddle off with Karl Heinz, the house steward, a rosy-cheeked Bavarian who had been his fishing companion for years.

That night, however, in the privacy of their bedroom, the full impact of what he believed to be going on inside his body finally struck home, and he wept. Nothing Celestine could say would dissuade him from the idea that he was stricken with a fatal malignancy. To Celestine he appeared suddenly very old and small. Not at all the vital man who had held her in his arms the day before, whose embrace had aroused her. She had never till that moment thought of him as old. Now suddenly his tears embarrassed her, and she loathed herself, for she could see that he saw her disgust.

Through his tears he pleaded with her to stay with him until the end, as if she had ever once entertained any thought of leaving. Dying alone, without her, terrified him and, in his terror, he offered, at last, to marry her. A small, private ceremony, he said, both Buddhist and Catholic. Only a few close friends would be present. There had been very few occasions during the long course of their relationship in which she had disliked him more.

She tried again to persuade him that he was not dying. The doctor had only said something to her about polyps, or possibly a bleeding ulcer. Nothing more, and in any event, that was no reason to marry. Still he pleaded, and finally, in the end, she relented. She said of course she would marry him. Her voice was dry and clipped, as she put him to bed with powerful prescription sedatives.

In another wing of the castle, Mariko sat by herself in her room, deeply shaken. On the one hand she had been relieved by the doctor's report on her father's general health. On the other, it was clear to her that the report, benign as it was, had triggered in him some emotional *crise*. It was no great thing to see that the health panic was the direct result of the collapse of Sujimoto, Ltd., combined with the tidal wave of legal entanglement that must inevitably follow.

A day ago she had finally resolved in her mind to leave Mendenhall, to strike out on her own, find a way for herself. Now, of course, there was no question of that. She could not leave Celestine to face these critical months with him alone. And, strangely, almost against her will, hating herself every moment for it, she grieved for him, having promised herself she never would. At the same time it occurred to her with terrible clarity that she wanted to go to Daughtry; wanted, even needed, to see the man who, like her father, was now facing critical times.

In the early morning hours as the gray of dawn streaked the eastern skies, Madame de Plevissier accepted a long-distance call from Tokyo, where it was then roughly 3 P.M. It was from Sujimoto's attorneys there. They had called to advise her to be on her guard. News had reached them from sources in Washington that U.S. Treasury agents were at that moment on their way to Vaduz with instructions to take Sujimoto out of Liechtenstein and back to the U.S. to stand trial. They would, of course, try to effect this through normal diplomatic channels, but if that didn't work, the Japanese attorneys advised Madame de Plevissier, the agents might very well then resort to less conventional means of bringing Mr. Sujimoto to book.

22

Lafayette, we are here.
—COL. C. E. STANTON, USA: *At the grave of*
Lafayette, Picpus Cemetery, Paris, July 4, 1917

Ordinarily, he would have gone directly to the Hampshire House and checked into his father's fourteenth-floor suite overlooking Central Park. On this trip, however, Kajumi Sujimoto had no wish for either comfort or luxury. Nor did he intend to seek out favorite Manhattan haunts or call up old friends. He had no desire to make his presence in the city known to anyone. Anonymity was what he wanted, and to that end he had, at great expense to himself, acquired a forged passport in the name of one I. Matsumura.

From Kennedy Airport, where he landed in the early afternoon, he made his way to Grand Central Station, where he proceeded at once to enter one of the many washrooms at the lower level. Once inside, he entered one of the small booths there and instantly proceeded to shed his outer garments. Gone now was the leisurely, unhurried air of the former man; every motion was swift and purposeful.

When he emerged once more from the booth, he was no longer attired in the smart tweedy business suit with the soft yellow lisle shirt and wool argyle tie. Indeed, he was not even recognizable as the Japanese gentleman who only a short time ago had stepped jauntily from Flight 407 from Zurich. The person now making his way out of the Grand Central washroom was attired in jeans, sneakers and leather jacket. He seemed more than just a bit disreputable.

Kajumi entered the subway at the downtown IRT station of Grand Central, then proceeded to make his way to lower Manhattan at a point just north of the Battery.

The Neptune Hotel stood at the corner of Bridge Street and

123

Battery Park. An ancient, ramshackle structure, it was built in the 1860s during the administration of Andrew Johnson and at a time when Mr. Herman Melville was inspector of customs at the Port of New York.

Having started out as a fashionable hostelry, it had, over the years, undergone a succession of reincarnations that inscribed what might be called a downward trajectory. Starting from that of restaurant and livery stable, becoming next a warehouse, it had descended to its present incarnation as a "Seaman's Shelter"—or what less charitable people might be inclined to call a marine flophouse.

A rickety, insubstantial three-floor Victorian structure, part wood, part rose-brick over which tendrils of unruly ivy crept, its large bay windows looked out over New York Harbor with a prospect south to the Verrazano, Governors Island, and the broad shimmering Atlantic beyond. In the weed-choked garden a lichen-stained Diana with a cracked nose and poised on a pedestal stood ringed by a pack of marble hounds. A large cast-iron urn on the sagging wooden porch, containing a spray of parched geraniums, suggested that the Neptune, hard times notwithstanding, still struggled to assert some few pretensions to gentility.

The desk clerk at the Neptune scarcely looked up to acknowledge the presence of the Oriental gentleman standing there before him. A perfunctory glance had already yielded an impression of a Japanese merchant seaman, probably unemployed and waiting for a boat back—a not uncommon sight these days. The Merchant Seaman's union card identifying him as one Itakomo Matsumura, seaman's number L 835-698-0370, more or less verified that impression.

The desk clerk registered him in his own shrewdly crafted shorthand as Mr. I. Mats, assigned him to room 6, and collected $4 in advance. No words passed between the two and at the conclusion of their transaction, a heavy brass key stamped 6 clattered noisily onto the desk between them, where the room clerk had simply flung it.

Once upstairs, Kajumi unpacked his small piece of hand luggage. It contained no more than the business suit he wore that afternoon when he departed Kennedy—a fresh shirt and tie, a change of underwear, socks, shoes and minimal toiletries. In addition, it contained the loaded P38 pistol he was accustomed to carrying about in the glove compartment of his Aston-Martin.

One additional, seemingly inconsequential item remained unpacked in the bottom of the suitcase. It was a small, candid photograph of Charles Daughtry that his half-sister Mariko had taken. He had stolen it from her drawer at Mendenhall just before leaving Vaduz. It was a picture of Daughtry and his father taken at a dinner party in Tokyo. They were seated at a long wood banquette in conversation, Daughtry leaning forward, elbows on knees, chin propped in the palm of his left hand, appearing the soul of attention all the while Sujimoto, in white ceremonial robes, hands gesturing broadly, appeared to be making a point forcefully. They sat amid a crowd of people, yet their isolation from that crowd appeared to be inviolable, so engrossed were they in each other's company.

Inconsequential though it was, the photograph infuriated Kajumi, and he kept it for just that purpose—to pique his rage. It seemed to point up his own estrangement from his father. It made him feel slighted and disowned. Furthermore, it was that night, at that particular dinner party to which he had been summarily commanded to appear (having first declined the invitation), it was there that his father had humiliated him in front of Daughtry and all the others, referring to him as "my poor son," "my poor benighted Kajumi, whom no amount of assistance can help." He could still feel the color rising to his cheeks, his scalp tingling. He could hear his father's high mocking voice and then, strangely, his own self-deprecatory laughter, resounding hollowly in the catacombs of his mind.

"I believe it was Clausewitz who maintained that great military genius never occurs among primitive, warlike societies, but rather only in the highest epochs of civilization, arguing that war—war, that is, brought to a level of high art—is a manifestation of only the most civilized of peoples."

The night was June 9, 1978, the place, Sujimoto's penthouse in Tokyo, not far from the Kabutocho—the heart of Tokyo's financial district. Mr. Sujimoto, presiding over a table of rapt dinner guests, was expounding, as was his wont before large captive groups, on some erudite subject of which he had made certain in advance to know more about than anyone else present in the room.

"He was speaking, of course," Sujimoto continued, "of Rome and the French Empire—of geniuses such as Caesar and Napoleon—but I think the same may be said of our time. We have brought war to the level of high art. We have come a long way in the art of war as well as that of high finance."

A portly Belgian diplomat at the other end of the table asked, "Do you then equate the two?"

"Why not?" Sujimoto smiled, sensing quick engagement. "Are not the similarities inescapable? Have you never noticed that the tactics of war and those of finance are remarkably similar?"

"Finance, however, is benign," said a Philippines banker, sitting across from Daughtry. "No one ever died from high finance."

"Quite the contrary, my friend." Sujimoto rose to the scent of lively disputation. "Murder is the common medium of the boardroom, just as it is of the battlefield."

Wine was passed. They were on a fish course. Daughtry sat at the opposite end of the table. There was laughter and the wife of the Belgian diplomat beside him fidgeted nervously. In profile and shadow he glimpsed the girl.

"Civilization is at its height when you can wage both war and high finance well," Sujimoto continued. He enjoyed goading his guests. "No one can argue that the one does not engender the other. The French economist, Colbert, reminded us that trade is the source of finance, and finance the vital nerve of war."

Madame de Plevissier frowned. "What a sorry comment then for civilization."

"And for the morality of financiers at large," remarked one of Sujimoto's colleagues.

"I don't believe that anyone has ever accused the business of business of being particularly moral," an American pharmaceutical manufacturer said. "To expect that would be childish."

"The same could be said of war," Sujimoto replied.

"I was brought up to believe that civilization implied the antithesis of war," Madame de Plevissier persisted.

Several people murmured assent. Sujimoto smiled sardonically and nodded to Madame de Plevissier. "Ah, now, the distaff side has spoken." The old financier's eyes wandered down the table to where his son sat with eyes lowered, his fingers slowly rotating crumbs of bread into tight little balls. He had not uttered a word all evening. Seated there, he sensed his father's eyes upon him and grew visibly tense. He appeared to know exactly what was coming next.

"What does my esteemed son say?" Sujimoto asked.

Madame de Plevissier's eyes fluttered. A sudden pause in activity descended upon the table. Kajumi's fingers slowed their rotations. Eyes lowered, he appeared to be fighting back panic. "I think, father—" he said, after a moment struggling for control of his voice, "that I would prefer to play at more lighthearted games than at the game of war."

Enfolded in his capacious white robes, Sujimoto's smile was diabolically mocking. "With such an unheroic outlook, my son, you will never win at anything."

Kajumi's eyes lowered back down to the table where the tiny breadballs lay strewn recklessly about his setting. A long, uneasy hush settled over the group. Sujimoto, at last, spoke again: "And what does our esteemed guest, Mr. Daughtry, think?"

Daughtry's mind had been elsewhere, his eye caught in the lambent flicker of long wax tapers.

"Mr. Daughtry?"

He glanced up to see Sujimoto smiling at him, and twelve expectant faces turned in his direction, one of which was the girl's.

"You are a veteran of war, are you not, Mr. Daughtry?" Sujimoto went on in his playfully taunting way.

"I spent some time in Southeast Asia."

"How much time?"

"Three years."

"That certainly qualifies as time, to my mind," Sujimoto remarked. There was mild laughter. "You saw battle then, I presume?"

"I did," Daughtry replied laconically.

"What sort of unit did you serve with?"

"Armored. I was a tanker with the 11th Armored Cavalry."

"And your rank?"

Puzzled, vaguely annoyed, Daughtry could not imagine why he'd suddenly become the object of interrogation. Sujimoto, however, appeared to have his reasons and, as he persisted, his line of questions grew more searching. As it went on, the lively dinner conversation of moments before turned slowly into a faintly antagonistic duel between the two.

"What was your rank?" Sujimoto asked once more, a distinct edge to his voice.

"I arrived in Vietnam as a first lieutenant, was breveted to captain a year later, and mustered out with the full rank of major."

A squadron of Japanese waiters swirled noiselessly round the table with platters of Kobe beef on beds of wild rice. Corks popped and very good Bordeaux was decanted.

People did not eat, however. All conversation was held in abeyance while Sujimoto and Daughtry carried on their quiet conversational joust.

Sujimoto, glancing in the direction of his daughter, continued to question Daughtry. "What are your thoughts on our thesis regarding war and finance?"

"They're not at all dissimilar," Daughtry replied curtly.

"Come, come, Mr. Daughtry. We won't let you off that easily. As both soldier and financier, surely you can do better than that."

"Well," Daughtry said, "by that I mean both grow out of a basic competitive spirit. The object of both is to take possession of something that belongs to someone else. In order to accomplish this, tactics and strategies must be brought into play." Daughtry's eyes challenged the venerable figure at the head of the table. "And, of course, the strategic principles of both are reducible to mathematical formulations."

Sujimoto's pale, watery eyes lit up. "Computer war, you mean?"

The attention of the table shifted, like a palpable tide, toward Daughtry. There was a kind of galvanic surge from the direction of Mariko, followed by Madame de Plevissier's shrewd, disapproving gaze. No one was at all aware of Kajumi sitting there, in a torment of self-hate, wringing his hands beneath the table.

Daughtry took a deep breath and plunged ahead. "By that I mean strategic war can now be easily expressed in terms of concise mathematical formulas that theoretically should make war as it's presently waged look like the simple minded sticks-and-stones affair of Neanderthals."

Sujimoto was clearly aroused. He leaned forward. "A war of machines? No further need of generals?"

"No further need of men at all. The entire engine of war will be driven by computers. Ships, planes, tanks, rocketry—the full arsenal—"

"But, surely men would have to instruct this fearsome engine you speak of, Mr. Daughtry," said the Belgian diplomat.

"Not at all. We now have computers that are designed to collect information, analyze it and, based on that analysis, extrapolate instantly a set of probability formulas which not only anticipate enemy strategy, but recommend a number of suggestions to contravene it."

"Horrible," murmured the Belgian lady, with a tone of sanctified disgust.

"A futuristic nightmare," remarked another.

"A child's board game," quipped the pharmaceutical manufacturer.

"Too ghastly to contemplate."

"Nevertheless, a distinct possibility," Sujimoto beamed. "And an exciting challenge. I, for one, am tired of all these simplistic platitudes about the evils of war. No one can tell me that man is not at his best in times of war. He's more productive in life-threatening situations than during the lethargy of peacetime. His unit-work capacity increases. His ingenuity has unlimited scope for expression. Was it not war, after all, that gave us heavier-than-air flight, jet flight, the science of rocketry—war which gave us interspatial flight? Was it not as a result of military research that the atomic age was born, and from there fission as a source of domestic power, and now laser technology and transistor communications? All born of war. And, a little-known fact—was not the first large-scale skin graft the work of surgeons working under battlefield conditions? No—" Sujimoto waved his hand. "Please do not preach to me of the immorality of war. Surely not if it gives mankind all of this—plus prosperity, full employment, abundance. And now, finally, we achieve the zenith of civilization—humane war. Prosperity without suffering. War minus the anguish and displacement of men. Men in war, totally obsolete. Marvelous."

"You must forgive me if I cannot thrill to the glories of this brave new world of computer warfare." Celestine's face had grown pallid and taut. "I have seen mothers disemboweled on the bayonets of the invading heroes of Nanking; tiny children flayed of their skins from incendiary bombs in Dien Bien Phu. As a correspondent in Nagasaki I had the dubious honor of walking in with the Americans after the bomb drop. I saw sights there too horrible for the niceties of this dinner table."

She paused a moment to glance at Daughtry. Then, having reflected on the wisdom of continuing, she plunged right ahead.

130

"You must forgive me if I tell you that your view of war—and Mr. Sujimoto's as well—is the strutting, posturing stuff of little boys at territorial games. You see the parade and hear the music, but not for one moment do you pause to take in the human tragedy."

Daughtry stared at her quietly. There was a surprised and chastened look on his face. "You're right," he said. "I'm sorry. I'm afraid I do get carried away when I think of the limitless technological possibilities of the future. Even those, I'm afraid, must inevitably be destructive."

Mariko watched him as he spoke and felt an enormous sense of satisfaction at his chastisement. He appeared repentant, but she knew very well he wasn't. Not really. "Perhaps the computers will make currency traders obsolete, too," she suddenly interrupted. "Since, as you say, soldiers and financiers are one and the same."

The breaking of her silence was startling. Even to her. She flushed after the words had burst unexpectedly from her.

"*Touché.*" Celestine laughed with a husky lilt and clapped her hands. "Bravo, Mariko. What the computer can do to the general, Mr. Sujimoto, it can also do to the banker and the arbitrageur."

"It can't come soon enough for me." Daughtry smiled, staring directly at Mariko. "The moment I see the computer beginning to outguess me, that's the moment I quit."

"Hopefully, that time is not yet at hand, ay, Mr. Daughtry?" Sujimoto chuckled delightedly.

"Not yet. But when it is, I'll be the first to confess it and then go quietly."

The Belgian diplomat shook his head with an air of futile dismay. "The triumph of machinery—little gears and sprockets, flashing lights and blinking transistors."

"All destined for the scrap heap of time, Mr. Huygens," Madame de Plevissier remarked drolly. "Take my word for it."

"But not before they've annihilated us all," retorted the banker from Manila.

131

"Let's eat our beef and drink our wine before that happens," Sujimoto said and clapped his hands.

The sound, like the clap of doom, echoed hollowly through the shabby darkened room of the Neptune Hotel. Kajumi dragged the painful scene back, dwelling on it obsessively, as if picking at a scab.

Something had happened that evening between his father and Daughtry. A bond, a covenant, tacit but profound; something, try though he might, he could never hope to penetrate.

Then later that evening, after all the guests had left, he recalled stealing up to the third floor, treading noiselessly in sandals down the narrow, camphor-scented corridors of the north wing where his half-sister slept, standing outside the door listening, breathless, full of self-loathing, and with that horrible sense of his own excitement, to the scuffling, grunting and ecstatic moaning of Mariko being ravished by the barbarous American. The door had swung partially open of itself, but all he could see in that thick moist dark was the sharply delineated square of the window on the far wall with the star-littered sky beyond and a thin slice of silvery-yellow moon in the upper quadrant of that square.

After dark on Bridge Street the mist creeps in off the ocean over Battery Park. During late November, around the Martinmas, and well into December, the fog there is particularly dense, a sinuous, milky, coiling thing that hunkers down in corners and inches forward along the narrow streets and alleyways. All night the foghorns boom; the channel buoys toll mournfully, a sad sound, like some lost and stricken child seeking the comfort of its mother.

In the cheap and slovenly garb of an unemployed seaman, Kajumi Sujimoto slipped out the front door of the Neptune and into the fog-shrouded night. The heir to the Sujimoto millions ate supper that evening in a beanery on Pine Street—a cup of thin chowder and a roll, followed by a glass of water, savoring as he did the odd exhilaration that comes of a self-imposed ascet-icism; feeling for a moment the attractive uniqueness of want in a life that had long since wearied of the sensation of plenty.

Later, he walked round the corner into the ghostly vacancy of the financial district. Empty lanes and alleyways, dimly lit by periodic streetlamps; a pale moon ringed with a white halation rode above the low scudding clouds. His footsteps resounded down the empty pavements that only hours before crawled with teeming humanity spilling out of office buildings, creeping back down into subways, slouching wearily homeward from daily toil. Now a shaft of moonlight fell upon the brokerage houses, poked through dirty casements and wandered through the tellers' cages. The exchange floor was vacant, as well as all the bond and commodities houses with their armies of qualified techni-cians and drones—all now still—the Big Board, Amex, Comex, Nasdaq, Forex, capital taken in and given out; the vast, pitiless maw of commerce with its common fuel of money, momentarily slaked and sated—resting now for tomorrow's onslaught.

Kajumi's solitary steps rang down Pine and William to Wall Street, where they came finally to rest before the shrouded massive granitic face of the Confederated Trust Bank tower, soaring like some ancient Druidic monument amid the fog-blown stars.

What a succession of specters swirled about the tower that evening. Not only the angry hectoring specter of his father, but that of Daughtry, the hated Celestine and her bastard, miscege-nate daughter. There, too, was the reproachful phantom of his own disdained self—the washed-out naval cadet and the sham-bling, inept shadow of his aborted career at Sujimoto, Ltd. Around the tower, too, whirled and whispered classmates, relatives, old friends buzzing and gossiping derisory things in his name.

Such specters were not at all uncommon to Kajumi Su-jimoto. As a boy of fifteen he had started to suffer from a variety of punishing phantoms—all of them somehow engaged in the business of pointing up to him his failures and inadequacies. Now, on this January evening, all of these phantoms appeared to converge upon the Confederated Trust building—a deadly confluence of hatred and self-recrimination.

23

They say soldiers and lawyers could never thrive both together in one shire.
—BARNABE RICH: *The Anatomy of Ireland, 1615*

"And you still maintain you have no idea of Sujimoto's present whereabouts?"

"None whatsoever."

"You haven't heard from him?"

"Why would I hear from him?" Daughtry's voice rose angrily. "Those newspaper headlines you just read to me say he's in Liechtenstein."

"They have a holding company there, don't they?" Arthur Littlefield, Daughtry's lawyer, went on.

"Protocorp. Just outside of Vaduz. He owns a château there, too."

"Very neat." Littlefield smiled knowingly and shook his head. "We have no extradition treaty with Liechtenstein."

"Undoubtedly why he chose to have a château there."

"Undoubtedly." The lawyer consulted his notes on a small spiral pad. He was a large, crisp-looking man with clipped hair and a florid splotchy complexion that gave him the stuffed, inflated look of someone holding his breath. They were sitting in his cramped, airless offices on Pine Street. "And you haven't had contact with anyone else in the immediate family?" He squinted down at a note in his pad. "Who's this Madame de Plevissier, anyway? Companion? Mistress?"

"Little of both, I'd imagine."

"What about the son?"

"Kajumi?"

The attorney glanced at his pad. "Right. Kajumi Sujimoto. You know nothing of his whereabouts."

Daughtry frowned. "I don't think anyone knows anything of Kajumi's whereabouts."

"Why?"

"He keeps his whereabouts very much to himself."

"You mean he's secretive?"

"I mean he's strange. He comes and goes," Daughtry added by way of explanation.

Littlefield scribbled something in his pad, then sucked his pencil eraser reflectively. "What does he do, this Kajumi?"

"Professionally?"

"Right."

Daughtry had begun to show signs of wear and tear. "Nothing."

"Nothing?"

"Nothing much that I could see when I was there. Occasionally he'd come down to the office. But that was only for appearance's sake. More likely, just to collect a check and light out for the weekend."

Littlefield smiled whimsically. "Not bad."

"If you like that sort of thing. I think Kajumi was bored to tears with it."

The lawyer's eyes rose from his pad; at first they'd been amiable and a trifle evasive; now suddenly they were hard. "Did you know that he was charged with the murder of a medical student in Tokyo?"

"Kajumi?"

Littlefield nodded. "Twenty years ago, 1960. With two other young men. Fairly brutal business. Hammers and defenestration. The charges were subsequently dropped. The gist of the story is that Sujimoto bought off the family and pressures were brought on the police to drop the investigation altogether." The lawyer waited. "You know nothing of that?"

Daughtry shook his head. He couldn't say why but the

information had left him a little breathless. "Well, I told you. He's a funny one," he murmured again.

"How so?"

"He's secretive. Elusive. Sleeps all day. Goes out all night. You hardly ever see him. All the time I was there, he seldom appeared."

"And your relations with him were amiable?"

"I don't know," Daughtry reflected. "As I say, you never knew with him." He moved uneasily in his chair and gazed round the office. It was a small, untidy room but expensively furnished.

"And Miss Sujimoto . . . ?" Littlefield pursued him.

"Mariko."

"Mariko." The lawyer glanced at his pad again. "Yes—Mariko. What about her?"

Daughtry's lips pursed slightly. "What about her?"

"Your relations with her? They were amiable?"

"Amiable enough."

Littlefield watched him as though he were awaiting something more. "My notes here . . ."

". . . refer to something more than merely a professional relationship."

"You might say that." The lawyer's eyes danced wickedly. "Who said so?"

"Somebody."

"Somebody?"

"Does it matter? Somebody close to the family."

Daughtry wondered who that might be. Then he thought about the myriad house servants and corporation employees that could have been questioned in Tokyo or Okitsu. He threw up his hands and capitulated. "There was nothing to it."

"Nothing to it?"

"Flirtation. Sporadic heavy breathing. Fits and starts. Nothing much."

"What did Sujimoto think of all this?"

"He didn't much care for it."

"Didn't much care for it?"

"That's what I said, didn't I?"

A harsh, mirthless laugh burst from the lawyer. "You haven't heard from her since?"

"No, and I don't expect to, either."

Littlefield snapped his pad shut and tossed his feet up on the desk.

"That's all?" Daughtry asked.

"For now." The lawyer exhaled noisily. "You're in a peck of trouble, you know, Charley. We're going to have to know more about the actual transactions. Specifically, how you and Sujimoto worked out these foreign exchange deals."

"I've already told you that a dozen times," Daughtry suddenly flared. "Sujimoto told me exactly how he wanted the transactions executed and I carried them out."

"To the letter?"

"To the letter. He was the boss."

"And you obeyed?"

Daughtry fumed. He disliked the intonation in the lawyer's voice. Littlefield went on. "Millions of dollars have been lost or either just disappeared. The reputation of a great bank is compromised. The SEC, the comptroller, Federal banking agencies staffed by influential, politically ambitious men have been made to look stupid and lax. I warn you, Charley. If they don't get Sujimoto on this thing, they're going to grab the nearest thing at hand."

"That being me?"

"More likely than anyone else."

"Others are involved."

The lawyer smiled sympathetically. "We know that, too."

"What are the chances of getting Sujimoto over here?"

"I'm trying. We're putting pressure on the State Department."

"My chances would be better if you had him here?"

"Obviously, but I must be perfectly candid. Short of a declaration of war, I don't believe the Liechtenstein authorities are going to turn him over to the U.S. They've been very prickly in the past about extraditing residents."

"Particularly residents," Daughtry interposed, "who maintain accounts in Liechtenstein totaling billions of dollars."

"Particularly that sort of resident." Littlefield smiled drolly. "You understand?"

Daughtry pondered that a moment. "Perfectly." He rose and started out.

"Daughtry," the lawyer called from behind. "That thing I told you about Sujimoto's son."

Daughtry turned. "What about it?"

"I told you that because I think you should know. This Kajumi character is the only one of Sujimoto's immediate family, as of now, we can't account for."

"You don't really think . . ." Daughtry paused there in mid-thought.

"I don't think anything, Charley. Forewarned is forearmed. That's all."

24

"Go in anywhere, Colonel: You'll find lovely fighting along the whole line."
—MAJ. GEN. PHILIP KEARNY, USA: *To the colonel of a reinforcing regiment at Seven Pines, May 31, 1862*

A short time later Daughtry was back at the main branch of the bank located on the ground floor of the Confederated building. It was 2:45 P.M., fifteen minutes from closing. Typically, on a normal day, bank activity at this hour should have been slow to virtually nonexistent. But today, just as yesterday and the day before, and for several weeks before that, queues snaked from the tellers' cages, across the length of the bank floor, outside the front doors, and around the block.

The lines had been proceeding like that for several weeks.

Reports that twelve major New York banks had ponied up $250 million to help bail out the Confederated, and that the Fed had opened credit lines of $1.7 billion had done little to allay the fear of depositors. The news media did not help much. If anything, they helped to fan that fear.

People stood in columns and lines, bank books open, waiting to withdraw precious life savings. In newspapers, on radio and television, they had heard each day the most dire reports on the status of the bank. Harried and badly pressed, the tellers had been working steadily since opening at 9 A.M. that morning, and still the lines did not diminish. The atmosphere was not one of panic but, rather, one of reasonably contained anxiety.

Occasionally, quarrels broke out on the lines; people accusing one another of pushing and line-breaking. At one uptown branch, an elderly man, after waiting several hours on line, expired just as he reached the teller's cage.

But it was not only tellers who were overworked that day; bank guards forced to mediate line-crashing arguments, executives and senior officers going about the grim business of divestiture in order to ease the bank's liquidity crisis—all were equally pressed.

Fear spread like contagion, not only amid the ranks of depositors but also amid Confederated's 4,000 employees, from the ranks of the janitorial staff upward into the highest echelons: rumors suddenly abounded of massive layoffs if the deposit drain continued to go unabated.

Daughtry stood on the bank floor for a while, observing the activity.

"Never thought I'd live to see this day, Mr. Daughtry."

Daughtry glanced up to see the sad, bewildered eyes of an elderly bank guard.

"Been here thirty-four years," the man went on sorrowfully, "and never seen the likes of this."

It was 3 P.M. and one of the tellers closed his cage. Several others, taking his lead, quickly followed suit. The move infuriated people who'd been waiting on line several hours.

"I'm not going," someone shouted. "They'll have to carry me out."

An elderly woman shook her head sadly. "I went through this in '29."

"Let 'em go get the police to put me out," someone else shouted. "The only way I'm leaving is with my money.",

There was a surge forward and suddenly, more shouting. Three or four guards moved into the fray.

"You've had a call, Mr. Daughtry," said Mrs. Gaynes as he swept past, a short time later.

He half turned, looked back, and frowned. "Anything important?"

"I'm not sure." Mrs. Gaynes paused. "He wouldn't leave his name. I asked him several times, but he only wanted to speak with you."

"Did he say about what?"

"No." Mrs. Gaynes, normally self-possessed, grew flustered. "He wouldn't tell me anything. Only that he'd be in touch."

Daughtry pondered a moment, something nagging at the back of his brain.

"He spoke with an accent," Mrs. Gaynes went on, striving to clarify.

"What sort of an accent?"

"I'm not sure, but it might have been Oriental."

Daughtry hovered there—poised on the threshold of his office. "Oriental?"

At the Schloss Mendenhall, Mr. Sujimoto's condition took a sudden turn for the worse. The bleeding increased. The doctor was summoned. Sujimoto was ordered to the hospital where transfusions were administered in the early hours of the morning. The doctor departed with the reassuring sentiment that there was no "immediate" danger. It had the look of a bleeding ulcer.

140

Still, Madame de Plevissier was alarmed. Sufficiently so to ring the Ritz in Monte Carlo in order to summon Kajumi home. It was at the Ritz, after all, that he said he would be staying. Great was her surprise when she was informed that no Mr. Sujimoto was in residence there, nor, indeed, the desk clerk assured her, had any Mr. Sujimoto made arrangements to be present there in the foreseeable future.

Celestine did not inform Sujimoto of this. In the first place, he was sick and she did not wish to upset him further. Secondly, even if he had known where his son was, the fragility of his health would have made it impossible for him to do anything about it. Could he have ordered his son home by telephone or telegraph? Possibly, but understanding the nature of Kajumi's derangement, it was certain that his son, bent on mischief, would not be easily deflected. Therefore, Celestine chose the moment to confide in her daughter instead. Concern registered in Mariko's eyes the moment her mother broke the news about Kajumi. First the girl stalked and fumed round the room. "New York," she kept muttering over and over again with an almost obsessive intensity. "New York."

"New York?" Celestine demanded. "What about New York?"

"Call New York," Mariko finally put the words together. Tears glistened in her eyes. "Warn Daughtry."

25

All is lost to me save honor.
—FRANCIS I: *Letter to his mother after the Battle at Pavia, February 24, 1525*

Jerk. Crook. Get lost. Drop dead. If I loos my job becaus of you your life aint worth beens. May the DA lok your ass up for the nex 200 years

Guess who?

It was in a clumsy, barely literate scrawl on a piece of lined loose-leaf paper soiled with dark-grease thumbprints. It had come through the interoffice mail and lay on his desk amid a pile of more imposing correspondence. The epistolary style and syntax suggested that it was the work of one of the janitors or handymen.

In truth, however, the volume of his mail had been declining over the past few weeks. What he had found waiting for him this day was hardly the typical end-of-week avalanche of correspondence he was accustomed to: communiqués, reports, summaries, cables, confidential intelligence gathered by overseas branches indicating trends in international currency trading. This was in great part due to Edelbach's having appointed Ricardi to assume most of Daughtry's responsibilities until the grand jury would resolve the question of Daughtry's status one way or the other.

He had noted, too, in past weeks, that many of his colleagues, particularly those on his own staff, traders and currency experts, and even secretarial personnel, had begun to shun him. There was nothing of a conscious or concerted action about this. Rather, it was a deeper, more instinctual drawing away from a marked man.

Daughtry made a point of going to the trading rooms twice daily—early in the morning, then late in the afternoon, after the second fixing, and chatting freely there with the traders as he'd always done. It was a matter of genuine pleasure for him to check the daily rate sheets, to review the entire international market, Eurodollar and Libor rates, then return to his office with fresh data and project future rates and purchasing trends in the currency markets—all as if nothing had happened.

The noise, the din of shouting, ringing phones and blaring squawk boxes had never failed to exhilarate him. In the past, his relationship with his own staff, while professionally distant, had always been colored by a keen sense of fraternity. A mutual passion was shared and mutual interests were at stake.

Nothing of that former spirit prevailed now. Instead, his appearance in the trading rooms produced sudden awkward lapses in activity. There was an air of embarrassment. He had betrayed his people, they felt. They had given him their best, and in return, he had plundered and deceived them. He had sullied their good names and jeopardized their livelihoods. That was their understanding of the situation, at least, and Daughtry was not the sort to get up and clarify things or plead his own innocence.

At higher levels, his colleagues—those who were compelled to deal with him in the course of their daily work—were barely civil. Certainly no one at that level felt secure enough around Daughtry to have the courage to be supportive or even just friendly. As key witness in the upcoming hearings, it was understood that by virtue of his testimony Daughtry could hurt you badly. Knowledge of that among jittery senior executives, with much to lose, inspired fear, contempt, hostility, or simple nervous obsequiousness.

For many at Confederated, particularly those who knew little of the facts of the situation, Daughtry had already been convicted. He was guilty, along with Sujimoto, of conspiracy to embezzle and misapply bank funds to conceal huge foreign exchange losses. Both men, the consensus agreed, deserved to go to jail. But Daughtry, because it was understood he was prepared to go to court, implicate his colleagues and sing his heart out in order to save his neck—for this he was even more contemptible than his master, Sujimoto.

The media, of course, made the situation worse, reporting on every financial page, and on every evening news show, with the pounding regularity of the daily football scores, the New York Clearing House figures reflecting drops in Confederated's deposits each week, fanning the general hysteria, and increasing the panic run on the bank.

At Confederated headquarters in lower Manhattan, senior executives were locked in boardrooms all day, striving to find ways of staunching the huge hemorrhage of capital. Enraged voices could be heard shouting from behind closed doors. Threats and recriminations abounded. Clerical help, driven to exhaustion, careened headlong in and out of offices, staggering under files and papers, trying to keep up with the requisitions of lawyers, auditors and Federal investigators seeking confidential records. At the same time the Niagara of paperwork generated by the drain of deposits had to be processed.

Coming home night after night to three floors of empty brownstone, Daughtry tended to feel himself more betrayed and isolated than ever. He had not thought for several days of Kajumi or of the possibility that he might be in New York bent on some morbid act of vengeance. Nor was he anxious any longer about the mysterious phone call from the unidentified stranger. If Kajumi was, in fact, in New York, he had made no special effort to contact Daughtry. What effort there had been, if one might call it that, was limited to a single ambiguous phone call to the office—clear indication that if Kajumi Sujimoto was actually nearby, he had nothing very compelling on his mind.

Watching the news that evening with a tall Scotch, Daughtry learned that Confederated's assets had dropped by $845 million during the last six months of 1980. The report had been made public in response to a request by the Currency Comptroller. The ongoing investigations by the SEC and the comptroller's office had forced the bank to withhold publication of its final quarter financial statement. Stockholders were enraged and close to revolt.

Daughtry was privy to a great deal of this, and considerably more. Total assets of the bank he knew to be somewhere in the neighborhood of $4.5 billion a half-year ago. A series of frantic confidential reports crossing his desk recently painted the bleakest picture of continued, irreversible erosion of the bank's assets. Loans outstanding: $2.63 billion at year's end, down from $2.77 billion in June. His own breakdown of Confederated's present assets reflected a cash due from other banks amounting to $487 million at 12/31/80, as compared with $1.2 billion six months earlier.

The late evening news reported the most ominous figure emerging to date from the Clearing House officials. At the conclusion of business that week, the Confederated had posted new deposit drops representing a total outflow of $1.45 billion, or a staggering 48.5 percent of all the bank's deposits.

When he had flicked off the news that night, Daughtry was, for the first time, frightened. Something very much akin to loneliness had descended upon him.

That night in his roiled and troubled sleep, he dreamed as he had not in several years of the East, and the Sea of Japan. It lay before him beneath a pale, lemon wafer moon, unfolding like a long gray scroll on the soft undulant beach at Okitsu—on that vast, untrafficked beach where one's feet sank to the ankles in pink powdery sand and crabs scurried sideways on the shore's edge before the racing spume.

The lips upon his fevered forehead were cool, and there was something strong and urgent in the electric tension of the coiled body moving beneath his. Through his gray dreams, the small, childish teeth glinted in the moldering shadows of a crumbling bathhouse where two figures lay on an old quilt, their hectic urgent breathing gradually conforming to the quiet surge and lap of tide. Afterward, they shivered together beneath the quilt.

Then along about 3 A.M., the phone rang, and then her voice—stilted, and curt, and a trifle high from embarrassment, intruded like an extension of that dream, so that in his still drowsy consciousness, he could not immediately separate them.

"Daughtry?"

He knew at once who it was and, curiously, he was not in the least surprised. It all had a perfect continuity and logic—just picking up the phone that way, and hearing her voice, clear and immediate, without the typical crackle or whine of long-distance wires, and no operator to announce the call. She had simply dialed direct.

"Daughtry?" she said again.

"Where are you?"

"Vaduz. Don't ask questions. Is my brother there?"

Daughtry was sitting upright in bed now, the fog of sleep slowly lifting from his head. "No—I mean—not here with me.

Someone told me today he might be in New York. What time is it there?"

"Nearly 9 A.M. Who told you?"

"My lawyer. Why? Is anything wrong?"

"Nothing is wrong. Why would anything be wrong?" The snarl of impatience sounded like evasion. "Only—"

"Only what?"

"Listen—he's not where he's supposed to be. I mean—not where he said he was going. My mother and I wondered—"

"Where did he say he was going?"

"Oh, for Christ's sake. Does that matter?"

"I had a call the other day."

"You had a call?"

"At my office. Nothing really. Just a bit odd." It occurred to him that he was happy to be talking with her, the cables in the air, and fathoms beneath the sea bonding them in some mysterious unity. "I wasn't there. Gaynes took the message. She said the man wouldn't identify himself. That he'd call back. But he never did. She said he sounded Oriental." He could hear the agitation in her breathing. "Do you have any idea why he'd come here?"

"I don't know." Her reply sounded evasive. "What else did this lawyer say?"

"Nothing. Only that they knew where everyone else was, except for him. Your father didn't send him here, did he?"

"Don't be idiotic. Why would my father send him?"

"How the hell would I know?"

"My father doesn't know anything about this. He thinks Kajumi's in Monte Carlo. Listen—call the Hampshire House, will you, and check? He might be there. Then cable me here."

"But why would he—"

"I don't know, I told you," she shot back. "Listen, maybe you'd better call the police instead."

"The police? What the hell are you talking about?"

"Don't ask me—I told you not to ask a lot of questions. Just

146

do as I say. He's"—she sought for the word and found it—
"unpredictable."

"So am I."

"Don't be a fool."

He laughed, trying to conceal his uneasiness.

"Just don't be a fool," she fretted. "That's all."

"How's your father taking all this?"

The question brought her up sharply. "The newspapers here
are full of the whole stinking mess. It's very ugly."

"For me." Daughtry laughed again. "Not for him. He's home
free in jolly old Liechtenstein. They're going to try to nail me for
the whole ball of wax."

"Not if he goes over there to testify." She had blurted that out
before she could stop herself.

"You think there's a chance he might?"

"Not a chance in a million." Her voice was hard again. "A—
he doesn't acknowledge that he did anything wrong, and B—his
health is poor."

For a moment they listened to each other breathing. Then, as
an afterthought, she said, "How have you been?"

"Okay, considering everything." He was about to ask more
about Sujimoto's health, but then suddenly, incomprehensibly,
he said, "Remember Okitsu? Just before you called I was
dreaming of it."

When he left for work about 5 A.M. that morning, he stepped
out his door into the still darkened street and did something
most uncharacteristic. He stood on his front stoop, out of the
perimeter of illumination from a nearby streetlamp, and scanned
the entire street, east to west, seeking out every niche and
shadow where someone bent on mischief might secrete himself.
Only after he had satisfied himself that the street was safe did he
then step off the stoop.

147

26

The small disc of yellow light glided across a line of silhouetted ducks moving in single file across the bottom of a glass screen. On the screen a forest and a marsh were painted in lurid electric pastels with a lake and mountain in the background. In the lower right-hand corner of the screen was a stilted depiction of a crouching hunter concealed in a duck blind, shotgun at the ready.

The small yellow disc was projected from a rifle barrel that fired a beam of light instead of a deadly bullet. Every time the disc passed over one of the duck silhouettes a loud buzzer sounded and a score was tabulated in bright digital figures across the upper quadrant of the screen. At that particular moment a large number 22 pulsed urgently on the screen while bells and buzzers were going off all around.

With an air of dreamy abstraction, Kajumi Sujimoto studied his score flashing on the screen. Shortly, he reached into his pocket, withdrew a handful of coins, discovered the quarter he was looking for, and inserted it into the machine.

Still attired in faded jeans and leather jacket, Kajumi blended inconspicuously into the general surroundings. It was a penny arcade in the Times Square area—a place crammed full of garish electric games—pinball, ski ball, target shoot, fan-tan, even a coin-operated gypsy fortune teller in a glass cage, who blinked her wax eyes, moved her head from right to left, and with her spastic, bejeweled hands, pushed a planchette round on a Ouija board.

The people in the arcade were mostly young, a combination

148

of rowdy adolescents and tourists, as well as a wide assortment of shadowy, predatory local types.

The various game machines buzzed and rattled, rang loud bells, and posted numbered electric scores up on screens, while a frightful din of acid rock throbbed from loudspeakers over-head. Harmless though it all seemed, there was about the place an undercurrent of the sordid and something vaguely menacing; a sense of assignation and creatures preying one upon the other.

Kajumi had spent the last three-quarters of an hour there. He had drifted in from the street, having spent the earlier part of the day viewing pornographic films in the seedy little cinemas abounding in the area.

Fourteen ducks toppled while the yellow disc glided smoothly over the glass screen. Kajumi's eye squinted above the sight hairs, his finger slowly squeezing the trigger of the penny arcade gun. The machine buzzed and bright numbers zoomed like meteors over the screen, trailing off into infinity. The senseless din of music pounded overhead.

Shortly he was out on the street again, walking north up Eighth Avenue, his comfortable, outsized musette bag clattering at his hip. Attired in a turtleneck, jeans and sneakers, he spoke to several prostitutes hovering in doorways, engaging them in titillating conversation as if he were a prospective client.

At Fifty-seventh Street he turned east and strode briskly for several blocks. Reaching Third Avenue, he turned north, on his way up to Sixty-third Street. There was in his mind then a feverish and exalted sense of personal mission; a task to perform; an exercise from which there could be no rest, until there had been successful consummation.

Far away now seemed the penny arcades and the porno flicks of Times Square, the prostitutes and the furtive, predatory figures haunting the street corners. Far away too was the mean little second-story room at the Neptune Hotel, where the desk clerk dozed in his chair and the register read "I. Mats, unemployed seaman," in parentheses beside it. Up in the darkened room of Mr. I Matsumura, the high-powered P38 service pistol waited, like something quivering and alive crouching in the darkness. And on a rickety night lamp beside the unmade bed, propped against a lamp base, stood a photograph of two men—one elderly, the other young, both conversing earnestly at a dinner party in Tokyo.

At Sixty-third Street he veered sharply into the block. The address he sought, he'd taken from the telephone directory, and now, several times he walked up and down the block, reconnoitering the house, marking the points of entrance and egress, pegging the site in relation to adjacent houses and rooftops. The operation, with its air of the clandestine, aroused in him a strange, giddy excitement.

Before he finally left the location, he took photographs of the front and rear of the house with a tiny Minox, and noted with quiet satisfaction that the upper bedroom windows had been left open even though it was obvious no one was there.

27

We are not interested in the possibilities of defeat.
They do not exist.
—QUEEN VICTORIA: *During the Boer War, 1899*

Canvas garden chairs beneath a hard blue Alpine sky. Huge, fleecy, pendentive clouds overhead. The turreted masonry of a seventeenth-century château set flat and dimensionless like a postcard photograph against the dreaming landscape. Unseasonably warm, springlike weather. The click of croquet mallets. Bright colored balls shuttling through steel wickets, bobbling over a vast rolling green lawn.

Madame de Plevissier's mallet rose and fell all in a single uninterrupted motion, inscribing short definitive arcs. Like the process of her mind, her strokes were clean, concise, emphatic, as opposed to her daughter's, which were choppy and brusque, like one trying to get through unpleasantness fast.

Mr. Sujimoto's strokes were grandiose, with something Byzantine in their complexity. Executed on a grand scale with more than just a mere hint of the theatrical, Sujimoto's mallet would rise to the apogee of his stroke, and hover there in defiance of gravity. When at last he chose to let the mallet drop, it came down guillotine-like, impacting with a loud crack on the wooden balls, sending them careening across the lawn, leaving deep grassy tracks in their wake.

Dressed in a striped mariner's shirt, a scarlet scarf tied raffishly about his throat, in espadrilles and topped by a white straw boater, Mr. Sujimoto suggested the gay, holiday air of an Impressionist canvas. At his heel, the dutiful Karl Heinz trailed, like a golf caddy, carrying several mallets in a canvas bag. Bounding rapidly over the field, keeping up a ceaseless disquisition on tactics and strategy, Sujimoto could instantly turn a croquet course into a battleground and a simple lawn game into Gallipoli.

The old man's mallet rose to play a skillful *roquet*. The crack of impact rang upward into the clear blue air. Mariko's orange ball careened from the mouth of the wicket, making way for Sujimoto's green ball to hurtle through. Beaming, the financier paused to accept Karl Heinz's effusive praise.

"Watch what I do to your position now, madame" he boasted to Celestine. His mallet cracked sharply on Madame de Plevissier's yellow ball, sending it skimming wildly across the lawn. Sujimoto roared gleefully and set out after it at a frantic pace. Karl Heinz and his mallets clattered along at his heel.

Celestine sighed. Mariko frowned. They didn't mind the exuberance, but they were confounded. Was this the man so recently hospitalized with internal bleeding?

Sujimoto came up to his ball and made ready for the next shot. The wind gusted, fluttering his white flannel trousers, swaying the tops of the tall spruce surrounding the parklike grounds.

"Your shot, my dear," Sujimoto cried out to Mariko from across the course. Sullenly, she approached her ball. She didn't know her position, nor those of the players around her. What's more, she didn't particularly care. Her mind was not on the game. It was on the article she had read in the *Deutsche Zeitung* that morning, and the photographs of her father and Charles Daughtry she had seen in the *New York Times*. The pictures had a grainy, rather lurid quality, like those in a cheap tabloid. They made her father look imperious and Daughtry, smug. Both of them looked guilty. She could not read the German in the *Zeitung,* so she had Karl Heinz read it aloud to her, which he did with a great deal of stammering and embarrassment. Most of it she knew. The worst of it she had already surmised. Of the part played by her father in the Confederated scandal, she suspected it to be sizable. What she wanted to know was the part played by Daughtry. Was it willing, or unwilling? Ignorant or intentional? She had a great need to settle those questions in her mind. The only new information in the *Zeitung* and the *Times* was the fact that the FBI had now definitely identified Daughtry as the trader directly involved with Mr. Sujimoto in the unauthorized currency transactions.

As for Daughtry himself, she felt a great deal of ambivalence. On first seeing him staring out at her from the front page of the *Times,* her immediate reaction was fury that he had got himself into such a predicament. Then she recalled that this was also the man whose grand jury testimony would implicate her father as the architect of gross misapplication of bank funds and bring her family into public disgrace. She had not yet admitted to herself the fact that she had any special feeling for Daughtry; only the fact that she could not get the man out of her mind.

When at last she hit her ball, she didn't even bother to aim it at the wicket. Instead, she bashed it violently. It went bobbling over the lawn, with Karl Heinz and his funny limping-rolling gait in hot pursuit.

Sujimoto barely noticed, so intent was he on his own strategic positions. "Now to *roquet* you, madame," he piped gleefully at Celestine. Mariko seethed. Here he was playing lawn games while great multinational banks and cartels were reeling from the repercussion of his actions over the past several weeks. Heads would roll, reputations would be lost, people were about to be charged, perhaps unjustly, with crimes for which they could be jailed. Worse yet, her own mad half-brother had bolted, was running loose, unchecked, in New York, bent on mischief, born, she suspected, of some demented sense of personal injury and a lunatic Japanese codal compulsion to redress it.

"Shoot, shoot," Sujimoto cried at her across the lawn.

"Don't tell your father," Celestine had pleaded that morning, watching her daughter's gathering restiveness. *"At least not yet. If not for my sake, then for his. Another row now with Kajumi would be too much."*

"Shoot, shoot. What are you waiting for?" She heard her father crying at her distantly. Mechanically, she approached the ball and shot.

"I promise you," Celestine had continued. *"If it comes to any real threat to Daughtry, I will personally notify the New York police. But right now, for the time being, your father doesn't need the additional worry of police involvement. Not only would it look bad at this particular moment, while the investigation is going forward, but it would just about kill him to have people say—"*

"Say what?" The daughter had seized her mother's unfinished thought. *"Say what?"*

"That he—that he sent his own son to New York to somehow— Oh, it's just too incredible."

"Incredible? For him to send his son to silence the only key witness against him? That's hardly incredible. It's practical and shrewd. My father is nothing if not practical and shrewd."

"Stop it, Mariko."

"Not incredible at all. It makes damned good sense—if you happen to be guilty."

"Stop it, I said." Celestine's shrill cry echoed in her head.

And that's the way it had ended. With an agreement to hold off on notification of the New York police. Instead, she would call Daughtry herself and attempt to ascertain whether or not Kajumi had been there. Who knows, she reasoned. He might be in any one of a dozen places. Why necessarily New York? And why this nagging, inescapable notion that if indeed he were in New York, it was with some violent purpose? Her call to Daughtry was intended to put those fears to rest. Having spoken to him, the moment she hung up the phone, she was more uneasy than ever.

"Shoot, mademoiselle, for God's sake, what is delaying you?" Exasperated, Sujimoto whined at her across the lawn. "Please do shoot and let the game commence."

That evening Mr. Sujimoto was in high spirits. He felt well. Deceptively so. There was a touch of color in his cheeks, and more than a mere hint of his old breakneck vitality. Celestine and Mariko were worn out trying to keep up with him.

At table he spoke of the currency market and the intervention of the Japanese Central Bank to brake the fall of the plummeting dollar. All currency markets in general were in disarray as a result of the collapse of Sujimoto, Ltd., and rumors were spreading like wildfire of the impending collapse of the Confederated. The Japanese and U.S. money markets in particular were experiencing chaos, and the U.S. banking system, under investigation now by a joint banking committee of the House and Senate, was suffering its greatest crisis in public confidence since October of 1929.

"The public sector must demand greater Federal regulation of these gigantic, monolithic banks." Sujimoto wagged his finger, and went off on a tirade against opportunists and the "unsavory elements" that had recently penetrated the world banking system. He hinted darkly of organized crime working in sinister collaboration with the OPEC nations. Coming from him,

154

it was either brazen hypocrisy, or the most pathetic self-delusion.

Celestine's eyes caught her daughter's incredulous gaze and begged forbearance. At dessert fresh strawberries were served. Over Celestine's protests, Sujimoto insisted upon a large dram of kirsch. He then had a second while Celestine and her daughter exchanged worried glances.

"Stop fretting, the both of you." Sujimoto waved his hand at them. "I can see in your faces what you're thinking. For God's sake, madame. What are you frowning about? I tell you, I'm fine. Never felt better. You saw me out there today, Mariko. Did I not trounce you both? Don't I still wield a mighty mallet?" He giggled merrily.

Celestine moved uneasily in her chair. The color in his face was florid and he was ranting uncontrollably. The kirsch had loosened his tongue and deadened some of the fear. "I don't think I'm ill at all. I know that idiot Swiss physician thinks I'm ill. I could tell by looking in his eye. But he's wrong. They are a plodding people, the Swiss. Except in the area of finance, where they are very good indeed. Not as good as they think, however." He laughed. "Once during the battle of Kwajalein I was hit four times by American tracer bullets. In the stomach, in the lungs, and two bullets in the legs, for which I still bear little purple mementos on my shins. In addition, I took a great deal of fragmentation and lost blood. The ship's doctor gave me up for lost. Two weeks later I was alive in a base hospital in Nagasaki, sitting up in bed and taking nourishment. Admiral Inoue himself came to visit me. 'Miraculous,' he said. I can hear him even now. 'Hiroji—you are indestructible. Absolutely immortal.'"

Having evoked that warm remembrance, Sujimoto's eyes glowed. He clapped his hands and roared heartily. For a moment, so great was the sense of vitality and conviction he conveyed, they actually believed him.

Shortly Mariko excused herself and went outside to smoke

and pace fretfully up and down the long flagstone patio. She thought about Kajumi and his probable whereabouts at that moment. And then she thought about Daughtry, and she worried.

Inside, Celestine worried too. Still at the dinner table amid half-eaten plates of berries, uneaten cakes, a decanter of unfinished wine and cooling coffee cups, wound in ribbons of smoke from her own Gauloise, she listened uneasily while Sujimoto called for another kirsch and declaimed.

He was now talking about their impending wedding which he'd decided should occur as soon as possible. From a small affair involving only the immediate members of the family, it had evolved under Sujimoto's feverish, pyramiding imagination into something quite grandiose. "Several hundred guests, at least," he said. "Diplomats. Bankers. Industrialists. International celebrities." They would do it in the lovely little chapel at Mendenhall and later have the reception in the grand salon which could easily accommodate upward of 500 people.

Celestine was appalled. "My darling," she pleaded, "but don't you see how impractical that is?"

"Impractical?"

"Well, I mean—at this particular time."

"Madame." He laughed lightly. "Have I not told you to forget about my health? Put it out of your mind entirely. I intend to live forever. If not forever, then at least thirty years more." His hand fell across hers.

Celestine's head drooped dejectedly into the palm of her hand. When she spoke, her voice had a muffled quality— something halfway between exasperation and tears. "I didn't necessarily mean your health, Sujimoto. But, of course, that is a consideration. Also a consideration is the disposition of your affairs."

Sujimoto stiffened. "My affairs?"

"Your legal status, for God's sake."

"Put that out of your head, too, madame." Sujimoto waved an

arm impatiently. "Banish it from any further consideration. I will be vindicated."

"Of course you will. Still—however, I must insist—"

"When all this is over," Sujimoto ranted on, "it shall be seen that I acted unimpeachably in the best interests of the bank." He gulped the dregs of his kirsch and grew more voluble. "I must admit I was deceived badly by my subordinates. But when I perceived that there were irregularities . . . and mind you, I was the first to discover them . . . certain things . . . improper things . . . unorthodox . . . I uncovered these things . . ."

Sujimoto raved on, his hands cutting wild flourishes through the smoky air. It occurred to her at that moment that he was unstable. His own irrational interpretation of the doctor's diagnosis and the sudden insistence on a marriage he had rejected for thirty years were all symptomatic of a major dislocation in his mind. She fought back a sudden panic, an urge to run—not just from him, but from Mendenhall and the whole situation.

"Even now," Sujimoto continued, "at this very moment, I am acting to save the bank. I have notified my agents in Tokyo to approach the Confederated with an offer to guarantee a new stock issue. Upward of $50 million of my own personal funds I have offered. My own personal funds, madame. Does that strike you as immoral?"

28

No operation of war is more critical than a night march.
—WINSTON CHURCHILL, *The River War, XII, 1899*

In New York it was just past 11 P.M. when Kajumi Sujimoto lay down on his narrow rumpled cot at the Neptune and smoked a cigarette. Wearily, he took up the *New York Times* he had brought home that evening and started to read. On the front

157

page were photographs of Daughtry and his father. The story went on to identify Daughtry as the dealer who had participated in unauthorized currency speculation, which had cost the Confederated nearly $42 million in losses. Spokesmen, the story reported, were insisting that senior officials at the bank had never authorized, and were completely unaware of, the "dealer's highly irregular transactions," while Mr. Daughtry was insisting that every transaction he consummated was "authorized and directed by Mr. Sujimoto, owner and board chairman of Confederated, and tacitly approved by senior management."

The story went on to discuss further disclosures by the FBI, the SEC, and the Currency Comptroller regarding the mysterious Japanese financier-industrialist. There were rumors that he had absconded to Liechtenstein with millions of dollars in yen and other foreign currency. "Mr. Charles Daughtry," the story concluded, "had agreed through his attorneys, Littlefield and Pace, to disclose to a blue-ribbon grand jury panel, everything he knew of Mr. Sujimoto's 'unorthodox' currency dealings."

Rising from the bed, Kajumi stripped off his trousers, shorts and skivvy, and treated himself to a long, leisurely bath. Returning to the bedroom, he proceeded to dress.

It was going on toward midnight now. The later the better, for Kajumi Sujimoto planned to go out again that evening, and the fewer people up and about the hotel lobby, the fewer there would be to observe him.

There was still a bit of time to kill and so he took up his writing tablet and began:

Honor comes to the man of action. So it is written. My father has always been the man of action. But action comes uneasily to his son. His son has preferred to live (or hide?) in the province of the mind where all action may be forestalled or played over and over again on a number of different themes, always with different conclusions, and with no unpleasant, irrevocable consequences. A cowardly arena indeed, for the blood heir of samurai and shogun. My esteemed father has now presented me with a golden opportunity to change all of that.

Who is this man Daughtry to me, and why at this particular moment has it been ordained that our destinies are to intersect? It is written that a son's duty is to preserve and perpetuate the honor of his ancestors. Indeed, anything that jeopardizes that familial honor, that acts in such a manner as to sully it—that thing must be eliminated.

What my father has done, it is not for me to question. What he has done is a debt he must settle with the ghosts of his forebears and his own conscience. It will be sufficient for me to vindicate my father's honor only. Perhaps, too, this is my final chance to vindicate myself. Many will say that the chance I have been given is a horrendous one; far more immoral than anything Daughtry did to bring about the need for such bloody vindication. Many will be appalled and outraged by the course that has been set for me. Still, I am happy. I am content. If I can effectively silence this man before the name of Sujimoto descends into even greater dishonor, my life will not have been a complete waste.

At the conclusion of this manifesto, written in a tight, curiously crimped little hand, Kajumi signed his name, closed the writing tablet and packed it carefully away in his musette bag. In the next moment, he rose and prepared to leave. When he went out he left a light burning, and a radio playing music softly beside the bed.

29

The designs of a general should always be impenetrable.
—VEGETIUS: *De Rei Militari, III,* 378

"I have reason to believe he's in New York."

"Impossible—he's in France."

"That's what I thought. I wasn't going to tell you. But now—"

"Why in God's name would he be in New York?"

"I don't know. You tell me."

Standing before her father in the top floor conservatory, Mariko seemed very small. Possibly it was the oak desk Sujimoto sat behind that made her appear so. It was a great plank of highly polished wood with deep grains and great brass fastenings that glinted greenish gold from the antique coach lanterns that hung above it. An imposing desk from which one imagined portentous acts to be regularly consummated.

Dressed in a silk paisley robe, Sujimoto sat before large ledgers, his fingers tremulous above the foolscap pages. Behind him stood a bank of wide curved clerestory windows opened to a gusty Alpine evening.

"You speak sharply, daughter," Sujimoto said, his eyes lowered to the ledgers on the desk. "I am unaccustomed to such a tone from my own child."

Mariko disregarded that as if the words had not been uttered. She merely stood there, small, erect, and defiant before him, her expression glaring. "But I have told you, Father, Kajumi may be in New York."

"Well, what of it? What would you have me do?"

"He's supposed to be in Monte Carlo."

"I know very well where he is supposed to be. But I fear your brother is far past the age where I have any control over his whereabouts. If Kajumi chooses to go to New York rather than

160

Monte Carlo, what in God's name do you expect me to do about it, chase after him?"

The glare in her expression changed to one of puzzlement. Possibly he was sincere. Perhaps he really didn't know.

"Oh, I see now—" Comprehension suddenly flooded his eyes. "You don't seriously suggest that I sent Kajumi to New York to harm Daughtry?"

"The thought had crossed my mind, Father."

"So that is the depth to which my daughter's opinion of her father has sunk."

"Answer the question, Father," she probed ruthlessly. "Did you send Kajumi to New York?"

"I already told you I didn't."

"I have your word then?"

"Mariko." His eyes rolled heavenward.

"Your word, Father."

"Yes," he snarled. "Yes. You have my word. If I'd really wanted to silence your friend—"

"Kindly leave all such talk of Mr. Daughtry out of this. My friend, as you put it, is none of your concern."

The effect of those last words registered sharply. She was suddenly aware of the hurt and uncharacteristic vulnerability in his eyes.

When at last he spoke again, it was with an air of weary resignation. "As your father, I was merely trying to ascertain the extent of your affection for this man."

"And I told you"—her irritation mounted—"my affections are a matter of no concern to you."

"Mariko—" The sudden supplication in his voice startled her. "If I ask personal questions regarding your involvement with Daughtry, it is because I am concerned for your happiness. Unsatisfactory as I have been as a father, I cannot help caring very much what happens to you."

His words, intended to subdue her, had accomplished even more; they had touched her.

"Very well, Father." Her voice trembled as she spoke. "My

affection for this man is of an indeterminate nature." She heard her voice coming at her as if over great distances. Suddenly, she recalled a time when she was twelve, and had been rude to guests and sent to her room. Later, summoned before her father, she recalled how he first scolded, then corrected her. Contrition was what she had first felt, then afterward a sense of healing relief, and finally, love for him when at last he dismissed her.

"Nevertheless," Sujimoto probed deeper, "there is some feeling there, undeniably."

"Undeniably."

"When he was a guest in my home, you know—under my very roof—"

"Yes, I know, Father." She forced herself to meet his gaze. "But I was the instigator of that. Not Daughtry."

Again the old man sighed and a breeze from the open window behind him stirred wisps of his thick white hair. "But of course. You must forgive me if I sometimes forget you are a woman now, Mariko. Still, despite what you may think, what happens to you is very much a matter of my concern. When you are happy, I am happy. When you are hurt, I hurt. I am content to live my life as I have with Madame de Plevissier in defiance of certain codes of propriety. I realize by doing so I have not made your life easy. I believed, whether rightfully or not, that your way would be smoother if the world believed that you had been conceived the daughter of a Japanese mother and father—and full-blooded Japanese yourself. You know as well as I do how miscegenate Japanese are looked upon in the homeland. Treated civilly enough, to be sure, but always outsiders, belonging neither here nor there. I did not want that for you. Even though I had fallen in love with a foreigner, I hadn't the courage as the descendant of noble ancestors to take a foreigner for my wife. Nor did I wish my daughter to be looked upon in her native land as a foreigner. Perhaps that was hypocritical of me. I suspect now that it was. Nevertheless, that was my choice. Ridiculous and inconsistent as that may be, it is my hope that you will marry a Japanese. I am not so foolish as to think I can compel you to do that, and if I thought your happiness were at stake, I would do all in my power to help you marry anyone you truly loved. But I must caution you strongly against any sort of alliance with this man Daughtry."

Sujimoto's voice rose with sudden emotion. He paused as if to gain strength. "Believe me, I know more about this man than you can ever hope to know."

She started to protest but he silenced her with a wave of his hand. "I have looked deep into that heart," he continued, "and seen the worm that inhabits the center of it. He is ambitious, and ruthless. He has systematically cheated, duped, and misled his superiors at the bank, gambled and speculated away fortunes, misrepresented his role in this matter, and brought a noble institution to the brink of ruin. Now he seeks to lay the blame for this catastrophe at my feet. Oh, I know that he claims that I ordered him to carry out a number of questionable transactions. Some of my . . . procedures may have been slightly unorthodox, but I assure you, however, that Daughtry's actions far exceeded any of my instructions."

He gazed at her obliquely through glassy eyes. "I know what goes through your mind. And you're right, daughter. But I never claimed to be a pillar of virtue. I have cut corners in this life. I have made compromises and sometimes taken the low road. What businessman has not? Wealth and power in this world are seldom achieved through noble acts. Noble acts are the stuff of martyrs and lunatics. Noble acts in this world go mostly unrewarded."

Sujimoto's hands fumbled restlessly across his ledgers. He extruded his tongue to lick his dry lips. "I admit all this," he went on, "but that is not to say that what I have chosen for myself is the same thing I would like to see for you. This fellow Daughtry is amiable enough. Talented. Undeniably so. But I have looked enough into my own heart to know precisely what is in his, and he is not for you."

Mariko had given up trying to silence him, and now merely stood there listening in rapt obedience.

"I know this man far too well," Sujimoto went on. "Far better than I care to. He has nearly ruined me, and I warn you that any union with him would be ill-considered. Oh, it's all right. You've had your fling now. I understand all that. As far as I'm concerned, it's forgotten. But I ask you not to be impulsive." The old man had unconsciously fallen into his finger-waving, didactic postures. "My position now, as you very well know, Mariko, is extremely sensitive. I don't ask that you suborn yourself or lie in court. All I ask is that you give me my chance, before you declare me guilty and consign me to the gallows. I have not been all evil. Surely, there have been things in the past that have been pleasant between us."

His dry, gnarled hand crept across the back of her own. "I ask you to help me. I have no idea how much time is left me. I don't mean by that that I have any intention of expiring in the foreseeable future. But I am not young any longer. I realize this. And what I want now more than ever, what I long for in the time that's left me, is to redress past wrongs—to at last do the honest thing—to marry Celestine and to make you and her the two happiest, most fortunate women in the world. Is that unreasonable of me? Very well, then, I'm unreasonable. You are both, after all, the only things on this earth that matter to me. Kajumi, as you know, is my constant sorrow. If I feel any sense of failure in my life, it is there. No one knows better than I how lost he is. So it is your loyalty I need now, daughter. And your support. I need this as I've never needed it before."

He rose, tottered slowly forward and kissed her. There was something shy and a little tentative in the gesture, as if he were afraid he was going to be rebuffed. But he had not kissed her in quite so pure and sweet a fashion since she had been a child.

"Now what I want to know"—his smile was radiant and beaming—"is if you will oblige me by giving the bride away at your mother's wedding?"

When she left him that evening she was in tears. Recognizing that some covenant had transpired between them—some deal, tacitly made, but nonetheless binding. For all that, she remained uneasy, uncertain what she had agreed to, and what concessions had been extracted from her. She did not know whether she had been either deeply touched, or merely ruthlessly conned; whether having pledged loyalty to her father, she had not betrayed Daughtry.

For some time after she left, Sujimoto sat motionless at his desk. The fingertips of his hand forming a bridge while he pondered. Several times he started to compose a cable, and each time broke off. Addressed to Mr. Kajumi Sujimoto, care of the Hampshire House in New York, the gist of each cable was principally the same: WITHDRAW. TAKE NO RASH ACTION. RE-PEAT—TAKE NO ACTION. But, each time he composed a new cable, he tore it up, and as a result, no cable was ever sent.

In the early morning hours, Sujimoto was on the long-distance phone to Shanghai, where it was 10 A.M. and trading was just about to get underway. At the highly esteemed Bank of Shanghai he purchased $50 million in pound sterling on the spot market, then rolled his sterling over to Deutsche mark at the Deutsche Bank in Hamburg, where the sterling-mark cross-rate was yielding a spread of nearly two points in his favor.

The agent in Hamburg who consummated the deal never knew the identity of his long-distance client. All he knew was that the gentleman calling in the order had instructed him to forward credit in Deutsche mark to a numbered account at the Privatbank in Vaduz. With nearly 900 multinational corporations dealing out of Vaduz, it could have been anyone. But in a transaction such as this—one involving the currency exchange of $50 million—the identity of the purchaser was not of particular importance, only the authenticity of his money. He put the order through.

For Mr. Sujimoto it was a handy piece of work. A few minutes on the long-distance phone and he was nearly a half-million dollars richer.

30

No great art yet arose on earth but among a nation of soldiers.
—JOHN RUSKIN: *The Crown of Wild Olive, III, 1866*

One evening, in the spacious empty basement of 302 East Sixty-third Street, on a piece of plywood, 18 by 24, Daughtry began to fashion a battleground. There, in his basement, below the level of a bustling residential street, out of such improbable materials as wood, sand, cardboard, brick, papier-mâché, plaster of Paris, he proceeded to replicate with passionate authenticity a North African topography. On a scale of one foot to every fifty miles, running from Mazagan in northwestern Morocco, eastward across Algeria, Libya, Tunisia, to El Alamein in the northeastern corner of Egypt, Daughtry crafted mountains, deserts, seas, and a grand host of shattered, battle-torn cities— Oran, Benghazi, Derna, Gazala, Tobruk, Tunis, Bir Hacheim, Bardia, Tripoli, Sidi Barrani, Mersa Matruh. He laid out cities with feverish diligence, like the itinerary of a trip one has waited far too long to take. It was his intention now to re-create the entire Desert Campaign from the disastrous early days of the British 8th Army under Sir Archibald Wavell, to the giddy trimphant days of Montgomery and Patton, when the Allies squeezed the life out of Rommel's forces at El Alamein. This, he reasoned, at this painful juncture of his life, would save his sanity, and perhaps his soul.

Once his plywood was assembled and laid out on sawhorses, Daughtry began to lay out the major sectors of the battleground. Quadrants of warfare were cordoned off in black crayon. After that, the landscape took shape at a frantic pace. Deserts were a simple affair. Sands brought down in pails from the beach at Montauk, mounded, hummocked, and lovingly sculpted, became the Cyrenaican desert, the western and eastern Sahara, the Qattara Depression, and the hellish moonscape of the Boiling Cauldron. All were created there in loving detail.

The chain of mountains known as the Atlas he raised up out of a combination of granite detritus scavenged from a quarry in New Jersey, and a good simple New York clay harvested after a rain from mud puddles near the Central Park boathouse. He capped his mountains with snow made of flour and egg whites.

The great 700-mile escarpment stretching east and west between the Libyan desert and the Mediterranean, he modeled out of plaster of Paris, following with obsessive detail the topographic survey made by the Royal Articifers in 1942. He worked at fever pitch, completely losing himself in the task at hand.

The sea he created was a great slab of gray crafted out of slate and simple bathroom mirror. At the confluence of the Mediterranean and the Atlantic Ocean, off the Moroccan littoral in the region of Tangier, he indicated the great turbulence of the sea at that point by rearing whitecaps and breakers out of gray-blue clay sprinkled with flour and water to suggest spume.

Within that sea he floated a huge armada of warships—the Allied Western Task Force laying off Mazagan, the Center Task Force off Oran, and the Eastern Task Force off Tébessa in Algeria.

In his desert, Daughtry raised great cities. It was his intention to show the bones of a city after it had been flayed by the modern engine of war—its proud antiquity reduced to powdery rubble. Here was Alexandria, Tobruk, Tripoli and Casablanca, fashioned out of plaster, clay and brick, papier-mâché, mortar made of paste and water. Domes and minarets and ziggurats, cheek by jowl with warehouses, office buildings, whitewashed huts. Here were seaports lined with toy tankers, oil refineries, aerodromes, tiny HO gauge railroads with toy freight cars hauling military equipment up to the front.

Great coastal roads Daughtry laid down with narrow wood planks over which convoys of trucks, tanks, troop transports, ambulances and jeeps moved steadily. Next came military

167

installations, depots, airstrips, armories, barracks, sheds. Into these he insinuated contingents of the British 8th Army, the U.S. 7th Army, the Italian Ariete Division, Von Arnim's 15th Panzer Army and, from the crack Afrika Korps, Rommel's 7th Panzer Division.

Daughtry felt a surge of excitement as he proceeded to move his tanks up into position spearheading the troops—the 30-ton British Matildas with their two-pounder turret guns, the unwieldy Italian M13/40s dubbed by their own tankers as the "mobile coffin," the swift and awesome Panzer IIIs and IVs, and the U.S. bruisers, the Grants and Shermans.

For several hours as he mounted the battle, Daughtry's problems appeared to vanish. Not once did he think of Mr. Sujimoto, Leon Edelbach or the grand jury. Pips and spreads, hedges forward and the plummeting dollar were mercifully far away.

There was room for none of that in his mind at the moment. Only the battle lay before him now; the awesome tactical problem at hand, deployment, logistics, the task-force boats to be landed at Mazagan, Oran and Tébessa, the U.S. 7th Army to slog its way ashore against the shore barrage of the resisting Vichy forces. And best of all, there were the great sand Goliaths, revving up in the scorched earth, spinning their tracks, swinging their gun turrets, racing their engines in anticipation of the gorgeous conflagration of battle that lay ahead.

He started to unbox and line up his troops. Guided by his careful sense of tactical design, battalions began to assume formation. Regimental masses, proud ensigns unfurled, began to fall into place. Huge naval task forces took up their positions opposite hostile shores where heavy gun batteries were beginning to uncap their artillery. The clang of field infantry jostled into motion, rang sonorously in his head. Here were the U.S. II Corps, the 4th Indian Division of the British 8th Army, the 1st New Zealanders and the British X Corps. Next came the Argyll and Sutherland Highlanders, the U.S. 1st Armored, the 1st and 9th Infantry Divisions, the 5th Corps and the 34th Infantry

Division, followed by the French 12th Corps, the British 2nd Armored, the Australian 4th Light Infantry, along with the 3rd Indian Motorized Brigade.

On the other side was the Italian Ariete Division, under General Gariboldi, the 15th Panzer under Von Arnim, the German 5th Light and the total staggering might of Field Marshal Rommel's Afrika Korps.

Daughtry will never know what made him turn when he did. His absorption was that deep. But eerily, uncannily, something had nudged him. It was well past midnight and there was certainly no sound. Yet he turned like a man responding to sound. Possibly it was subliminal, a warning buzzer that goes off in the mind. Call it one of those inexplicable acts of self-preservation like canceling on impulse reservations on a doomed flight, or unwittingly stepping backward onto a curb, thereby avoiding an onrushing car.

It was only after he turned that he both saw and heard. Heard first the small tinkle of glass shattering on the basement floor; then saw the silhouette, squatting and hulklike—a dark mound framed sharply in the narrow transom window that looked up out onto the street.

Whatever it was, whoever it was, he could not say, but after the breakage of glass he stood petrified beside his plywood battlefield with the toy lead troops massed and the armor all poised on the brink of cataclysm, even as he watched something round and metallic drop through the broken casement and bobble toward him, rattling lightly, almost delicately, over the concrete floor.

The fact that it was some sort of detonative device with a rapid timer, a grenade as it turned out, did not particularly surprise him. What did surprise him was the swift paralysis that overtook him—the paralysis of a nightmare robbing one of the power of flight. It froze him in place, watching transfixed the small, toylike object rolling toward him over the concrete floor like some fierce rampaging roach. And then, of course, the silhouette, the shadowy shape framed in the transom, watching too the progress of the thing—the three of them joined just then—Daughtry, the figure in the transom, and the thing, now animated, consciously malevolent, rushing toward him over the floor—all joined in fatal trinity.

31

My sentence is for open war.
—MILTON: *Paradise Lost, II, 1667*

"I have lived so long with an assumption of personal guilt that I have actually achieved guilt. The point being, therefore, that one becomes the sum of all one's assumptions about oneself, whether those assumptions be taken personally or imposed upon one from the outside."

Kajumi Sujimoto sprawled prone on the sour, sagging cot in the little lazaretto room he occupied at the Neptune. The photograph of Daughtry and his father stood propped against a lamp on the night table beside him. Periodically he looked up and regarded it.

It was nearly 5 A.M. A clammy predawn chill had seeped into the tiny space through cracks in the rattling casements and, outside in the first dull gray of early morning, foghorns boomed across the Verrazano Narrows. Even as he scribbled in feverish haste, fearful he could not get it all down, he could hear the mocking laughter of the gods and see his father's pitying, scornful face. "My poor, benighted, feckless Kajumi."

Then as the laughter and the grievous words subsided, his eye saw the grenade. He watched it roll and bounce over the floor, veer sharply off its course, and then saw the face of the man in the basement below the level of the street, the body frozen, the eyes transfixed.

Then came the bright sudden luminescence, the puff of smoke, and the faint, barely audible crackle—the fizzle of the

170

grenade. A pathetic, silly fizzle—the wildly funny fizzle of his worldly hopes. The end product of all his careful calculations. All hope of redemption gone up in smoke. Laughable. Absurd. He saw it as some grand cosmic joke of which once again he was the butt. He even laughed himself.

The gods howled delightedly with their plaything. For a moment he gazed sideways and down at the photo of Daughtry and his father engaged in earnest solemn talk—the conversation of men of substance and achievement—men of action who stood astride the world. His cheeks burned.

Then, once again, he saw Daughtry, wavering beyond the gray smoke and the dud grenade rocking gently on its side; Daughtry beyond it looking up at the transom, but unable to see him in that light, the expression startled, but not at all frightened. Then he was up and running, feet clattering, scuffling over the damp pavement. Running through the vacant, early morning streets, past darkened brownstone residences where people slept unmindfully. Shortly he broke out onto Madison Avenue, loping past dimly illuminated storefront windows where pottery, rugs, antique chinoiserie, glazed fruits, sumptuous berries, brightly beribboned boxes of French chocolates, and boutique manikins flew past him as he whirled by. The red and green of traffic lights in untrafficked streets flickered eerily, and only the occasional cab hurtling toward some secret destination to remind one of life. And he was running.

Daughtry was running too. That was his initial instinct. Panicky, headlong flight. The bags he had started to pack earlier, he closed and made ready for departure. His head reeled with a variety of far-flung destinations—safe houses, cities of refuge, wilderness outposts in remote, northern climes.

But then, moments after, Daughtry put aside the packing, and was on the phone to Arthur Littlefield, who ordered him to stay put. In something under an hour a U.S. marshal, a tall, broad slab of a man with an iron jaw and something bulging portentously beneath his coat, had taken up a position outside his front door. Several of his colleagues followed close on his heels, deploying themselves at key locations about the house—across the street, even on a rooftop across the way. They were all of a type. Large, stolid, laconic men, they spoke little, yet there was something instantly reassuring about their presence there. Only when Daughtry addressed them directly did they deign to utter words, and even then, most begrudgingly.

After that came the police. Plainclothes detectives asking questions; then smoothly efficient technicians in a mobile lab to whisk away the undetonated grenade and gather up tiny shards of glass from beneath the shattered transom.

When Daughtry left the house to go to work that morning, one of the marshals fell into stride beside him. Daughtry turned and looked quizzically at the man. The fellow cracked a stiff smile.

"I'll be getting into a cab at the corner," Daughtry advised him. "Are you coming with me?"

"If it's all the same to you." The fellow smiled affably. "Otherwise, I'll just have to follow in one of our own cars."

"Are those your instructions?"

"Yes, sir."

"In that case, be my guest."

"Why not? It's a helluva lot easier that way."

They didn't converse much in the cab going downtown. Only the most perfunctory talk, nonetheless very civil.

"Are my movements restricted?" Daughtry asked at one point.

"You can go anywhere you want."

"But you'll be nearby?"

"If not me, then one of my friends."

"Twenty-four-hour guard?"

"Till the hearing anyway, is what they tell me. Your lawyer called up Judge Whittaker 4 A.M. this morning." The marshal whistled softly and laughed. "That takes guts. The judge assigned us indefinitely. For the duration."

Later at the Confederated, when he was upstairs in his office, behind closed doors, he panicked. Seized with regret that he hadn't fled, his decision felt portentous, an augury of doom.

Mrs. Gaynes appeared, bustling foward with a pot of fresh coffee, correspondence and the daily morning ratings. He lit a cigarette and was suddenly calm.

Ricardi came in a short time later.

"What's moving?" Daughtry spoke, signing papers at his desk, trying to control the small tremor in his voice.

"Gold. They're dumping the dollar like mad. The Tokyo Central Bank just bought $150 millions' worth, trying to prop it."

Daughtry didn't look up. He continued to scribble. "Anything else?"

"DM are up—1.9232 and we're taking all the Swiss francs and kroner we can get. Everything's up except the dollar which is down, down, down."

"So, what else is new?"

"New?"

"Here, I mean."

Ricardi leaned back in his chair, emitting a long sigh. "Deposit withdrawals slowed a bit this week to $65 million, if that's what you mean."

"Are you scared?"

"Who me? Scared?" Ricardi laughed nervously. "Why should I be scared?"

Daughtry leaned across the desk and poured his colleague coffee. "I gather we're selling off a portfolio of municipal and corporate bonds to the FDIC at book value."

Ricardi quickly scribbled some figures on a tag of paper. "That comes to approximately another $100 million which guarantees the principal amount of our Eurodollar loans portfolio, if we choose to sell it."

"We'll have to. No choice in the matter. Then use the proceeds to repay the Federal Reserve Bank the $1.7 billion we borrowed."

Ricardi stroked the area above his glazed, reddish eyes. "They say the next step will be to dismantle international operations."

"Then, after that, we can all go looking for work." Daughtry stacked a pile of signed letters and contracts before him.

They were silent for a moment while Ricardi moved uneasily in his chair, averting his eyes from Daughtry's. "There's a rumor going around," he began at last, "that a stockholders' suit has just been filed in District Court against us. The charge is that $45 million of Confederated funds were squandered improvidentially."

"Improvidentially." Daughtry laughed out loud. "Whose word was that?"

"There are nearly twenty people named as defendants— Sujimoto, Edelbach, Wainwright, Michaeltree, Villiers—the whole crowd."

Daughtry's eyes rose from a currency contract before him. The Argentinian moved uneasily in his chair. "I'm not sure if you're included, Charley. I wouldn't be surprised, though."

"I wouldn't either. Anyway, we'll know soon enough, won't we? How's Leon?"

"Pretty shaky. They say he's taken to sleeping up in his office."

"Afraid to go home to Mrs. Edelbach, I should imagine."

"More likely afraid if he does, Halliday will have his desk moved out into the hall."

They started to laugh.

"I went in there yesterday," Ricardi went on soberly, "and sure enough, he was sleeping. But with one eye open."

They roared.

"Does it amuse you to know," Daughtry remarked, "that I'm being guarded twenty-four hours a day?"

Ricardi's laughter sputtered to a halt.

"Guarded by whom?"

"U.S. marshals. Someone tossed a grenade into my basement early this morning."

The Argentinian's head swung left and right in disbelief. The phone rang.

"Charley?" It was Arthur Littlefield. Before he could respond, the lawyer had repeated the name Sujimoto four times.

"What about him?" Daughtry asked.

"Kajumi Sujimoto is not registered at the Hampshire House. According to the desk clerk, they've had no indication that he's even in New York. U.S. Customs has no record of any entry here in the past two years. Doesn't mean he couldn't be here under an assumed name, of course. And you know what else?" Littlefield sounded breathless as he spoke. "Sujimoto, the elder—"

"What about him?"

"A pair of U.S. agents in Vaduz tried to snatch him."

Daughtry's breath caught in his throat. "Good God. When?"

"Early this morning. He was taking a drive near the Swiss border before breakfast and these two Treasury men drove up behind him and tried to force his car into Switzerland."

"What happened?"

There was a pause and he could hear Littlefield's irregular breathing on the other end. "I'm afraid the dummies blew it, Charley."

Daughtry could feel the momentary surge of hope take flight, then vanish forever as if it were some tangible, feathery thing.

32

*To insure victory the troops must have confidence in
themselves as well as in their commanders.*
—NICCOLÒ MACHIAVELLI: *Discorsi, XXXIII, 1531*

"Then they sprang. Simply rushed up at us out of nowhere and tried to force us over the border. 'Hiroji Sujimoto?' one of the lunatics shouts at me from his car and whips out his papers . . ."

"That's when the security forces at the border gate stepped in."

"A good thing, too, Karl Heinz, or I shudder to think where I'd be at this moment."

"No doubt on a plane, halfway across to New York, Father."

"No doubt. No doubt about it. Shackled to my seat between those two Treasury idiots. It means they've been monitoring our movements for some time. You should have seen it, madame. I tell you, it was a sight." Mr. Sujimoto laughed. There was an air of slightly hysterical triumph about him.

They made a lively party, all seven of them—Sujimoto, Mariko, Madame de Plevissier, Karl Heinz, the two administrative assistants brought from Japan and Aito, the giant valet-bodyguard from Sakhalin.

They were seated round a large glass table on a flagstone veranda, set beneath a black-and-white-striped awning that ran almost the full length of the castle's west wall. Sujimoto spoke rapid-fire, nonstop, half-Japanese, half-French, with occasional bursts of German proffered out of deference to Karl Heinz, whose French was of course far superior to Sujimoto's.

Sujimoto had drunk nearly a full bottle of champagne by himself, on the claim that after the harrowing events of the morning he needed sedation. His cheeks glowed, his eyes were a trifle glassy, but his energy and animation were astonishing.

"You appear to have enjoyed the experience, Father," Mariko remarked sarcastically.

The sarcasm was lost on Sujimoto as he refilled the gamekeeper's glass, then started to refill his own. "It was, I tell you, exciting. Exhilarating. Ay, Karl Heinz?"

Celestine attempted to stay his hand. "You've had enough now."

Her keen eyes told her that, belying the mirth and boastful laughter, he had been deeply shaken by the events of the morning. The glow in his cheeks, far from the flush of animal vitality, looked more like the fever of disease. "We'll hear more about this at dinner," she went on. "Time for a nap now."

"A nap?" Sujimoto scowled. "In midafternoon? Am I an infant? Or an invalid? Why should I nap? Come, Celestine. You're quite ridiculous. Let's have more champagne." He clapped his hands and a butler appeared.

"Please," she implored.

"Father, you've had enough."

"Ah, has this now become a matter for my daughter to determine?" the old man asked icily. "I must stay up. I'm awaiting a report from the national police on the identity of these two harebrained agents. They promise me a complete dossier. The American consul here remains strangely silent on the episode. Only the Americans could employ such amateurs. Who do they think they're dealing with? Imagine—these buffoons tail one's automobile, then try to herd one over the borders. Believe me, my good friend Gainsville, the American ambassador at Bonn, will hear of this."

"Father—" Mariko interrupted his tirade. "Go upstairs. I'll bring you the report the moment it arrives. Take a nap now."

"I don't want to nap, I tell you," he shouted, more ruffled than ever. "I want more champagne."

Celestine rose. "I will not sit by and watch you drink any more. The doctor was quite explicit about alcohol."

"Oh, bugger the doctor," Sujimoto boomed. "The doctor's a dolt, I tell you. Let him look up his own colon. I know what's right for me."

The others at the table lowered their eyes and sat uneasily.

Celestine started to move off. "I'm going upstairs. I have a dreadful headache."

Mariko rose too.

Sujimoto defied, appeared to swell, and grow purple. A great trembling rigidity consumed his slight frame. Then, just as suddenly, he went limp, lowering his head, sagging in his chair. When he spoke again, his voice was dry and rasping. "Celestine, please come back and sit beside me."

Baffled, a torrent of conflicting emotions, Madame de Plevissier, wringing her hands, gazed down at Sujimoto.

Sujimoto murmured a few words beneath his breath and the others rose and dispersed quickly in different directions. Mariko lingered a bit longer, then, abruptly, turned and left.

Sujimoto and Madame de Plevissier were now alone. She stood nearly twenty feet away, observing him uneasily where he sat amid the wineglasses and the fruit bowl, the half-empty coffee cups and rumpled napkins. He had the sad look, she thought, of the host of a party after all the guests have gone. Tired and alone, he was. "Come sit beside me, Celestine."

Her lips, too bright and scarlet, smudged from her napkin, moved slightly as if in protest. No words came.

She shrugged instead and moved quickly to the table, an air of apprehension about her, like a mother coming to succor a stricken child.

That night Celestine sat with Mariko addressing invitations. She scribbled envelopes with smoldering irritability. Glasses balanced severely on the tip of her nose, she worked in swirls of smoke curling upward from an ebony cigarette holder.

Her teeth gritted the stem of the cigarette holder. "Has he gone to bed?"

"Directly after supper. He was exhausted."

178

"One doesn't live through kidnap attempts every day." Celestine pushed a mound of envelopes aside. "This is madness. A circus. Three hundred people. A gown of lace. A hundred kilos of caviar. Cases of champagne. He asked me to find *ortolan*. *Ortolan*? Can you imagine? For three hundred people, no less."

"He can't be serious."

"You don't know your father when his mind is set on something. A dressmaker and a tailor will be here first thing in the morning."

"For you?"

"For you, too. A first fitting. It's insupportable." Celestine sighed and flew back at her envelopes with a vengeance. For a time all that was heard in the conservatory was the furious scratching of pens.

Mariko glanced up suddenly. "You don't really want any of this, do you?"

"I've forgotten what I want." Celestine shook her head back and forth helplessly. "But, of course, we'll go through with it. We have no choice."

They returned to the invitations until Mariko looked up once more. "You don't think they'll try again?"

"Why not? If once, why not twice? Or three times? This is all your friend Mr. Daughtry's work."

Mariko's back stiffened. "Daughtry? Why Daughtry?"

"Oh, come."

"If you mean they want to bring Father to the States to indict him, I can't say I blame them."

Celestine did not look up. Instead she continued her angry scribbling.

"If he's blameless," Mariko went on, "then he has nothing to fear."

"Your father is not well, Mariko."

"All the more reason that he should clear his conscience now."

"His conscience is perfectly clear. Why do you simply assume his guilt?"

"I don't. That's why I want him to go and put to rest any doubts."

"There are no doubts," Celestine snapped. Color rose to her cheek. "And don't think otherwise. What would you have him do? Go to New York? Put his head in a noose? All for Mr. Daughtry?"

"Please don't shout at me," Mariko's voice was quiet.

"You assume your father is guilty."

"So do you. That's precisely why you're so furious with yourself at this moment."

"Mariko—" Celestine rose from her chair and paced fretfully the length of the room. "I don't know. I don't know what I believe, any more."

"And if you did know, would you be content to stand by and watch this other man bear the whole blame?"

"This *other man*? You cannot even say the name, can you? Your feelings about him—"

"My feelings about him are not the issue here. Forget about Daughtry. The point is, knowing your husband's guilt, would you permit another man to go to prison for him?"

"Things aren't quite so clear-cut."

"Ah." Mariko looked at her mother strangely. "I see. Then you would."

Celestine appeared flustered.

"For all of your noble sentiments," Mariko continued, "your lofty moral postures . . ."

"Mariko—that's unworthy of you."

"You're no different from all the others. Lofty, noble principles are fun and easy to proclaim when there's nothing to lose from espousing them."

"How unkind—"

"Unkind, indeed, Celestine. Nevertheless true. The fearless, outspoken journalist. The unyielding advocate of justice with her grand reputation for precise and impartial observation."

"Mariko—"

"A farce."

"Mariko, please."

"A farce."

Celestine's head drooped. An expression of desolation crept across her haggard features. "Hand me more envelopes, will you, please?" she murmured after a moment, and from where the girl sat she could see tears coursing down her mother's lined, pasty overrouged face.

Sometime much later that evening, actually in the dark early hours of morning, a night call was put through to Mr. Sujimoto's bedroom, now a private suite apart from the one he customarily shared with Madame de Plevissier. It was from the Japanese embassy in Washington.

The gentleman from the embassy in Washington excused himself profusely for interrupting Mr. Sujimoto's sleep but he felt it was imperative to advise him that the Japanese consul in New York had just notified the embassy that the FBI in Washington and the New York City police were conducting a nationwide manhunt for Kajumi Sujimoto. They had reason to suspect that he had entered the United States illegally and that he was now in New York.

"What has he done?" Sujimoto asked guardedly, and the gentleman in Washington proceeded to inform him of the abortive attempt on Charles Daughtry's life. Kajumi had not been directly accused of anything. In view of the pending grand jury hearing, the police and the FBI were merely being cautious.

Later, after Sujimoto had put down the phone, he lay for some time peering into the close, thickly muffled darkness. A dull throb had commenced in the area of his side. Momentarily he thought of Daughtry, and ground his teeth.

33

Grant stood by me when I was crazy, and I stood by him when he was drunk, and now, by thunder, we stand by each other.
—Attributed to GEN. WILLIAM TECUMSEH SHERMAN, *ca. 1870*

Several weeks after the excitement of the grenade incident, Arthur Littlefield called him.

"Suspicious." He enunciated the word between gritted teeth. "Suspicious is the way they put it. They were absolutely unwilling to say any more than that."

He had been on the phone to the FBI and after that the police. The result of those calls had clearly disquieted him.

"Suspicious." Daughtry pondered the word aloud. "Someone tosses a grenade in your front window and they call it suspicious?"

"So I think it's time you thought about a temporary change of address."

"Change of address?"

"Exactly. Or, to be more precise, just get the hell out of there fast."

"Ridiculous."

"Just temporarily, I said. Just until this thing blows over. As you say, Charles, a hand grenade is a good deal more than vague, unsubstantiated suspicion. Furthermore, even if this is not Sujimoto's son, the guy who did toss the dud grenade through your window is quite real and he's still at large. And remember, too, the grenade was a Jap. Type 97 war surplus grenade."

Daughtry fumed. "I'm not moving. The hell with that. I stay put. I've got a half-dozen U.S. marshals staked out all around me. They look like the Pittsburgh Steelers. Who the hell's going to bother me?"

"Charley," Littlefield's voice pleaded, "if this Kajumi character is out there somewhere, and the police have every reason to believe he's right here in New York, the fact that he's not at the Hampshire House where he would typically be but instead gone to ground can mean only one thing. He has important business to finish, and I'm absolutely certain you're that business. A grenade tossed through your window may be only the beginning. I told you about the murder charges in Tokyo."

"Arthur, I am not leaving this house, and that's that. Not for Kajumi Sujimoto. And not for that half-demented old pirate, his father, either."

It was a standoff. For a moment they merely hovered there on the phone, glaring at each other through the wires. When Littlefield finally spoke again, all the pluck had gone out of his voice. "Why don't you take my cabin up in New Hampshire for a week or so—"

"No way."

"—at least, until we can get a fix on this guy. He can't be far."

"A few weeks ago I would've gone, Arthur, but now I wouldn't give them the satisfaction. I'm staying put right here. That's final."

"Charley."

"Final, Arthur." He flung the phone down onto the cradle and stood there in his bathrobe, glowering. After a moment he realized he was in a cold sweat.

It had been going on like that for several weeks, the marshal out in front of the house when he left each morning; the marshal in the cab; the marshal sitting outside his office all day with the secretaries and the other office personnel gawking and buzzing; and, later in the evening, leaving the bank, the marshal following him out, big and silent, treading at his heels. Unshakable. Annoying, yet oddly comforting it was, when thinking of the possibility of Kajumi still at large, prowling about the city, the knowledge that someone was always standing at his unprotected back. Still, there was no evidence at all that Kajumi was actually in New York.

Then arriving home. The changing of the guard. The new marshal coming on duty in the sad, brilliant glow of late February dusk, murmuring a set of muted instructions for the man departing, while several others deployed themselves on the street, and on the rooftops across the way.

And the newspapers. There were stories every day. Daughtry's name figured prominently in each, always preceded by the obligatory adjective, "alleged." By this time he had become notorious—something of a celebrity in the true American sense.

Littlefield was furious and tried to put a stop to it. He had even gone to court to take out an injunction against a handful of tabloids inveighing daily against the American banking system at Daughtry's expense. The newspapers, television, indeed all the media, were responsible, he charged, for creating an aura of guilt around his client, thus badly prejudicing his case. The final straw was when Edelbach called Daughtry in and suggested that he take a brief vacation until the outcome of the hearing resolved things one way or the other.

"I take it, then, I'm relieved of duty?" Daughtry inquired.

"In a manner of speaking. As of today, Ricardi will assume your daily responsibilities."

"I note you're not being asked to take a brief vacation," Daughtry remarked pointedly.

A wry, enigmatic smile crossed the ruddy features of the president and chief officer of Confederated Trust. "My time is coming, Charley. Don't worry about that."

For Daughtry, the sense of continuity he experienced at the office each day was all that had made the present situation tolerable. It affirmed for him in his troubled mind some illusion of control over his own destiny. In a curious way, it also bespoke his innocence. If the courts and the bank permitted him to report to the office each day, go about his appointed tasks as usual, like anyone else, it signified to him, and to anyone else who took the trouble to look, that the law and the bank had still not judged him guilty.

Now, however, that he had been banished from the office, what were people to think? Undoubtedly that the bank, if not the law, had finally made up its mind on the question of Charles Daughtry.

It was 10 A.M. Friday morning. Had this been an ordinary working day, he'd have been at his desk at the bank nearly five hours ago. The skies over Sixty-third Street were clear and sun poured in benevolent, mote-filled beams through the bedroom skylight windows.

Showered and shaved, attired in jeans, sneakers and an old sweater, he went downstairs to make coffee, bacon and eggs, inviting two of the marshals stationed round the house to join him. They declined. Under no circumstances would they consider leaving their posts. They compromised instead by accepting steaming cups and hot plates to be gulped outside on the street while standing vigil.

Their diligence was reassuring, but it only served to make Daughtry lonelier. He felt completely isolated—apart from the others at Confederated, a man alone singled out for special punishment, while all other guilty parties had scurried safely down holes, all home free.

For his crimes, Sujimoto would now spend the rest of his days rich as Croesus, honored by cronies and retainers, leeches and hangers-on. Power undiminished. Reputation untarnished. All hint of scandal or impropriety quickly forgotten. Only some hapless underling, indigent and defenseless, would be trotted out and compelled by clever expensive lawyers to face the executioner.

But this would not be the case here, Daughtry vowed. If he was brought down by Federal prosecutors, he meant to bring as many as he could along with him. Kajumi Sujimoto notwithstanding, he meant to live, at least long enough to get into court and have his day.

Having breakfasted and smoked several cigarettes, it dawned upon him with the most gloomy sense of urgency that he had no place to go for the day, nothing to do, not even a friend to call and visit for lunch. More than that, it occurred to him that he himself had erected the isolation with which he had surrounded himself over the years. Now, without a job to go to each morning, he found himself suddenly and frighteningly alone.

34

The flags of war like storm birds fly, the charging trumpets blow.
—JOHN GREENLEAF WHITTIER, *1807–1892*

"In desert warfare," Field Marshal Erwin Rommel used to say, "illusion is everything." As commander of the 7th Panzer Division, spearhead of the fearsome Afrika Korps, he gained a reputation as something of a sorcerer. The 7th Panzer, dubbed "The Ghost Division" for its lightning-swift *blitzkrieg* tactics, wreaking havoc in a few devastating seconds, then evaporating just as quickly into the desert, sadly bedeviled the British and American forces who had daily to contend with it. Rommel's maxim was *"Stürm, Schwung, Wucht"*: "Attack, Impetus, Might."

Poorly supplied and often dangerously undermanned, Rommel, nevertheless, had the uncanny gift of making his presence felt throughout all the broad wastes of the desert, even when he was nowhere in sight. One of his most fiendishly clever tricks was to mount cardboard armor onto the chassis of Volkswagens, thus creating an illusion to British reconnaissance pilots of a desert literally crawling with huge armadas of German Mark III and Mark IV tanks.

Mr. Sujimoto was nowhere in sight. Yet most people appeared to know very well that he was in Liechtenstein. If not Liechtenstein, then certainly one of the Benelux countries with their splendid climate and scenery, and of course their special banking arrangements for those requiring a screen of secrecy. For the time being, people said, Mr. Sujimoto had dropped out of sight. He was only licking his wounds now, and waiting for a chance to break out.

Daughtry knew that Sujimoto was 4,000 miles away in Liechtenstein. Yet, from that awful morning when Daughtry turned just in time to see a grenade rolling toward him, he sensed the presence of the wily old fellow nearby, his treacherous hand inching closer toward him with each day. In response, he began to mount his campaign in the desert against a dangerous adversary—the invisible, but no less palpable Mr. Sujimoto.

And just as the approaching confrontation between himself and Mr. Sujimoto loomed larger and more imminent, so his preoccupation with the toy *Kriegspiele* grew more intense. Either for reasons of escape or for some unconscious need of outlets for the imagination, Daughtry's craving for the war circus in his basement became insatiable. It had all the earmarks of obsession. He would spend hours there, orchestrating the grand encounters of the desert war. Like a superb chess player, he would study the tactics of the board from both sides, alternating between playing Field Marshal Rommel's hand, and then Field Marshal Montgomery's. Subconsciously, he identified with the British, beleaguered, bedeviled, outgunned and badly demoralized by the lightning hit-and-run blitz tactics of the Afrika Korps.

Outside, snow fell silently on Sixty-third Street. The windows of brownstones glowed warm and orange into the cold blasts of February nights. In Daughtry's basement world, the Allied forces were in disarray. Confusion and disunity prevailed. During the bitter fighting in Kasserine, Daughtry sensed his own paralysis and indecision—his inability to produce out of the chaos of his life, some coherent strategy. He had the British and the American air units spread out over the entire front, instead of concentrating their full force against Rommel's main threat, as he should have. On February 18, the Kasserine fell to Rommel, the same day on which Arthur Littlefield informed Daughtry that all attempts to compel the government of Liechtenstein to surrender Sujimoto to the U.S. ambassador there had failed.

That evening, as Eisenhower, still on the defensive, began to build his forces, so too did Daughtry. Sensing his own position fragmented and dangerously strung out, he began to consolidate and concentrate his resources, probing for a soft spot in the tough underbelly of Hiroji Sujimoto. Though he was not conscious of it then, the strategy of Eisenhower and Patton became the strategy of Daughtry. The period of waiting and watching was nearly over.

35

A beaten general is disgraced forever.
—FERDINAND FOCH: *Precepts, 1919*

In the world beyond Daughtry's basement, financial money markets were reeling. The cumulative impact of the Sujimoto-Confederated debacle was having wide repercussions. With the sudden failure of the world's largest steel producer, steel prices soared on the rumor of impending shortages. The effect was felt at once in the automobile and housing industries. Prices rose immediately in order to accommodate the runaway price of steel. Analysts spoke of the "inflationary fallout" surrounding the "Sujimoto-Confederated bust."

In Zurich and London gold rocketed upward 34 points in a single day and the dollar fell across broad fronts throughout the world money markets. In New York the Dow Jones took a sudden dip of 47 points, continuing its sickening slide all throughout the final week of February.

Industry and enterprise experienced the shock waves everywhere. Bauxite mines in Jamaica, copper mines in Rhodesia, rubber fields in Indonesia, coffee planters in the Andes, diamond mines in South Africa, steel mills in Indiana—all with strong credit lines to Confederated Trust Bank—suddenly found themselves financially threatened.

At an automobile assembly plant in Manchester, hundreds of workers were laid off, and at a tiny diamond mine in Chad, fifty-five natives were called up out of the deep tunnels and paid off, merely because the credit needed to continue operations could not be found elsewhere. Their credit liability to Confederated was that overextended.

At home in the U.S., the Secretary of the Treasury murmured reassuring words and cautioned calm. The American banking system, he maintained, was never healthier. Had the banking industry been compromised? people asked. Had the Federal agencies set up to monitor abuses within the industry failed at their jobs? Had the American people's faith in the banks been sadly misplaced? To all these questions, the Secretary replied with a resounding "No."

At the same moment, however, that the Secretary was proclaiming the soundness of the American banking system and particularly Confederated, privately, unbeknownst to that bank, he was awaiting responses from ten to a dozen other banking institutions eager to take over all or part of Confederated's domestic operations. Among them, Manufacturers Hanover, Chemical Bank and a consortium of financial institutions known as the Trans Asian Bank. The prestigious Deutsche Bank informally leaked news through the fast-moving money market grapevine that the moment the Currency Comptroller declared Confederated insolvent, at that time it would bid for control of the bank's total assets.

In the next week the New York Clearing House would report that Confederated deposits were down again another staggering $35 million. In its continued effort to bail out the deeply troubled bank, the Federal Reserve Bank of New York would immediately assume full responsibility for Confederated's still outstanding contracts to buy and sell $800 millions' worth of foreign exchange within the next twelve months. At the same time, the bank would be compelled to appeal to the SEC for yet another ten-day suspension of public trading in its securities. The prestigious accounting firm of Begley-Smythe, conducting just then a comprehensive audit of the bank's books, was unavailable for comment.

Within the eighteenth-floor executive suite of the Confederated tower, at a full conclave of the bank's board of directors that commenced at one o'clock in the afternoon and endured a grueling thirteen hours until shortly after 3 A.M., Leon Edelbach was notified by acting board director, E. Daniel Halliday, that the parent corporation of Confederated Trust Bank was to put all of its shares into a voting trust. The trust was to be named by the FDIC, the Currency Comptroller and the Federal Reserve Board. For the once-proud bank, the handwriting was on the wall.

The following morning, without having slept in forty-eight hours, the ex-president and chief operating officer of Confederated sent a hastily written memo through the various departments that the bank would be moving out of its 200 Park Avenue headquarters because it could simply no longer afford the rent. The Park Avenue operation was to be vastly reduced. There would be personnel changes—a euphemistic phrase for wholesale firings—and the new operation would move to smaller, "more pleasant, convenient quarters" at 130 Pearl Street.

After the dissemination of that memo, Leon Edelbach had lunch with a few friends at his uptown club, the Metropolitan. They talked about everything from politics to deep-sea fishing—everything, that is, except the fate of the doomed bank. When all this was over, the bank president laughed, he meant to get in some good tarpon fishing down in Florida. He was back in his office late in the afternoon where he found on his desk the long-awaited audit from Begley-Smythe, as well as a subpoena ordering him to appear for questioning by the grand jury scheduled for the following week. The subpoena came as no surprise.

The Begley-Smythe report was 228 pages long, single-spaced, full of graphs, charts and figures. Mr. Edelbach began reading it shortly after 5 P.M. when most of the bank personnel were just starting home. He completed it, the medical examiner's office estimated, somewhere shortly past midnight. His body was found by a cleaning lady in the early hours of the morning, slumped forward over his desk, the auditor's report open and scattered beneath him, the right side of his head completely shattered from the impact of the .45 caliber bullet he had discharged into it.

36

There is a gift of being able to see at a glance the possibilities offered by the terrain . . . one can call it the coup d'oeil militaire *and it is inborn in great generals.*
—NAPOLEON I: *Memoirs, 1815*

Mr. Sujimoto, late of Tokyo, took tea on the veranda of the Schloss Mendenhall in late-afternoon Vaduz. Impeccably swaddled in white ceremonial robes, his cup rose in short, unhurried arcs to his lips. Squinting, he watched the transit of the sun across the Alpine sky. Already six hours past its meridian, the fiery red ball had just started to take its dip behind the craggy peaks of the Malbun.

Below, within the vaults mortared so deep within the vast, winding cellars that very few members of the household knew their specific location, innumerable crates and elephantine luggage, bulging noticeably through the middle and girded with thick, flexible steel straps, had all been stored at easy access, ready to go at a moment's notice. All were crammed to the gunnels with gold, negotiable papers, and various currencies in staggering profusion.

Upstairs, in Mr. Sujimoto's bedroom suite, a small suitcase containing toiletries and a complete change of clothing, sat ready and waiting in the event of hasty departure. Never one to indulge a sense of false security, Mr. Sujimoto, having survived one attempt to snatch him from the refuge of Liechtenstein, redoubled his vigilance as well as his mobility. He hired a force of some thirty-odd trained mercenaries of rather questionable character to provide for him 24-hour surveillance all about the grounds at Mendenhall. A fully fueled Lear jet stood hangared at the small airport outside of Vaduz, with two private pilots in constant attendance. In the event of any real emergency, Mr. Sujimoto was prepared to leave the country on less than a half-hour's notice.

As the molten bubble of sun dipped behind the sawtooth peak of the Malbun, Mr. Sujimoto's fingers drummed uneasily on the tabletop. Something restive and unsettled gnawed at the innards of the septuagenarian financier. The long-dreamed-of and long-sought retirement he had earnestly believed he wanted, he was finding tedious. Fishing was fine. Picnics and lawn games with his bride-to-be and daughter were fine. But they were simply not enough. He missed the machinations of daily enterprise. His fingers itched for the sensation of barter for gain.

His situation was ludicrous. He had hundreds of millions of dollars at his immediate disposal, with additional millions stashed in secret unnumbered accounts round the world, yet there were few places he could go. Few sovereignties would accept him within their borders. Few people would take his gold, except possibly criminals. Add to this the fact that within one month's time Charles Daughtry would stand up in an American court and proceed to reveal all he knew about the Japanese banker-financier, which was not inconsiderable.

Behind Mr. Sujimoto, in the Schloss Mendenhall, the servants had begun to light the lights. Fingers still drumming agitatedly on the table, he watched the golden shafts of the fallen sun radiate fiery spokes of light into the darkening sky— like the evanescent ghost of some receding god.

*   *   *

In New York the market had closed on the downside. Dollars had again retreated on a broad front. In the money bazaars of Bahrein and Abu Dhabi traders in djellabas hectored each other and howled in their effort to unload dollars in which they were perilously long. While several thousand miles away in Tokyo, the still drowsy attendant in his green rumpled uniform threw open the doors of the Kabutocho and stood aside to avoid being trampled by the stampede of panicky humanity that had been gathering there. By the close of that trading day, the Central Bank of Japan would have to buy up $200 million U.S. in an effort to halt the sickening slide of that currency.

On East Sixty-third Street, Charles Daughtry organized files of personal correspondence and records, prepared affidavits and consulted for hours with his lawyer.

When he was not preparing his defense, Daughtry prowled the streets, the U.S. marshal trailing not far behind—browsing in shop windows, pausing at a kiosk to buy a newspaper or a magazine, trying to fill the long, agonizing inactivity of his days.

Often he went to department stores, having contrived long lists of items he had absolutely no use for. Wandering up Third Avenue, he would visit antique shops in search of old lead miniatures. Or, he would go to museums, principally the Metropolitan, and then only to the hall of armaments in the basement, where he would linger for hours, or stand struck in wonder before some glass-encased twelfth-century Flemish knight masked behind a bronze morion, attired in full armorial splendor—chain mail, pike, cuirrass, mounted on a massive, caparisoned charger, heraldic flags and banners hung all about the silent, untrafficked hall. To Daughtry, those dummy martial figures, posed in stilted, vainglorious representations of battle, were real. He viewed them in grateful, baffled wonderment, while behind him the big, lumbering marshal, perplexed and weary in his tight black shoes, paced uneasily back and forth over the cold stone floors.

Standing there, Daughtry felt a strong affinity for all the vanished warriors. Like these mercenaries, he too had no strong allegiance to country, no family, no devotion to home or hearth. All he had was his work for hire at the bank and, like Sujimoto, he recognized that to be only a pale surrogate for the pure exultation of war.

Craving vengeance, he thought often of Sujimoto. Despite deep-seated mutual antagonism and distrust, they had gotten on well; liked each other, enjoyed the verbal and intellectual jousting of two highly competitive spirits. Their regard for one another was wary, and begrudging, but nonetheless real, like adversary pugilists assessing one another's skills.

And like Sujimoto, when the pure elixir of battle was no longer available, he too had fixed upon the chancy numerical games of high finance as a likely, but no doubt slightly tamer, substitute.

Later, at night, after the shopping and the museums, after the terrible business of getting through the day, Daughtry would invariably return to his basement, transported from the enforced tedium of the day to a place 5,000 miles away in the vast, stretching wastes of the Tunisian desert where the Battle of Tobruk was just about to get underway.

37

I engage and after that I see what to do.
—NAPOLEON I: *Remark during the Italian campaign, 1796*

A huge pale disc of silver moon hung low in the purple sky. It cast a chalky luminescence over the undulant dunes riding like watery rollers into the distant west. In the chill gray-blue dawn the long line of Panzers had the look of herds of dozing cattle stirring in their dreams. The camels and the pack mules had slept beside the tanks, petrol cans and crates of ammunition still lashed to their backs. With the first tentative growl from one of the big Mark IVs, one of the camels coughed. Several of the pack mules brayed and wobbled to their feet.

Shortly, several more Mark IIIs and IVs of Rommel's 7th Panzers growled engines and skidded their great spiky treads. Clanking, slipping about like sleepers just awakening, unsteady on their feet, they gouged great ruts into the powdery sand behind them.

Nearby, within a detachment of Italian Lancia trucks from the Ariete Division, the Italian drivers sat up in their cabs where they'd slept all night and drank coffee and brandy.

Eighteen miles away, over the dunes, at Field Marshal Montgomery's headquarters, contingents of the Royal Hussars were up and moving stiffly about in gusty 30-knot breezes, lashing trucks and tents against the airborne sand. The smell of frying bacon and coffee from the mess tents mingled with the suffocating stench of cordite and fresh camel dung.

Off to the west, radio signals from a forward American outpost to General Anderson's gun batteries several miles off commenced the battle. In the next moment, the sky opened with the pummel and growl of howitzers. Somewhere near the Lancias a shell burst, sending up a hail of sand and orange sparks, incendiary blossoms—like sprays of orange-red deCaen poppies.

Daughtry watched the regiments moving up eight abreast, sixteen deep, marshaled forward, out of their torpor by the barking noncoms. *Flags, pennants flying, the Chasseurs wheeling on the flanks, cannons trundled forward on the mule caissons, the animals tripping hurriedly, small hoofs embedded in sand, braying with fear, as the air sprang alive with the sharp, scattered crack of rifle fire.*

Next came the heavy armor—half-tracks, tanks, ambulance lorries, transports, motorcycle dispatchers, the sky starting to fill with the German Feister-Storch planes droning overhead, and in the distance, a dirigible hovering, languid and dreamy like a whale suspended beneath the sea. All the gorgeous panoply of war.

195

Austerlitz. Manassas. Sarajevo. Quatre Bras. Marengo. The names rang silvery and sonorous in his head as he mounted the basement stair, the exhilaration of battle still upon him. Sevastopol. Marathon. Actium. Château-Thierry. Chancellorsville. Bastogne. Benghazi. Tobruk. A line of soldiers and warriors marched behind him. The regiments and brigades of a glorious long-vanished past. Leaving would be easy, perhaps because he had at no time ever consciously contemplated it, so he had spared himself the struggle of long inner debate.

It was past midnight when he'd finished Tobruk, and he'd thought only to go up to bed. Now, instead, he was ascending the stair, animated by some fixed and unswervable purpose. It was more invigorating than anything he'd experienced in two nightmarish weeks of mandatory inactivity.

At the top of the stair, turning toward his room, the dying roar of artillery rumbled distantly in his head. Somewhere near 12:45 A.M. he was suddenly, improbably, unaccountably preparing for flight.

Several times he gazed down from his bedroom window at the unhatted marshal, collar up, slouching in a shadow near the front door; on the rooftops across the way it was possible to see the glow of cigarettes from several others huddling there against the cold. It gave him pause, momentarily, but only momentarily. In the next moment he had completed his perfunctory packing and was slamming the lid on his small piece of hand luggage. By his bedside he left a brief note for Arthur Littlefield. "Dear Arthur," it went, "Had I asked your permission to do this, you would have denied it. So I think you know where I've gone and why. If I'm not back in two weeks, please notify U.S. consul in Vaduz and the police. Yours, etc."

Once on the attic stair, small suitcase in hand, passport in vest pocket, along with assorted credit cards and several hundred dollars in cash which he always kept secreted round the house, whatever doubts he might have harbored quickly disappeared. Cautiously, he pushed open the little door at the head of his attic, and in the next moment he stepped out onto the puddled tar roof of his own house.

At every step of the way he expected to be confronted by marshals or police guards. Winding furtively toward a ladder on the far side, he awaited the cry of marshals from the rooftop across the way hailing him back, or the shrill alarm of whistles. No such thing happened.

Moving thus, unimpeded, over the roof, a gusty wind buffeting his back, he glimpsed twinkling stars through the cold, dirty metropolitan sky and a prospect of huddled rooftops stretching northward before him—a clutter of antennas, chimney pots, the occasional laundry line with a sheet waving fitfully like a phantom. He saw no sign of the law. It was all free riding.

And all so easy. Crossing several rooftops. Moving east toward the river. The swift, silent descent by roof ladder to the street below—Sixty-fourth Street—a block farther north and a whole city street east of where the marshals had gathered to protect him from untimely annihilation. Then the quick hailing of a cab to Kennedy, the purchase of a flight ticket at the Lufthansa desk, then moving smoothly, unhurriedly through the departure area. When he'd cleared customs and boarded the plane, his head felt light and giddy. On takeoff, feeling the roar of the jet engines in the pit of his stomach, he had a vision of Panzers rolling up onto the Mareth line before him.

Sujimoto and the Imperial fleet, drawn up in semicircle at anchor in Tulagi Harbor, their big 16-inchers unmuzzled and already targeted, the Zeros and the Mitsubishis revving up on the flight decks, all waiting. The Allies looked northward to Sicily and Italy. And Daughtry had decided to take the war to Liechtenstein.

PART III

38

Find, fix, fight, follow, finish.
—MILITARY MAXIM

"Yes, I think I'll take this one."

"An excellent choice, Fräulein. The piece is quite unique. The bagettes are fine, the stone of a quality seldom encountered."

The object under discussion was a nineteenth-century scarab lavaliere, about which the pretty German saleslady chattered on with considerable animation.

"It's one of a kind, Fräulein. I can assure you."

"Yes, I see that," Mariko replied. "I'll take it along with me."

The saleslady glowed. "Will you be paying for it direct, or shall I put it on Mr. Sujimoto's account?"

The moment the question emerged, she could see the girl stiffen and the warm expressive features suddenly darken. Mariko appeared to be on the verge of a nasty retort, but it never came. Instead she said, "I shall be paying for it myself, thank you."

There was an awkward pause in which the gazes of the girl and the saleswoman engaged. The saleswoman looked away first.

"Very good, Fräulein. Shall I wrap it?"

"That's quite all right. I'll wear it out." Mariko turned and in that moment saw reflected in a smoked mirror behind the woman the figure, almost wraithlike, of a man. It hovered momentarily amid the reflected clutter of antique clocks and ormolu bric-a-brac, a shadowy, anonymous presence, yet bearing with it a vague, disquieting sense of recognition.

201

"I do think you've made a very good choice, Fräulein."

"Yes," Mariko stammered, fighting back excitement. "Yes. I think so—"

She'd been counting a number of bills. Now suddenly she whirled, gaping at the spot she'd seen reflected in the mirror. The figure, or whatever it was, had vanished, leaving in its place only an aura of some former presence having occupied the space.

Mariko turned back to the saleswoman. Her face wore an expression that might have been either amusement or fright. "I'm sorry. I—" She turned and looked back at the spot again, half expecting the thing she'd seen to reappear. But all that she saw there now was a sunny prospect of the fashionable Rheinstrasse with crowds of noonday pedestrians perambulating slowly by. A collection of old clocks tick-tocked and bonged the horary.

When Mariko turned back again, the saleslady was frowning. "Is everything quite all right, Fräulein?"

"Yes, quite," she replied curtly, then finished peeling off her bills. "You didn't by any chance happen to see—"

"Fräulein?"

"A person. A man."

"A man?"

"Yes. Standing right there, I think. Outside the window." Mariko pointed at the vacant spot.

"No, Fräulein. I don't believe I did." The saleswoman was apologetic and uneasy. "There may well have been. Many people stop to look in our window. But I'm afraid I didn't see—"

Before she was able to complete the sentence, the girl had flung a handful of bills on the counter and rushed out of the shop into the sun-flooded street.

The saleslady pursued her out onto the pavement. "Fräulein—Your change . . . Fräulein."

But by that time Mariko had turned a corner and was out of sight. Somewhere, a block or so away, she stopped running, came to an abrupt shuddering stop, her eyes sweeping wildly up and down the broad boulevard, seeking something. She didn't know exactly what.

Twenty yards or so up ahead, on the right, she spied a narrow alleyway cut between two wide boulevards. It was there she headed. If it were he, and she was by no means certain that whom she had seen reflected in the smoked mirror of the curio shop was Charles Daughtry, that would have been the most logical place for him to go. An easy place in which to vanish in a brief space of time.

It was past noon in Vaduz. People were spilling out of shops, offices and large banks. The avenues were beginning to fill with workers and tourists. The thought of locating someone in such a crowd was overwhelming.

The little alleyway Mariko had spied was one of many such in Vaduz. Cuts, they were, between the large fashionable boulevards, lined on both sides with tiny cafés and boutiques and crammed with prowling shoppers.

"*Merde*," she muttered and plunged into the swirling tide, pushing and muscling her way past startled pedestrians. With her coat open, her eyes flashing left and right, dashing in and out of shops, she gave the appearance of being demented. She didn't know herself what impelled her—fright, anticipation, a strange, giddy joy. Barging into shops, hovering there on the threshold, she frightened people with her angry sweeping gaze.

In no time she covered the entire alley. At the end of it she'd found nothing. If he'd been there at all, he wasn't there now. Somehow he'd managed to elude her. Well then, she reasoned, he'd never been there at all. She'd imagined it. What she'd seen in the window of the little shop on the Rheinstrasse was completely chimerical. But if so, then why was her heart pounding?

Overheated and panting in the rush of noon, she retired to the small outdoor café of the Hotel Adler for a lemonade. Sitting there, she tried to absorb exactly what had happened, if indeed, anything had happened at all.

*   *   *

At the Schloss Mendenhall, a huge gaily striped tent was about to go up on the lawn. Dozens of workmen were sinking tent poles; others were laying a dance floor; banquet tables were being unloaded from trucks. Hordes of merchants and delivery vans swarmed on and off the grounds. An endless stream of wine and champagne crates were being unloaded and carried into the cellars, while a profusion of personnel flowed all about. In the midst of all that turmoil, harried and unkempt, stood Celestine. Besieged by workmen and officious merchants, she appeared exhausted, well nigh at the end of her rope.

Not far away, but comfortably sequestered from the noise and confusion, in a shaded dell, Mr. Sujimoto sat at a tile table beneath a gay orange umbrella. He was playing a set of backgammon with one of his young Japanese assistants. Their conversation was minimal and their concentration intense. Periodically, a gleeful manic shriek burst from the old man. It issued under high pressure, like the whistle of a boiling kettle, followed by a grunt of admiration from the assistant. After that was silence broken only by the raucous bark of rooks in the towering spruce overhead.

From time to time the shape of a figure would appear momentarily through the dense surrounding foliage. Crunching heavily over the branches and pine spills, it would then vanish just as quickly. A closer inspection of these peripatetic phantoms would have revealed them to be, for the most part, large muscular men, mostly Corsicans of a fierce mien, uniformed in khaki fatigues and bearing on their shoulders U.S. Army surplus Browning automatic rifles.

They passed unnoticed by the backgammon players, and certainly by the hordes of people besieging Madame de Plevissier, clamoring all about her like famished hounds, several hundred yards away on the vast rolling lawns of the Schloss Mendenhall.

These men, these walkers of the woods, had been conscripted for money paid in the form of a sizable bonus by Mr. Sujimoto, then instructed by his assistants to be vigilant and painstaking, but also to stay well out of sight. Mr. Sujimoto had no wish to have his home turned into an armed camp, nor did he wish his guests to be discommoded or made uneasy by the unsettling presence of armed men.

If Mr. Sujimoto felt secure surrounded by this newly acquired force of mercenaries, it was because the broker in Vaduz who had consummated the deal had assured him that these were the very best to be had. Thoroughgoing professionals, they attended to their duties unobtrusively and with impressive dispatch. They moved with an éclat reminiscent of crack drill teams. Regular 24-hour daily patrols swept over the grounds, armed to the teeth and augmented by braces of large barking Alsatian dogs. All visitors to Mendenhall had to be cleared by the house security. For cars wishing to go on or off the grounds, there was a road check and a rigorous document validation shack two miles from the residence at the main gate. Entering Mendenhall was not a little unlike clearing customs at a foreign border.

Returning from Vaduz, Mariko didn't bother to conceal her impatience at being flagged down by the guard at the gate who nodded to her courteously, but nevertheless used the occasion to make a quick visual search of her car.

Driving up the long, poplar-shaded gravel approach, she was still deeply troubled. While common sense told her that what she had seen in Vaduz was merely a mirage, she could not dispel the disquieting notion that Charles Daughtry was somehow near at hand. Breathlessness and a curious mounting excitement made it for her almost a certainty.

But even if the figure in the shop window that morning was chimerical, it still posed for her a distinctly uncomfortable dilemma. Wasn't it her duty to promptly advise her father even of what she thought she might have seen? Barring that, she must at least notify the chief of house security so that strong precautionary steps might be taken.

39

*Next to victory, the act of pursuit is the most
important in war.*
—CLAUSEWITZ: *Principles of War, 1812*

The bell in the tiny temple rang three times in quick
succession. Several shaved votives kneeling in silent meditation
on the bare sandalwood floor rose and quickly padded off. They'd
been worshipping before a large stone representation of the
Buddha. The figure was impressive, at least four feet, and hewn
out of a smooth dark basaltic substance. Arms folded, the
divinity sat on its stone haunches in lotus position, gazing
serene and imperturbable into the incense-laden shadows.

Before the Buddha was a small teakwood altar with elaborate
scrollwork. A number of small figurines, lesser deities, stood
amid a clutter of jeweled boxes, reliquaries and guttering
candles.

Behind that was a triptych screen upon which a scene of
Mount Fuji had been painted. Snowcapped and mist-shrouded,
a chalk-white luminescence hovered above the scene, so pale
and tenuous that the massive granite summit with its few
stunted, wind-tortured trees, appeared to float in space. The
painter, an anonymous Japanese of the seventh century, had
been able to infuse the barren, windswept scene with an
unearthly, hallowed aura, so that the place appeared truly to be
the habitation of a god.

In the next moment, shuffling was heard and a priest
appeared in voluminous white robes. Silently, he lighted votive
candles to the Buddha and to a whole pantheon of lesser gods.

He went about his work intently, looking neither right nor
left, mumbling invocations as he did so. It was late and the
temple appeared to be deserted. Not many people were about at
that hour. It was bitter cold outside and, besides, the neighbor-

hood on the upper West Side, near Riverside Drive, was known to be dangerous after dark.

The priest extinguished several small electric lights on the altar, dropped swiftly to his knees and, for several moments, with eyes shut and hands clasped before him, meditated before the stone deity. Shortly, he rose and moved off to the side of the altar. His robes rustling behind him, he exited by a small door at the rear.

Except for the sound of an occasional auto rumbling past outside, the temple was now completely still. Only Mount Fuji, remote and timeless, glowed throughout the dense incense-laden shadows with a strange preternatural light.

In the next moment a barely audible creak sounded from the rear of the room, followed by a figure stepping suddenly and stealthily out into the open. Wavering, the figure hovered in the center aisle, then moved swiftly toward the Buddha and fell noiselessly onto its knees before it.

Kajumi Sujimoto wore white ceremonial robes beneath a warm, fashionably cut overcoat. His head had been completely shaven.

Like the priest who had preceded him, he closed his eyes and clasped his hands in meditation. He asked the great Buddha to bring peace to his troubled spirit, and for yet one more chance to redeem himself in the eyes of his noble ancestors.

Kajumi was returning to Liechtenstein that evening. There was dread in his heart at the prospect of seeing his father. His way home would not be easy. From newspaper and TV reports, he knew that the New York police were looking for one Kajumi Sujimoto. By this time they had no doubt already advised every airport and airline, every customs inspection point out of the country to watch for a person bearing a passport issued in that name. Whether or not they were on to Mr. I. Matsumura, he did not know.

His shaved head, he knew, would serve him well for purposes of clearing U.S. customs, where passport officials had been supplied with large five-by-seven glossies of one Kajumi

Sujimoto. But he had no idea that at the same time the police of several nations, as well as Interpol, were also actively seeking him. Destiny was rushing up at him fast. He had failed so often, and now more than ever, he had the nagging, implacable sense that this was his one final chance for salvation.

40

In the art of war there are no fixed rules. These can only be worked out according to circumstances.
—LI CHÜAN, A.D. 7

In the back of Charles Daughtry's mind a plan had been slowly evolving. It was daring, simple in concept and probably impossible in execution. He meant to snatch Sujimoto out of Liechtenstein and bring him, forcibly if necessary, back to New York to stand trial. He had given himself thirteen days to carry out this task. How it was to be achieved, he had not yet the slightest idea.

Having flown to Zurich, he rented a car and drove down the length of Lake Zurich to the small Swiss village of Ragaz at the mouth of the Rhine, almost directly athwart the border of Liechtenstein.

In Ragaz he stayed at a small inn where, happily, they did not ask too many questions. Registering at the desk, he let it be known that he was on vacation, come to Switzerland to do a bit of hiking along the Alpine trails.

There is about the small principality of Liechtenstein a disarming informality. To be sure, there are border checks and customs, but travelers are rarely, if ever, questioned by border officials and papers are simply not checked. People move back and forth from the Swiss and Austrian borders, unhampered by the authorities. And so did Daughtry. Dressed unremarkably as an Alpinist, with heavy shoes, an alpenstock, a Tyrolean hat set at a jaunty angle, he gave the impression of a vacationing bachelor pedagogue on spring vacation. Slightly eccentric but certifiably harmless.

Setting out from Ragaz that first morning, he'd driven the four or five miles into Vaduz where, as chance had it, he stumbled across Mariko in the little curio shop, and was very nearly detected by her. When she'd stormed out of the shop, clearly in search of him, he was already seated in the car across the way, observing her.

Still in the car, he followed her up to the alleyway into which she'd disappeared, then sped round the corner, waiting for her to reappear on the other side. When she did, he followed her to the little outdoor café by the Hotel Adler, where again from the cover of the car he watched her drink lemonade. Then later, when she reclaimed her Volkswagen at a nearby garage and drove out to Mendenhall, Daughtry, at an unobservable distance on the windy mountain roads, was still behind her.

When Mariko stopped to be checked by the house security at Mendenhall, Daughtry merely drove on a mile or so, pulled his car off the road into a wooden glen and retraced the route on foot.

Anticipating that Sujimoto would be well guarded, he did not go back to the Schloss by way of the road, but instead made his way through the deep pine forest running parallel to the road. Reaching Mendenhall, the first thing he heard was the deep throaty baying of a large dog in the distance. Shortly, he was confronted by an eight-foot cyclone wire fence with an additional three-foot tier of barbed-wire canted inward at the top. An armed guard, automatic rifle slung at his shoulder, with a huge, nasty-looking Alsatian, was just then strolling the inner perimeter of that fence.

Concealed by heavy foliage, Daughtry, crouching, observed for some time the rotation of the guards, counting eight that passed in the space of an hour—an average of seven and a half minutes from one passage to the next.

From his vantage point he had a clear prospect, too, of the inspection shack at the front gate, noting the steady flow of commercial traffic that streamed through it, in and out of the castle. Mostly, they were delivery trucks—butchers, poulterers, bakers, confectioners, wine merchants, florists. Given the fact that Mendenhall, granted its size, was still only a residence for three, or possibly four, plus staff, so much produce going through at one time struck Daughtry as distinctly odd.

By that time he had taken the lay of the land. He contemplated several additional reconnaisance trips, while a strategy to invade the place was already taking shape in his mind. He would be back that night.

41

We have retired far enough for today: you know I always sleep upon the field of battle.
—NAPOLEON I: *To retreating French troops before the counterstroke at Marengo, June 14, 1800*

At Ragaz by dusk, Daughtry had a shower and changed quickly for dinner. Sipping an apéritif on the small veranda, he replayed in his mind the events of the day. It occurred to him that, for a man facing professional ruin and a possible prison sentence, he was in strangely good humor.

It was curious the way he'd stumbled on Mariko in Vaduz. He hadn't expected to. It had been his intention to pick up maps at a local tourist bureau, make a few discreet inquiries regarding the route to Mendenhall, then make his way out there. Then— seeing her like that, after two years—the odd glow of satisfaction in merely watching her unobserved.

After that came the apprehension and misgivings. He had counted on her being in Tokyo. Her being here now, in a sense, complicated things. It was not that he harbored any residual feelings for those days in Okitsu. He liked to tell himself that he had never been all that involved, but the excitement he felt suddenly seeing her there, belied all that.

Now he'd come to take her father from her. Possibly put him away in a cell for a long time. There was nothing particularly heroic about what he was contemplating. And the girl being there made it just that more awkward. Not at all in the scenario.

Sipping his vermouth, he replayed the scene once more—coming upon her in the little curio shop, seeing her first in profile through the window. The first thing that had caught his eyes was the long, sable hair draped like a curtain over narrow, elegant shoulders. She wore a blouse and peasant skirt and clogs. Her legs were bare.

In Tokyo she was merely someone who was about all the time, with her father, in some sort of vague, quasi-professional capacity. There, she'd affected a kind of outwardly chaste reserve. He saw no sign of that here. She was, at that moment, unquestionably striking, the ultrasmart way of Oriental women who become deeply Westernized.

Then seeing her that morning. Just the back of her head. Knowing it was her before he'd actually even recognized her, before it had registered on the mind's eye. And then, that warm pleasurable glow of surprise and anticipation and running for the car in near-fright.

It was nearly 10 P.M. when she'd found him in the card room playing five-card stud poker with Karl Heinz and Aito. She'd been looking for him but only halfheartedly, waiting for an opportunity to get him off by himself.

"Pair of nines and two knaves," Sujimoto snapped, and flung his cards triumphantly on the table. In a broad gesture reminiscent of an embrace, he swept a pile of chips toward himself, merging it with an already toppling heap.

Dispiritedly, Karl Heinz tossed his cards in while the big fellow from Sakhalin shook his shaved head.

"Illusion, my good friend Abbington, the British admiral, used to say to me." Sujimoto puffed at his Monte Cristo and dealt cards swiftly, squinting against the smoke. "Poker played well is illusion. Sortilege. Necromancy. Stratagems. The stuff of life." He looked up suddenly to see his daughter framed in the doorway, regarding him oddly.

His smile faded and he grew suddenly cross. "Yes?"

She didn't reply but merely gazed at him in that defiant, quizzical manner. Her silence made him more peevish. "Well, Mariko?"

"Father, may I see you?"

"Is it important? I'm busy."

Her heart thumped and she felt thirteen years old again. "Father, I'd—"

"Yes. Yes. Get on with it. Can't you see I'm engaged? Can it wait?"

Her mind reeled, seesawing dizzily between her need to warn him, and her innermost instinct to say absolutely nothing. "It's not important," eyes lowered, she stammered. "Of course it can wait." Even as the words came out, she could not believe she had said them.

Sujimoto regarded her, his face impassive. He appeared calm. Laying his cards face down on the table, he sighed. "Come now. I see something is bothering you."

"No, Father. Nothing of the sort." The silhouette of Charles Daughtry flashed unnervingly in her mind.

"Why then, may I ask, daughter, are you here now?" Sujimoto frowned.

Standing there, observing her father, whatever certainty she'd felt about seeing Daughtry that day turned quickly to confusion and doubt. She laughed uneasily. "I'm sorry, Father, I haven't been myself these past weeks."

Sujimoto's taut bluish lips relented into a pinched smile. "Understandable, given the circumstances of the past several weeks."

"I've been nervous. I don't sleep well. I just felt like seeing you."

"Of course. I understand perfectly. You were right to have come." His cool, silken palm covered the back of her hand. She had a sudden image of him, small and childlike, reposing in a satin-lined casket.

"Have a brandy and go to bed. We have a busy schedule tomorrow."

"Yes, Father." She started to back off, then returned and kissed him.

"Good night, child." He reached up and patted her cheek. It was, for him, unguarded and touching.

When she left him a great weight was upon her. She'd failed to warn her father and had thus betrayed him. She had then, she understood, made some conscious choice between Daughtry and her father. The knowledge of that appalled her. Worse even, she felt distinct relief at having kept the information to herself.

When she went upstairs it was getting on toward midnight. She'd been up since six that morning, photographing a series of Alpine scenes for a German travel magazine, then working in her developing room until roughly ten, at which time she had driven into Vaduz.

Ordinarily, she'd have been exhausted by this hour. This evening, instead, she found herself alert, restive, strangely apprehensive.

In a robe and slippers she went back downstairs in search of a glass of milk. Her father's brandy sedative came to mind, and she veered from her course to the pantry, to that of Sujimoto's well-stocked bar.

She had been aware all that afternoon of making a conscious effort to keep her mind off Daughtry. The thought now that the effort was proving to be so great was exasperating. Still, she had no certainty, other than a deep, feminine instinct, that he was even in Vaduz. Actually, despite the danger that it suggested, it was her fervent hope that he was.

In her mind she acted out a little scene in which the two of them would meet. Fortuitously, as it turned out, on the street, or in a little café. She imagined him walking toward her, nodding and smiling, with that irritating smugness of his. She disliked his smile; it was crooked, or perhaps the line of his teeth was. In any event, it was a brash smile, and she had always perceived it as patronizing—a sign that he looked upon her as amusing or possibly even slightly ridiculous.

"How are you," he would say, and then he would extend his cold, unresponsive hand. There was certainly nothing attractive about him. What it was, she deduced, that appealed, was that kind of eerie prescience he projected, as if he knew her thoughts before she did. Like her father's mind, she found Daughtry's also intimidating. Encyclopedic but without any special depth. Cataloging facts and numbers in the matter of the committed collector—for the sake of merely being able to display them. Inhuman, she thought, or possibly even antihuman. She hated the fact that she was frightened by him.

She imagined herself taking his hand without deigning to acknowledge his question. He would pull a chair up to her table and sit down.

"What are you doing here?" she would demand.

"I thought you'd be happy to see me."

"I would, if I thought you'd come simply for that. Leave my father alone."

"You don't expect me to go to jail for him, do you?"

"If you come near him, I'll have you killed." She heard herself say and, to her dismay, realized it was ridiculous. Posturing heroics.

"How are you, Daughtry?" She started the scene over, then wondered why she could only address him as Daughtry. Why not Charles? She hated the name Charles. What was there about him that prohibited the simple civility of first names? It was stuffy and priggish. Overly formal. Exactly the way he was.

"How are you, Charley?" she said instead, and laughed out loud. "I know what you're here for. And I might as well tell you, if you go anywhere near him, I'll have your legs broken. Those apes he's got up there with him are not exactly choir boys."

Why was she going through all this? What was the purpose of these silly rehearsals? Clearly, Daughtry had her raddled. The thought that he was somewhere nearby made her fidgety and irritable. She had not been able to put him out of her mind for two years. Why couldn't she acknowledge it? Why couldn't she just go to him and say, "Look, Daughtry," or Charles, or Charley, or whatever. "I like you. I think you like me."

She had a woman's intuition that in matters of the heart he needed the jarring of direct confrontation. "Why not give it a chance," she went on prodding him in her head. "Forget about my father and whatever he's done to you. Let's put all that aside for the moment and concentrate on us."

It sounded fair and to the point. She liked the ring of it. She wondered if in fact she'd ever find the chance or the courage to say it.

She poured herself another brandy, then took her snifter and walked out into the garden, where the bright myriad stars studded the lofty dome of midnight sky.

Later that evening, Kajumi Sujimoto's plane landed in Zurich. When he disembarked and cleared customs, he was still using the passport of Mr. Matsumura.

In the terminal he bought a late newspaper, then strolled out into the parking area where he hired a car. He could not yet get himself to go to Mendenhall. The thought of creeping home with his tail between his legs made him physically ill. Apologies and hollow explanations of the feckless, wayward son were simply insupportable. Later, he thought, later. Better tomorrow, or the next day, after he'd had time to work out in his mind exactly what he would say. How he might explain things to his father.

The car, at last, drew up beside him. He slipped in and when the driver asked him where he wished to go, he didn't say Vaduz. Instead, he asked the fellow to take him down to Sargans, a tiny Swiss village next door to Ragaz.

215

42

*The only quality which is known and constant is the
will of our leader.*
—ERICH LUDENDORFF: *My War Memories, 1919*

Long after Sujimoto had fallen asleep, Madame de Plevissier
sat beside his bed holding in her palm the small smooth aged
hand. It was light in her palm, ghostly light and feathery, like
the paw of a cat. From time to time, his eyelids fluttered, but his
breathing was deep and regular. She could detect no trace of
anger in his face, or fear, even though she guessed that
Sujimoto's days were now comprised principally of those two
emotions.

Once again she marveled at his capacity to control the
turmoil of his life, to regulate destructive emotions, and somehow make even adversity work for him.

He was wanted now for questioning by courts in several
jurisdictions; the evidence of guilt against him, she suspected,
was considerable and mounting each day. Beyond that were the
lawyers, the creditors, the accountants and his many accusers.
He was not, it was obvious, in very good health. But still the life
force would not yield. He did not quail. He was up all day,
talking on the phone to money markets round the world,
trading, building up his positions in precious metals or in one
currency or another, and reading everything pertinent to money.
Then outdoors, attending to his land, fishing, inventorying his
household possessions. At night, she'd put him to bed with a
warm glass of milk and a sedative the doctor had prescribed for
bedtime. Then, afterward, she would sit quietly talking with him
until he drifted off.

"Remind me to call Crédit Lyonnais first thing in the
morning. I expect the franc to make a real run: .4832." His head
nodded on the pillow and he spoke in a lispy little singsong,

distantly from a twilit world, as if he'd already crossed beyond, yet lingered there reluctantly. Still, the numbers spilled from his lips like a sacred litany; incantatory magic that evoked for him a sense of personal indestructibility.

In bed, lying beneath the quilted counterpane, he appeared very small, doll-like. His skin had the dull yellow sheen of waxed fruit. He was nearly eighty and she had given him thirty years— the better part of her youth. She didn't regret it. Not one bit. In some peculiar, implausible way, she had loved him, and in time that love had matured into a deep, unswerving friendship. The paradox of it all now was that she could not see for the life of her any purpose in marrying him, except possibly for Mariko, who perceived it as some kind of vindication for herself.

She recognized that the wedding, this gross, unwieldy circus they were about to produce, was merely a gesture to placate the whimsy of a frightened old man. She resented deeply the part she was now compelled to play.

They would go through the ceremony like mummers in a masque. People—her friends and his—would come to congratulate and ogle, then go off and gossip. They would say cruel, sniggering things. People delighted in that sort of mischief. People were mostly ungenerous. She understood that. They could not hurt her. But they could hurt Mariko, who desperately wanted the wedding. So much had gone wrong for her already. As a result of their unconventional arrangement, she had suffered far more than they. It would be a pity now to have the child hurt any more. Oddly, she still thought of her daughter as a child.

When she turned out the light above Sujimoto's head, she knelt and kissed him on the brow. He stirred and mumbled something that sounded vaguely like more numbers.

Outside, Celestine moved numbly through the long, unending corridors of the castle. Strange it all seemed, and alien. A home that had never been a home. A habitation, rather, which she had shared with several others. She would soon be the mistress of the manor. Rather than any feeling of positive joy or satisfaction, she experienced mostly a keen sense of desolation.

The servants were now extinguishing lights. Passing through the main ballroom, she paused and stood in the center of the bare, darkened room. All of the furniture had been removed for the gala reception. The place had a forlorn, abandoned look. A shuddering chill seeped into her bones from off the cold marble floor.

Outside, just beyond the veranda, she could see the great striped tent erected that afternoon. A single flambeau left there by the workmen illuminated the place, with a dim, ghostly glow.

Standing in the shadows within the great French doors, Celestine saw a figure moving there. At first she couldn't see who it was, but in a moment the figure of Mariko swung into view. She was standing within the tent staring upward into the lofty roof. Celestine watched her daughter walking about, twirling slowly within an intricate nexus of ropes and guy lines, like a dancer in a dream, a look of rapt, childish wonderment on her face.

Driving to Sargans from the air terminal, the cab driver drove through the village of Ragaz. It was past midnight and the simple Swiss burghers of the town had long since gone to bed. But on the main street of the little toylike village a few lights, mainly from hostelries and bars, still glowed and twinkled warmly.

At one point, Kajumi's cab rattled past a little Weinstube called Nick-Nack. It catered largely to tourists and, in season, to skiers from Davos and Chur. Since it was off season, the place was fairly quiet. A quaint little spot in the style of a chalet, it was long on such Teutonic oddments as mounted stag's heads and cuckoo clocks.

The bar in the basement was small and snug. Pewter mugs hung from the low timbered ceiling, and a fire crackled in a stone hearth. At one corner of the tiny bar, recessed into a corner, Charles Daughtry sat ruminating before a tall stein of Schieffen bock. He scarcely heard the sound of the cab rumbling past on the untrafficked street outside. Kajumi sat in a corner of that cab, unaware that at the moment, he was within no more than fifty feet of the man he wanted more than anything in the world to lay hands on.

Once in Sargans he checked into a little guest house frequented mainly by adulterous Italian couples who slipped regularly over the border from Como for assignations. Exhausted, and sick with worry at the prospect of seeing his father in the morning, he sought eagerly now the oblivion of sleep.

While he undressed and prepared for bed, his eye happened to stray to the newspaper he'd picked up in the terminal. It lay on the bed where he'd tossed it, and now he lay down and took it up. Without looking for anything in particular to read, he browsed listlessly through the sports pages, then came, almost by chance, to a page upon which he immediately recognized an aerial view of Mendenhall. Beneath that was a photograph of his father and Celestine. The headline above it in bold, capped letters read: FINANCIER TO WED PROMINENT CORRESPONDENT.

Kajumi's eyes swam as he read word for word, then over again, a story detailing the whole sordid history of his father's "intimate friendship of 30 years."

Reading, he ground his teeth so hard that his jawbone ached. Something very much like tremors began to wrack his frame. What perfidy. What betrayal. And had they not picked the moment to consummate this abomination too perfectly, too cleverly? Thinking him thousands of miles away, his father had chosen the safe moment to legitimize his relationship with the Parisian whore. The bile rose in his gorge. What an insult to the memory of his mother. This adventuress and his wicked, selfish father. This was indeed the ultimate humiliation, and he would not accept it.

Seething, he tore the newspaper in shreds, wadded it into a ball, then flung it violently across the floor where it burst with a dull thud and drifted downward to the floor like ragged confetti. Hot tears sprang to his eyes, coursed down his cheeks, seeping salty into the corners of his mouth. This could not happen, he

219

vowed. This would not be. Having made that resolve, he grew suddenly confused. For a moment he imagined he was back on Sixty-third Street in the frigid February air. Suddenly flames leapt and crackled gorgeously before his eyes. Great sheets of sparks showered upward into the bright, frigid night. It was all so lovely and exciting. He caught his breath. Fireworks, he recalled, as a boy in a park in Osaka. Within the lambent flames shapes moved. They resembled blood-red butterflies, fluttering, pirouetting, lighting here and there. Watching the fire, mouth open, stunned by its beauty, like a spectator enthralled, he laughed triumphantly.

43

Be audacious and cunning in your plans, firm and persevering in their execution, determined to find a glorious end.
—CLAUSEWITZ: *Principles of War, 1812*

"Christofson—Mr. and Mrs. Table 8."
"Christofson—Table 8."
"Myerbeer, Lord and Lady, Table 6."
"Myerbeer—Table 6."
"Lord and Lady Hazeltine. Table 4."
"Hazeltine, 4?" There was a jarring pause. "Surely not at the same table with the Peronellis?" Karl Heinz blushed. He always blushed when he was obliged to correct his superiors.

"Why not?" Mariko asked. They were seated in a small room—an office off the scullery of Mendenhall. Mariko was surrounded by Karl Heinz and three other gentlemen of the kitchen staff. With their eyes lowered to a huge parchment unrolled on the desk, they gave the appearance of a general staff studying a battle plan. In actuality, the scroll bore a floor plan of the Grand Tent and the surrounding gardens. They had gathered there to work out seating arrangements.

"All due respect, Fräulein," Karl Heinz stammered. "There's known to be a history there. Some unpleasantness. Many years ago. The Hazeltine boy and the Peronellis' daughter. Nasty business. Very unpleasant."

There was an air of tension in the little room, and the four men hovering above Mariko seemed uneasy. She wore dark glasses and a crisply tailored pinstripe suit. A wisp of hair tumbled on her brow and she appeared more peevish than ever. "I see," she murmured, compressing her lips. As she spoke, she suddenly looked up. A figure passing the door caught her eye and then moved on, losing itself in the whirl of activity in the kitchen beyond. Moments after the figure had vanished, she was still watching the spot—aware of Karl Heinz and the others watching her, but unable to avert her gaze. What she had seen, in that fleeting instant, appeared to be a cook—or possibly a pastry chef—attired in white coveralls and a large, floppy toque. But what struck her as unusual was that this particular individual wore sunglasses. It was unusual, she knew, almost unheard of, for any of the Mendenhall kitchen staff to wear sunglasses while at work. It would have been looked upon by the implacably rigid Swiss gentleman who was chief chef, as a sign of the most flagrantly, unprofessional behavior.

She couldn't say why but, quite inexplicably, something grim and chilling had taken hold of her.

44

I am quite happy, thank God, and like Lawrence, I have tried to do my duty.
—CHARLES GEORGE GORDON: *Postscript to his last letter from Khartoum, December 29, 1884*

That evening Mr. Sujimoto took a quiet supper with his daughter and his bride-to-be in one of the smaller dining rooms of the castle.

During most of the day he'd been busy, on the phone, dealing with major money markets round the world—New York, London, Zurich, Bahrein—and even now, he was awaiting calls from Tokyo and Singapore where he was about to roll over millions of dollars in pound sterling.

Later in the day, the eminent financier had been off with Karl Heinz on an auto tour of his vast properties, inspecting fishing streams, and the condition of fences used to discourage poachers. Outdoors, he'd been cheerful and energetic. Now, suddenly, he grew morose and withdrawn as if the effort to keep up a good face had exhausted him.

Throughout dinner he scarcely spoke. Celestine believed he was preoccupied, uncharacteristically nervous—far more so than he cared to reveal. She imagined that he was suddenly feeling himself trapped, propelled into a situation he could no longer reverse nor, indeed, even contain.

"Are you well, Sujimoto?" she inquired.

He scarcely looked up.

She tried once more. "Sujimoto?"

"Father," Mariko tried now. "Do you like the suit Señor Ruffino made for you?"

"You know I really don't care for formal dress. I don't look well in it."

"Nonsense." Celestine smiled. "You're very attractive when you dress up."

Sujimoto made a wry face.

"Is everything all right, Sujimoto? You don't—"

"I don't regret anything." Anticipating her question, he cut her short. "Nothing."

Madame de Plevissier's smile waned and she felt courage ebb from her. Desperately, she sought ways to take his mind off things. "You know, Sujimoto, Mariko has promised to take pictures. We'll have photos for a scrapbook. We shall be able to look at them for years to come . . ." Her voice trailed off. Even as the words were pouring out, she could see the bleak, abject look in his eyes. Mariko lowered her gaze. Sujimoto merely sat there, mute, frozen, staring straight ahead, peering at the multiple images of himself shimmering in the facets of a crystal wine decanter.

A butler and two waiters entered from a side door, cleared dishes and served coffee, then disappeared noiselessly with the efficient dispatch of people who know when to make their presence scarce. Afterward, the three all sat together in strained, uneasy silence. The only sound to be heard was the anxious tinkle of spoons swirling sugar rapidly through the demitasse.

"You know, darling," Celestine said with sudden, artificial brightness, "there's no need to go through with this."

"How so, madame? What do you mean, no need—"

"I mean—" She sensed his growing vexation. "If, for any reason—any reason whatever, you should choose not to—I mean, I would not be upset—"

"Father—Celestine doesn't mean—"

"I know perfectly well what Celestine means, Mariko. Please not to be ridiculous. I asked for this because I myself wanted it." His face suddenly brightened. "It's going to be the grandest day of my life." Suddenly, he clapped his strong little claw hands and cried out: "Aito."

Outside in a shadowy corner of the veranda, another individual stood viewing the scene through the large French windows. Still unable to confront his father with charges of treachery and betrayal, Kajumi Sujimoto had stolen onto the castle grounds by means of a little-known jogging trail that commenced some three miles off, meandered through the spruce forests surrounding Mendenhall, and came out not far from the rear approach to the château.

Observing the intimate little family gathering through a wide French door, Kajumi's raging, jealous mind immediately assumed that the three individuals sitting there round the dinner table were ecstatically happy. Chattering, laughing, looking eagerly forward to the coming festivities, and making plans for the future.

He saw himself as excluded, cut off from the happy three-

223

some. In a still more disturbing way, he perceived the individuals posed within that little vignette as utter strangers. He knew them but did not recognize them as any natural extension of himself. His father appeared to have forgotten him completely. It was as if he no longer existed. The vile Frenchwoman dominated him now. She had gelded him, turned him into a docile, compliant ass. She could do anything she wished with him. She had even made him dishonor the memory of his beloved mother.

And the girl—the one they dared to call his half-sister, the whore of the American, Daughtry—how had she managed to so completely displace him in the affections of his own father?

Thoughts of Mariko led inevitably to thoughts of Charles Daughtry. The face, sharp, perceptive, the jaunty little spade of beard, so full of pride and self-assertiveness, flashed before him. In his fevered mind he watched Daughtry's head tilt toward that of his father's, the two of them sharing a confidence or an anecdote, from which he had been pointedly excluded. How that rankled—the thought that he had come within a hair of annihilating the detestable fellow, and failed. Fate mocked him. It was true—Daughtry had eluded him by scarcely even trying.

He saw it all now with a piercing, agonizing clarity. How these foreigners, trespassers and intruders, had killed his beloved mother, insinuated themselves into his father's life, blinded him to all familial loyalty, then finally usurped from his son his own rightful place beside his father.

When Kajumi looked down, something hard and bright was glinting in his hand. It was the P38, but he could not say how it got there. Standing there in a cone of shadow, aiming it at his father's head, seemed so simple, so correct. It had such a clear unassailable logic to it. It was even poetic, the way his arm rose and stood straight out from the shoulder, the hard, bright thing glinting at the end of it with the dazzling refulgence of a diamond.

The motion had a strangely familiar air to it, as if in his head, or somewhere perhaps in a dream, he had gone through precisely the same motion over and over and over again. This now was only just another dreamy replication of the same.

His finger applied the slightest pressure to the trigger, holding it that way tantalizingly for seconds, protracted exquisitely until within his mind the seconds had the duration of geological eons. His arm extended rigid and straight, grew numb. It ached, and started to tremble.

In the next moment the huge silhouette of Aito loomed beyond the leaded casements, moving toward his father. It was then that Kajumi lowered the pistol and, almost catlike, slipped silently off the flagged veranda, disappearing into the wooden shadows beyond.

45

The officers of a Panzer Division must learn to think and act independently within the framework of the general plan and not wait until they receive orders.
—FIELD MARSHAL ERWIN ROMMEL: *The Rommel Papers, I, 1953*

Arthur Littlefield stood amid the turmoil of his office and glared at the ringing phone on his desk.

"I'm not here," he roared at an unseen presence beyond the half-open door.

"What shall I say?" the unseen presence, an exasperated female voice, cried back.

"The same as you said to all the rest. I'm out of town. You don't know when I'm expected back."

He kicked the door shut and proceeded to prowl. The office had the appearance of a ransacking—as if someone had come along and tilted it on end. There was a great deal of paper strewn about—reports, cables, memos marked urgent, in red.

On his desk bedlam reigned. Pink call-back slips, stacks of affidavits, confidential testimony and, most prominently atop it all, a copy of the *New York Times* open to the business section. It bore a picture of Charles Daughtry beneath banner headlines which read KEY WITNESS IN CONFEDERATED SWINDLE VANISHES.

It was not yet 10 A.M., but Littlefield's phone had been going all morning, starting at 6 A.M. when he himself arrived at his office in order to elude the calls at home. Early the night before he had had the first intimations of disaster. A *Daily News* reporter reached him at home in Rye and baldly asked if it was true that Daughtry had fled the country. Certainly it wasn't true, Littlefield snarled back just as baldly, and slammed down the phone.

The reporter called back the next moment and said if the bit about Daughtry wasn't true, was it true then that Confederated was on the brink of insolvency?

"How the hell should I know?" Littlefield yowled. "Go ask Confederated."

It was now six days before the opening of the grand jury hearings and Littlefield had not had one word from his client. Nor did he expect to. Postcards and phone calls were not in the nature of a man who was morbidly private. Still, Littlefield's fury knew no bounds. Without bothering to inform his counsel, Daughtry had bolted. His disappearance just at that moment placed his lawyers in an embarrassingly awkward position. The U.S. District Attorney prosecuting the case for the government had even gone so far as to intimate that Littlefield himself had engineered the disappearance, and that if Daughtry didn't show for the inquiry, the government would move to prosecute Littlefield instead for obstruction of justice.

Littlefield ground his teeth while the District Attorney proceeded to denounce him in crazed nasalities. Exasperated, the lawyer slammed the phone down in the middle of a particularly bitter exchange. That was the last call he deigned to accept.

"It's the *Washington Post*," his secretary called now from without.

"Tell them I fled with Daughtry," he snarled, and trudged like a condemned man to his desk. Then, for the next few minutes, he sat plowing his fingers through his hair and staring balefully into space.

Charles Daughtry had promised to return in approximately two weeks. In five years of client-lawyer relationship, Daughtry had never once given his attorney cause to doubt him. While it was true you could never get close enough to the man to feel you had his friendship, Littlefield nonetheless knew him to have an unflagging sense of duty. In terms of such niceties as punctuality and the strict fulfillment of verbal agreements to the letter, his word was solid gold. The attorney had no reason to doubt that Daughtry would return in time for the opening of the hearings. But the fact that he had bolted without first notifying his counsel—the fact that he had stolen off into the night, vanished from under the very eyes of six U.S. marshals guarding him—this looked bad to outsiders, who didn't know the man. Very bad indeed.

Beyond that was the uncomfortable fact that one attempt—albeit bungling—had already been made on Daughtry's life, and every moment he walked about in the world unguarded, the risk of yet another soared in geometrical progression.

During Daughtry's brief absence, the Confederated situation had deteriorated markedly. With the news of Leon Edelbach's suicide, demand deposit withdrawals began to avalanche. After that, true panic was afoot. Rumors began to fly like myrmidon locusts darkening the sky.

It was known that the bank had started to eliminate its international operations, and was now considering cutbacks in its national divisions, particularly Manhattan. Littlefield had heard from the bank's holding corporation's attorney, an old classmate of his, that the Confederated's board had ordered the ailing bank to roll back its payroll by $12 million.

There was, too, the rumor, more solidly founded, that four more senior officers—Whitelaw, Kavanaugh, Peck and Daughtry's old nemesis, Michaeltree—had suddenly elected by mutual agreement with the bank to take early retirement. Several others

227

were quietly negotiating their departures. A senior vice-president who'd grown drunk and disorderly at a Pine Street bar, proclaimed to one and all gathered there that a major staff reduction, involving 500 to 600 jobs was imminent. This, he maintained with that air of statistical infallibility common to businessmen in high places, represented a reduction of 20 percent of all jobs, and was in identical proportion to the bank's loss of resources to date.

The hottest rumor of all, however, springing whole cloth out of the steamy rumor mills of Washington and Wall Street, had it that several banks were at that very moment contesting heatedly with the appropriate Federal regulatory agencies to take over the Confederated's assets. The banks included were Manufacturers Hanover, Chemical Bank, Citibank, Bank Leumi, and the Trans Asian Banking Corporation. The dismemberment of the bank had begun in earnest.

Littlefield thrust aside the summary of the Begley-Smythe auditing report, folded his arms, and resolutely fumed. Given the bleakness of Daughtry's outlook, he could not say he blamed the man for bolting. Nor would it surprise him greatly if he declined to return. The verdict was virtually in. As of now, everyone considered Daughtry guilty. By no means the chief architect of a conspiracy to defraud, he was clearly guilty of full complicity in such a conspiracy. This was certainly the attitude of the bank. At Confederated, Littlefield had been told that the door of Daughtry's office, closed and padlocked after his departure, had several times been defaced with obscenities scrawled in red crayon. "Stoolie," "Fink" and "Crook" were some of the more felicitous epithets.

Attempting to bring Sujimoto to book in the U.S. seemed improbable at best, but Littlefield could not see that Daughtry had much choice in the matter. The amount of incriminating material amassed against him by the comptroller, the SEC and the District Attorney's office was known to be awesome.

On the other hand, Littlefield had in his possession two years' worth of interoffice correspondence, the thrust of which were persistent, sometimes impassioned, pleas from Daughtry to his superiors, regarding what he judged to be the questionable character of Sujimoto's foreign exchange dealings. All extenuating, to be sure, nevertheless the fact remained, the records showed—Daughtry had participated in what he knowingly understood to be a criminal activity. True, he himself never gained personally from this activity, but he had clearly acquiesced in it. That fact was inescapable, and the only thing that could significantly improve his present position of grave risk was for the Grand Dragon himself to be carted in by the ear to Federal Court and forced to tell all. Obviously, the Grand Dragon had no intention of coming voluntarily. Viewing it in a certain light, what Daughtry was now attempting to do had a certain ruthless, ineluctable logic to it. He was simply resorting to his last resort.

46

The word of a scout—a march by night,
A rush through the mist—a scattering fight.
—RUDYARD KIPLING: "Ballad of
Bah da Thone," 1888

It was some time after dark before Kajumi stirred. Until then, he had secreted himself in what appeared to be an empty coalbin somewhere beneath the west wing of the castle. The scullery dumbwaiter had set him down directly below the kitchen in a well-trafficked area that turned out to be his father's wine cellar. It was a deep, high repository of stone and timber, lined with racks of bottles and noble old casks that creaked and twanged in the shadows. The air was dry and cool to the point of chilling, with the acrid, earthy scent of mold.

Overhead, he had heard voices, people moving about. He was somewhere beneath the kitchen, he knew, at the point where, disguised in a cook's outfit, he had descended by pulleys into the Mendenhall netherland. The wine cellar where he now stood bore all the signs of mortal activity. Crates of vintage champagne, recently pried open, still packed in overflowing excelsior, stood randomly about, along with the hammers and crowbars that had been used to pry the lids. Several clarets stood open on a table where the wine steward had decanted one or two in order to sample vintages. Damp corks lay about here and there, along with several small copper tasting cups with droplets of wine still beading their bottoms. A sommelier's leather apron lay draped over the back of a tall stool, a sign that the owner was gone but could be returning at any moment.

Kajumi stole back deeper into the complicated network of tunnels that appeared to lead him farther down into the dank earth beneath the castle. There were several distinct sections of foundation, each built at different periods of Mendenhall's 300-year history. Each additional section had been added along with each new extension to the castle, each lying at a different depth. Moving through the chill, clammy air, he sensed himself dropping deeper into the earth, the sound of voices and movement overhead receding markedly.

Tiny mullioned windows set within stone walls permitted sufficient light for him to descend several flights of stone steps and arrive finally in a dark, lofty space within which he could hear the sound of what resembled fast rushing water.

Lighting a match, he looked around, and found himself in a tall hollow rotunda, windowless and full of dank gloom. When first conceived several centuries ago, it might have served as a chapel. Roughly cruciform in shape, it bore the marks, now largely vanished, of transept and nave. There was even an elevated stone platform that might have once served as an altar.

But if the original function had been votive, its present use was far different. Crates stood about here, too, but they contained no wine. Several were open, and when Kajumi lit a second match, something glittered instantly out of the top of one. Kneeling for a closer look, he caught his breath as he peered down into a hoard of gold coins.

A half-worn candle stood within a small niche. With his

dying second match, he lit it. The flame leapt up, casting huge guttering shadows on the dampish mortared walls above him. He moved from coins to bullion and paper tender in every conceivable currency and denomination. Stacked high against the wall were bars of silver and platinum, sixteen-kilo gold bricks, all in staggering profusion.

On the altarlike structure were scales for weighing metals, calipers for sizing gems, even bagging machinery for the handling of gold dust. Kajumi had stumbled upon his father's countinghouse. He had known of such a room in the Mendenhall cellars, but his father, as a sign of dissatisfaction with his son, had never chosen to bring him down there. Computing mentally the dollar value of what he saw there now, he estimated it to be something in the neighborhood of a half-billion dollars.

A sound, indeterminate and distant, brought him up. It was seemingly harmless, but he waited for it to come again. It did, however, only some time after he had resumed the examination of his father's treasures. How much of it, he feverishly wondered now, belonged rightfully to him? When the sound came a second time, it had direction and a certain ring of intent. There was an unmistakable furtiveness about it, like that of a moccasin or a soft slipper scuffing lightly over stone.

This time he took heed, snuffed out the candle and slipped quickly back behind a long retaining wall at the rear of the chamber. In a dank low vault behind the wall he waited, crouching in the penumbral light through which he could perceive shape but no color—only gradations of black in varying planes.

Waiting there he heard nothing save only the inner cadence of his own breathing and from somewhere far off the rushing of water. There was too a dirty trickle of seepage on the floor.

Still he heard nothing quite resembling the furtive steplike sound he'd heard before. A clammy sweat beaded his forehead. Breathless, he waited for what seemed an interminable period. The air in the altar room was chill and miasmal. There was a disagreeable odor of sulfur. Hunkered down beneath a joist, his legs started to cramp. He was aware of an overwhelming need to move.

He never did for in the next instant the altar room on the other side of the retaining wall suddenly flooded with light and though he could see nothing from the lair in which he crouched he was aware that someone was now standing inside the room.

Whoever it was, that person had entered as if he'd clearly expected to surprise someone there. He could hear the person breathing, then suddenly footsteps heavy and swift, grating over the stone. Kajumi fell back farther into the shadowy recesses of the vault, aware that the footsteps were coming at him on the far side of the wall. More than coming, they rushed toward him and he could feel vibrations in the floor trembling beneath him. The steps produced a frantic, scurrying, strangely feral sound like that of a large angry creature, butting and charging mindlessly about. The person responsible for those steps appeared to move all about the chamber, darting here and there, shifting crates and boxes, pausing momentarily, then plunging forward once more, as if he were searching for something.

Next the steps moved in a circular pattern, clockwise, then counterclockwise, coming to rest finally on the other side of the wall nearly directly opposite the place where Kajumi sprawled flat, face down, the P38 pistol cocked and ready. Guttural sounds like grunting were followed by what he knew to be the sound of someone vigorously sniffing. Suddenly, it occurred to him with a sense of sinking dread that the person on the far side of the wall was sniffing, just as he was, the odor of candle wax freshly melted and no doubt still warm.

His mind whirled. At any moment, he expected the person out there in the altar room to turn the corner and appear in the rectangle of gray light between the wall and vault.

Shortly the footsteps commenced again. This time they were slow and had taken on the character of careful premeditation, as if each additional step were being cautiously weighed. Kajumi could hear them creaking toward the far end of the retaining wall, then pause without turning. If whoever stood at the far end of the wall were suddenly to turn the corner, there was little doubt he would see Kajumi crouching there. He fully expected that. But, incredibly, it didn't happen. Instead, the footsteps turned and slowly receded, retreating back over the cold stone from whence they had come, leaving him behind, panting like a winded dog in the dark.

47

. . . two o'clock in the morning courage.
—NAPOLEON I: *Quoted by Las Casps, 1823*

Mariko had always been uneasy around her half-brother. Frightened would, perhaps, be a more precise description. They had never had strong familial ties. Possibly they'd even regarded themselves as strangers who happened to share a mutual father and thus inhabited a number of the same residences. Otherwise, they had nothing in common except perhaps the animosity and suspicion with which they eyed each other. In recent years, Mariko's unease had deepened even as Kajumi's behavior had grown increasingly secret and bizarre.

It was now past midnight in Vaduz. Mariko stood outside the door of her mother's bedroom. There was a crack of light under the jamb and noises emerged from within.

The wedding ceremony was scheduled to take place in four days at the little private chapel of Mendenhall. The reception for 300 was to commence directly after. It surprised Mariko that her mother was still up. Her day had started that morning at 6 A.M., overseeing all the preparations and ironing out countless last details. From there on, she had moved from one potential catastrophe to the next, never pausing to rest or take a bite of lunch. Now she was still up, with the full day ahead of her tomorrow bound to be even more taxing.

Mariko's hand rose to knock, then paused in mid-air. She heard her mother cough, and then the scratch of a match across a carbon strip to light a cigarette.

Mariko had not intended to go to her mother. At least, not on this night. She had no wish to add to Celestine's already full bundle of cares. But, something had prevented her from speaking to her father of her encounter, real or imagined, with Daughtry in Vaduz.

Moreover, that very day, seated in the little pantry office off the scullery, working out seating arrangements with Karl Heinz and Dieter, his assistant, another terrifying apparition had appeared. Momentary it was, and evanescent, the figure this time in white coveralls, a black leather apron and a chef's white toque, with a pair of sunglasses concealing the eyes. Knowing Kajumi, it was a ludicrous costume and yet she was certain that the wraithlike figure fleeting past the door was truly him. But why in heaven's name would he suddenly return to his own home in such outlandish disguise?

She had sat there, gaping at the empty space, her mind still unable to grasp what she had clearly seen with her own eyes.

Embarrassed, clearing his throat, Karl Heinz had to address her several times before she responded. At last she stood up, the two men staring after her, and walked several steps outside the pantry door, peering down the scullery in the same direction the figure had disappeared. Unable to shake her fears, she dialed house security and informed them that she had seen a stranger wandering about in the kitchen. They assured her they would check immediately. She never thought to identify the stranger by name. Still, her confusion persisted.

It was something of that feeling of confusion she wished to convey now to her mother. Celestine coughed again, and then came the high, fragile tinkle of cosmetic and cologne bottles.

Her fist still poised, Mariko suddenly heard a sigh from within—more a sound of despair than fatigue. For some inexplicable reason, she was unable to bring herself to knock. As with her father that morning, something deterred her. Instead, she turned abruptly and left.

The big winding catacombs beneath Mendenhall had always struck her as inhospitable. Even as a child, when her father had first taken her down there, she'd found the cellars gloomy and foreboding. There was the vast sprawling designlessness of the place, the sense of crushing weight atop her, and the wet streaked ancient masonry with its air of a dark history steeped in unspeakable secrets. Frequently Kajumi tried to lure her there in order to terrify her.

At that time the far-flung network of tunnels and countless lateral vaults feeding into the main corridors like vertebrae into a spine, was in a state of imminent collapse. The walls were mostly rubble. Rodents slithered noiselessly over the detritus of ages. Water leached in from the outside, bringing with it the rank putrescent odor of rot.

Since Mr. Sujimoto had taken occupancy, however, the place had undergone extensive renovation. Modern plumbing lines and central heating had been installed. Most of the tunnels had been rebuilt and electrified, and a system of pumps and dehumidification devices had dried out the place.

Standing at the head of the steep cobble stairs leading down to the cellars, Mariko experienced a sinking feeling at the prospect of descending. At 1 A.M. in the morning the place was as forlorn as a graveyard. Yet she deeply suspected Kajumi to be hidden somewhere down there, bent on mischief, a mischief born of morbid irrational hate.

Her father's personal bodyguard, Aito, whom she sent earlier to check the cellars, had found nothing. That should have allayed her fears, but instead, only heightened them. Try as she might, she could not shake the notion that Kajumi was nearby.

At the top of the stair descending into the cellars was a master switch controlling the lights throughout the entire tunnel system. She flicked it on, took a deep breath, closed the door behind her and started down the narrow vertiginous stairs.

The lights and small flambeaux niched in the stone walls glowed faintly, producing more shadow than illumination. Dressed only in a light robe and slippers, Mariko shivered in the cryptlike cold that gripped her at the first level of descent. Once below, she wasn't at all certain where to begin her search. Still, something prodded her forward and deeper into the lower levels of the catacombs. What she intended to do when, and if, she encountered Kajumi, she had not the slightest idea. Possibly try to reason with him. Deflect him from any contemplated violence. If he appeared in a truly dangerous state, she would then have to notify her father and, of course, the police.

Proceeding down a dimly lit corridor, she heard the sound of water trickling down a wall, the scurry of tiny animal feet in one of the vaults off to the right, and then the baying of a guard dog outside. Ruefully, she gazed backward through the dim tunnel and thought of retreating.

At a second level the tunnels grew uncomfortably narrow and oppressive. The icy chill of the stones crept upward through the soles of her slippers. The effort of will needed to continue increased steadily.

"I'm not going to let this thing throw me," she said to herself. "There's nothing here that frightens me. The dark doesn't frighten me. Kajumi doesn't frighten me. If he's here, I'll find him."

A board in one of the distant vaults contracted with a sharp ping, amplifying many times the sound as it reverberated through the subterranean tunnels. She froze and felt a fist close over her heart.

"Kajumi?" she called into the bleak, vaulted chambers ahead. Her voice coming back to her through the tunnels moaned horribly.

Descending another steep, cobwebbed stair, she was now at the third level, full of a sudden, terrifying sense of her own vulnerability. If she did encounter trouble, who was there to hear her cries?

236

Yet, what did she have to fear from Kajumi? If he was there, he surely hadn't come all this way to harm her. His business in Vaduz, she knew, was with her father and mother. The lights at this point were more sporadic and there were long, terrifying distances to cross between one point of illumination and the next.

She turned a corner, and there in a dim, sepulchral light she suddenly found herself on the threshold of the ancient altar room that served as her father's countinghouse.

She had often heard her father speak of this room. Once, during a school vacation, she'd asked him to show it to her. He laughed, winked his eye waggishly, and called it her dowry, but he declined to take her down there. She repeated her request on several occasions, but he'd always found some excuse not to oblige her. It had remained, therefore, a part of the catacombs forever off limits to her.

Standing there now, she forgot completely her initial terror. What she felt, instead, was a sense of mounting anticipation, a leaping excitement, mingled with the uncomfortable sense that she was about to learn something she would have preferred not to.

She stepped down the four stone stairs into the circular room, her eyes fixed directly before her, afraid to look, yet unable to avert her eyes from the crates and boxes, the great chests of currency and precious metals, the surrounding walls aglow with the ghostly sheen of kilo bricks of bullion running from ceiling to floor. In a slow, almost stately gait, she progressed from one heap of treasure to the next, fighting back as she went a sense of growing anger. This countless wealth buried here—how was it come by? She was neither gullible nor a fool. The fact that it had to be buried and kept out of sight seemed to tell all. Here, at last, was her father's true church, and there the altar at which he worshipped. Here was the sum of his life's efforts and, to Mariko, ample evidence of his guilt. If she had entertained any lingering childish hope of her father's self-proclaimed innocence, she did not any more.

When she started moving again, she had no idea that she was crying; only that she felt this sense of profound sorrow. It seemed to her that her life had arrived at some kind of culmination, as if innumerable wild unruly streams, coursing in a multitude of directions, had flowed together at the point where she now stood, all united at this fatal confluence to form a thunderous, surging cataract.

Her quickening footsteps had led her, independent of any conscious willing, to the end of the retaining wall that stood as a support between the altar room and the low narrow beehive of vaults standing behind it.

The illumination at this point was rudimentary and, for a moment, Mariko stood at the wall's end, trying to adjust her eyes to the sudden deprivation of light. The small beehive of stone cells beyond had a distinctly threatening air. For a moment they gave her pause, but the vacillation was only fleeting. Without further hesitation, she took a bold first step in. When she had managed that, the rest was easy. Mariko was not tall, but she found that she had to stoop when she entered this close, uncomfortably restrictive area.

"Kajumi," she whispered into the shadows. The name sounded alien and faintly menacing on her lips. She moved from one coal cell to the next, looking for some sign, any telltale evidence. "Kajumi," she called again. "Are you there? Kajumi? It's me."

She had scoured four bins and found them devoid of any sign of recent habitation; at the fifth, she fought back her doubt and disappointment. At the farthest one, the sixth, she lifted her robe, crouched on her knees, and groped blindly along the floor, all the time whispering "Kajumi" a little frantically as she went. "Please answer me. I know you're down here."

She waited, but no answer came. The doubt of moments before gave way to full-fledged despair. At last she rose, fighting back her confusion and anger. There was nothing. He was not there. And as she made her way out of the bin, half stooping beneath the low joists, her foot struck something. She shrieked.

If was soft and airy, infinitely yielding. At first she thought it was some kind of living creature. But in the next moment she pounced on it as if it were a treasure, her fitful hands groping for it in the dark. When at last her fist closed triumphantly round it, she knew what it was, even before she'd actually seen it. Brought up level to her eyes, she examined it. It was a big, white floppy baker's toque.

48

Take your time. Stay away from the easy going.
Never go the same way twice.
—GUNNERY SERGEANT CHARLES ARNDT, USMC:
(Rules for successful reconnaissance, Guadalcanal,
1942)

"I'm dissatisfied with the camellias."

"The absence of rain, I'm afraid, sir."

"Last year we had prize camellias. These are puny. Trivial."

"We watered each day, sir."

"Not enough, I fear. Too little and too late."

The gardener lowered his head and followed, mortified in his master's wake. In the face of rebuke he was flushed and pitifully defenseless. "We tried hard to bring them back, sir. But it was an unfortunate combination of unseasonably warm weather and draft."

"I am unimpressed with such excuses." Sujimoto lifted his robes delicately and swept forward. Having detected some sign of dereliction in his rank, he became an avenging angel. "Show me at once the agapanthus and woe unto you, if they are poor."

The two men moved together through the long formal aisles of spring flowers. Sujimoto, toddling forward in his robes and gesticulating at the waving flowers, kept up an endless stream of condemnation, while the gardener, chastised and gloomy, trailed along behind at a discreet distance.

At the same moment, not more than several hundred yards off, well concealed behind the screen of towering spruce surrounding the perimeter of Mendenhall, a solitary man lay prone in the grass. Attired in lederhosen and desert boots, he toted a knapsack full of picnic sandwiches and wore a camera and binoculars round his neck. As he lay there uncomfortably in a bed of pine spills, he busied himself by observing the two garden strollers through a pair of high-powered binoculars.

Had he been challenged just then by any of the grounds-keepers or the private security guard, he would have identified himself as an American tourist who had set out from a nearby inn that morning for a day's outing along the Alpine trails above Lake Constance, and had inadvertently lost his way. A call to the inn would have quickly corroborated this.

But had anyone chosen to make more careful, more strenuous inquiries, they might have uncovered the fact that the gentleman Alpinist was, in fact, Charles Daughtry. This had been his third surveillance mission to Mendenhall, and while he knew perfectly well he had no real authority to move against the fugitive financier in the jurisdiction of Liechtenstein, or anywhere else for that matter, he had resolved in his mind that the moment Mr. Sujimoto was so foolish as to leave Liechtenstein, he'd be right there to pounce upon him.

A short time later, several miles away in Ragaz, Daughtry was back at the inn, sprawled full-length on the floor of his room. Surrounded by sheets of discarded paper and pegboard and while his impressions were fresh in his mind, he scribbled hectically a number of diagrams and schematic drawings.

One drawing showed four different elevations of Mendenhall indicating points of entrance and egress. Another showed the immediate environs of the castle within a radius of three miles; another was a rough organizational chart of the house staff, broken down in terms of butlers, chambermaids, maintenance personnel, groundskeepers, security forces and personal body-guards. Code numbers had been assigned to each category, designating their hierarchy of importance based upon physical proximity to Mr. Sujimoto. The same chart also showed anticipated daily frequency of personal contact with him.

240

From public records in Vaduz, Daughtry had secured maps and surveys of the castle. The survey maps showed topography, wood trails and a number of lakes and streams crisscrossing the deeply wooded property. Also shown there was a derelict pumphouse, made obsolete now by the recent installation of modern water lines.

Daughtry had meticulously compiled several charts, attempting to graph the daily movements of the security force. One dealt exclusively with manpower (twenty-six according to a head count he himself had carefully conducted while secreted in the vast encircling forest), a second made a rough inventory of the security's various weaponry described in terms of number and type. Still another charted the route, with a 24-hour timetable for each security patrol of the perimeter. This information Daughtry had carefully gathered and collated over three successive days of patient surveillance.

To a wall above his bed he had taped a large, tattered square of parchment at the top of which the word STRATEGICS appeared in large handprinted block letters. Various geometrical symbols had been scrawled there. Thin red-ink lines ran from one figure to the next. To all rectilinear shapes, he had affixed a large S indited in the center, standing, no doubt, for Sujimoto. Circular figures bore a P for Plevissier. The M for Mariko appeared within equilateral triangles. Aito, whom Daughtry knew well from Tokyo, was assigned a trapezoid; the octagonals with K stood for Karl Heinz, whom he knew not at all. A rhomboid shape with a large X signified Security. Daughtry depicted himself in short chunky cylinders with a large D.

The geometrical figures were cutouts with stickum on the obverse side for easy movement round the pegboard. Lying in bed on his back, he could move the symbols about to show their manifold interrelationships.

On the same parchment, in columns off to the side, were two lists; one headed ALLIES, the other FOES. Allies were listed in black, foes in red. Under Foes first came Sujimoto, followed by Plevissier, followed by Mariko, Aito, Karl Heinz, and finally,

Security. Under Allies he listed himself. Directly beneath that the name Mariko appeared again, but this time in small letters followed by a question mark.

Daughtry's perception of the tactical situation before him commenced by placing the rectangle with the large S in the center of the board securely encircled by all of the geometrical symbols listed under Foes. Assembled on the board they gave the appearance of satellites swirling in orbit round a common sun.

The cylindrical figure standing outside that protective, seemingly impregnable perimeter hovered there in paper space, solitary and watchful, seeking a soft, vulnerable underbelly through which it might penetrate.

49

Look to the front.
—Motto of the Rifle Brigade, British Army

It was Sujimoto seated facing the wood who saw him first, the gray solitary spot moving boldly up the gradual acclivity from the forest without any attempt to conceal the fact. It merely came on marching with an air of jaunty resolution.

Sujimoto had been discoursing widely on currency fluctuations and the impact of discount rates on the recent volatility in the money markets. Then his eye happened to glimpse the solitary figure moving up the hill toward them.

It was late afternoon. They'd been taking tea outdoors in the garden—Sujimoto, Celestine and Mariko. The sun dropping in the west was at a position roughly behind the solitary walker, thus making identification all the more difficult. The sweet roll, moving on a course from the table to his lips, paused in midflight. Sujimoto had no sense of alarm, and yet the abrupt termination of his talk tended to convey a sense of alarm to the others.

At first he thought it was a dog or a large animal and he glanced up sharply.

"Father—"

"Sujimoto—" Celestine and Mariko both spoke at the same moment, but he raised a finger to a point above his eye; a light, swift, definitive gesture that had the effect of silencing them. All the while they followed the line of his unswerving gaze to the gray figure moving inexorably closer.

By the time the figure had reached the table, Sujimoto had regained sufficient composure to say, "You have your gall walking in here like this, Mr. Daughtry."

"It is a bit unorthodox"— Daughtry smiled—"even for me." He nodded to both Celestine and Mariko, both of whom gaped at him incredulously.

Daughtry turned back to Sujimoto. "I realize this is not the most opportune moment for a social call."

The air of good-natured mockery was not lost on Sujimoto. "My sense of humor, Mr. Daughtry, does not transcend my sense of survival. Give me one good reason why I shouldn't have Aito come out here and break your back."

"Because, whether you like it or not, you don't want the world to see what a villain you really are."

"That is impertinent." Madame de Plevissier rose. She was livid and trembling. "May I ask how you were able to elude the guard posted all around here?"

"Easy." Daughtry smiled exasperatingly. "They're not very good. Actually, I came right through your backyard."

Sujimoto fumed.

"Oh, by the way," Daughtry lilted wickedly, "may I offer you both my belated but heartfelt congratulations."

"So that *was* you skulking around Vaduz yesterday," Mariko finally chimed in.

"I regret that."

243

"This is all very cynical and underhanded," she went on.

"I tend to get cynical and underhanded when I feel threatened."

"I wonder who's threatening whom." Celestine's gaze was withering.

Sujimoto gaped at his daughter more baffled than ever.

"I should have told you, Father. I was in Vaduz yesterday. In a jewelry shop. And I saw him in the window."

"You saw him"— Celestine sank back into her seat—"and you said nothing?"

"I wasn't certain. One moment he was there, and the next, he was gone." She rushed on breathlessly, aware that the story as she recounted it had the tinny clink of implausibility. "I know I should have said something. I didn't want to get you all alarmed. Particularly if I wasn't certain. But, I should have at least alerted the guards."

"Not to concern yourself." Sujimoto grew expansive and consoling. "I will attend to the guards. Aito will make up for their complacency." He reached for a small handbell used to summon butlers and valets, but Madame de Plevissier stayed his hand.

"Wait, I'd like to know a little more of this before we have Aito in. Will you kindly tell us, Mr. Daughtry, why you chose this time to come to Vaduz?"

"I came here to take Mr. Sujimoto back with me to New York." Daughtry's self-possession was stunning. "I want him to testify with me before the grand jury."

"You do have a certain audacity, Mr. Daughtry. I admire this blunt frontal attack. But did you really expect me to simply get up and go with you voluntarily?"

"I had hoped you would. If not, I'm prepared to take you by force."

Sujimoto stared quizzically at the impertinent young man, uncertain whether to laugh once more or shout for the guards.

Mariko rose and came toward Daughtry. "Why don't you

244

leave now, before there is a great deal of trouble?" She glanced at him uneasily, wanting to stave off any sort of physical encounter with Aito or the guard. "Please go."

"Sit down, Mariko." Sujimoto's voice behind her had a shrill edge.

"I won't. Not until he leaves."

"Aito will soon attend to that." Once more Sujimoto reached for the bell, but again Celestine deterred him.

"I think you'd better hear him out," she said, all the while her eyes fixed steadily on Daughtry, taking for herself the true measure of his intent. Observing him standing there, she had come to one of those swift precise appraisals that are forced inescapably upon one during the course of an emergency.

Sujimoto stared up at her. He looked baffled and a little hurt. His own instinct now was to dispose of Daughtry as neatly and expeditiously as possible.

Celestine continued: "I think we'd probably better hear everything Mr. Daughtry has to say. Put down that bell, Hiroji. Mr. Daughtry, will you have some tea?"

Several hours later when Daughtry left, Mariko saw him out. A pale lemon sliver of moon had risen up over the rim of distant mountains to the east. Daughtry had phoned for a taxi to take him back down to Ragaz, and together now they stood in the gravel dirt beneath the twilight sky.

"This is really too idiotic of you, Daughtry," Mariko fumed.

"Given my present situation, I don't see that I have much choice."

"Your present situation?"

"Professionally, I'm ruined. There's not a bank of any significance that would touch me with a barge pole. In addition, I face the unenviable prospect of spending the next six to ten years in jail. Your father happens to hold the key to how well I make out before the grand jury next week."

Until then she had scarcely ever taken into account Daughtry's heavy embroilment in the Confederated scandal; she had only considered that of her father's, which might well, in turn, affect her. Now suddenly Daughtry's brash, almost careless enumeration of woes struck home.

"It won't happen," she said. "None of that is going to happen."

"It's nice to have your assurances," he replied acidly.

"My father won't let that happen. Do you think he'd let someone else take the full blame—" It occurred to her she was pleading her father's cause and that dismayed her. "The other night on the phone—"

"Yes?"

"You said something about—"

"Kajumi. Yes. In New York. He made what the police describe as an attempt on my life."

The expression on her face wavered between wariness and despair. "He didn't really?" was all she could say, but she didn't doubt it for a moment. All the pluck had gone out of her, and she said it again. "He didn't really?"

"I can assure you he did. I suppose to prevent my testifying." He watched a multitude of thoughts rushing behind her eyes. "Your father—by any chance, he didn't—"

"No." She cut him short. "And don't dare suggest it. Under no circumstances would he ever consider—"

A wicked gleam pervaded his bright, unsympathetic eyes.

She had started to tremble. "You have no proof—nothing. And yet—"

"True," he conceded. "I don't even know for sure that Kajumi was in New York that night. The police are not at all certain, either."

"And yet you dare suggest—" Even her indignation, he thought, was attractive.

"On the other hand, what proof do you have that he wasn't in New York?"

The question caught her off balance. Daughtry, seeing the advantage, continued: "Didn't you tell me on the phone that he was untraceable in Monte Carlo, where he was supposed to be?"

246

"Yes, but—" A vision of the white toque lying limply on the floor of a coalbin flashed before her eyes.

At that moment the crisscrossing headlights of the taxi appeared at the crest of the drive, swept round the wide arc of gravel and drew up to the portê cochere where they waited. Daughtry pulled open the rear door. "But what?"

She stammered something about "No proof" and "My father would never," then suddenly, as if it had been the last thing she intended, she blurted it out. "Be careful, Daughtry. He's here."

Daughtry's eyes narrowed. "Kajumi?"

"Yes. Right here. Probably on the grounds."

"Where?"

"I don't know. Someplace. But concealed. My father doesn't even know yet. Believe me, I'm certain."

Whatever doubts he'd had, the force of her last line had convinced him. The cab waited, while the driver, stolid and uncaring, stared straight ahead.

"You didn't have to tell me that," he replied. "But I'm very happy you did."

"My father would never—" Before she could protest again he'd pressed a finger to her lip as if to silence her. "Come see me. I'm at the inn in Ragaz."

50

. . . two o'clock in the morning courage.
—NAPOLEON I, *Memoirs, 1815*

"I sleep beneath the stars. I take my place amid wheeling constellations. I scrape my head on the roof of the sky. I float free in boundless, gray silences. I am embedded in glacial ice—cold, removed, unreachable. I join my most noble ancestors here amid the dazzle of stellar light. Where am I now, Mother? Closer to you. Noble Grandfather, Isamura—embrace me, welcome me.

Succor me. I have stumbled badly. I have caused embarrassment to departed uncles, cousins, venerable grandparents, and all proud ancestors before them. All my noble antecedents, here with me in the star-blown sky. Kajumi is a constellation rising in the eastern sky. Kajumi is a seven-star figure kneeling in the night sky—a hunter crouching—legs coiled tight as springs, one arm thrust forward for balance on the ground, the other cocked rearward as if holding a sling, a catapulting device. The hunter crouches in the night sky, poised, ready to pounce. Frozen in gray time like some fossil creature entombed in ice. He sleeps there, dreaming and waiting for the moment he will wake and slay the dragon."

A thin, pale sliver of moon hung weightless above the jagged, sawtooth line of Alpine peaks. Stars flickered in the mauve-gray predawn sky.

Kajumi Sujimoto lay on his back in the sodden grass of an open meadow, shivering in his damp clothes. His eyes half-drowsed with sleeplessness, he watched the whirring stars, and heard a fox bark in the distance. Limbs stiff, clothing heavy with dew, he had been lying there several hours. After the scary encounter with the unseen searcher in the coal cellar, and then the pistol episode on the terrace, he had fled, frightened that his presence would soon be discovered.

He had no place to go and no clear idea of what he wished to do. For the time being, he sought refuge in an unused cow pasture several miles or so from the main house. At times he knew all too well what he wished to do—knew it with burning, incandescent clarity. But shortly he would forget what he had known only moments before, his mind lapsing into dreams; then he would have to work very hard to recall his deadly purpose. While drowsing in the tall meadow grass, he imagined he was in Sapporo in his mother's house, lying in bed in early morning, looking across at the tiered roof of a pagoda reflected upside down in the still pond outside his window. Confoundingly, his orientation shifted once again to New York. He imagined himself at the Neptune Hotel on Battery Park in the squalid little

248

room with the sour bedding and the sound of someone coughing in the room next door. But again, in the next moment, he was amid a rude crowd of pushing, gawking people in a fetid Tokyo back alley. Onlookers watched the fantastic shapes and colors of a spectacular conflagration. On the retinal screen of his eye, flames leaped brightly upward into the frigid heavens, blades of exquisite fire filling him with a warm, thrusting, sexual excitement.

It confused him the way the scenes shifted so quickly. Sometimes they would collide and run together, then burst into millions of kaleidoscopic fragments bearing no thematic relation to one another. He wondered why his mind played such tricks on him.

"Deceitful, treacherous mind," he murmured softly at the receding flames and counted to ten to steady his nerves. Calm again, he watched the profusion of stars gliding overhead, experiencing, as he did, a sensation of disembodiment. At first he fought back the terrifying sense of losing control over himself. Then he succumbed to it eagerly. Suddenly he was airborne, free of gravity, a gay balloon cut free of all its earthly moorings, free of the oppressiveness of his own flesh; free, amid the chaste, serene stars. Looking downward from a great height, he could see his body, a heap of noisome rags, lying lifeless and limp below.

Amid the bright clear night of stars, countless planets, meteors, glowing trillions of miles away, he felt secure and protected. Abruptly the scene shifted again and he was earth-bound, alone and shivering in the damp meadow. Shivering in his rumpled clothing, his limbs stiff and aching. Wracking his befuddled mind, he tried to recall how he had come there, and what it was exactly he was going to do. Rising inadvertently and rolling sidewards, he felt the hard jarring of the pistol in his pocket push against him, and then he knew.

51

Force and fraud are, in war, the two cardinal virtues.
—THOMAS HOBBES: *The Leviathan, 1651*

"What do you mean, Kajumi is here?"

"I mean just that. He's here in this house."

"Now?"

"If not in the house, then somewhere on the grounds."

They were in Sujimoto's study upstairs beneath the old clock tower; he, Celestine and Mariko. Karl Heinz hovered anxiously in the background, wringing his hands.

On Sujimoto's wide-planked oak desk a white chef's toque, crumpled and soiled, lay limp, like some newly murdered creature.

"And now you tell me this incredible story about Kajumi masquerading about in the kitchen as some sort of cook. And then, this extraordinary business about Daughtry and a hand grenade."

"Exactly, Father. That's exactly what's been going on. It's all true. I notified the guard immediately. They scoured the grounds. I sent Aito down to search the basement. And several hours ago"— she held up the toque—"I found this down there myself."

Pursed-lipped and glaring, Sujimoto scrutinized his daughter as if he'd never set eyes on her before. Baffled, he shook his head, shrugged his shoulders, and gazed appealingly at Celestine.

"We must notify the police," she said, after a moment.

"No." Sujimoto's hands flailed the air. "I don't want any of that."

"You must, Father. There's no telling what he'll do. He's clearly deranged."

250

"I don't want the police, I tell you." Sujimoto's voice was shrill. Karl Heinz wrung his hands all the harder as the atmosphere in the lofty, book-lined study heated up.

"I agree with Mariko. You can't permit it to go on like this any longer." Celestine clasped his hand and patted it across the desk. "You know how badly Kajumi has slipped over the past year."

The old man pursed his bluish lips and raked his fingers through his hair. "I didn't want any of this now," he murmured with an air of self-pity. "I don't need it. First Daughtry. And now Kajumi, with a wedding to get through in a few days."

"None of us needed it, Father. The point is, we've got it. The only sane, responsible thing is to get hold of Kajumi fast before he does anything rash."

"Rash?" The word had the effect of a lash on Sujimoto. He glowered first, then smirked at his daughter. "Such as what, Mariko? You mean such as harming your precious Mr. Daughtry?"

"There's no need for any of that," Celestine continued a little desperately. "No need at all."

But her words went for naught. Sujimoto was smoldering. "Is that the rash act you're thinking of, Mariko?"

She was clearly frightened, and when at last she spoke it took all of her will to control the quaver in her voice. "Since you mention it, Father, that is a distinct possibility."

"Ah ha." Sujimoto leaned back and clapped his palms triumphantly. "So now at last we have it."

Celestine rubbed her temples fretfully. "Please, please."

"And since you are unkind enough to suggest such a thing"—Mariko's eyes glistened—"I must tell you that Daughtry, and apparently the New York police, too, believe that it was *you* who sent Kajumi to New York to silence Daughtry."

Sujimoto's jaw dropped. He sat silent for some time, slouching in his chair, his fingers drumming tattoos on the desk top. When he looked up again, at last, scrutinizing Mariko, there seemed little left of the father and daughter between them. At that moment they were clearly adversaries.

"And you, Mariko," Sujimoto persisted with almost ominous quiet, "what do you believe?"

"Sujimoto," Celestine implored.

"You believe this, Mariko?"

"It's a question that must now be fully explored."

"I didn't ask you that, Mariko," he bore down ruthlessly. "I asked if you believed—"

"How can she possibly answer that?"

"Madame," Sujimoto hissed through clenched teeth, "please not to interfere between my daughter and—"

"She is my daughter, too." Celestine's voice rose. "And please let us not forget that."

Ill-accustomed as he was to any form of defiance, Sujimoto's eyes fluttered. Momentarily flustered, however, he quickly regained his composure. "Karl Heinz," he snapped, "notify the security to make another complete search of the grounds. Send the chief of security to me. I personally want an accounting of how Daughtry was able to walk on to this property, virtually unchallenged. After that, send Aito to me."

For some time after Karl Heinz had left they were silent. Sujimoto shuffled a number of portentous-looking documents about on his desk top, aware of, but not acknowledging, the two women seated there, regarding him quietly. Adversity, he thought, had drawn mother and daughter together in some kind of alliance against him. So this is the way it is to be, he thought, feeling betrayal percolating all about him.

The area in his stomach that had given him such pain had started to throb beneath his belt. It had commenced with a sharp jab, causing him to stifle a gasp before he could speak. When at last he did, his voice had a husky, uncharacteristic breathiness.

"One further question, Mariko, and then we may terminate this conversation." He gazed back and forth from daughter to mother like a magistrate cautioning defendants on their rights.

252

"I think I know now where you stand regarding the matter we just discussed," he went on grimly. "Tell me, daughter, knowing what you do of Daughtry's reasons for coming here, do you still intend to continue seeing him?"

"Seeing him?"

"On a social basis, that is?"

"Father—" she commenced, but he waved her to silence at once.

"For I must tell you that if you do, you must leave this house forever."

"Dear God," Celestine gasped.

"I will go now." Mariko rose.

Sujimoto was startled by the swift decisiveness of the reply. "So, that is your loyalty . . . your support."

"While I had no special plans"—Mariko's eyes blazed— "to see Daughtry, I will not stay in this house under any limitations to my freedom."

Sujimoto stiffened. "No Japanese child—"

"I am neither Japanese," Mariko lashed out, "nor a child." Her eyes filled and words clogged in her throat. In the next moment she was up, half striding, half running across the room. The huge, oak-paneled door banged thunderously behind her.

Afterward, Sujimoto and Celestine sat alone, opposite each other. Neither spoke. Eyes lowered, once again shuffling papers, Sujimoto pretended to be unperturbed. The throb in his side had intensified until he could feel all the pain, like the point of a drill, concentrated in a single burning spot.

"Sujimoto," Celestine began. She was as gray and ashen as he'd ever seen her.

"If you are going to say something unpleasant about the wedding, I prefer that you save it for the morning."

"I think we must talk about it now." She could see the hurt and bewilderment in his eyes. "Is it still that important to you?"

"I'm not happy, Celestine." He broke suddenly into French. "I don't like it here. I want to go back to Okitsu. To my home. . . above the beach. . . ." His voice trailed off wistfully.

"Answer me," she pressed him hard. "Do you still want this wedding?"

"More than anything," he gasped. The pain soared through him like a knife blade. "It's the only thing I have left that I care anything about."

"You may very well have lost your child today."

"Oh . . . she'll be back." Sujimoto laughed with hollow bravado.

"I wouldn't be too sure." She paused a moment, reflecting. "Between you and Daughtry, I can't say who is victim and who is victimizer. I suspect there's something of each on both sides. In any event, I will not be a part of this wedding with my own child banished from my home. And I can assure you she will not return here under the terms you impose. I'd be very much disappointed in her if she did. I suspect you've succeeded now in driving her right into Daughtry's arms. So if you do still want this wedding, my darling, you had better start thinking about suing for peace with Mr. Daughtry. It strikes me he holds the key."

Shortly after Celestine's departure, Sujimoto was still seated where he'd been, elbows on desk top, face buried in upturned palms. He recognized all too clearly his predicament. He was neither so foolish nor so blind that he failed to see that by a single stroke that afternoon, Daughtry had effectively driven a wedge between not only Mariko and himself, but now also between Celestine and himself. Very real questions, he could see, now existed in their minds as to the extent of his real involvement in the collapse of the Confederated. With a bold, deft thrust, Daughtry had managed to alienate Sujimoto from his closest and most valuable allies.

The trick, he knew, was to regain their sympathies. This could be accomplished by a rush of humility. He might accept, or appear at least to tolerate, his daughter's friendship with Charles Daughtry. A bitter pill, indeed, but undoubtedly necessary if he was to regain the support of his loved ones. A picture of Kajumi, fugitive and secreted somewhere nearby, flashed through his mind. His heart ached at the same moment that it leapt with some new barely defined hope. The idea of both salvation and destruction suddenly overwhelmed him.

A faint knock sounded at the door. "Enter," Sujimoto said in Japanese without looking up. Locks clicked hollowly in the high, cool room and, in the next instant, the enormous bulk of Aito loomed in the open doorway.

52

In all the trade of war no feat is nobler than a brave retreat.
—SAMUEL BUTLER: *Hudibras, 1663*

When she left Mendenhall, Mariko drove directly to Vaduz and checked into a small *pensione* she knew there. It was full of students and cyclists and young people with knapsacks and vague plans to walk across the Continent or at least over the Alps.

She had no idea how long she would stay there or where, in particular, she intended to go. She only knew that she needed time to assess her situation. Departing Mendenhall that night had an air of finality about it. If the experience had been frightening, it had also, in the most improbable way, been exhilarating.

The little room in which she found herself now, with its narrow cot and night table, was spotless, austere and smelled faintly of antiseptic. It might have been the room of an acolyte in some rigorously self-abnegating religious order. It did not depress her. Quite the contrary, it produced a decidedly pleasant jolt to her drooping spirits. Later, departing her room to use the common lav at the end of the hall, she felt a camaraderie with her fellow residents lingering there. Their footloose independence, their brave, cheerful poverty, rather moved her.

Her flight from Mendenhall had been precipitate. She had taken nothing with her but a few toiletries and a change or two of underwear, all tossed haphazardly into a small overnight bag. She took everything out now and set it methodically out on the bureau opposite her cot, taking mental inventory as if these were all her earthly possessions. After that she sat stiffly on the edge of the cot, hands clasped, and wondered what she would do next.

She thought of the impending wedding and then of her mother, and her heart ached. When she thought next of her father, the ache intensified. She felt no anger toward him, only a sharp hurt, like that of a recent wound. It occurred to her that this hurt had always been there, but that through a curious act of self-denial she had for years been able to disregard it. Now that wound, or breech, had grown too wide ever to be sutured. She could not then envision a time when she could ever go back to live under her father's roof.

Lastly, there was the question of Daughtry and the nagging ambivalence she felt toward him. She suspected that her ambivalence grew out of her mother's—not her father's—negativity on the subject. She trusted Celestine's negativity to be objective, while she knew her father's to be the product of self-interest.

She both envied and admired Daughtry; envied him that easy air of self-assurance he appeared to convey; that mystique of omniscience that hovers over individuals within whom a large body of complex information resides. Be it real or illusory, its impact was considerable on Mariko, who felt mostly powerless in a world in which she had stored up very little by way of a fortress for the ego.

Sitting there at the edge of the rickety cot, hands clasped as if in prayer, another facet of her ambivalence toward Daughtry emerged. While she never regarded him as particularly attractive, nonetheless he exerted upon her a powerful sexual attraction. Analyzing that, she realized that the attraction sprang from the fact that he had traits she greatly admired but sadly lacked;

qualities in Daughtry that intimidated her, just as they did in her father. The truth being that despite her father's strong distrust of the man, she knew very well that he admired Daughtry, even feared him, and that was the basis of her envy.

It had been that same envy that had driven Kajumi to the desperate act of making an attempt on Daughtry's life. Even more than his half-sister, Kajumi had felt displaced by the young currency trader in the affections of his father. And if Mariko felt resentment toward Daughtry, Kajumi felt hatred—a very big, unreasoning, all-consuming, ungovernable hatred. The kind of hatred that is powered by one's own sense of utter worthlessness and defeat.

Kajumi had already made one attempt on Daughtry's life. Mariko had no doubt that there would be others. Further, she knew for a certainty that Kajumi was somewhere at Mendenhall; if not actually within, then somewhere dangerously nearby. The fact that he had gone to the trouble of secreting himself was alarming enough; whether or not he had yet discovered that Daughtry was also in the vicinity was too terrifying to contemplate.

Without much additional soul-searching, and with virtually no qualms at all, her first instinct after flight from the nest was to fly directly to Daughtry before Kajumi himself might reach there.

53

Counterattack is the soul of defense.
—JULIAN CORBETT: *Some Principles of Maritime Strategy, 1911*

Still attired in robe and pajamas, Mr. Sujimoto in his study commenced his morning reading. That involved the financial pages of several newspapers, journals of politics and geopolitics, consumer price indices, interest rates, rates of unemployment,

257

trade balances and deficits, plus reports of the ever-shifting policies of central banks and *bourses* round the world.

For him, reading of this nature had almost a ritual air about it. Conducted in the solitude of his study, no day could begin for Sujimoto without first the solemn ceremony of this daily, matutinal rite. On recent tips from highly placed, well-informed sources, he had learned that as a result of the plummeting dollar, the Fed planned shortly to raise the discount rate significantly and buy up sizable amounts of dollars. This meant that gold prices would fall and the dollar, which had nose-dived so drastically as a result of the Confederated-Sujimoto debacle, would soon start to rise. The question was *when*.

He intended that very morning to begin divesting himself of millions of dollars in yen so as to build up a long position in the U.S. currency. He had four ways he might go about that, those being the purchase of dollars in *outrights, spots, forwards* or *swaps.*

Another ingredient of this heady brew was that if Sujimoto intended to purchase U.S. dollars in a forward transaction (he was now leaning in that direction), he had to figure into the equation whether the *forward* exchange rate for dollars was higher than the *spot* rate. If so, the currency would be trading at a premium; if lower, then the currency would be trading forward at a discount.

As of that moment, with U.S. dollars on currency and money markets still sagging badly, forward exchange rates for them would be trading at attractive discounts, and it was here where Sujimoto would likely strike.

Additional facets of the same problem led the old man to study the spread in yen on the London, Tokyo, Hong Kong, New York markets over the past several days in order to try and predict the general direction in which that currency was now moving.

Sujimoto knew that he held several hundred million in yen in accounts round the world. A sizable amount of that was stored right there in his cellars at Mendenhall. The divestiture of

258

such a large sum of yen would have the effect of depressing the price of the currency on the world market. People fleeing the descending yen would, of necessity, flock to the rising dollar. Quite simply, his plan would be to make a simultaneous, spot/forward purchase of U.S. dollars financed by a simultaneous forward/spot sale of his treasure trove of yen.

The only question that remained in his mind was the crucial one of pegging both value dates correctly so as to maximize the profits from this transaction. Science could not help him here. This could only be accomplished by a kind of inspired wizardry.

That morning, however, Sujimoto could not summon up the requisite wizardry. His mind was not clear. Quite the contrary; it was badly fragmented. All the domestic-legal buzz of the past several days had taken its toll. He had no idea of Mariko's whereabouts, although he guessed she was with Daughtry. His wedding was the day after tomorrow, and Madame de Plevissier was still coldly aloof. More than that, the throbbing pain in his side, bearable and contained only by powerful painkillers, appeared to be reaching out into other parts of his body. His small fingers trembled up and down the daily rate listings while he attempted to make tabulations with a small desk computer.

A knock sounded at the door and in the next moment Aito entered. He wore the breathless, slightly sheepish look that always overtook him in the presence of his master.

Sujimoto glared up impatiently. "Well?"

"She is in Ragaz, Sujimoto-san."

"Alone?"

The big fellow grew flustered and looked away.

"Oh, come, Aito."

"Not alone, Sujimoto-san."

"With him then?" Sujimoto spoke with that trace of irritation that obsequious groveling invariably aroused in him.

"Yes, san. In Ragaz. At the inn."

"The same room?"

Aito wrung his thick, stubby hands.

"For God's sake, man . . ."

259

"Yes, san. The same room."

Sujimoto sighed slowly, a thin, exquisitely protracted hiss, and tipped backward in his chair. For some time he sat like that, tilted back, eyes closed, as if meditating, while the big sweating man, shifting from foot to foot, hovered about him in a state of miserable anticipation.

When Sujimoto's eyes opened again, he appeared strangely tranquil, like one coming out of a trance. Having resolved some outstanding question in his mind, his manner became composed and matter-of-fact.

"Now hear me carefully, Aito," he snapped.

54

War without allies is bad enough—
with allies it is hell!
—SIR JOHN SLESSOR: *Strategy for the West, 1954*

"Why do you stare at me so?"

"Do I?" His smile carried a question. "I suppose because it gives me pleasure."

"Please do not do so any more. It's disconcerting to look up and find your eyes fastened on me."

"You make it sound unwholesome."

She flicked her long hair petulantly and glanced quickly round at diners at surrounding tables. "Not unwholesome. Just damned embarrassing."

It was a little Swiss bistro near the inn at Ragaz where they were staying. He paid the check now and they walked out under a star-cluttered sky into a parking lot illuminated by floodlights.

Mariko drove the Volkswagen while Daughtry, eyes closed, sat back in his seat smoking. Lulled by wine, strangely contented, he had been completely unaware of the van that had pulled out of the parking lot shortly after them.

"Why don't you say something?" she said after a moment.

The narrow ribbon of mountain road unfurling like a scroll before them glowed a chalky luminous white.

"I'm very happy we're here together," he said after some lengthy consideration.

"You've already said that."

"It bears repeating."

"Having now repeated it on at least five separate occasions, will you now tell me just what your immediate plans are?"

"Regarding your father?"

She moaned miserably and adjusted the rearview mirror so as to diminish the glare reflected there by headlights from the car just behind them.

"I have no plans regarding your father."

"You said you were here to take him back to the States. You said you were prepared to take him by force."

"That was all bravado."

She shot him a sidelong skeptical glance. "So you're going home empty-handed then, I take it?"

"I didn't say that."

In the faint green glow of the dashboard, she appeared suddenly uneasy. "You know he believes he's innocent, betrayed by everyone, including his family. Why should he leave?"

"He won't." Daughtry leaned his head back and closed his eyes. "But you will, won't you?"

He glanced up at her, smiling, but she continued to drive, wordless, unresponding, her eyes riveted to the road ahead.

"Won't you?" he asked again.

His strategy suddenly became clear.

"I want you to know, Daughtry, that whatever my father is, whatever he's done, I won't permit you to use me as some sort of leverage against him. I've hurt him quite enough already."

"You haven't answered my question."

She pushed hair off her forehead. "No. I will not go back to the States with you. And if those are the terms of our relationship, I think we'd probably better terminate it right here and now."

261

The car behind them suddenly moved out as if to pass them. In response, Mariko moved to the far right of the road but, instead of passing, the car, a gray Chevrolet van, started to crowd them toward the side of the road.

"Jesus . . ." Mariko clenched her teeth and blared her horn. Still the van kept shoving them implacably to the side. At last they came to a screeching halt, the Volkswagen horn still blaring and just inches from a rock ledge at the side of the road.

Suddenly doors opened and slammed. Figures streamed back and forth through the dust-blown headlights. In the next moment the doors of the little Volkswagen were flung open. Mariko screamed and Daughtry felt himself lifted bodily from his seat. Wildly, without aiming, he flung a fist out at one of his assailants, clipping him hard on the chin, sending him spinning back into the person just behind him. The next he knew, he was caught up in a windmill of flailing arms. Out of the corner of his eye he caught sight of Mariko being hoisted over a pair of broad shoulders, her legs thrashing. His own arms he felt being wrenched cruelly behind him.

Somebody trying to force him into the rear of the van banged his head on the top of the doorframe. In order to brake himself, he dug his heels in and kicked. A sour-smelling figure above him grunted and went down. In that instant he felt a short hard jab from a billy club applied to the back of his neck and suddenly everything went gray and then dark.

55

Men begin with blows, then have recourse to words.
—Address by the Athenian Ambassadors to the
Lacedaemonians, 433 B.C.

"You appear chastened, Mr. Daughtry. Not quite so cocksure of yourself as you looked the other day." Mr. Sujimoto chuckled, then pushed a box of tissues across the desk. "There's a bit of blood under your right eye."

"That happens when people hit me there." Daughtry sat rumpled and groggy in Sujimoto's top-floor study. "You now add assault and kidnapping to your list of crimes."

"I do regret this. I gave explicit instructions. But Aito, poor fellow, doesn't know his own strength."

Daughtry's head throbbed from the blow he'd taken to the back of his neck. "I'd noticed that. Where's Mariko?"

"Resting comfortably in her own room, thank you. Her mother's with her at the moment."

"May I ask," Daughtry spoke while dusting clouds of dried mud from his jacket sleeves, "just what the hell this is all about?"

It was nearly 2 A.M. Dressed in a silk robe, Sujimoto smiled and tilted his head sideways. It was a coy, rather droll posture, serving to heighten the old fellow's sense of sinister playfulness. "It's really very simple." He rose and crossed the room to a marble pier table upon which assorted decanters of whisky sat. "You look as though you could use a good stiff one."

He poured two large drams of whisky into glasses with ice, spurted soda from a siphon into each, and thrust one at Daughtry. He took one for himself and proceeded to pace slowly up and down the room.

"I read about you daily in the papers, Mr. Daughtry," he commenced. "You're famous, or should I say, infamous?"

"No more so than you," Daughtry raised his glass in toast. "I take it you know you've made the FBI's Ten Most Wanted List."

Sujimoto's lips pursed, but he preferred to overlook Daughtry's impudence. "Like you, Mr. Daughtry, I find myself in a tight situation, and perhaps for two fugitives, such as ourselves, so to speak"— he winked at Daughtry—"it is better for us to join forces rather than to increase the number of enemies we already have at our flanks."

Daughtry daubed a tissue at the welt beneath his eye. "Speak plainly, please."

263

Mr. Sujimoto regarded the soiled, untidy figure with pointed distaste. "I fully understand there's no love lost between us, Mr. Daughtry. To put it simply, I'm saying that since I decline to have my daughter live with you as a concubine, and since she appears determined to be in your company at all costs, and since it is a matter of some importance to Madame de Plevissier that her daughter be present at this time, I invite you to remain here as a guest in my house. At least until the wedding."

Daughtry's mind was whirling. "And if I decline?"

"There's always Aito to put the invitation more forcefully."

The smoke from Sujimoto's Monte Cristo curled sinuously before his sad, runny eyes.

"And after the wedding?"

"You are free, of course, to go your own way."

"What about Mariko?"

"Forget about Mariko."

"I want to know about Mariko." This time Daughtry's voice had an unpleasant edge.

"Mariko remains here. With her parents."

"As a prisoner?"

Sujimoto nodded his head sadly. "There are ways of making her detention very appealing."

"You can't just lavish gifts on her and expect—"

"She's a very practical girl, Mr. Daughtry."

"But she's not a fool. Soon she'll tire of that and want to leave."

The weight of Daughtry's message left Sujimoto unimpressed. For the reply he merely shrugged and raised his palms in question.

"I'm due back in New York to face a grand jury."

"What would you have me do, go back there with you? Face litigation? A sick old man. To go to jail? For what possible purpose?"

"For your own sense of conscience. For how your daughter and wife will perceive you after you're gone."

Sujimoto's hand flew upward in exasperation. "Why do you

264

taunt me? I did nothing wrong." He whirled furiously, on the brink of a shout. When he turned back, there was Daughtry quietly regarding him.

"The law takes a different position on that." Daughtry spoke softly. "You overlook one thing. I am just as determined to be with Mariko as she is with me."

Sujimoto's nervous pacing halted abruptly. A snort of mirthless laughter burst from him, and he squinted through curling smoke at Daughtry. "Forgive my amusement, Mr. Daughtry. These expressions of affection for my daughter I find very touching. Suddenly you find her presence indispensable. With your extraordinary mathematical gifts you have no doubt computed to the last penny the size of her dowry."

"Give her nothing." Daughtry's gaze was steady. "She wants nothing from you. Not now. Not as a criminal. I certainly want nothing, except my self-respect back. You've lived long and well for many years. I'm still relatively young. I still have to live and make my way. Come back to New York with me. Tell the truth. Tell the jury everything and offer to make restitution. You have millions. Billions. It would mean nothing to you. Given your age, your health, I'm certain the jury would recommend clemency. They might convict you, but they'd certainly never sentence you."

"That's precisely it!" Sujimoto pounded his palm with a fist. "I will not be convicted. I will not stand for that—that blot against my name. And even if I were to make restitution, as you say, that would be as good as an admission of guilt."

"But you are guilty. Everyone knows that."

Sujimoto held a hand up as if averting a blow. "I did nothing. I am innocent."

"There are documents in New York—"

"I am clear—"

"—in the possession of my lawyer. Very explicit documents detailing—"

"Fraudulent—all fraudulent."

"—negotiations with the Weiler Bank in Zurich. Self-dealing

265

operations between Protocorp and the Confederated. Fiduciary accounts with your banks in the Bahamas."

"Not true." Sujimoto's voice grew shrill. "That was you. I did nothing. Entirely your doing. Your ego. Your megalomaniacal ambitions. You acted beyond your authority. You know that. Look into your own heart. I did nothing. I know nothing."

Hands clasped, Daughtry sat silently in his chair, a mask of impassivity on his lean, pallid features. At last he threw his hands slowly upward, as if to suggest there was nothing further to discuss. "You appear to hold all the cards. I trust you'll permit me to leave here in time to get back to New York for the hearing."

Slumped over his desk, Sujimoto gazed wearily into a shadowy corner of the room. "On that you have my word."

"And Mariko? I still expect her to come with me."

"Impossible." Sujimoto's hand fluttered before his eye, waving the thought aside as if it were an unpleasant smell. "Never."

"You surely don't believe you can keep her here under lock and key."

"Why not? Why not, Mr. Daughtry? Better bondage at home than see her commit a tragic mistake."

"I don't agree that I'd be a tragic mistake."

"You're a criminal." Sujimoto half rose to his feet, then sat again. "Despite what happens in court. In the eyes of the world you are judged guilty."

Daughtry could not resist a smile. "So are you, for that matter."

"Never mind me," Sujimoto fumed. "It is my daughter's future that is at stake here. Forget her, Mr. Daughtry. Put her out of your mind. She's not for you."

At that moment Daughtry heard what he thought was a cry from a distant wing of the castle. It sounded once again but he concluded that it was only some nocturnal bird. He turned slowly to leave, then turned back.

"About your son?"

A frown slowly clouded Mr. Sujimoto's strained features.

266

"Have you any idea of his whereabouts?"

"Your ideas ought to be more up to date than mine. I gather you've had some contact with him recently."

Daughtry was amused by the Oriental understatement. "I simply wanted to make it clear that if any harm were to come to me, those documents I spoke about, in the possession of my lawyers, would immediately be released to the police."

The cloud over Sujimoto's brow darkened. His jaw was visibly clenched. Outside, a wind soughed through the deep encroaching forest. "Such a despicable insinuation scarcely warrants reply."

"Good. So long as we understand each other. Your daughter is virtually certain that Kajumi is here right now. Somewhere on the property. She's seen him."

"My daughter has a vivid imagination." Sujimoto sat ramrod erect at his desk. "In any event, kindly leave the matter of my son to me, Mr. Daughtry. As long as you are a guest here in this house, you are perfectly safe. Aito will show you to your room."

The words appeared to signal the conclusion of their talk.

"Will there be a guard posted outside my door?" Daughtry asked somewhat spitefully.

"Unnecessary. Every point of exit is posted with a sentry. And, oh, yes, there are some large, rather nasty dogs roaming the grounds freely at night."

Daughtry in his dusty suit mused for a moment in the open doorway. "Not much fun living that way, is it?"

56

Guerrilla war is far more intellectual than a bayonet charge.
—T. E. LAWRENCE: *The Science of Guerrilla Warfare*

Behind a sack of sphagnum, Kajumi watched a pair of security guards stride crisply past the greenhouse. They moved on in a straight line, then wheeled and yawed sharply toward the greenhouse, moving directly at him. Kajumi wheeled at the same moment, ducking beneath a potting table. From where he crouched, eying them warily, and the position of the sun in their eyes, he could not tell whether or not they had seen him. They moved briskly as if they were coming on specific business. Kajumi dropped his head and placed his right hand above the P38 pistol secreted inside his shirt. At a distance of ten yards the guards veered again, and strode off toward the low fringe of distant woods.

Not far from the greenhouse, in the pavilion area before the main building, the tents and tables and bars, all erected now for the impending ceremony, stood deserted. It was still too early for the staff to be out completing final arrangements for the following day. Kajumi used the time he had now to dispose of his discarded cook's costume. Finding a small spade, he dug a hole into the base of a nearby mulch pile and interred the garments within it. It occurred to him that something was missing, but in his confusion and haste he could not recall that it was the toque which he'd left behind in the cellars.

Some sixty feet off, he watched two more guards promenade the gravel walk between the greenhouse and pavilion. From their leisurely gait they appeared to have no pressing business with him. But he could not depend on that kind of good fortune much longer. Mariko had almost certainly seen him the day before in the kitchen. So his best chance was to get out quick, go to ground somewhere else on that vast wooded preserve. In the next moment he'd snatched up a pot of camellias and had stepped outside the door into the warm sunlight. To the unwitting observer he appeared to be no more than one of the house staff transporting a pot of flowers from one part of the grounds to another.

His course led him round the fringes of the vast open lawns at the rear of Mendenhall, where he could see the tents swelling their sides capaciously in the gentle winds. It was slightly past 8 A.M. and shortly, he knew, kitchen and household personnel would arrive and start to work purposefully around the large empty banquet tables. His feet sped quickly over the bright sward, round the less-trafficked east side of the main building. His camellia pot he held waist-high just at a level designed so that the giant yellow blooms screened his face. He moved quickly, but with a modicum of restraint so as not to call attention to himself. If his feet moved fast, his mind raced while his eyes swept the area for a place in which to vanish. At any moment he fully expected to hear the bark of dogs, the shouts of pursuing guards and the clap of a hand on his shoulder.

At the rear of the building, in the vicinity of the kitchen, a number of vans and catering trucks were parked. Several had been left open with their keys still in the ignitions. Nearby, a pair of guards caroused among the trucks, wolfing morning rolls and coffee.

He saw them pause like a pair of watchful hounds and gaze boldly at the fleeting figure with the large pot of flowers. It seemed to Kajumi that one of them frowned and started up. He kept his eyes straight ahead and moved quickly on in the direction of a piny fringe of woods directly behind the kitchen. Behind him he heard one of them call out. Still, he kept right on going as if he hadn't heard. There was a second call. He closed his eyes and moved ahead with a plan firmly in mind to bolt for the woods in the event they came after him.

But instead of pursuing footsteps, he heard loud raucous laughter, as if the guards had meant only to taunt him. He turned quickly off the gravel walk and onto a narrow dirt path cutting through the forest.

He trod about a hundred yards through a stand of big spruce, emerging finally at a weedy circular clearing, at the center of which stood a shack. It was small and brightly painted, about the size of a large doghouse, and from within it came a high whirring electrical sound, like that of a compressor or generator.

The thought of pursuing guards had not left him and he was not about to quibble with opportunity. Without further pause, he marched directly up to the shack, seized the doorknob and

269

twisted. In the next moment he stepped inside, kicking the door shut behind him.

Enveloped in sudden darkness, bright gaily colored pin-wheels spun before his eyes. The high whirring sound, mercifully muffled by walls when on the outside, was now disconcertingly loud. Standing there in the dark, clutching his pot of camellias, he felt the sound vibrate and expand inside his head. The noise came from the generator that powered the pumps, raising water out of the deep cisterns surrounding the estate.

He knew the shack well. A pumphouse in the woods not far behind the château. It was a small, cramped, narrow place, tidy enough, but not uncomfortable. A cozy, dreamlike sense of boyish nostalgia overcame him. Outside, not at any great distance, he thought he heard the baying of nearby dogs. He did not care, however, for there in the cramped airless dark he felt safe and calm.

 All soldiers taken must be cared for with magnanimity so that they may be used by us.
—CHANG YÜ, *1000*

Daughtry rose shortly after eight. Actually he had not yet been to sleep. Leaving Sujimoto at approximately 3 A.M., he was taken directly to a large, comfortable bedroom with a large adjoining bath, complete with sauna and expensive toiletries, in the upper wing of the castle, and fitted out with a pair of silk pajamas. A robe given him bore the monogram *KS* by which he quickly surmised that he'd become the unwilling heir to Kajumi Sujimoto's room and wardrobe.

True to Sujimoto's word, no guard was placed at his door, but at a night table where a phone had obviously sat, now only the wires, useless and dangling, still remained.

Mariko, he knew, was in another wing of the house, but she might have been on the other side of the earth for all the accessibility he had to her. His head still throbbed from the blow he'd taken at the base of his skull. Too agitated to sleep, too tired to get up and move about, he spent the several hours until dawn sprawled on his back in bed, watching shadows shifting on the ceiling above him.

Later, shaved and showered, he went downstairs in search of coffee and juice. At that early hour the place was already a hive of activity. Outside, swarms of people moved under the large tents adjoining the main house; linens and napery were set out; the finest bone china was being uncrated; great chests of Georgian silver had been hoisted on pulleys from the basement vaults and were now being inventoried by the house steward, shortly to be trundled off in barrows to a large burnishing machine.

Amid all of the bustle and chaos stood Madame de Plevissier, haggard and drawn but, nonetheless, organizing and directing. Beside her, directly inside that gray dizzy swirl of motion stood Karl Heinz. Just behind, like a beacon several feet above the milling crowd, Aito towered.

Still Daughtry could see no sign of Mariko. Had Sujimoto imposed a kind of house arrest on his troublesome daughter? It was too medieval and hard to believe and, yet, wasn't that exactly what had been imposed upon him?

He was given breakfast in the kitchen with the staff, where a sumptuous sideboard replete with assorted fruits, eggs, sausage, bacon, toast and a variety of marmalades and confitures had been laid on.

Afterward, he strolled outside under the tents, lingering for a while to watch a group of workers struggling with poles and ropes under the billowing canvas. From there he moved out over the spacious grounds, aware as he went that two guards, with a brace of massive Alsatians, strained along behind at a discreet distance.

At 10 A.M. a butler came out from the main house to advise

271

him that he had been summoned to Mr. Sujimoto. Taken through a side entrance of the castle, down a steep, narrow stair, then led through the cellars along a nexus of dank, gloomy corridors, Daughtry could not help feeling a twinge of apprehension. That persisted until at last they emerged into the brightly lit converted subterranean chapel that now served as Mr. Sujimoto's countinghouse and base of operations.

Characteristically unfazed in the face of sizable quantities of money, Daughtry was truly stunned to see the vast, yet strangely unselfconscious, display of wealth stored up there.

Within the center of it all sat a bank of video screens with up-to-date exchange rates posted, several highly sophisticated computers clicking purposefully, in addition to the half-dozen phones with open transatlantic lines manned by several of Mr. Sujimoto's prize traders imported from Tokyo.

Behind a huge travertine desk, swathed in white robes and clearly at the head of operations, sat the old captain of the *Aoba*. The dour, decidedly ominous mood of several hours before appeared to have lifted, and the old fellow sat beaming now, clearly delighted with the royal fireworks show he was staging for Daughtry.

"Ah, good morning, Mr. Daughtry." He was all affability and smiles. "Not bad for an amateur operation, ay?"

A box squawked; a phone rang, and he picked it up. He nodded to Daughtry. "Excuse me, one moment please—" then tilted his ear to the receiver. "I take one mil at .0143, value date two weeks hence." When he dropped the phone back onto its cradle, he was still smiling. "We've just had a report from Frankfurt that the Italian Central Bank sold 120 million in dollars, following sales of 6 million yesterday."

"They're propping the lira," Daughtry remarked offhandedly.

"They have no choice." Sujimoto was animated. "The lira will have to be devalued if one takes into account the present Italian inflation rate. My sources tell me to watch for the Crédite Commercial de France to cut prime lending rates to 12¼. It was 12¾ yesterday."

272

"French money market rates are going to start slipping shortly," Daughtry remarked and, listening to the squawk boxes, the shouting traders and the low whirr of computers, he experienced a pleasant shock of excitement. It was as if, for a moment, he were back in the Confederated trading rooms, making the market in pounds or Deutsche marks, up to his ears in the old game.

Sujimoto's eyes glowed brightly. "Are you sure? I mean, do you have any hard information?" All of the animosity of the night before had boiled off, and it was just like old times in Tokyo as the two men continued to sit there and trade the latest money market gossip. "What is your feeling regarding the dollar, Mr. Daughtry?"

"Futures?"

"No, spots."

"Going up. The Fed's raising discount rates."

"And the yen?"

"Going down. The dollar's bottomed out in both Tokyo and New York."

"Then you'd recommend unloading yen and building a long dollar position?"

"Naturally. In spots and forwards, using DM and Swiss franc cross-rates. But why ask me?"

Daughtry stared quizzically at the elegantly robed figure and realized suddenly he was being tested.

"You could have given me the wrong information," Sujimoto replied. "Or, for that matter, even denied me any information. But you didn't."

"How can you be certain?"

"Because obviously it seems I'm privy to the same source of information as you. Quite apart from that, I have independently arrived at the same conclusions. In my country it is said that one outcast is harmless, but two are unbeatable. Something to dwell upon, ay, Daughtry." Sujimoto laughed. "Have a seat, please."

Daughtry never moved. "I prefer to stand, thank you. It was my understanding I'd be permitted to see Mariko today."

273

"And so you shall. I give you my word." The phone rang again. This time Sujimoto flagged one of his assistants. "If it's Hammamura or the Deutsche Bank, we're offering yen at .6113, not a pip less." He turned back to Daughtry. "It appears we shall have an exceptionally fine day for the wedding tomorrow. I have been on the phone to the Meteorological Bureau and they tell me that sunshine is virtually assured." Sujimoto spoke as if he himself had just cornered the market in fine weather.

"I'm delighted to hear that. When shall I be permitted to see Mariko?"

"But any time you choose." Sujimoto appeared aggrieved. "You've been invited to the ceremony and the banquet. I trust you will find it all very much to your liking."

Daughtry watched the old man warily, puzzled by the highly conciliatory tack he was suddenly taking. "Then, if there's nothing further, I'll go up and see her now."

"By all means," Sujimoto trilled, waving with one hand to his assistant to lead Daughtry out, while with the other hand he reached for the ringing phone.

Shortly after Daughtry's departure, he was on the phone to London where the bid rate on dollars was preferable to that of New York. Next, in Hong Kong, where the yen had not yet started to slide, he unloaded several millions of that currency for dollars and repeated this simple transaction throughout the day in over a half-dozen money markets until he had divested himself of roughly $100 millions' worth of the Japanese currency. All the while he had been scrupulously careful not to call too much attention to his actions by trying to unload too much of the currency in just one market.

These actions were bound to have an impact on the already deeply troubled yen. By midday the dollar had zoomed up against the yen in both Tokyo and New York and he knew that traders sitting around in Zurich, London, Frankfurt and New York were bound to start asking questions about this sudden flood of yen. It was time, he thought, to quit for lunch.

Before leaving his subterranean headquarters, however, he

took a portion of his already considerable dollar gains and rolled them back, as Daughtry had suggested, into the powerful, prestigious Deutsche mark and Swiss franc. It was a matter of a single phone call and, in a matter of several moments, he'd had a net profit of slightly over $1.2 million. Not bad for a morning's work and it hadn't even required his withdrawing so much as a single dollar from his own private accounts.

He had no idea how long he'd sat there. He couldn't see his wristwatch, but he estimated it was close on to an hour. With the door shut as it was and the sun beating on the dark asphalt roof, the cramped little space soon grew intolerable. The barking dogs he'd heard had receded now into the distance, yet he had no guarantee they would not return.

In the hour or so that Kajumi sat there, his mind was strangely lucid. Sweltering in the airless dark, he brooded over many things. What had brought him to this desperate turn? And what part did a young American exchange expert play in the strange, ineluctable weave of fate between his father and himself? Whether or not that fate would be gloomy or bright rested squarely on whether or not he succeeded here. The odds, he knew, were heavily against him. This was his last chance and failure was inconceivable.

58

In war we must always leave room for strokes of fortune, and accidents that cannot be foreseen.
—POLYBIUS: *History, II*

By midafternoon preparations had reached a crescendo. A constant stream of delivery trucks flowed in and out of the front gates. Nerves were frayed, tempers were short, and quarrels broke out over matters like floral arrangements. In the kitchen where temperatures soared to over 100 degrees Fahrenheit, the

275

mood was even more volatile. A 300-pound, six-tiered wedding cake was just in the process of being unloaded from a van amid an awesome din of threats and imprecations. Pots banged, lids clashed, and sweaty soup chefs stirred caldrons of steaming consommé.

Outside, Daughtry wandered distractedly through the din, looking for Mariko. He was in the area of the tents where he'd been told she was last seen. And, indeed, that's where he found her—in the Grand Tent itself. She'd spotted him just as he saw her. For a moment their eyes questioned each other; then suddenly they were both edging their way across the swarming, congested space.

"You're all right?" he asked, feeling an enormous sense of relief.

"Fine," she said, a little breathless and embarrassed. "I'm fine. And you? The last thing I saw was three men kicking and hauling you into the back of a van." She studied him now, assessing the damage. "You're okay?"

"Fine." He laughed, in spite of his apprehension. "Actually, nothing is fine. Everything is rotten."

"Like what?"

"I'll tell you later."

She tugged at his sleeve. "Tell me now. I want to know." She appeared determined to hear the worst. All attempts to dissuade her were fruitless.

Wordlessly, he led her out to a secluded bower at the bottom of the garden, where together they sat on a little wrought-iron bench. They spoke in whispers, both aware of the two security guards lingering conspicuously, not more than seventy-five feet away.

"Forget them." Mariko tossed her head in their direction. "Have you had any more contact with my father?"

"I spoke with him last night and again this morning. There's no chance that he'll consent to go back with me and testify in court."

"You didn't seriously expect that, did you?"

276

Daughtry shook his head and paused, watching her. "He also forbids you to leave here with me after the wedding."

"Oh?"

He watched the shift of expression on her features. Something in her quick transition from defiance to that of merely quiet resentment made him uneasy. He prodded further: "I tried to tell him that there was no way he could keep you here."

Daughtry watched her more closely. Still, she was silent.

"That is true, isn't it, Mariko?"

She stared resolutely downward, her hands clasped in her lap.

"True, he may try to keep you here under some sort of house arrest, but he knows that he can't hope to hold you indefinitely. I'm sure all this has a great deal to do with me."

Watching her doggedly avoiding his eyes, evading reply, he grew angry. "Mariko—"

"Don't ask me, Charles. Please—"

"When you came to the inn the other night—"

"I was angry then. Furious with him."

"And you're not any longer?"

"Don't make me choose now. Please don't put me into that position. It isn't fair."

"Mariko, I thought—"

"I know what you thought, but you were wrong." Her voice was curt and emphatic. "We have no agreement. No understanding."

"But two nights ago—"

"Forget about two nights ago. My father is in grave difficulty and all you can think of is putting him in jail."

"Right," Daughtry suddenly snapped. "Why the hell should I have all the fun?"

She started up, but he pulled her roughtly back down. "You agree he's guilty?"

"I do." Her eyes suddenly watered. "But he's still my father. What do you expect me to do? Desert him? Betray him?"

"Christ," Daughtry fumed, started to reply, then sighed

instead and leaned back on the bench, suddenly exhausted.

Her moist eyes trailed off into the distance. "You have no brilliant mathematical formula for solving this problem, do you?"

"You can't put ethical dilemmas on a computer. There are no punch keys for conscience."

In her expression he could see a whole tangle of thoughts and emotions flying chaotically. "He's old. He's not very well. How much longer can he live anyway?"

"If that's so," he spoke at last, "then all the more reason for him to make a clean breast of things now."

"To whose advantage?"

"To mine, of course. Given his age and condition, they'll never sentence him. But I'm going to be around for awhile. After all this, I still have to go out and somehow pick up the threads of my life."

Stunned by the uncharacteristic note of entreaty, she watched him drum his fingers on the edge of the bench. "What do you expect me to do?" she asked.

"If you won't come with me, then just don't interfere when I try to take him."

"You'll never get him off the grounds. There are thirty security guards and a kennel full of dogs. What do you think they'll do to you when they get you?"

"I'll take my chances."

"Even if you do get him off the grounds, he'll never survive the trip."

He nodded, weighing the force of her point. "I still must try. I don't see that I have much choice."

He had a desire to reach out and put a hand on her, but he withheld himself.

"It's hot here." She turned to go.

He caught her by the arm and pulled her back, then glanced back at the guards observing them warily. "All that time in Tokyo and Okitsu . . . it was impossible then. Living in your

278

father's house. My position in his bank . . . you understand, it was wrong. All wrong then."

"And now—not wrong?"

"If I get out of this thing, Mariko"—the sense of crisis flooded back upon him—"I'd like to try again. Just you and me. By ourselves."

He watched her for a time, skepticism and belief alternating in her face. Suddenly she laughed out loud. It was a harsh, unkind laugh.

"You don't think too highly of me, do you, Daughtry?" she mocked. "Mariko is offered the undying love of a man she admittedly admires. All she has to do is accede to a conspiracy against her father."

"I didn't ask you to accede to any such thing."

"No. Just to look away when it happens. Pretend ignorance. Doesn't that amount to the same thing? Betrayal?"

Daughtry shook his head despairingly. There was an edge of anger when he replied. "Whatever I do here is wrong. I'm damned if I do and damned if I don't."

He was about to continue, but her rueful, accusatory look brought him up sharply. "Do what you have to do, goddammit," she bawled. "Don't ask my advice." She rose suddenly and started out.

"Where are you going?" he cried after her.

"I must get back. They'll be looking for me."

"Wait."

But she was gone.

That night, the night before his wedding, Sujimoto startled everyone by appearing at dinner in his Imperial Navy uniform. Bristling with decorations, ribbons and captain's insignia, the effect of putting it on after thirty-some odd years was subduing. It caused a certain degree of startled embarrassment among Mariko, Daughtry and Madame de Plevissier. Sujimoto spoke little thoughout dinner and he drank virtually nothing. For the most part he seemed very far away.

Whenever Celestine or Mariko addressed him, he would nod or respond quietly in as few words as possible, then withdraw again into himself. At the completion of the meal, after coffee had been served, he rose suddenly as if responding to some eagerly awaited call, and strode slowly, eyes closed, round the room. His walk had the curious stilted air of ancient ceremony. In truth, there was something a little ludicrous about it—the old man in his forty-year-old captain's uniform, kept spotlessly clean as if its owner were expecting to be recalled to the fleet at any moment. Then, too, Sujimoto had put on four decades of girth since the time he'd last worn it and the jacket, taut, and slightly askew, did not button properly down the front. Finally, the most ludicrous stroke of all was the captain's saber banging at his thigh as he strode solemnly up and down the room.

There was a touch of Gilbert and Sullivan about it all—the great Nipponese industrialist-financier in his tight uniform and saber—a comic admiral in an *opéra bouffe*. But if it was comic, there was also something majestic, and not a little sad. At one point, he cocked his head as if he could hear for a moment the rumble of distant gun batteries and the rich, thrilling growl of Zeros and Mitsubishis revving on a flight deck. It was as if the wild drone sounded in his belly, and he were gazing back over the years, over the gulf of time in that heroic fading twilight where he had lived once with the certainty that youth and energy and hope would never forsake him.

Something jarred his concentration. His head snapped and his eyes sprang open with the dazed, disoriented look of a man waking from sleep. The first thing he saw was Mariko and Celestine regarding him uneasily, then Daughtry frowning farther down the table. A sweet almost childlike smile suddenly suffused his features. The smile touched Celestine oddly, made her want to go to him, protect him. But at the same moment, she experienced a chill breath of air, dank and unsettling, as though some augury of doom had wafted between them, then quickly passed on.

In the next moment, Sujimoto was back at the table, splashing cognac into snifters, laughing and raucous, proposing a round of gin rummy with Mariko and Daughtry.

59

Time spent on reconnaissance is seldom wasted.
—British Army Field Service Regulations, 1912

The first car arrived shortly before noon. It was a vintage Daimler, forest-green, with a beige canvas roof and a great expanse of chrome grille. The high whine of its engines climbing the steep drive in second gear preceded by several moments the auto's actual appearance.

Suddenly, the Daimler breasted the hill; a flash of coruscating light reflected from its circular hood insignia as it swept round the large gravel drive and drew up before a porte cochere outside of the main building. A liveried attendant strode smartly down from his post at the main entrance, opened car doors, and helped a party of four out. Another uniformed figure materialized as if out of thin air, then drove off with the Daimler, presumably to some parking area provided for guests. It was all very efficient.

By that time a second and a third vehicle had droned up the drive and turned into the porte cochere, suggesting that a steady stream of arrivals had begun.

The day chosen for the Sujimoto nuptials could not have been more felicitous. Bright sunlight, a sky blue and clear save for a feathering of high-altitude cirrus clouds, streaked on the sky in long, attenuated mackerel patterns. A coolish day, the air was pungent with the sharp resinous breath of tall thrusting conifers.

Even the Schloss Mendenhall had dressed for the occasion. Its brooding towers and turrets, its generally sober mien, appeared uncharacteristically gay—a dour maiden aunt known principally for black attire, suddenly tricked out in tango skirts. Flowers, balloons, colored banners and lights garlanded the grounds and main building. Gaily colored wreaths were draped over fearsome gargoyles and stone garden satyrs all about the grounds. Three vividly striped dining tents dotted the expansive lawns, surrounding the larger Grand Tent to be occupied by the wedding party and its closest relatives and friends.

Shortly the drive was clogged with traffic. More cars drew up to the front. People alighted, gathered in small clusters on the broad verandas, chatted in low voice. A tall, aged Franciscan in white vestments stepped from a car. His silken gown swelled gently in the mild gusts outside the castle, while bells peeled unceasingly from the little chapel within.

Promptly at noon, as if a wand had been raised, the crowds suddenly vanished into the chapel, leaving the grounds to foraging birds and the sizable staff of service and security personnel bustling purposefully about.

"The collar is too stiff. Get me something softer."

"I regret, sir. There is nothing—"

"I won't wear this. It will sever my head."

Two gentleman's valets fluttered about Sujimoto like a pair of sparrows agitated by a stalking cat. They stood in the musty little vestry outside the chapel, hissing frantically to each other while people filed past the open door toward the chapel, moving to the muted plangencies of a Handel organ mass.

The valets fussed and frowned. They wielded whiskbrooms and snarled instructions at one another, trying to assuage the master's wrath. But the master would not be assuaged. His voice rose, thin and strident. Several late arrivals passing the open vestry door peered in. Mr. Sujimoto glowered back at them, whereupon they retreated hastily to the safety of the chapel.

Not far away in a small wardrobe off the chapel, Mariko

pinned a small corsage of orchids on the delicate old peau-de-soir lace of her mother's bridal gown.

As usual, Celestine had applied her makeup too liberally. An untidy smear of lipstick at the corner of her mouth set her features slightly askew. Mariko rubbed and daubed with a tissue to correct the situation.

"Are you all right?" she asked, not for the sake of information but merely to calm herself. She was still thinking of the crumpled white toque she'd found in the cellars.

"I'm fine," Celestine replied grimly and stared straight ahead.

"They're all here, you know."

Celestine appeared not to have heard. But then, after a moment, she replied distractedly, "Who? Who's here?"

"Your family. All the Plevissiers. Your cousins from Rambouillet. The fat family from Périgord."

"Ah, Marcel. Christ—I'd forgot I'd asked them."

"And your former in-laws—"

"Oh, my God." Celestine palmed her forehead. "I sent an invitation. I surely didn't think they'd accept. Finish, finish, Mariko. The ceremony will begin shortly."

The slow, muted piping of the organ wafted funereally in upon them from the chapel.

"There's still time. You don't have to go through with it." She had a sudden, pressing need to relieve her mother of any sense of obligation. "You mustn't do this for me."

A smile creased Celestine's haggardly fine patrician features. "Don't be foolish, child. I do it for myself. And, there is no time left. No time at all."

At first she assumed that her mother was referring to her father's uncertain health. But the remark, tossed off with a kind of cheery glib defiance, appeared to resonate with all kinds of ambiguity.

"What do you mean, no time? You mean my father—"

"Of course. That, and—"

Mariko waited. "And what?"

283

The organ music had stopped and they could hear the hurried footsteps of late arrivals outside the door.

"And what?" The name Kajumi was suddenly on the tip of Mariko's tongue. And then at last she blurted it out. "Mother— he's here. Kajumi is here. On the grounds somewhere."

Instead of surprise or fright, Celestine merely nodded with weary resignation.

"Do you understand, Celestine? Kajumi is here. I saw him in the kitchens the other day. And the fact he's concealed himself makes me extremely uneasy."

Celestine shrugged. "I'm not surprised."

Mariko stared at her mother in disbelief.

"Why shouldn't he be here?" Celestine continued. "It is his father who is being married today. He feels estranged from us. Displaced. He is deeply hurt and we have a duty to make it up to him. I don't think he's here to harm us. But if he is—we'll have to get used to that fact, Mariko."

It was not exactly the reaction she had expected. Anger, fright, rage, anything, but not this tired capitulation. Such passivity was totally out of character.

"Mother, look. You can ask the house security to make a thorough search of the grounds. Find him, before he finds Father. Or you, for that matter."

One ear cocked as if to hear what was going on in the chapel, Celestine shook her head. "Why? There's really nothing much he can do to me. And your father may well yet have to face justice."

Gazing at her mother, Mariko barely recognized the slightly stooped, suddenly aged-looking lady standing before her in the mauve lace gown. "You do believe he's guilty, then?"

"He is, my darling. Of everything they say. You know that as well as I."

For answer, Mariko merely hung her head.

"I've known it for years." Celestine's voice was husky. "Your father's business practices have always been . . . irregular—to say the least. It was only a matter of time before things caught up with him."

Mariko's agitation mounted by the moment. "If you knew this, you could have forced him to correct his ways. He would have done it for you. He adores you."

Another weary smile. "Your father knows I care far too deeply about him to turn him over to the tender mercies of jailers. Come now. Don't be silly, child. Of course I've known all the unsavory, lurid things. Confederated is only one item in a long list. There's a bank in Zurich, and another in Milan. There is also right here in Vaduz dealings with a huge munitions consortium of unspecified nationality that specializes in arming what is euphemistically referred to as 'paramilitary operations.' There's all that and probably much worse. I hesitate to question too closely. To your father it is all commerce. He's lost the ability to discriminate." Celestine's eyes glistened brightly. "It doesn't matter. He's still precious to me. The only thing that matters now is to protect what remains of his life. Perhaps I shall not be able to do that much longer. In any event, I will not permit Kajumi or Mr. Daughtry or the goddamned bloody money market to ruin this day for me. Come, Mariko—" She kissed her daughter with ineffable tenderness on each cheek and hugged her closely. "My legs are trembling," she giggled. "Take me out there now, child. By God, I'm going to my wedding."

Kajumi Sujimoto had been hearing the music for hours—the proud blaring martial brass, the trumpets and hautboys, the tympany and clash of symbols. It was all so stirring. It made him want to be a part of the music; to march to it in lockstep; to enact heroic deeds to the exalted strains of it. At first he thought the music was in his head, until it occurred to him that he had risen from the moldy earthen floor of the pumphouse, where he had lain for hours, and now started walking toward it. All the while its sound grew louder and even more stirring.

Attired once again in the white priestly robes he'd worn as a disguise onto the Swiss airliner in New York, with his shaved head, he moved through the woods now like some wraithlike presence. Branches and thorns tore at his flowing gown; burrs clung to him. At one point a branch lashed his face and laid open a cheek. He was impervious to it all, marching as he was, blindly and exultantly toward the music.

For some reason, it made him recall that period of desperately wanting, for his father's sake, to become a naval cadet. Now, as he perceived the painful episode in retrospect, he was no longer the man who had washed out ignominiously because of a punctured eardrum. Instead, he was a bright young cadet, hugely admired by instructors and fellow classmates. Just like his father before him.

So it was. The music drew him on—seductive and lethal. It drew him like an invisible leash through the forest, across the vast rolling lawns to the glittering teeming banquet tents of Mendenhall.

Surprise—the pith and marrow of war!
—SIR JOHN FISHER: *Memories, 1919*

The Grand Tent sat in the center of a large outdoor atrium in the shape of a *U*, the stone arms of which formed the east and west wings of Mendenhall. The midsection of the *U* joining the wings comprised the main rooms and salons of the noble old edifice. The roof above this section had been gabled with steep turrets at both ends and covered with copper sheets, anodized by wind and the elements, to a pale cuprous green.

The copper roof, pitched steep in the manner of a French mansard, projected out over the central wall terminating in a wide ledge designed to carry rain and melting snow away from the building's foundation. Between the ledge and the open side of the Grand Tent nearest the main house spanned a distance of some hundred odd feet.

For this occasion lights had been installed high up on the ledge, along with gaily colored heraldic banners that snapped back and forth in the wind with loud concussive cracks.

Daughtry found himself a spot beneath the copper over-hang—an observation point from which he could reconnoiter the field. From where he stood in a murky corner behind a serving stand, he had an unobstructed view of the backs of people seated on the banquet dais. He had never seen such an array of the mighty mingled with the exotic—the princely and imperious, figures swathed in djellabas and saris, kings and oil sheiks, shipping tycoons and assorted world shakers, plus the standard cannon fodder of the society columns.

The Sujimotos were up now and walking about the tent, greeting people. Celestine moved with a worn, stately radiance, heightened no doubt by the yards of silk and lace trailing behind her. Smiling for her guests, she pushed wisps of hair off her face—flushed and giddy like any new bride. Sujimoto himself, strutting and glowing like a sunrise, appeared boyishly happy.

The bodyguard Aito towered behind them, fully seven and a half feet, several hundred pounds, with the awesome girth of a classical Sumo wrestler. When they walked, he walked. When they paused, he paused, standing there patiently like a trained bear, uncomfortable in his tuxedo and black pumps, glancing constantly over his shoulder.

The more Daughtry studied the field, the more the assess-ment of his chances grew increasingly gloomy. Faced with a force of thirty armed guards, he himself had nothing in the way of firepower. Even were he to successfully bag old Sujimoto, there was then no easy flight out of Mendenhall, not to mention the additional impediment of Aito. Moreover, in the brief time that he had been standing there, he noted that a number of the security force had managed to string themselves out and ring the outer perimeter of the atrium. In the midst of all the noise and gaiety, they were scarcely noticed.

The newly wedded Sujimotos stopped to greet guests and chat with old friends. Occasionally, the old man would stoop to embrace someone. He did not look like a person who had just lost or finagled away the lion's share of an industrial empire. Nor did he look like a man in frail health. Quite the contrary, he exuded vitality and spectacular inner confidence. Begrudgingly, Daughtry had to admire him.

Faced with the problem of trying to remove Sujimoto from his impregnable fortress, Daughtry had a momentary flash—a recollection of Lafayette at the Battle of Yorktown. Pinned down by the withering fire of a sizable force of Hessians and Grenadiers, desperate to get his men out, Lafayette exhorted his general staff to stop seeking audacious solutions, and look merely for what was simple and there at hand.

Festivities had reached a peak in the Grand Tent. It was all a bright blur of motion—people dancing, milling about, straying from one tent to the next. In the next instant Daughtry caught sight of Mariko, her lean, strapless back to him, chatting with a Middle Eastern gentleman.

Daughtry came up on her from behind, startling her momentarily. He bowed from the hip in the European fashion, and stood there a little oafishly while she tried to ignore his presence, and declined to introduce him. At last, the Middle Eastern gentleman, perplexed, and a trifle miffed, withdrew.

She looked at him as though he were mad. "Aren't things confused enough? Why in God's name did you have to attend this thing?"

He smiled irritatingly. "Your father invited me and wouldn't take no for an answer."

She started to protest, but just then the music stopped, in order that the Brazilian samba band might take a breather. Out of the corner of his eye Daughtry could see the Sujimotos moving slowly through a throng of guests and a hail of good wishes. Mariko watched their approach with a look of sudden unaccountable sorrow.

"I don't trust you," she mumbled at him beneath her breath,

while people whirled by. She appeared to him just then somewhat smaller, more compact than he recalled, and quite beautiful.

"Why should I believe a word you say?" she continued. As she spoke she wadded a cocktail napkin up into a tight little ball in her fist as though she were about to fling it at him. "Leave," she fumed. Several passing people turned. Flustered, she looked away. When she resumed her tirade, her voice had a softer, somewhat entreating air.

"For God's sake, go away. Please."

"If you come with me."

"Don't be ridiculous. You can't expect me to leave him."

"But I do."

"You must be mad. Go, go."

"Not without you."

"Unfair. Unfair." She wrung her hands. "I told you—don't ask me to choose. Not now. Not when he needs me."

"I need you too." He looked at her miserably. In Kajumi's outsized tuxedo, which had been given to him spur-of-the-moment to wear, he looked slightly ridiculous. "Come with me," he whispered, this time more urgently. "I'm not asking you to betray your father. Let's forget him now. I'm just asking you to be with me."

"How can I possibly be with you, without betraying him?"

"You're not betraying him by simply standing beside me. Helping me to see things through."

She'd never seen him in the position of a supplicant. He could see her wavering, starting to come over to his side, then consciously pulling herself back into the old intransigence, the open antagonism of her doubt.

The small band of Brazilians returned to play more sambas. People started up again, moving past Daughtry and Mariko to the dance floor. From where he stood he caught a quick but rather poignant glimpse of the Sujimotos seated together at the head of a nearly empty dais. Everyone else had gone to dance and the two of them sat there, heads inclined toward one another. Laughing occasionally as if they were sharing secrets, they conveyed a strangely youthful, carefree appearance— merry, a trifle irresponsible and utterly unto themselves.

"I'm due back in New York next week for the hearing," Daughtry murmured. "If it goes badly for me, I won't ask you to stay. I'll send you home."

"Fool!" she glowered. "Why would I bother to go all the way to New York with you only to walk out in hard times?"

He laughed at her indignation, sensing that they were approaching some sort of an accord. He started to reach for her hand, only to recall how incongruous that might strike outsiders who didn't know them.

It was then he heard it—a sharp crack that seemed to have originated from outside the tent. At first he thought it was a glass shattering, or possibly a champagne cork. No one appeared to notice, and the dance music tended to drown it. Then came a second crack, somewhat louder than the first, but still not enough to distract the festivities. When he looked next across the dance floor, he had a view of Sujimoto slumped on the table, his arm outstretched, as if reaching for something. Celestine was sprawled atop him.

Someone screamed and a number of baffled dancers spun to a halt. Others, however, continued to dance. Mariko, facing the other way, looking over Daughtry's shoulder, had not yet seen what had happened. In the next moment, he saw clearly a vivid splash of red on Celestine's gown. Paralyzed, trying to distract Mariko's attention from the mounting excitement on the dance floor, he watched the red splash leech outward into the absorbency of old lace and intensify in color like a poppy bursting into bloom.

Out of the corner of his eye, Daughtry was suddenly aware of a blur of gray motion, too swift to convey meaning. He looked back at Mariko, who'd seen it too. But neither knew what it signified.

There was a crack and another crack. The gray blur fled sidewards, then rushed back. It wasn't that, however, that riveted Daughtry's racing mind. It was, rather, the spectacle of people fleeing the dance floor, scattering, screaming, streaming outward from the center like nocturnal roaches fleeing sudden light.

Daughtry was immediately aware of a commotion behind him; a loud rattle of commands in demotic Italian, and feet thudding. Mariko was the first to see the half-dozen or so security guards, carbines unslung, shouting and streaming round the sides of the tent, impeded by the crowds of panicked guests stampeding for the exits. Several of the guards collided with them as they fled. Loud, angry altercations ensued.

Mariko whirled to watch, but instantly Daughtry spun her back round to face him. They stood there locked in a kind of tug-of-war, while he tried to block her vision with his chest. By this time she knew something had happened. She stood there for a moment, glaring at him, then turned. At first she saw nothing. Just the commotion. Then, for a millisecond, the crowd parted and she had a sudden prospect of the horror. She muttered something. Then followed what came at Daughtry like a high distant keening, something sounding like a prolonged and grievous wail.

She started back now toward the dais. Daughtry thrust himself before her, once more pulling her tight to his chest. All the while she kicked and scratched and bit at him, stampeding people jostled them aside in their effort to flee the tent.

A large man in a tuxedo, terror in his eyes, came thundering at them like a runaway bus. He hit them broadside. The impact was terrific. It bowled Daughtry over, head over heels. Miraculously, Mariko, a trifle stunned, was still standing, even as the tuxedoed fellow went barreling past. Briefly, she regarded Daughtry sprawled full-length on the floor, a querulous impatience stamped on her features. Then, having resolved which way her duty lay, she turned and hurried toward the ghastly scene at the banquet table.

Flat on the floor, trying to recover his balance, Daughtry had to look sharp to avoid being trampled. Several waiters had also been knocked down; trays of food overturned. One of the sidestands containing hot plates went over with a resounding crash, only inches from Daughtry, spraying his trousers with tendrils and filaments of some hot runny substance. The air rang with screams and cries. That more than anything cleared his head, brought him to his feet where he took his bearings. In the next moment he was streaking across the tent after Mariko.

There was more shouting from the Corsican guards, and several additional sharp cracks which Daughtry took to be gunfire. Still, he had no idea where it was coming from. However, when he emerged at the far side of the Grand Tent, the question was quickly answered. High up on the copper overhang, above the atrium, like a circus aerialist, a white-robed figure with a shaved head, arms outspread beatifically, stood Kajumi Sujimoto. A small pistol gleamed in his hand as he scrambled back and forth along the coping of the roof. Transfixed, Daughtry watched the small bright orange blaze from the pistol's barrel rain hot lead solemnly down on the Sujimotos. The focus of fire was exactly at the point where Mariko stood.

When Daughtry reached her, she was struggling to bodily lift her mother. He joined her but Celestine was unbudgeable. Dead weight. A bullet had torn through her back just beneath her shoulder. Where it had entered a small pulsating fountain of arterial blood seeped out into the white lace of her gown and spread. She sprawled in an ungainly attitude, completely covering Sujimoto, as if she had died trying to shield him.

Another sharp crack and one of Kajumi's 9mm shells gonged horribly off a silver champagne bucket. Mariko screamed as Daughtry hauled her roughly up from Celestine. He had literally to peel her off like an orange rind and, when at last he separated her, shreds of torn bridal lace clung to her clawing nails.

The moment he'd felt her, he knew Celestine was dead. Still warm she was, but clammy and limp. To his horror, his concern was more with the man sprawled beneath her. He rolled her sideways off Sujimoto. Behind him, Mariko pounded his back with little mallet fists.

292

Sujimoto's eyes fluttered; his bluish lips moved soundlessly. A bullet appeared to have struck him below the ear. Blood streamed down his throat into his collar. There was no way of telling how seriously he was hurt.

"Leave him alone," Mariko shrieked, still pounding Daughtry's back with her fists. "Take your hands off him. Don't you touch him."

"You're crazy." Daughtry flung an arm at the roof. "He'll kill him."

She looked up at the robed figure flowing about on the copper overhang, then saw for the first time the blood spattering the front of her party dress.

Daughtry saw it too and his heart sank; then he realized it wasn't her blood at all but Celestine's. Once more, Mariko clawed toward her mother while Daughtry kept fending her off, blocking the shattered, bloodied view with his own body. She cried and tore and kicked at him. Another shot whistled past.

Suddenly, Mariko turned, giving up her struggle with Daughtry, and bolted toward the copper overhang toward Kajumi. Directly beneath her half-brother, she planted herself and shouted up at him in Japanese. The white-robed figure paused to gape down at her, a bemused, somewhat startled expression on his face.

Daughtry waded right out after her, trying to pull her back under the ledge, out of the line of fire. But she stood firm as a rock, rigid, unmovable, shouting up at her half-brother, mindless, unheedful of any danger. The next time Daughtry glanced up at the ledge, he realized that Kajumi was no longer alone. Aito was now up there with him.

Looking up from Daughtry's perspective, an angle of some sixty degress, the giant appeared even more massive and gigantic than he was, curiously elongated as if seen through a distorting mirror.

Inching his way out on the ledge, Aito appeared to be clearly uneasy with the height. But his rage to lay hands on the pistol-firing robed figure far outweighed his fear of heights.

293

The Corsican guards who'd been jabbering and scurrying about to no great purpose suddenly stood silent, gaping up at the two men. They hovered just behind Daughtry and Mariko, watching the large, stiff, blocklike silhouette of Aito groping its skitterish way toward Kajumi, looking more crazed and demonic than ever.

Daughtry could hear Mariko whimpering softly beside him. Aito was near the center of the overhang now, a foot or two from Kajumi. The ledge, no more than a thin sheet of copper, began to sag and buckle from their combined weight. Kajumi, wary of the man approaching, kept one wild eye on him and the other transfixed on his targets below. Attempting to evade the giant bearing remorselessly down upon him, he inched off to the right, suddenly raised his pistol ceremoniously and fired another shot. Celestine's limp soiled body shuddered on the impact, moving slightly off its perch, giving the impression she was still alive.

A hoarse, gagging sound tore from Mariko's throat. She made another lunge toward her mother, but was yanked cruelly back by Daughtry, half dragging, half shoving her, kicking and screaming behind the protection of an upturned table.

The Corsicans jabbered and jumped up and down, pointing up at the roof ledge. By now it was sagging perilously. Several of them had their carbines up but could not get a clear shot at their target.

Kajumi's pistol rose once more. The guards scattered, but this time he was no longer aiming at his father, or his step-mother, or even at Aito, but at his own temple. It was at that moment that the giant reached forward—and his great paw shot out, catching the hand with the pistol.

What followed was odd and funny in a rather ghastly way. Aito towered nearly two feet above Kajumi and when he reached and first grabbed him, the two men teetered and struggled on the ledge for a while. Queasily, Daughtry watched the deepening curve of sagging copper, and the two men slowly descending as if their feet were mired in quicksand.

294

It appeared to Daughtry that Kajumi had finally sensed his danger and was trying now to get away from Aito. The more he struggled, however, the more the giant appeared to be hauling him in like a big, hooked fish, enfolding him ever closer to himself, until at last the two men appeared to be embracing, then, ludicrously, even dancing with each other.

Daughtry looked away momentarily, his eyes fixed midpoint on one of the spired gables of the roof. Directly above the action on the overhang, two of the Corsican guards had suddenly appeared at a window and started to climb out onto the roof. There was another shot. Mariko screamed. Daughtry turned back in time to see a grayish blur hurtle through space, followed inseparably in time by a thud. The flat, concise, emphatic sound of it made Daughtry sick.

There was a time, directly after (it seemed, however, interminable) that no one moved. Guards, Daughtry, Mariko—all poised motionless like characters struck on a frieze. A number of guests who'd fled the Grand Tent, and others from the surrounding banquet tents, started to move haltingly back to the main tent.

Curiosity overcoming fright, they gathered and milled about at the open sides and peered in. The balloons, the confetti, the gorgeous floral displays, the flashing pennants and the bright flambeaux still celebrated the gay event.

Suddenly, a small Corsican guard with swirling mustaches, bolder than the others, swaggered jauntily up to the ghastly mess huddled on the tent floor beneath the overhang.

At the point where the two men hurtled down, the overhang, unable to bear the weight and struggle any longer, had given way. The copper sheet dangled from above like a long broken vine. Directly below on the flagged patio the huge carcass of Aito thrashed feebly, his head lolling at a sickening angle where he had most certainly broken his neck. An unearthly, inhuman bellowing came from somewhere deep within him, like the boom of a kettle drum.

In all his pain and rage he still clasped Kajumi to him, as if

295

he were some rich prize, unaware that Kajumi was dead; that he
had no doubt expired before he'd even hit the ground. Dead
from his own hand, from the bullet that had torn fully half his
skull away. Shortly, in a nearby hospital in Vaduz, the huge
heart of the Sakhalin giant, severely overtaxed by the shock of
traumatic bodily injury, would itself expire.

61

Victory is a moral, rather than a material effect.
—B. H. LIDDELL HART: *Thoughts on War, 1944*

They sat in the back of the car, Sujimoto between the two of
them, with Karl Heinz up front, driving. They had no trouble
getting off the Mendenhall grounds. At the inspection shack
they were waved quickly on and two of the security guards were
waiting there with motorcycles to escort them to the American
military hospital in Zurich.

Although Sujimoto was conscious, he was by no means
aware of what was going on about him. Several times he
attempted to sit upright while Mariko tried to keep him lying flat
and quiet, all the while kissing and cradling him, dabbing his
bloody cheeks and throat with a small lace handkerchief. In
between, she whimpered to herself and murmured words in
Japanese. Words of grieving, words of endearment. Daughtry
imagined she was blaming herself and begging forgiveness. She
had just lost a mother and a half-brother; now in her highly
distraught state, she assumed she was also about to lose a
father. Throughout most of the drive to Zurich she sat numbly
staring ahead.

Destiny, fortune, Lady Luck had played fantastically into
Daughtry's hand. He had Sujimoto now. Shortly, they would be
out of the jurisdiction of Liechtenstein. Once in Switzerland, all

he need do was notify the American consul in Geneva and Sujimoto would be taken quickly into custody, then flown back to the States. Paradoxically, without having even the ghost of a plausible strategy and badly outmanned, events had gone all his way.

The car lurched and bounced and sped along the narrow winding mountain roads while up ahead the motorcycle sirens wailed dolefully. At one point the big Bentley careened down a hill and lifted, all four wheels, over a hump in the road. The heavy chassis came down hard, sending their heads rocketing up to the roof. Sujimoto, stirred, shook his head and looked at them out of woozy, unfocused eyes. Like a man shaking off sleep, he resumed conversation as if he had not once for a moment stopped.

What he said made little sense; largely mumbling and disjointed phrases in Japanese, French and English. At no time did he ask after, or even mention, the name Celestine.

Mariko he appeared not to recognize. Several times he stared at Daughtry with a strangely puzzled, distant look and called him Kajumi.

"Father," Mariko cradled the aged, doll-like figure in the crumpled tuxedo to her breast. "Father, Father, dear, it's me— Mariko."

Later at the hospital he was taken upstairs, X-rayed and examined. Mariko and Daughtry sat below in a cold waiting room full of vinyl couches and plastiform chairs, waiting for word from the doctors.

Daughtry had still not called the American consul, and while instinct urged him to do so at once, something else, something as yet unspecified, deterred him.

Mariko stared down at her hands moving incessantly in her lap.

"Mariko, I should call the consul." He waited, watching her gravely. "If I call, they'll come now and take him into custody. He'll be sent back to the States."

If she heard, or even cared what he'd said, she showed no sign. She merely sat there staring down, her hands entwined and fingers spinning restlessly.

"If you'd prefer," he went on earnestly, "I won't call. The moment he's better, I'll take him back to Mendenhall. He'll be safe there."

"What if he doesn't go back with you? What will you do?"

"I must go back anyway."

"Why? What if you didn't. They can't extradite you from here."

A sister in immaculate starched white with the huge winged bonnet of a Carmelite drifted past and smiled at them incuriously.

"We could stay here now." Her face brightened. "Together. Forever."

For answer he turned a weary, almost grateful smile upon her. But she had known his answer even before she'd asked the question.

"It's so important to you, then," she asked softly.

After a moment, he nodded. "Whatever happens," he went on, "I want you to come with me. If you can't now, then follow me after you've settled everything here."

She continued to stare down at her fidgeting fingers.

"I think I want that, Mariko. Do you understand? More than anything, I think that's what's right for me now. If it doesn't work, I promise not to hold you to anything. But, at least, I'd like us to try and . . ." His voice trailed off as his mind sought desperately the right words. "I don't want you to feel—that any of this—any of it, in any way, depends on whether your father comes to the States or not. Somehow"—he laughed a little foolishly—"I don't care any more if he does."

Tears coursed down her cheeks. He tried to dab them with his handkerchief but she snapped her head away sharply.

"Mariko."

"What? What?"

"Don't be angry with me."

"I'm not angry with you. Don't be foolish."

He reached to touch her, but at that moment a young doctor in a long white jacket with a carefully trimmed beard arrived. "Sujimoto?" he inquired.

"This is Miss Sujimoto, his daughter. I'm just a friend of the family."

The doctor gazed down at Mariko, noting the blood spattering the front of her dress.

He turned to Daughtry and spoke in a low voice. "I gather there's been some kind of an accident."

"Yes—a shooting. Her mother was killed."

"Is she all right?" He pointed to Mariko, in her blood-smeared gown.

"I think so," Daughtry said. "Just numb. A little shocked."

"Do you have any idea of the old man's age?"

Daughtry shrugged helplessly.

"Seventy-six." Mariko stirred and suddenly spoke.

The doctor nodded. "Basically, he's okay. I mean, the wound is harmless. His vital signs—heart, blood pressure—are remarkable for a man his age. As for the rest—"

Daughtry watched him uneasily. "The rest?"

The young physician gave him a distinctly uneasy look. "By the *rest* I was referring to his mental state. . . . He's completely disoriented. Doesn't know his name, his address. Where he is or who he is. Whether this is temporary—a function of trauma—" He lowered his voice once more and spoke to Daughtry. "It could be simple shock," the doctor sighed. "But at his age it has the look and feel of deep senile dementia."

The young man watched Daughtry, staring hard into his eyes, trying to gauge his reaction. "If you don't mind, I'd like to keep him here overnight and have the neurologist go over him in the morning."

Daughtry wavered.

"Perhaps we ought to ask her." The doctor nodded toward Mariko.

"I don't think she's—"

"I'm fine." She sat up erect and tossed her fine dark hair off her shoulders, as if suddenly waking. "Yes, of course. That will be fine. I want my father to be examined completely before he's discharged."

Something about the authority and self-possession in her manner brought the young man up sharply. "Good," he said, a trifle flustered. "Then I'll see to the arrangements. He's resting comfortably now if you'd care to see him. But just for a few minutes. He's pretty tired."

He nodded to each of them and strode off, his cork-soled shoes squeaking down the green vinyl corridor.

"It will be all right, Charles," Mariko said, after a moment, the line of her jaw set firmly.

"What will be all right?"

"My father and I will go to New York."

Incredibly, to his amazement, Daughtry started to protest. "You haven't the right to make that decision for him."

"If what the doctor just said about his state of mind is correct, it appears I'll have to."

"He did say the condition may only be temporary."

"Nevertheless," she said with an air of finality, "I wish to take my father to the States for medical treatment."

"If you think you're doing that for me—"

"Don't be ridiculous," she snapped. "How egotistical. Of course I'm not doing it for you. I'm doing it for him, and don't forget that. Even if it's only temporary, he still needs the best medical treatment available and he shall have it."

"There's perfectly fine treatment to be had right here," Daughtry argued gently.

"It is not for you to say." She grew more vexed. "So long as my father is unable to make that decision for himself, the responsibility falls to me as his only surviving family—"

The memory of Celestine must have returned to her at that moment for she was unable to complete the sentence. "There is no need to notify the American consul now. There's no need to take him into custody, or fly him in handcuffs, under guard, to the States."

"Mariko—"

"Please, don't argue. I take full responsibility for his arriving in New York in time to testify. You go now. I must see first to arrangements for my mother and brother."

"Let me at least stay and help."

"No, you go. There's a 12 noon flight to Kennedy that puts you in New York at around 3 P.M. Go now."

He stared at her numbly. Sitting there, rumpled and small, she had taken on a stature and nobility he had never quite seen there before. It moved him oddly, in ways he could not articulate. He stood there watching her, wavering, uncertain.

"Go," she said, her voice raspy and impatient.

He stood above her, shaking his head back and forth. Suddenly he leaned over and pushed a wisp of hair off her brow, permitting his fingertips to linger there.

"I'll see you in a few days," he said.

62

Oh God! It's all over.
—LORD GEORGE GERMAIN: *On receiving word of Cornwallis's surrender, November 25, 1781*

Three days later, Mariko delivered her father to the Federal District Court in Manhattan. Their appearance there was startling. Reporters and television crews streamed out of the walls; photographers swarmed like termites. For several weeks thereafter, "The ruined and disgraced financier and his daughter" dominated TV screens and the front pages of newspapers from coast to coast.

Daughtry testified before the District Attorney, followed by Villiers, Wainwright, Michaeltree, and a number of other senior

301

officers who had been persuaded to take early retirements from the bank.

Mr. Sujimoto, while present for every session, was never called. On his arrival in the States, his lawyer, a formidable and flamboyant figure known principally for large fees and the defense of distinctly shady causes, presented to the court affidavits and medical reports of examinations recently undergone at the U.S. Military Hospital in Zurich. The gist of these findings revealed, not surprisingly, an advanced but completely treatable condition of bleeding ulcers.

More significantly, however, neurological and psychiatric reports, along with a number of brain scans, fully corroborated a condition of advanced atherosclerosis affecting the flow of blood to Mr. Sujimoto's brain. For purposes of testimony, Mr. Sujimoto was *non compos mentis*.

The elderly financier came to court each day with his daughter. He appeared frail but nonetheless natty in a pressed gray pinstripe suit and fresh linen. Silent and unspeaking, he would sit for hours at a stretch, a blank, almost dreamy expression on his wan features. Only his eyes would blink periodically, as testimony and cross-examination heated up in the room. At noon recess his daughter would feed him lunch in a small private chamber off the court, or try reading the newspaper aloud to him in the park outside, where the pitiless press would pounce the moment they appeared.

At the conclusion of the day a long black limousine would roll up to a side entrance of the Federal Court House and whisk them up the East Side Drive and west to the Hampshire House.

Over Arthur Littlefield's stern protests, Daughtry saw Mariko regularly throughout the course of the hearing. After bitter days of testimony, of recrimination and countercharge, he would taxi up to the hotel and have supper with the Sujimotos in the privacy of their suite, all of them like the best of old friends.

In the small Pullman kitchen of the suite, Mariko would prepare their dinner, then carefully cut up her father's food and patiently feed it to him. Docile, infantlike, the old man would

302

accept forkfuls of rice, bits of chicken, or fresh sashimi, gumming it abstractly as if he were millions of miles away.

Incomprehensibly, he would listen to the evening Wall Street report and the latest Forex quotes, following with his lips the progress of the dollar and yen, Deutsche mark and pound sterling. The numbers would drone on monotonously while Sujimoto mouthed them in silent repetition. Mariko maintained that she had no way of knowing whether the old man heard, let alone even understood, a word of any of it. Daughtry believed it was no more than an involuntary reflex to the sound of numbers. He could see no visible sign of cerebration. Still, it was therapeutic. The dull, hypnotic murmur of incessant numbers appeared to tranquilize him, prepare him for bed, rather like a lullaby or a child's bedtime story.

On weekends, Daughtry would come early to the Hampshire House and they would take old Sujimoto out into the park for a short walk or a breath of fresh air. With an arm locked in each of theirs, he would toddle along between them. Sometimes they would sit on a bench. Often, reporters would hound them and they would have to flee. It was mid-April now, lilac time. Apple and cherry blossoms burgeoned and bent the boughs of trees; stands of stubborn daffodils surmounted and ultimately triumphed over the uncollected rubbish strewn about the scraggly grass. Sujimoto appeared content. He spoke infrequently. Responding vaguely to a question from his daughter, he would stare at her blankly. Daughtry he still insisted upon addressing as Kajumi. Celestine he never mentioned. It was as though she'd never existed.

During the course of the hearings the fate of the Confederated hung in the balance. Rumors, like proliferating weeds, sprang up everywhere, the most persistent of which was a report that six or seven banks were at that moment still bidding wildly for the right to appropriate whatever remained after the insolvency procedures.

On the evening of April 16 the Currency Comptroller declared the Confederated Trust Bank insolvent, characterizing it as the largest failure in American banking history. One day later, the Confederated New York Corporation, the holding company for the bank, filed for bankruptcy. The SEC gave the bank ten days to file a list of its assets and liabilities.

All this occurred during the course of the hearing, sometimes exacerbating a judicial process that was already highly inflammatory. Hundreds of pages of affidavits and testimony were entered into evidence. An endless stream of witnesses came forward to plead ignorance and to exonerate themselves. Wainwright, Villiers, Bagwell, Michaeltree, even Ricardi, plus dozens of others—all depicting themselves as unwitting victims, all breathlessly eager to incriminate their colleagues. Then came Paul Selig, the night-school CPA who'd exploded the whole business in the first place.

Mr. Sujimoto, serene, unruffled, impeccable in gray flannel, sat beside his daughter, present—but not really present. Surrounded by attorneys, witnesses, reporters and curious spectators, his solitude was complete. He was far removed from the judicial battlefield now strewn with the innumerable corpses of so many of his unwitting victims.

An editorial writer in the *Wall Street Journal* described Sujimoto as having drawn a veil between himself and the proceedings. Indeed, his detachment appeared impenetrable— almost trancelike. Once, however, during the course of the hearings, Daughtry had occasion to glance the old man's way. Several times, instead of the "mask of impassivity," so frequently alluded to by reporters, Daughtry caught there instead the alert, canny expression of the dauntless captain of the *Aoba,* monitoring through binoculars the progress of the U.S. Task Force streaming toward Tulagi Harbor.

That evening at the Hampshire House, after dinner, they watched the late evening news—Daughtry and Mariko on a settee, Sujimoto in a large wing chair beside them in his robe and satin slippers. The big breaking story was that the Trans-Asian Bank had taken over Confederated's operation in an agreement that guaranteed no loss to any Confederated depositor.

There was to be no interruption of services to the public. At a news conference attended by the president of the Federal Reserve Bank of New York and the New York State Superintendent of Banking, the exact nature of the settlement was revealed. Trans-Asian had taken over $1.4 billion in Confederated deposits plus $1.58 billion of loans and securities, paying a combined premium of $125 million. The FDIC had taken over loans to the bank from the Federal Reserve Bank of New York, totaling $1.7 billion, as well as $2 billion of less desirable Confederated commercial paper and debentures.

The SEC, the report continued, was about to file charges against nine former officers, directors and employees of the now insolvent bank. Daughtry watched the screen unflinchingly as his name was reeled off among a list of other malefactors. Last to be named was Sujimoto, who took the news as apathetically as if the television commentator had been referring to someone else.

The suit would charge that false information was issued to the public and the SEC by the former chairman (now deceased), Leon Edelbach, and chief executive Walter Wainwright. The SEC would contend that the bank manufactured, then reported, a profit of over $2 million as a result of foreign exchange dealings between Confederated and a Swiss bank controlled by Mr. Sujimoto, the major shareholder in the Confederated New York Corporation. It would further contend that Confederated had reported first-quarter Forex income of $2.4 million when, in fact, they had incurred losses of $26.7 million in currency operations during that quarter.

The TV news conference dissolved to the progress of the hearing in the Federal Court building on Centre Street. Wedged between news of the embattled proceedings, Daughtry and Mariko watched themselves move across the flickering screen. Next Sujimoto appeared, hobbling on his daughter's arm. Seeing himself, unexpectedly, the old man pointed a finger and laughed out loud. Mariko looked at Daughtry, appalled. He, in turn, gazed back at her, but only smiled. It was not a mean smile, but rather sage and forbearing.

After that evening, however, Daughtry viewed Sujimoto

quite differently. More wary he was now, but with a grudging admiration, and unexpectedly, a strange affection for his old nemesis.

Toward the end of April with the hearings grinding to a close, news came that the Confederated's attorneys had filed papers in U.S. District Court, reporting that the parent corporation had left debts of $66 million. Manufacturers Hanover held a $30 million note. Morgan Guaranty was trustee for $35 million in notes held by investors. Creditors were to meet in New York on May 12 to elect trustees in the proceedings before a bankruptcy judge. The dismemberment of the once mighty banking institution had begun in earnest.

The final irony was the old Confederated tower itself—a tower that had dominated the skyline of lower Manhattan and the international banking industry for over a century. In an effort to raise money for creditors, executors for the bank tried to have the noble old Stanford White edifice designated a "dump" in the hope that they might demolish the building and sell the real estate under it to a giant plastics corporation for its general headquarters.

News of plans to raze the branch produced a public outcry. Incensed citizenry and enclaves of civic-minded socialites, their hearts set on a cotillion, declared the old tower to be one of the few architectural anchors in an area already "debased" by overcommercialization. They accused bank officials of demonstrating a perverse and cynical set of urban values in trying to exchange historical values for "plastic claptrap." Delegations of concerned citizens swarmed on City Hall, demanding to see the Mayor, claiming that the tower was one of the few redeeming sights left in lower Manhattan—already a wasteland of aluminum and plate glass. It was an election year and the Mayor found irresistible the image of himself as a defender of "the City's invaluable heritage." Immediately he announced a press conference. It took him nearly an hour and a great deal of gassy rhetoric to say that he was taking steps to have the old tower declared a historic landmark. The real estate promoters howled "foul."

306

63

In war as in love, we must achieve contact ere we triumph.
—NAPOLEON I: *Political Aphorisms, 1848*

$$D(N_1) = D(N_2)$$

$$D(N_1, N_2) = D(N_2, N_3)$$

$$D(M_3, M_1) = D(M_3, M_2)$$

$$\frac{D_s([M_1])([M_1, M_3])}{D_s([O_1, O_3])} = Y$$

Daughtry looked up from his pad of doodle computations. Mariko had suddenly appeared and stood leaning in the door-frame.

"Is he asleep?"

"Fell right off. He was exhausted. What time is it?"

"Almost eleven. What are you doing?"

"Working out my destiny."

"Your destiny?"

He pushed the pad across the coffee table, which she studied perfunctorily. "Very interesting," she said, pushing it back. "They look like hieroglyphics. What are they?"

"Equations of probability and set logic."

"What could logic possibly have to do with your destiny?"

He ignored the facetiousness. "You see the first set there on the top row?"

"Yes. Well—?"

"That tells me that the odds are 6–2 that I'll be convicted on twelve counts of fraud and conspiracy."

"Fantastic. And the second set?"

"Such charges generally carry with them a sentence of one to five years," he answered, speaking reflectively to the ceiling,

307

as if he'd seen the computations written there. "If you're convicted of such charges in this state, judges will typically rule that a person serve those sentences concurrently."

"Meaning that you could serve a minimum of one year to a maximum of five for all twelve charges."

"Exactly. And, considering that I have no prior criminal record; that I have lived until now a reasonably useful and constructive life; that I haven't made a pain-in-the-ass of myself to society; that I'm a veteran with a silver star and a purple heart, and a lame leg to boot; that I gained no direct profit from my participation in this conspiracy; and considering that the record will show sincere attempts on no less than six separate occasions to bring to the attention of my superiors—"

"For God's sake, Daughtry, get the point."

"Considering all of those factors—"

"Yes—"

"The second formula suggests that it's even money that I'll be invited to serve a year to sixteen months in prison. Of course we'll appeal."

"And?"

"There's an even money chance we'll get a suspended sentence."

She looked away, her fingers kneading uneasily the velvet piping on the divan on which she sat. "And my father?"

"There's no question that your father will be convicted on at least sixty counts of conspiracy to defraud." He watched her intently for any sign of weakness but detected none. "But given his age, his general condition of enfeeblement, the old rascal won't serve a day in prison. I have this on faith from Littlefield, who is paid large sums to know such things."

"That's hardly fair, is it?" Mariko said, turning back to him.

"I thought that bit of information would make you happy."

"It does, on the one hand. On the other—"

"Don't think about the other." He laughed, then suddenly grew solemn. "Don't be too hard on your father."

"I still love him, but I think about you, too. What are the other two formulas you have there?"

"Those pertain to you and me."

She stiffened visibly and looked away. "Oh, I see. And what do they tell you, Nostradamus?"

He leaned back, sighed and closed his eyes as if he were computing in his head. "You see the D and the M?"

"Yes."

"They're the dominant factors in the equation."

"D is for Daughtry, I take it? And M for—"

"Very astute of you." Daughtry's manner as he explained his equation had taken on a playful zest. "Given the certainty of my conviction, the even chance that I will go to jail; given the effects of a jail sentence on my chances of ever being employed again by a bank in a responsible position; given my age of thirty-three—not old, but certainly no longer junior—and, of course, my general good health—"

"Yes—and what does that all tell you?"

"It tells me that it would be imprudent for me to ask you to marry me."

"Oh." Once more her eyes strayed off. "I see. And what is the fourth equation?"

"Funny you should ask," he said, matter-of-factly. "The fourth equation takes into consideration the findings of the three preceding equations—"

"And—"

"And attempts to build in as coefficients of D and M, factors of chance Y. By that I mean certain intangibles, unpredictables—"

"I see." Her voice was tremulous and a little unmanageable. "And—"

"Working that out to ten-thousandths with a margin of error factor of plus or minus 6 percent, which seems conservative but is nevertheless prudent—"

"It sounds crooked to me, like cooking the books," she said quite pointedly.

"The art of statistics is the art of the possible." He smiled provocatively. "As any good statistician will tell you."

"Spare me all the coy stuff, Daughtry, will you, please?"

He had tried to be amusing as a way of managing fear and defending himself against the indefensibility of his position. The attempt had failed dismally. She was more antagonistic than ever.

When he spoke this time his voice was quiet and bore a distinctly portentous note. "The fourth equation tells me to disregard the findings of the three preceding equations and to ask you on the night before my almost certain condemnation by the court to marry me. Odds, probabilities, smart money notwithstanding."

"Accepted," she retorted sharply. His ears perked as the air in the room crackled and the scene took on the look of an auction. He sensed, however, that something was to follow.

"State your conditions."

"You understand my father is ruined. Several governments have moved to impound his money. What he has, he can't touch."

He felt his heart suddenly lighten. "Is that all? I was afraid for a moment there was some difficulty."

"There is," she said, her voice harsh and matter of fact. "Further, it is understood he has no family left, other than—"

"Yourself."

"Correct—I'm all he has, and he's old and in poor health."

"I see," he said, having quickly discerned the gist of her thought.

"In Japan, we do not discharge elderly parents, or banish them to institutions."

"He's welcome to live with us, Mariko."

Her wide, frank gaze regarded him skeptically. "In spite of what you have endured as a result of his transactions?"

"What's mine is his." Daughtry spoke outright, matching her frankness. "So long as his daughter is my wife." His acquiescence appeared to make her sad, as if she had almost hoped he would have exacted harsher terms. Now the quiet generosity of it all seemed to throw her.

"You're certain?"

"Absolutely."

She glanced over her shoulder at the room in which Sujimoto now slept. "I should perhaps go see if he is all right."

"You just did that."

"He always kicks the covers off—" She started toward the bedroom, then turned back. "I'm looking for some reason to get away from you just now for a little bit. You understand?"

"Is there any special reason?"

She was suddenly flustered and almost contrite. Outside, the evening streetlamps shimmered like diamonds strewn across the wide dark patch of park below.

"Make a new equation," she said, her eyes glistening. "Two people meet, starting from zero."

"$D = 0$, $M = 0$."

"With a testy old fraud of a Japanese father to contend with."

"S_1," Daughtry supplied the mathematical term.

"D has a jail sentence."

"DJ_1."

"M has no job."

"MJ_2—catastrophe," Daughtry said, scribbling the elements of the equation onto the pad.

$$\frac{\text{If } D_1 (M_1 + S_1) \times D_1 (DJ_1 + MJ_2)}{\text{Let } L_1 = L_2 (A)}$$

She hovered there staring at the numbers, awestruck and rather fearful, as if they bore some powerful and sinister influence over her.

"You were going to check on your father," Daughtry said after a moment.

"No need to any more," she laughed uneasily. "No longer frightened. It's after 11 P.M. Turn on the news."

He rose and flicked on the TV.

"*. . . dollar continues to gain,*" the financial commentator reported, "*advancing on a broad front against most major currencies. Traders attribute the turnaround to renewed confidence in the U.S. currency . . . in Italy, the dollar jumped to a four-year high against the Italian lira. In Tokyo, the yen* *plummeted to an all-time low. Traders attributed this to . . ."*

The numbers droned from the TV and wafted upward into the velvety air of a star-filled evening. Out the window and up to the right, Fifth Avenue, serene and uncaring, glittered like a birthday cake. In the mild evening below, people lingered round the splashing fountains near the Plaza and strolled toward its warmly lit cafés.

"Late dollar rates in other European money centers in-cluded: Frankfurt, 2,2080 West German marks, down from 2.2108; Zurich, 2.0175 Swiss francs, up from 2.0145; Paris, 5.2440, French francs up from 5.2325. In Tokyo, the dollar gained more than 2½ yen from Tuesday. . . ."

Beyond the door Sujimoto lay quiet. Eyes closed, breathing easily, he listened to the recitation of numbers, lulling and incantatory, suffusing his drowsy consciousness. Just as he'd anticipated, the yen had tumbled, the dollar had soared on recent news that the Federal Reserve had raised the discount rate.

His long dollar position had paid off handsomely. Several millions would wend their way mysteriously into secret fiduciary accounts in Vaduz, Zurich, the Bahamas. Unnumbered, un-named, they would be untraceable to him. It was a good day's work.

The TV went off outside, and now he heard the muted murmur of two voices beyond the door. They produced in him, oddly, a drowsy comfortable sense of well-being. He had already reconciled himself to Daughtry as a fact, if not of his life, then that of his daughter's. While the brash American trader was not, could never be, his first choice for a son-in-law, Sujimoto was sufficiently pragmatic to have started perceiving him in a new and somewhat more acceptable light. After all, hadn't it been that way at the capitulation? Hadn't they all had to stand there at attention on the deck of the battleship *Missouri* in Tokyo Bay that September morning in 1945, himself and Shigemitsu, the foreign minister, and old Umezu, whose hand trembled as he

312

signed the instruments of surrender on behalf of the Japanese Imperial General Staff. "We, acting by command of the Emperor of Japan," it commenced. What a day of humiliation, of disgrace, to have to stand there before haughty MacArthur and crusty Chester Nimitz, and have to swallow the indignity of it all. And yet, hadn't a realistic attitude, a working accommodation with the enemy worked out very well for the Japanese over the past thirty-five years? The future had borne them out. They had triumphed over their victors. Ingenuity and commitment had done it.

To be sure, Daughtry was an American. That was unfortunate. But the obverse of that coin was the fact that he possessed a highly bankable talent. He needed shaping, to be sure, but there was room for a talent of that magnitude in the organization Sujimoto had been envisioning ever since the demise of Sujimoto, Ltd.

This would be an empire—a vast, multinational conglomerate—banks, mills, mines, rails, oils, armaments, the works. In his mind's drowsy eye, towering glass and marble rose up out of barren desert. Intractable jungles fell away. Factories, shipyards, vast armadas of boats and planes, the frontiers of space and the ocean bottom all yielded their treasures up to him. He saw his own desalinization plants transform the graveyard of the sub-Sahara into fecund orchards feeding millions. Awesomely big coal gasification plants and nuclear-powered generators fueled the economy of the world. Huge pharmaceutical companies cured the sick and eased the pain of the dying. All bore the seal of Sujimoto.

The vision, vivid, almost palpable, roared past, and suddenly quiet ensued. Like a large cat who had just eaten, he curled comfortably in his bed and smiled himself to sleep.